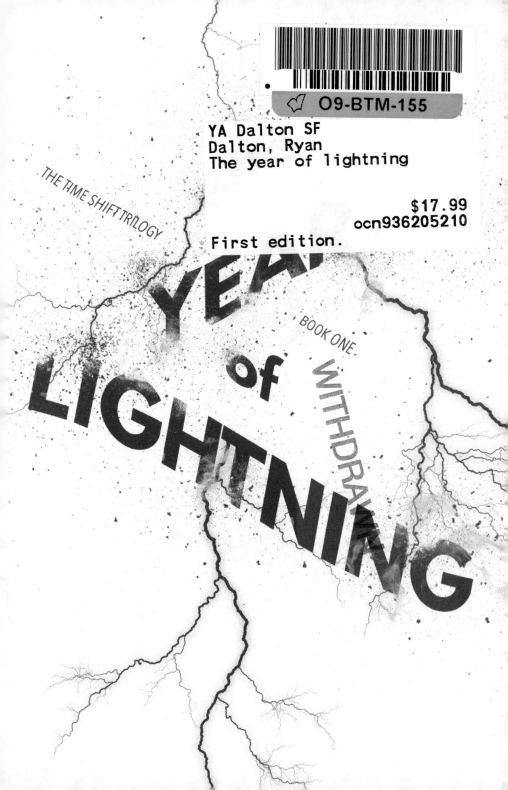

THE TIME SHIFT TRILOGY

YEAR

of

LIGHTNING

· BOOK ONE ·

WITHDRAWN

First Edition
Third Printing, 2016

Jolly Fish Press, an imprint of North Star Editions, Inc.

Jolly Fish Press
North Star Editions, Inc.
2297 Waters Drive
Mendota Heights, MN 55120
www.jollyfishpress.com

Printed in the United States of America

THIS TITLE IS ALSO AVAILABLE AS AN EBOOK.

Library of Congress Cataloging-in-Publication Data

Names: Dalton, Ryan (Young adult author) author.
Title: The year of lightning / Ryan Dalton.
Description: First Paperback Edition. | Provo, Utah : Jolly Fish Press, 2015. | Series: The Time Shift Trilogy ; Book 1 | Summary: "Thirteen-year-olds Malcolm and Valentine Gilbert must stop a crazed villain of the future who is bent on destroying their town and family to return to his time, while discovering that they are more than human in the process"--Provided by publisher.
Identifiers: LCCN 2015037460 | ISBN 9781631630507 (paperback)
Subjects: | CYAC: Time travel--Fiction. | Science fiction. | BISAC: JUVENILE FICTION / Fantasy & Magic.
Classification: LCC PZ7.1.D29 Ye 2015 | DDC [Fic]--dc23
LC record available at http://lccn.loc.gov/2015037460

For Mom and Dad,
who always let me dream.

Praise for *The Year of Lightning*

"Exciting plot, smart characters, and engaging prose; Dalton's writing jolts straight to your heart."
—Ellie Ann, New York Times bestselling author

"A rousing mix of science and fantasy that will thrill young and old alike! Dalton blends wit and emotion and adventure seamlessly in a tale that keeps your pulse pounding."
—Ryne Douglas Pearson, screenwriter and author of *Knowing* and *Simple Simon*

"With cheeky winks to classic time travel and a mind-bending central mystery, *The Year of Lightning* moves at a pace that lives up to its title and will keep your pulse pounding to the last page."
—Karen Akins, author of *Loop*

"Every page of *The Year of Lightning* is non-stop adventure that's, oddly enough, completely believable."
—Hott Books

"The emotional feelings in this book were so raw, and real."
— Maryam Dinsly, *onceupona-story.com*

the

YEAR

BOOK ONE

of

LIGHTNING

RYAN DALTON

CHAPTER 1

A torrent of lightning struck the roof of the old house. Malcolm had never noticed the place before, but now he stood transfixed at his bedroom window. Despite the storm's power, the house seemed strangely untouched—no damage, no fire, nothing.

The towering house sat across the street. Faded whitewash covered its three wooden stories, and tall brown grass curled around its worn wrought-iron fence. Malcolm guessed it had been abandoned for decades. Even the round window at the top revealed nothing but shadows.

Thunder boomed and his own window rattled. He rubbed his arms, feeling chilled. In the window's reflection, he saw his twin sister move her queen.

"Check," Valentine said.

"Two months of living here, and we didn't notice it until now?" he said. "How can that be? It's right across from us."

Valentine's eyes stayed on the chess board. "Noticed what, the storm?"

"No, that." He tapped the glass. "Aren't you listening?"

"I'm playing the game." Valentine smirked. "Which is why you're in check."

Malcolm tore himself away from the window. He grimaced at his remaining pieces. "I thought we agreed to slow-play this one."

"I had a good move."

He blocked with his knight. "You always have a good move. Science geeks shouldn't beat history geeks at chess. It's not natural."

Valentine grinned. "Well, maybe we should trade hobbies. I know some history."

"Really. Which empire first settled the British Isles?"

She stared down at the board.

"Can't answer, can you?"

"No, but I can do *this*." She advanced her rook, removing his last bishop. "Check. Again."

Malcolm winced and blocked with a pawn. His attention returned to the window. "How does it stand all that lightning? Shouldn't something that old just, like, catch fire and fall over?"

"Shouldn't what fall over?"

"Geez, Val. Come on, get up and look at this." Malcolm tugged on his sister's arm until she followed him to the window. "Look right there. Wait for more lightning and you'll see it better."

"Mal, I don't see—"

"Just keep looking, it's . . . there!"

A massive bolt struck the corner of the old house, and a crack of thunder rumbled through Malcolm's chest. For an instant, the sky lit up like mid-afternoon.

"Holy cow, that's loud," Valentine said. "The storms here are crazy!" Then she stopped, and Malcolm saw realization in her eyes. "Oh, wow. I hadn't noticed that place before."

"Right? That's what I've been saying."

"But it's just an old house. What's the big deal?" She squinted, leaning closer to the window. "Though, I wonder who'd build a place with—"

Malcolm nodded fervently. "With no front door."

"Actually, there aren't any doors at *all*. Now that I think about it, I saw the back from the main road once. I just didn't remember until now." Valentine shook her head. "Weird."

"Looks like each side has a window at the top. No doors, though." Malcolm's voice fell to a whisper. "No way in or out. Why would someone build that?"

Valentine stared for a moment longer, then turned away with a shrug. "Maybe Oma Grace knows."

Malcolm's shoulders fell. "You're not even curious?"

"A little, maybe, but old stuff is your department. Show me something new and you'll have my attention." She glanced at her phone. "It's getting late, and tomorrow is the first day of high school. I should go to bed. But first . . ." She moved to the chess board and slid a knight into position. "Checkmate."

Malcolm came to her side and stared at the board, crest-fallen. "Wait, wait, no way."

Valentine patted his shoulder in mock sympathy and crossed the hall to her room.

"Hey wait!" he called. "I think I see a move—"

"Bedtime, Mal. G'night."

Her bedroom door clicked shut. Malcolm studied the pieces a moment longer, sighed, and tipped over his king. Turning on the bedside lamp, he grabbed a book and settled onto the bed.

Hours drifted by as he let the historical adventure envelope him through the dead of night. Between chapters, he stretched stiff joints and watched the night sky battle on. His room had the best view of the storm, which appeared to be growing angrier by the hour. Lightning flashed constantly behind the dark clouds, and the air rumbled with rolling thunder. His brow furrowed as he noticed that frost had formed on the edges of his windows.

Frost seems odd for summer. Maybe we're close to the storm center.

Malcolm picked out the largest bolts of lightning and the most intense thunderclaps. Mentally he counted the seconds between them, hoping to guess their distance away. *Wait, that can't be right.* He counted again and got the same result.

The delay was identical every time—one and a half seconds between lightning and thunder. Strike-pause-boom, wait, re-peat. After twenty minutes of counting, the cycle still ran like clockwork. *Is that normal around here?* Valentine probably knew but must be dreaming by now. Maybe he'd ask her tomorrow.

As Malcolm turned away from the window, something brushed the corner of his vision. A burst of light, but not like the others. He whipped back around and stared into the night. A bolt of lightning and a crack of thunder greeted him again.

Whatever it was, it had looked different than the lightning—brighter, and a slightly different color. *Light must be playing with my eyes.* He rubbed them and moved to turn away again. *Probably just—no, there it is again!*

He saw it this time—a strange pulse of blue-white light. It hadn't come from the clouds. It had been closer to eye level and from the direction of—

Malcolm lunged at the shelf over his headboard. Grabbing an antique spyglass, he pointed the lens across the street, toward the house with no doors. He held deathly still, his eye trained on the front window.

PULSE!

A beam of light lanced from the window, piercing the inky

darkness. One-point-five seconds later the sky erupted in thunder and lightning. Malcolm felt like he'd been dunked in ice.

"Pulse-lightning-boom. House-sky-air, every time. What on earth is—"

PULSE!

A man's face glared at him through the window.

With cold fury, he stared into Malcolm's room and straight down his spyglass. Malcolm froze under those accusing eyes as they pulled him toward the window. His panicked breath came ragged and hoarse, his muscles refused to budge.

PULSE!

The face disappeared.

Malcolm snapped back like a broken rubber band, yelping as he fell from his bed. He smacked onto the floor and collided with the dresser. Antiques and picture frames toppled onto him as he sprawled on the floor, groaning.

"Mal?"

A moment later Valentine staggered in, squinting. "What are you doing? It's like two a.m."

Malcolm sprang up and dragged his sister to the window, shoving the spyglass into her hands. "Look across the street."

"At what?"

"You know what! Come on, just do it."

Sighing, Valentine held the spyglass to her eye. "What am I looking for?"

"You'll know. Shouldn't be long now."

Malcolm watched with her, determined to catch the next pulse. But after a moment, he knew something was wrong. *It should have happened already.* "These pulses of light were coming from the window across the street! I . . ." *What's taking so long?* Minutes passed as they watched absolutely nothing happen.

Valentine handed him the spyglass. "Well, this was fun. Go to sleep. Tomorrow is a school day." She glanced out the window as she turned to leave. "Hmm, looks like the storm broke. G'night."

Deflated, Malcolm studied the sky as his twin closed the door. The lightning had stopped, the thunder had quieted, and the house had become a dark, old shell again. He dropped onto his bed with a sigh.

Maybe the light just played tricks on me.

But the face in the window would not leave his mind. Sleep eluded him, and he found himself shivering at the memory of those eyes. Despite his efforts to believe otherwise, Malcolm knew what he'd seen.

"Someone's inside that house."

CHAPTER 2

First-day jitters. *That's all they are*, Malcolm told himself as he and Valentine entered their first classroom at Emmett Brown High School. They picked a lab table next to the windows and settled onto a stool.

Everyone has jitters the first day of school, he reminded himself. Being in a new town didn't make his own any better. Plus, they'd be scattering to different classrooms for every subject. Six classes, six teachers—that meant six chances of getting someone weird or mean or half-crazy. Or worse, someone boring. Malcolm perused his class schedule, trying to deduce if any of the names suggested evil tendencies.

The key is the first class, he repeated. *Just hit the ground running, don't look back, and it'll be smooth sailing.* The morning bell rang as the last few students filed in past the open door. *Oh, and try to forget about the mystery man inside the impossible house.*

Malcolm chuckled as Valentine fidgeted with her supplies, arranging and then rearranging them.

"Shut up," she said, brushing a lock of wavy red hair out of her eyes.

"No, I get it. I mean, how can you ace the class with your pen at the wrong angle?"

She shot him a fake glare.

Malcolm grinned at his twin. "Don't worry, Val. You know you're a science wizard. It'll be—"

The classroom door slammed shut with a boom. A man in his late thirties stood in the corner, staring out at the students with sharp eyes.

"Mal," Valentine whispered. "Was he behind the door the whole time?"

Malcolm nodded, transfixed by the strange sight.

The man's attention stopped on a sweaty, petrified student with braces. Lurching from his hiding spot, the teacher pulled a rough, gray stone from his pocket, charged toward the lab tables and hurled it at the student. A collective gasp exploded from the class, and the boy flinched as it bounced off his chest and fell lightly to the floor.

After a heartbeat of silence, the man in the jacket laughed. The boy bent to pick it up and let out a relieved giggle, showing the class how he could squeeze the trick "stone" flat in his fist.

The class joined in with the laughter, and the strange man sat on the edge of the teacher's desk with a satisfied sigh. Malcolm noticed that his feet didn't touch the floor. He couldn't have been more than five-foot-two.

"Ah, I love foam. So versatile," he said, revealing another surprise—a proper British accent.

"Pretty good trick," Malcolm whispered. "For a hobbit."

Valentine stifled a laugh.

The teacher wrote *Lucius Carmichael* on the chalkboard in large block letters. "Like some of you, possibly, I am new to the fair town of Emmett's Bluff. You may call me Mr. Carmichael, and this year I will be teaching you the secrets of the universe."

He faced the students with an impish grin. "My superiors like to call it Introduction to Chemistry. But what is chemistry, really? It is the key, the central science that connects all other natural sciences. Astronomy, physics, geology—the tools for unlocking the mysteries of our world—eventually they all come back to their master. That is what chemistry is, and that is what I will teach you—to be the masters of your own destiny, one molecule at a time."

He paused as if waiting for something, then seemed disappointed. Malcolm wondered if he'd expected them to cheer.

"Well," he said. "Let's unlock our future, shall we? First, we'll see what you already know. Who can tell me what chemical property describes the ability of an atom to attract electrons toward itself in a covalent bond?"

Twenty pairs of eyes looked everywhere but at the teacher. Malcolm watched Valentine fidget with a familiar gleam in her eye. She knew the answer, but couldn't bring herself to speak up.

"Should I answer for you?" he whispered. "Or just tell them what happened at homecoming last year?"

Her hand sprang into the air.

"Ah, a brave soul! Miss?"

"Valentine Gilbert. Um, electronegativity?"

Mr. Carmichael's eyes narrowed. "Are you asking me or telling me?"

"Well, um." She braced herself. "Telling?"

"Relax, Miss Gilbert." He flashed another easy grin. "You are most certainly correct. Round one goes to you!"

Valentine released the breath she'd been holding and gave

Malcolm a grateful look. An instant later, the door burst open. A tall, skinny boy stumbled into the classroom, nearly tripping over his low-slung sports bag.

"Whoa!" Half his textbooks tumbled to the floor. "Figures." He knelt to gather them and lost two more. A murmur grew among the class, and the boy stared up from the floor. "Okay, who moved the gym?"

The class burst into laughter. He straightened, looking proud of himself as he smoothed his blue and gray basketball uniform.

"Mister . . . ?" the teacher called.

"Fred Marshall in the flesh, dawg. Where can I park?"

"Unless 'dawg' is slang for 'brilliant one,' you will address me as Mr. Carmichael. Take any open seat. Quietly."

While Mr. Carmichael resumed the discussion, the new student chose a seat directly across the aisle from Valentine. He ran his fingers through strikingly blond, spiked hair that seemed to stick out in every direction, and then he peered around the room as if already bored.

Malcolm watched as Fred's gaze settled on Valentine, lingering for a moment too long. He leaned in her direction, and Malcolm grinned inside. This would be good.

"Hey, sorry 'bout charging in like that," Fred whispered to her. "Coach wouldn't let me go. 'Gotta start the year off right,' whatever that means. Y'know?"

Valentine barely glanced in his direction.

"So, uh, what'd I miss?"

"Oh, Mr. Marshall," Mr. Carmichael interrupted. "I assume, based on your attention level, that you are familiar with the basic concepts of chemistry. Tell me, how would you identify a chemical element by examining its nucleus?"

Fred's eyes widened like a deer in headlights.

"Care to venture a guess?"

Fred glanced around the room as if looking for the answer on the walls. His face reddened as he sank into the chair and folded his arms.

"You don't know?" The teacher's stare bored into him. "Well, at least you can throw a ball through a hoop. I'm sure that's everything you'll need in life." He let the silence drag, then turned back to the board. "Continuing . . ."

Three classes and a lunch period later, the hallways were crowded and buzzing with first-day energy. At their lockers, the twins changed out textbooks and tried not to drop anything in the sea of sneakers. Malcolm slowed when he grasped World History, easing it into his bag to avoid scuffs and bends.

"Wow." Valentine shook her head. "So much love, it's almost creepy. If history were a girl, you'd be staring in her window at night."

"Hey, for me, history would just smile and wave," Malcolm returned, zipping his bag. "But you'd get a face full of pepper spray."

"Good thing I only spy on electrons, then."

Malcolm glanced over her shoulder with an evil grin. "Tell that to *him*."

"Hey, what up?"

Malcolm choked back laughter as Valentine slowly turned, face frozen in an awkward smile.

"Oh," she said. "Hi . . . um, Fred?"

"The one and only." The lanky ball player held out his hand. "We didn't get properly acquainted. Fred Marshall, slammin' athlete."

"Hi," Valentine avoided his hand and grabbed for Malcolm. "Um, have you met my twin brother?" She took a step back and shoved Malcolm in front.

"S'up, player?" Fred leaned against the lockers. "So, you guys ever get social?"

"Yeah, sometimes," Malcolm replied. He felt Valentine poke him in the back and suppressed a smile. "Uh, but right now we're still helping our dad get the house organized."

"So gimme the stats. Where you from, where you live in town?"

"Came from Chicago. We live on the east side, in our grandmother's house. We're helping out 'cause she's, uh, kinda old."

"Awesome. You likin' it so far?"

"Yeah, it's pretty nice, even if the neighborhood's kind of odd. We're right across from that blank house."

"Blank house?"

"You know, the one with no doors. Big, super old, looks like . . ." Malcolm noted Fred's puzzled expression and trailed off. "You don't know. Never mind, it's nothing."

"Don't sweat it." Fred peered past Malcolm. "How 'bout you, Miss Chemistry? You likin' the neighborhood?"

Valentine shrugged and pulled out her phone, focusing on the screen.

"Well, maybe you'll like it after you come to my world-famous Start of the Year party. First chance to let people know you're somebody! You gonna come?"

"Are you recruiting for your wannabe players' club again?" a new voice said.

Malcolm turned to see a short, pretty Chinese girl stalking toward them. She fixed Fred with a stare through long, half-purple hair.

"Or do I have to warn them about your lame parties? Your slang isn't the only thing out of date."

Fred shrugged. "Yo, I gotta be me. And hey, be nice around the newbies." He gestured to the twins. "Malcolm and Valentine, meet Winter Tao. She runs the newspaper and believes every conspiracy theory ever. And say what you want, girl. You know you'll be there."

"Someone needs to make sure you don't embarrass yourself." Winter leaned toward Valentine. "Last year, a girl beat him at poker and pushed him in the pool."

"That was you!" Fred protested as Valentine laughed. "Man, why do I keep inviting you?"

"He knows he'd be bored without me," Winter said to Valentine. "I like your boots."

"Thanks." Valentine smiled back. "I like your hair."

"Nice to meet you," Malcolm said, then turned to Fred. "Yeah, I think we can be there."

Fred pumped his fist. "Sweet!"

Valentine tugged on her brother's bag. "We need to run or we'll be late for class."

"Oh yeah, we really should go."

"That's cool. We'll talk more at the party." Winter nodded to Malcolm, grinned at Valentine, and punched Fred in the arm.

"Ow!" Fred yelped.

The twins plunged into the crowd in search of their next class.

"You're not usually so ice queen-y," Malcolm said to Valentine's back as they hurried along. "He annoys you that much?"

"I'd have to care to be annoyed."

He grinned. "Careful, Val. You know who the brainy girl always ends up with in movies."

She cast a withering stare back at him and quickened her pace, though he could tell she was trying not to laugh.

THE twins' new neighborhood seemed so odd to Malcolm. Oma Grace's house sat on a straight road with only a dozen old houses, and not a single tree for a half-mile in any direction. While the rest of Emmett's Bluff exploded in lush colors, Pleasant Point Drive wallowed in the same drab, muted pallor that it had when the twins' dad was a kid there.

The school bus sped away from the Pleasant Point neighborhood entrance. Malcolm coughed as a cloud of exhaust swirled around them.

"I can't wait till we can drive," he said, waving the fumes from his face. They walked down the sidewalk toward their new home. New to them, anyway.

"You don't care for the luxury of the school transit system?" Valentine teased.

Malcolm snorted. "We're fifteen, Val. That's another year of taking the bus." Something cold and hard brushed against Malcolm's right hand. "Although, this is still better than the Chicago buses, and—"

Realization struck, and he stopped walking to stare down at his hand. Without knowing it, he'd been touching an old wrought-iron fence. He forced himself to look up.

The faded white house loomed over them. Despite the blue skies and warm afternoon breeze, the air around it felt gray and chilly, as if cloaked in perpetual shadow.

He gaped up at the house. "We almost did it again."

"Almost did what?" Valentine said, looking at her phone.

"Walked by without even noticing this place." Malcolm traced his hand over the gate. "Everything looks so old, but nothing's broken." He tried the handle, and the gate swung open without a sound. "Oh, crap," Malcolm grabbed the gate and swung it closed. He glanced up as it clanged shut, and he gasped. His grip froze on the handle.

A face glared down from the window.

"I bet Dad loved growing up here," Valentine said, still walking. "It's so odd, and you know how much he loves that."

It was the same piercing stare as before—glowering eyes half-shrouded in darkness. Malcolm felt as if a fist gripped his insides and pulled, locking him into the stare. His pulse quickened, hands sweating as he tried and failed to break away.

Examining her phone, Valentine stepped onto the empty street. "Let's get home. I want to finish my homework early."

Malcolm swallowed, throat dry. His pale skin went clammy. "Val," he whispered. "There's a . . . face . . . in the window again."

"A what in the what?" she whispered back. "Wait, why are we whispering?"

The man pressed closer to the glass. His expression changed, and Malcolm recoiled.

"Val, look! Look up at the window!"

"Hey, speak up." Valentine grabbed his arm and shook.

Malcolm's gaze broke away and warm air rushed into his lungs. "In the window," he said, shivering. "There was a man!"

She eyed him. "A man? Not just a shadow or something?"

"I saw him last night during the storm, and just now he was staring at me again!" He turned back to the now-empty window, searching. "I think he was laughing at me."

She looked up at the darkened window, then back at Malcolm with raised eyebrows.

"I'm telling you, I know what I saw!"

Valentine smiled. Holding his arm, she turned until the

house was at their backs. "I know it's weird, but it's just an old house. Okay?"

He hesitated, glancing back at the window. "But, there was a . . ." A cloud of doubt wrapped around him again. He rubbed his arms. "I'm so cold."

She tugged, leading them across the street. "Come on. Let's go play your Xbox."

He eyed her. "You never play video games."

"Well, you never see creepy faces in abandoned houses. It's a day for firsts."

Malcolm laughed and the cold seemed to dissipate as they walked toward home. A breeze blew again, and in a moment they were at their front porch.

"So, he laughed at you, huh?" Valentine opened the door.

"Yeah. Weird, right?"

She tousled his shaggy brown hair as they stepped inside. "Well, you are kinda funny looking."

"Says my twin."

CHAPTER 3

Malcolm turned from the front window of his new bedroom and got back to work. He'd found good spots for all his stuff except the last few things. Now an Apache arrow went on the shelf above his headboard, next to the brass spyglass. The antique Damascus steel daggers with leather and bone handles would have a special place.

"How's your room looking?" Valentine called from her own room.

Malcolm paused from hanging the daggers on the wall. "Well, I'm trying to finish here so I can go to one of the rock concerts in the front yard," he said. "Apparently, we got free tickets to all the shows."

"Ha-ha, nice try. I'll bet nothing's happened on this street in a century."

Malcolm plopped onto the foot of his bed and leaned against the front window sill. "Ever notice how it has a fence and a gate but no walkway?"

"What does?"

"That old house."

"There aren't any doors." Valentine appeared at his doorway. "Where would a walkway go?"

Malcolm shrugged. "Still seems weird we missed it for so long. I mean, it's right across from us."

"Technically it's across from our neighbor. Speaking of which," Valentine pointed through the left-facing window, "your old house isn't the only weird thing around here."

Malcolm peered at the squat brick house, which was situated directly across from the mysterious old house. On the porch sat a graying man in a worn leather chair. Like always, he stared out at the street with hardened steel eyes.

"Yeah, I've seen him," Malcolm said. "It is kinda odd. Is he looking for something?"

"Maybe he lost his marbles." Valentine grinned. "Or maybe he's just retired and bored."

"We could ask Oma Grace."

"Yeah, Grace the Immortal probably knows everyone. She's been here forever."

"And don't you forget it," a voice said from behind.

The twins whipped around to see their grandmother at the door. Tall for an elderly woman and slightly plump, she stood over them with the regal posture of a queen and wore her silver hair like a crown.

"Grandmothers know every*thing* and every*one*."

"And they're ninjas, apparently," Malcolm said. "I didn't even hear you come in."

Oma Grace chuckled. "What, you imagined old granny would need help on the stairs?"

Valentine smiled. "I can't imagine you needing help with anything."

"Well, you can help set the table. Dinner's almost ready. Oh, and please wake your father."

Malcolm sighed. "Again?"

"Yes, he's asleep in front of that computer. Honestly, how does he find time to write all those novels?"

"We'll get him up," Malcolm promised.

The twins crossed to the opposite side of the house and stopped at the closed door at the end of the hallway. Valentine reached out but hesitated just short of the handle. Malcolm stepped past her and grabbed the knob.

The door opened to their father's bedroom and office. On the opposite wall sat a tall wooden desk cluttered with papers, a computer screen, and their father's snoring head. He had fallen asleep on the keyboard and the screen displayed a cascade of Q's.

Valentine brushed his shoulder. "Dad," she whispered. Nothing.

"Dad," Malcolm said, louder.

Valentine grabbed his shoulder and shook. "Dad! Neil Gilbert!"

He woke with a start and grasped Valentine's hand. Brushing brown hair out of his face, he looked up with half-alert eyes.

"Emily?"

Valentine's face froze. She recoiled, shaking free of her father's hand. He stared confused for a moment before his expression straightened.

"Oh. Hi, baby. For a second, I thought . . . well . . ."

She blinked at him, speechless.

Neil forced an awkward chuckle. "Sometimes you look—"

"Dinner's ready," Malcolm broke in. "Are you hungry?"

"Oh hey, son." Neil's tone brightened. "Yeah sure, I could eat. Go on down, I'll just be a minute."

Malcolm gripped his sister's arm and aimed for the door. On their way downstairs, he cast sidelong glances at her dark, pinched expression.

"He didn't mean to—"

"Let's just eat."

Oma Grace and her legendary beef stew waited for them. Steam rose from the bowls in slow, lazy tendrils, filling the room with earthy aromas. Neil arrived and they dove in, the first moments passing in silence. Valentine ate head-down, clutching the silver pendant that hung from a chain around her neck.

Malcolm searched for any reason to break the mood. "So, that neighbor next door seems odd. Some people might say creepy."

Oma Grace raised a disapproving eyebrow.

"I-I don't mean me," Malcolm stammered. "But, you know . . . people. Do you know him, Oma?"

"For a long time now." She plucked a roll from the basket and tore it into pieces. "Walter's a . . . complicated man. He's seen a lot in his time."

"Always seemed kind of unfriendly to me," Neil observed. "Like he never really liked anyone, just tolerated them."

"Yes." Oma Grace's eyes grew distant. "War can do that to a man."

She looked off at something beyond the walls, her spoon hovering above the bowl. Silence fell again. Malcolm's stomach grumbled as he eyed a roll, but he wasn't sure if he should move. He jumped as thunder cracked outside and lightning flashed through the windows.

"I don't remember this place having so many storms, Mom," Neil said. "We've had several just this month."

"No," Oma Grace said, still distracted. "No, we haven't had storms like this for a long time." Her attention returned as rain came pouring down. She chuckled. "But when you're as old as I am, everything was a long time ago."

"How old are you this year?" Malcolm asked.

"A lady never tells, young man," she said, and rose to collect the dishes. "Now, you two come help me clean up."

Valentine pushed away from the table and darted into the kitchen. Neil leaned forward to call after her, but Oma Grace stopped him with a hand.

"Not now," she whispered, patting his arm. "Let her be. Okay?"

Neil leaned back in his chair with a sigh. "Can you help her?"

"She's closed up tight. Won't let anyone in, not even me."

"Or me," Malcolm lamented as he gathered more dishes.

Valentine went to bed early, leaving him to finish cleaning. Afterward, he settled at the table to pore over his World History textbook and let the evening tick away. Gusting wind splattered rain against the house, and before long his mind sank into stories of times past.

Outside, a dark figure drifted down the street, cloaked in shadow. Approaching the house with no doors, it touched the rain-soaked wall and melted through in a flash of light.

CHAPTER 4

Neil pulled through the gates of the sprawling Marshall estate on the northern edge of town. The driveway snaked through manicured trees and rolling hills and finally onto a wide, green glen. From the backseat, the twins gaped up at the house.

"Wow," Neil said. "I've seen mansions before, but . . ."

Valentine nodded. "You could park our house in the entryway."

Neil studied them through the rearview mirror. "You'll be okay?"

Malcolm faltered. "Sure," he said, forcing strength into his voice. "No problem."

Neil nodded. "Well, call if you need an early pickup. Remember, I'll be back at eleven." He smiled. "Have fun!"

The twins clambered out of the car. The sound of the engine receded into the distance, leaving them alone with the stone monstrosity. Lightning flashed overhead, creating an ominous scene, as if they were stepping into a horror-movie mansion. Except this mansion's doors and windows were open, pumping bass-heavy music into the air. They paused at the front door, regarding each other with a nervous grin.

"Well," Malcolm said, drawing himself up. "Mustn't keep our public waiting."

Valentine giggled as they stepped across the threshold. "Remember, they're just as scared of you as you are of them."

"Yeah. Don't make eye contact, and play dead if they charge you."

Fred appeared behind the twins and wrapped them in his lanky arms. "Hey hey, you made it!"

Pulling them through the gigantic foyer, he strode to the balcony overlooking a living room the size of the school gym. A sea of their classmates danced along with the pulsing music, dimly lit by strobes, colored spotlights, and a massive disco ball hanging in place of a chandelier.

"Hey!" Fred called out to the crowd. "My new favorite twins are here, yo!"

He grinned at Malcolm, then longer at Valentine. The twins smiled back, and Malcolm silently wondered if Fred realized he was a walking stereotype.

"Consider yourselves cool by association. Come on."

He led them down the curved staircase and through the crowd of dancers. Veering to the right, he cut into one of several broad hallways.

"That was where we get our dance on, obviously."

He pointed into side rooms as they walked. "Here we got a couple rooms to chill out. Video games and whatever in that room. Drinks and food in the kitchen, theater's across the way, billiard room's on right. Go anywhere you want, it's all good."

"Thanks for having us, Fred," Malcolm said. He elbowed his sister.

"Oh," she said, forcing a smile. "Yeah, um, thanks. This is really nice."

Fred beamed at her. "Hey, it's cool. Small towns suck without friends, but your boy's gotcha covered."

Valentine turned away and suppressed a laugh. She caught a glimpse of Winter in one of the chill-out rooms.

"So anyway," Fred continued, "Outside—"

Wordlessly, Valentine peeled off and entered Winter's room.

Fred paused. "Oh."

"She must've seen, um, cupcakes or something," Malcolm covered. "Can't resist them."

Fred recovered quickly. "No prob. Come on, I'll take you to the big show."

They backtracked to the main room. The mass of dancers parted for Fred as he strutted toward the three-story back wall, made entirely of plate glass.

Sliding doors opened to the backyard, where another crowd lounged on padded chairs or splashed in the Olympic-sized pool. Swimming didn't seem like the brightest idea to Malcolm, considering the increasing presence of lightning in the sky. A clattering noise echoed from the half-pipe adjacent to the pool, where someone had just wiped out.

"Nice move, Luke!" Fred joked at the skater, then glanced at Malcolm. "If you get this one jump right, you can land in the pool. You skate?"

Eyes wide, Malcolm shook his head.

"You all right, dude?"

"I guess I didn't expect all this. You know, small town and everything."

Fred followed his gaze around the patio, confused. "Oh!" he said finally. "You mean the house. Yeah, guess I'm used to it.

My dad owns some malls and part of the power plant outside town. Builds a buttload of houses, too."

Malcolm perked up at this. Maybe Fred's dad could shed light on his little mystery. "Do you know if he built the houses on my street? Or would he know who did?"

"Not a clue, dawg." Fred pulled out his phone. "I'll text him and ask."

Malcolm nodded his thanks and resumed marveling at the huge party. "I didn't know our school had this many students."

"It doesn't, but your boy gets around." Fred said. A moment later his phone beeped. Its glow lit his face as he read the screen. "My dad built four houses on your street, newer ones. Someone else built five. The other two are *way* old. Dad says someone built 'em before they started keeping records."

Malcolm's pulse quickened. "Which two?"

Fred exchanged another series of texts while Malcolm sipped on his drink, awkwardly searching the party for anyone he knew. *You've barely met anyone. Who are you expecting to recognize?*

"Yo, check it out." Fred slipped his phone into Malcolm's hand. His dad had sent an aerial photo of Pleasant Point Drive with two houses inside a red circle. Malcolm studied the screen and shook his head in disappointment.

Oma Grace's house—his house—and Walter Crane's house next door. The house with no doors wasn't even in the photo.

"I know these are old, but what about the place across the street? The abandoned one with no doors."

"Oh that's right, your urban legend." Taking his phone back, Fred tapped another message. He received a swift reply. "Naw, man, sorry. My dad's pretty sure there's nothing else on that street."

Malcolm's brow furrowed. He resisted the impulse to start shouting until someone acknowledged he'd actually seen the house. Had everyone in this town made some secret pact to pretend it didn't exist? Or was he just being crazy?

Fred's arm clamped around his shoulder. "You know what's a shame, bro? You been here for months and still don't have a nice Midwestern girl to kick it with."

Malcolm forced a chuckle, suddenly uneasy. Fred pulled him forward and aimed for the pool.

"Come on, let's see what we can do 'bout that."

VALENTINE approached the group lounging around the plush room's empty fireplace. Clad in variations of dark-rimmed glasses and ironic clothing, they appeared to be the town's young intellectuals. Four of them gathered closely around Winter as she reached the crescendo of a passionate diatribe.

"Sixty-three percent of the school's program budget goes to sports! Until they learn there's more to the world than football, we'll always be a backwater town with zero relevance."

The group nodded collective agreement. Valentine opened a soda can with a snap-hiss, drawing Winter's attention.

"Val! Meet the newspaper team. Guys, this is Valentine Gilbert. She's from the city, has a brain, and—get this—she actually uses it."

Valentine stepped into the circle with an embarrassed smile, feeling as if four pairs of eyes were weighing and measuring her. "Hi. But how do you know—"

"Oh, I read your transcript," Winter said as if it were nothing. "The firewall at school sucks. Right, Patrick?"

A mop-topped boy in a *Firefly* t-shirt nodded with a

smirk. Valentine thought she recognized him from her Intro to Chemistry class.

"That's Patrick Morgan, our computer geek." Winter gestured at each member of the circle. "Nathan's our cartoonist and pop culture guru. Carly knows all the gossip anywhere, anytime. And Brynne is so cute, no one has ever refused an interview."

Each of them tossed a lazy wave at Valentine—except the bubbly Brynne, whose blonde ringlets bounced as she squeaked an excited greeting.

"We mustn't forget the ringleader," said the fifth member, a thin boy with shoulder-length black hair that fell halfway across his face. He leaned back against the stone fireplace and adjusted his tinted round glasses. Deep brown eyes peered up at Valentine. "Winter Tao—alpha geek, wordsmith, and professional scary girl."

Valentine's gaze lingered on this one. His vibe felt different somehow—calm, not desperate to party his brains out like most of the others. His posture, expression, and tone of voice all radiated quiet confidence.

Winter gave an exaggerated sigh and rolled her eyes. "This is John Carter, the conscience. Not technically on the staff, but he has a talent for keeping me in line. I truly hate him. Anyway, open discussion, so feel free to jump in."

Winter resumed an authoritative stance and continued her speech. Valentine sat against the fireplace, feeling awkward in the unfamiliar group. A series of flashes drew her attention to the windows—yet another storm was coming, and growing quickly. *What is going on with this town?*

She tore her thoughts and attention away from the lightning. It wouldn't do for the new girl to spend the party gazing worriedly out the window. Her gaze slipped to the boy at the other end of the hearth.

John Carter glanced at her from behind his hair, looked away, then back again. Then away. Finally, he leaned toward her.

"Hello, Valentine," he said. "Welcome to the largest congregation of teenagers in the state. Be certain to go see the small lake they call a swimming pool."

"Thanks," Valentine laughed. "I just want to avoid getting lost in this house."

"I did that once. Somehow I kept walking into closets. Just keep making right turns, you'll escape eventually." His eyes shifted to the silver pendant around her neck. "I like your antique. Where did you find it?"

"My, um . . . someone gave it to me. A long time ago." Valentine tried to say more, but the words refused to come out. She looked away, reddening.

"You moved from Chicago?" he said, mercifully changing the subject.

"Yeah. You don't sound like you're from here either. Did you move from somewhere?"

"Probably." John shrugged.

"Oh, a man of mystery," she teased.

"Oh yes." Eyes narrowing, he looked around with mock suspicion. "I'm here incognito. Have you seen a man named Villefort?"

Valentine stared at him. "That's my favorite book."

John smiled. "There's no book I've read more than *The Count of Monte Cristo*."

A butterfly of excitement fluttered through Valentine's stomach. She pushed it away. *Stop that,* she told herself. Her phone buzzed in her pocket. Unlocking it, she read a new text and covered her mouth, laughing.

"What is it?" John asked.

"I'll forward it to you. What's your number?"

"I don't have a phone."

She gaped. "You don't have a phone?"

He shrugged. "I suppose I'm behind the times."

"Well, let's just say my brother needs backup."

Valentine stood to leave. Three steps away she hesitated. *Walk away.* She turned halfway back around and stopped again, chewing her lower lip. *WALK AWAY.* The doorway loomed at the edge of her vision. *Just go. It's better for both of you.* She forced her insides quiet. *No. This is a fresh start—we all promised that.*

She looked back at John. "Um, do you want to come?"

John sat up with surprise. He glanced over at the rest of the group.

"Oh, that's okay," she said quickly. "You're with them and—"

"Yes." He stood. "I would like that."

Slipping away, they made their way out to the pool. Valentine stood on a lounge chair and peered across the patio.

"What's happening with your brother?"

She caught sight of Malcolm and laughed again. "Only his worst nightmare. Come on."

She jumped down and picked her way through the crowd, John following. Fred's voice rose above the noise as they reached a clearing, the center of which had drawn a sizable audience. There stood Malcolm, staring at the ground as if he'd rather be six feet under it. Fred marched around him, calling into the crowd with his arms in the air.

"He's brand new from Chi-town and lookin' for love! Now,

RYANDALTON

which one of you fine honeys wants to take my man here on a date? Come on, look at that face!"

Valentine turned to a stout blonde. "Ten bucks if you volunteer."

The blonde's hand shot into the air. "Over here, Fred!"

"We have a winner, folks!" Fred announced. He patted Malcolm on the back and pushed him toward his "date."

Malcolm approached the blonde as if she were a guillotine. Grinning, Valentine slipped a bill into the girl's hand and stepped through the dispersing crowd. At the sight of her, his shoulders sagged with relief.

"Well, that was interesting," she said. "Have fun?"

"There are things I'd rather do," Malcolm replied. "Like face a firing squad, or an angry bear. Or a firing squad of angry bears." He noticed that she wasn't alone.

"Oh, right. John Carter, this is my brother Malcolm."

The two of them shook hands. Malcolm shot her a questioning glance, which she ignored. Mercifully, he let it go and turned to the blonde.

"Thanks for the rescue. Think I'll find a quiet corner and, you know, kill myself."

"Hold on, now." The blonde pushed the cash back into Valentine's hand. "You're cute, and I claimed you fair and square. You're my date tonight."

She wrapped a muscled arm around Malcolm and pulled him away. "You got a nice accent. Come tell me 'bout the big city."

Malcolm cast a pleading look back at Valentine before disappearing into the crowd.

"And they never saw him again," John quipped.

Valentine burst into laughter.

"Should we rescue him?"

"Probably." They began to walk. "But we'll let him handle it this time. A night with actual people will do him good."

"He's more of a loner?"

"Loner, bookworm, geek. We both are, I guess. He has trouble doing things and being with people these days. And he's afraid to talk to girls."

"All guys are, a little bit," John said. "They just never admit it."

"Does that include you?"

"No, I meant all guys except myself," he replied, a twinkle in his eye.

"Oh, of course you did." She pushed him playfully.

"So, you are brother-less for a while. What will you do for the rest of the party?"

Valentine stopped short, suddenly self-conscious. All at once she felt her insides slam shut, as if they'd just realized what she was doing. "Oh. Um, well, I'm not sure. I guess . . ."

She fell silent, searching the party as if desperate for an exit. A huge burst of lightning cut across the sky, making her jump. She realized her heart was racing.

John nodded, a faint smile playing across his lips. "I should probably join back with my group," he said. "It was a pleasure meeting you, Valentine."

She watched John's back as he slipped through the crowd, not sure whether to feel relieved or kick herself. Her heart wouldn't stop beating a thousand times a minute. Was she anxious? Upset? Worried? *I don't even know anymore.* She clutched the back of a chair for support. *Why am I such a mess?*

A crack of thunder split the sky and rattled the house,

drowning out the stereo. Then the house went dark. No lights, dance music, nothing. Cries of alarm echoed through the party, especially inside the house.

Fred appeared through the crowd, arms in the air and waving. "Chill out, dawgs, we got a backup generator! Ain't nothing to worry about."

Seconds later, a machine-like sound rumbled to life and the house woke up again. Lights came back, music thumped, and in no time at all the party was back in full swing. Though the lightning storm raged on, their momentary fear was forgotten.

Stopping at Valentine's side, Fred sighed in relief. "Now that was lucky. I was just guessing."

She gaped at him in disbelief. He just shrugged and grinned. "Good thing my dad actually did put in a generator, huh?"

Back home, Malcolm leaned against Valentine's doorframe while she gazed through her window, peering up at the angry sky.

"More lightning tonight," he said. "Storm was even bigger this time."

"Mm-hm."

"Can you believe how quiet this town is? They practically roll up the sidewalks at night. Even the gas stations were closed."

"Mm-hm."

Malcolm grinned. "Wow. Johnny Hipster must be smoother than he looks."

Valentine looked at him now, reddening. "I don't know what you mean."

"Sure you don't. Since when do you give any guy that much attention?"

Valentine bristled. "I do talk to people, you know. It didn't mean anything. How was your date with Country Strong?"

"Well, I learned about cattle farming, and it turns out my eyes are 'just darling.' So that's exciting."

"Wow."

"Yeah."

They both fell quiet. Malcolm rested his head against the doorway. At that moment, it all seemed more real than it had before. Their life was here now.

With a sigh, Valentine sprawled onto her bed. "I can already tell high school's going to be complicated."

In the deserted town square, darkened shops bathed in the light of the moon and a handful of street lamps. Dried leaves skittered across the ground on a warm, gusting wind.

Frantic footsteps echoed on the pavement as a boy dashed across the square. Panting, he swerved into a shadowed alley between two buildings.

The dark corridor was littered with overflowing garbage containers—he struggled to keep running between the debris. Fifty paces in, the alley cut sharply to the left. As he neared the bend, glass shattered behind him and the glow of the street lamp winked out.

In the sudden darkness, his feet struck the corner of a heavy box and flew from underneath him. His body smacked into the pavement, crushing the air from his lungs. A smear of mud stained his *Firefly* t-shirt. Pushing against the pavement, he begged his stunned body to move.

Come on come on come on, get up get up!

A garbage can flew overhead and split against the wall, raining trash and debris down on his back. With a cry, he heaved himself up and dove deeper into the network of alleyways.

An oversized metal dumpster sat at the meeting point

between three alleys. Gasping for air, he crouched on the dumpster's far side and flattened against the brick wall. In the refuge of shadows, the fear quieted and his breath slowly returned. He strained his ears for the slightest rustle, while a chill crept into the night air.

Shivering, the boy dared to wonder if he was now alone. If it was safe to move. He poked one eye around the edge of the dumpster, where only darkness and garbage greeted him. Sighing in relief, he stood and inched forward. He could see his own breath in the cold now.

Lightning flashed across the cloudy sky.

A darker mass of shadows detached from the night and charged forward, barreling into him. He flew backward and smacked against the brick. Colors danced behind his eyes and the alley seemed to spin.

The swirling mass of darkness pinned him to the wall, hanging above the ground. It loomed closer, and smoky black wisps reached out to brush against his face. He turned away, trembling.

"Oh god," he panted. "Please. Please, I swear I didn't see anything. I swear I didn't see anything!"

The shadow pulled his body away from the wall, then slammed it back against the gritty surface, rattling his vision. He cried out as something cracked in his shoulder.

The shadow leaned closer and a thousand angry voices shouted at him, the sound digging into his head. *"WWWEEE KNNNOOOWWW WWWHHHAAATTT YYYOOOUUU SSAAAWW, PPPAAATTTRRRIIICCCKKK MMMOOORRRGGGAAANNN."* The words crushed his thoughts. *"WWWHHHOOO KKKNNNOOOWWWSSS WWWHHHEEERRREEE YYYOOOUUU AAARRRREEE?"*

He shuddered against the assault on his mind. "H-how," he stuttered. "How d-do you know my—"

"*WWWHHHOOO KKKNNNOOOWWWSSS?*"

Patrick screamed, his resistance breaking under the invading voices. "No one! I'm just—" He caught his breath. "Just coming home from a party. I took a shortcut no one knows. No one knows, I swear!"

The voices roared into his thoughts, and he felt himself crumbling inside. "I-I'll go away," he cried. "Tomorrow, I swear, I'll go away and never come back. I'll never tell anyone. *Please, I'll never tell anyone!*"

"*NNNOOO. YYYOOOUUU WWWOOONNN'TTT.*"

Patrick suddenly dropped to the ground. Leaning against the wall, he barely managed to keep his feet. He looked up in confusion.

The shadow floated back and the air crackled around it. Overhead, the sky rippled with lightning. A pinprick of light appeared between the shifting shadows, pointed in his direction. Then a beam of silvery blue light lanced out from the darkness and struck Patrick in the chest. He shrieked.

In the blink of an eye, a shimmering bubble of blue energy enveloped him. It swirled around him, distorting his surroundings, spinning faster and faster. He felt an instant of panic as everything in the bubble warped impossibly—including him. Something beyond perception opened and sucked him in.

In the next blink, the bubble twisted and collapsed into a pinpoint of light. The tiny glow rippled, winked from existence, and Patrick Morgan was gone.

The shadow melted back into the night.

CHAPTER 5

"Donald Blake?"
"Here."
"Kaylee Frye?"
"Here."

Mr. Carmichael scrawled instructions for their next lab experiment on the blackboard. As he wrote, he called the roll from memory.

"How does he do that?" Malcolm whispered.

"Do what?"

"He's doing, like, eight things at once, and perfectly."

Valentine grinned. "Being brilliant has its perks, I guess."

"Austin Giffin?"

"Here."

Malcolm arrayed vials of multicolored chemicals next to the Bunsen burner while Valentine clicked away at her laptop.

"I hope *you* understand this," he said.

"Don't worry, I'll make sure you stay *not* on fire."

"Malcolm and Valentine Gilbert?"

"Here," they called.

"It's pretty easy." Valentine showed him the screen. "These are all the steps."

"Luke Harris?"

"Here."

"Patrick Morgan?"

Malcolm leaned over and studied the notes.

"Patrick Morgan?"

Amazingly, some of them actually made sense. Malcolm realized that, for the first time, he might not have to fake his way through a science class. He smiled. Even though the year had just started, having a brilliant teacher was coming with perks.

"Still no sign of Mr. Morgan," Mr. Carmichael said. "Well, if anyone happens upon the young truant, please tell him it's only civilized to send a fake note when you skip two weeks of school."

"Dude, he's missing," Fred said. "Never came home after my party. Cops came to my house to ask about him an' everything. You ain't heard? It's been on the news."

Mr. Carmichael's wry grin faded. He leaned back against his desk for support. "Oh. How dreadful."

Malcolm leaned over to his sister. "Did you hear about this?" he whispered.

"Yeah, Winter's been freaked out about it," she whispered back, her brow scrunched. "Police still haven't found him. She's been searching, too, calling all her reporter contacts. But it's like he just disappeared."

Malcolm sighed. "Is it just me, or does this town keep getting weirder?"

"Not just you." Valentine shook her head. "Something's really not right."

"Well," Mr. Carmichael said, drawing himself up. "We shall hope for his safe return. In the meantime, let us continue in the name of science. Miguel Jaco?"

"Here."

The twins were soon mixing fluids and working through equations, doing their best to put the town's troubles out of their minds. Malcolm finished stirring the next solution while Valentine plugged in their numbers.

"It's these next, right?" He plucked two vials from the table.

Valentine glanced up. "This one, yes." She gestured to his right hand. "Not the other."

A small shadow fell across the table.

"Can you explain Pauli's neutrino postulate?"

Malcolm looked up, and Mr. Carmichael fixed him with an impish grin.

"Uh, well, you know, it's where you, um—" His shoulders slumped. "No."

The teacher slid over to Valentine with eyebrows raised.

She sat straighter. "It's about the radioactive beta decay of an atomic nucleus."

"And how does Pauli account for the missing energy?"

"He guessed that a particle of zero charge and zero mass is released."

Mr. Carmichael beamed. "Truly, the future is in good hands, Miss Gilbert. And do not be discouraged, Malcolm. In this you may struggle, but I hear you're quite the prodigy when it comes to history. A subject in which you'd likely dominate, were our roles reversed."

"I do feel smarter in that class," Malcolm admitted.

"I quite understand, only when studying theories and equations." The teacher's eyes focused on him like a laser. "Yet each day I sense your hesitation, and I have concluded this comes from fear. That will not do. Science may not be your best friend, sir, but it will never be your enemy. So I make you this promise: commit to learning all you can from me, and I will open the universe and its mysteries to *you* as well." He held out a hand. "Are we agreed?"

Stunned, Malcolm reached out and grasped Mr. Carmichael's hand. The teacher gave a smile and a brisk shake, patted him on the shoulder and turned away.

"Mr. Marshall!" he snapped. "Stop that this instant!"

Malcolm turned to see Fred's Bunsen burner at maximum, the flame over a foot high. A beaker sat in the center, awash in the orange heat.

"Bigger flame means I'm done quicker, dawg!"

"Just do the experiment in the way your betters have instructed, and no argument!"

Fred rolled his eyes and reached for the knob to reduce the flame. Malcolm heard Valentine giggling beside him. Returning to their work, he struggled to contain his own laughter.

He heard a cracking sound, then something shattered and Fred yelped. Malcolm whipped back around to see Fred clutching his left hand, blood dripping from a cut across his knuckles. The glass beaker lay in pieces on the lab table.

"That's messed up," Fred said as he examined the wound.

"And there you have it," Mr. Carmichael said, brow furrowed. "Go see the nurse, young man. When you've returned, try not to endanger my classroom."

By the end of their third week, Malcolm and Valentine were settling into a solid academic rhythm. Mr. Carmichael's oddities had left the biggest first impression, but he was proving to be both a genius and an understanding teacher.

Other teachers stood out for their own reasons.

At twenty-five, the beautiful Madame LaChance was in her second year of teaching French. A native French speaker born in

Marseille, she seemed a perfect choice to teach the class—mostly because she hated everything about the English language.

Mr. Boomer's take-no-prisoners style of gym class turned average games like dodgeball into epic battles for survival.

Then there was Miss Miranda Marcus, teacher of history and professional oddball. On Monday, she'd given everyone historical nicknames. Valentine was now Pocahontas, likely due to her red hair, fair complexion, and total lack of resemblance to any Native American. Malcolm, a brown-haired boy of average height and build, had been dubbed Old Ironsides after the famous warship. He shook his head, wondering what universe he had wandered into.

"FOR SPARTAAAA!"

Malcolm snapped to attention. At the front of the class was Miss Marcus herself, bellowing a defiant battle cry and stabbing the air with a yardstick, gray hair flying.

"The Battle of Thermopylae!" she exclaimed, spinning and stabbing to punctuate each word. "Three hundred Spartans against an—*unstoppable—Persian—force*! Who can tell me what really happened?"

Malcolm sat like stone, half afraid to move. He wasn't the only one. The teacher squinted at the class.

"No guesses? Are you all secretly Persian?" She sat at her desk, smoothing her hair. "Well, much of history comes down to interpretation. It's a tragedy, but also an opportunity. A chance to investigate the past and discover hidden truths. Which leads me to this." Miss Marcus turned to the blackboard and wrote *Year Project* in large block letters. "This is my subtle hint that you're all about to get a project, which will be due at the end of the year."

A collective groan went up from the class. Except for Malcolm, who smiled for the first time.

"You will each choose a period and a region, then create a model to demonstrate the changes to that region during your chosen era. For example."

Miss Marcus set a rectangular box in front of the class. A wedge was cut from the front, showing an old turntable inside. She flipped a switch and the turntable began to spin. A cityscape rounded into view, showing stone buildings and the skeleton of a tall clock tower with the date 1843. As the city spun, the buildings took on a more modern style, and the clock tower was gradually completed.

Valentine gaped at the box, then at Malcolm, then back at the box.

"Last year, young Copernicus presented this model of Big Ben's construction. Use it as inspiration, but be original!"

The final bell rang. Most students were already packed and fleeing the classroom for their lives.

Valentine slung her bag over her shoulder. "I'm going home to put my head in the microwave."

"No, come here." Malcolm led them toward the teacher's desk.

"What are you doing?" Valentine hissed.

"Getting you an A. Miss Marcus?"

The teacher looked up from her papers. "Yes, Old Ironsides?"

"I was wondering if Val and I could do sort of a joint project?"

"I'm sorry, who?"

"I was wondering if Pocahontas and I could do the project together. Since we're new, I thought we'd learn the history of Emmett's Bluff."

"Forming alliances already, eh, young battleship?" Miss Marcus leaned back in her chair with a grin. "Very clever. I approve. But make sure to impress me. Now, off with you."

Valentine breathed a sigh as they left the classroom. "You're a lifesaver."

"Yes, I'm very valiant. I should wear my shining armor tomorrow. Now, where did I leave my faithful steed?"

"If you mean the bus, I think it's outside. Away from all the crazy."

Malcolm shook his head and opened the exit door. "I gotta tell you, Val—I like the studying and projects and stuff, but Miss Marcus is just—"

"Ten pounds of crazy in a one-pound box?"

"Yeah! I mean, when have you seen my mind wander during History?"

They turned toward the bus lane.

"I thought only college professors were that eccentric," Valentine said. "And what's with that pin she wears? The hospital symbol."

"Hospital symbol?"

"Yeah, the little staff with two snakes around it and wings on top. I've seen it in hospitals."

Malcolm pondered. "Maybe it's a caduceus. Looks like the hospital thing, but it's the symbol for Hermes. He's messenger of the gods in Greek mythology."

"Hmm. Okay, so I'll stick with our 'she's just weird' theory."

"Good choice."

"Although, if she can push your limits, I've gotta respect her a little. That woman's hardcore."

MALCOLM searched for the courage to step outside. His hand rested on the doorknob as he reviewed the plan one more time.

"If you're waiting for him to knock, you'll probably be there a while," Oma teased as she walked by. Despite her age, she glided forward with ease, footsteps not making a sound.

"He's scary!"

"Yes, very scary. Just go talk to him, dear. You might learn something." She glanced over her shoulder. "If he doesn't eat you."

Counting to ten, he forced himself to turn the knob. Once outside, he walked fast to keep from changing his mind. Crossing into the next yard, he mounted the porch steps and pressed the doorbell. Something clicked and the door cracked open.

"Hi, sir, I'm Malcolm from next door!" he began, loud and fast. "I have a project about the history of the town and I was hoping to maybe interview you about how it's changed and things that you've seen over the—"

"Slow down."

The door swung wide and Walter Crane stepped into the daylight. Tall and wiry, with close-cropped, steel-gray hair and sharp eyes to match, he pierced Malcolm with a hard stare.

"Take a breath. I'm not a blasted computer," he chided in a deep, gravelly voice. "What do you want?"

"Um." Malcolm swallowed. "I was hoping to talk to you for a history project if—"

"I'm busy."

The door slammed shut.

Malcolm turned to leave, more relieved than offended. His foot hit the bottom step and the door flew open again.

"Malcolm from next door. You Grace's kin?"

"Yes, sir."

Mr. Crane stared him down for what seemed an eternity. Grunting, he motioned Malcolm inside, then turned and disappeared into the house.

Malcolm crept inside, half expecting to be kicked back through the door. If he hadn't already guessed Walter's background, one look inside would have told the story. Although decades old, it showed not a crack or scuff, and the antiques were arranged with military neatness and precision.

"Close the door, boy," Mr. Crane's voice called from somewhere. "I know Grace taught you better than that."

Malcolm closed the door and followed the voice down a long hallway. Polished wood creaked under his feet as he made his way toward the back of the house. The walls displayed vintage posters, black and white photos, and cases filled with medals and ribbons. Malcolm leaned in to examine one.

"Purple Heart."

He jumped as the old man appeared over his shoulder. Then Malcolm gestured to a Silver Star. "What's that one for?"

Mr. Crane looked where Malcolm had pointed and ignored it. He turned and stomped into the next room. "You coming or not, boy? Don't have all day."

Malcolm followed him into a study. Smells of old leather and polished mahogany greeted him as they settled into overstuffed chairs, surrounded by old memorabilia. Much of it was unfamiliar until he spotted something on the table next to them.

"Hey, you've got a Little Mack!"

Mr. Crane stared at him, blank faced. Feeling awkward, Malcolm pointed at an old coin in a small display case.

"The 1863 General McClellan Civil War token? These are pretty rare. Did it always have that crack?"

Leaning back, Mr. Crane looked him over as if he were evaluating a new recruit. Malcolm shifted.

"Were you planning on asking me any questions?" Mr. Crane snapped. "You've got twenty minutes."

"Uh, yeah. Sorry." Malcolm fumbled in his pockets until his iPhone and a folded sheet of paper fell out. Activating the voice recorder app, he set the phone between them. "So, to start, I was wondering what the town was like when you got here."

CHAPTER 6

Malcolm dove to the floor and rolled for cover. Panting, he pressed his back against the makeshift wall and glanced around the corner. A hail of red foam balls bounced inches from his face. He stifled a yelp and ducked back.

"Dodgeball is war," Coach Boomer had declared at the start of class. "And today, you're in the trenches!"

"I'm out of ammo!" Malcolm called across the open "trench" between the stacks of foam mats and football practice barriers.

His sister peered around her own corner, focused as a hawk. A ball smacked against the brick behind them and bounced to the floor between the twins. Malcolm stared at it longingly, reluctant to give up safe cover.

Valentine vaulted from cover and sprinted toward the ball. The enemy caught sight and foam missiles whooshed over Malcolm's head. Flowing like a cat, Valentine darted past the first attack and ducked under the second.

As the third and fourth converged on her, Valentine leaped forward, tucked and spun into a front handspring. One hand planted on the floor while the other grabbed the ball and pulled it to her chest. The incoming balls bounced wide of her spinning form. Her feet arced through the air and touched back to the floor, and she sprinted toward Malcolm.

A fifth volley hurtled toward her face. She spun on her toes, palmed the ball from the air, and came to a crouch next to Malcolm. Laughing gleefully, she set both balls at their feet. Malcolm gathered in the three that had missed her, silent as old images played through his mind. Valentine peeked over the wall of mats and surveyed the battlefield.

"Four of us, seven of them. If we're careful, I think we can do this."

He didn't move. She looked up and saw his face. "What?"

Malcolm tried to seem nonchalant. "Oh. It's just been a while, you know, since I've seen you do something like that."

Valentine looked at the floor. "I know. Did it bother you?"

"No!" he stammered. "No, it was, uh, nice to see it again."

"Did you see that?" they heard from across the gym.

"She didn't even slow down!"

The twins shared a laugh, and the awkwardness ebbed.

"They're scared now," Malcolm said.

A wicked grin crossed Valentine's face. "Let's send 'em running."

He nodded and held a hand to his temple. "Sergeant."

She mirrored him. "Sergeant."

They leapt up with a ball in each hand and let loose. Two enemies went down immediately. The battle reached full force as their allies joined in.

"By the way," Valentine called over the din. "Winter invited us over tonight."

Malcolm paused mid-throw. "Really."

"Yeah, to study and have some pizza, maybe watch a movie."

He flung another ball and smiled as it glanced off a larger opponent's shoulder. He avoided looking at Valentine.

"You do want to go, right?"

"Uh, well, who's going to be there?" He bounced a ball off the one in his hand, "deactivating" it, and grabbed it from the floor.

"Winter's family, a few others from her group." She dodged a ball, flung one of her own, and gave him a significant look. "Maybe Fred, too."

Malcolm nodded but didn't answer, a heavy weight pressing on his chest.

"Mal, you can't leave me alone with that guy."

They attacked simultaneously. An enemy went down with hits to the thigh and shin, and the teams were now three-on-three.

"It's just, I've got this book on the Battle of Marathon that I really should start. So I think maybe I'll . . . anyway, Fred'll be busy taking abuse from Winter."

Valentine hurled a ball with both hands, smacking a yellow-haired girl square in the chest. "That's great, Mal. Pick a book over making friends. Again. Is that how you're going to be from now on?"

"Hey, going to Fred's party was my idea," he defended, ducking away from a ball.

"Yeah, and it'd be nice to keep that going." She held up a hand, halting his response. "I know. I didn't want to go then, but that was a huge party. We need to make real friends, and that means doing things like tonight. I mean, do you want to hide behind your books for the rest of your life, or actually make some history of your own?"

Malcolm's response was drowned out as a crack of thunder

slammed against the gym roof. Through tall windows, they watched lightning burst from the clear sky.

"Did you see that?" Valentine said.

Malcolm nodded. The bolts grew to sheets of silvery light. Rolling thunder rattled the decades-old walls around them. He jumped as a popping sound echoed overhead. The lights went dark.

"Cease fire!" Coach Boomer called out into the dark.

"Come on." Valentine stepped out from cover. "Let's get a better look."

The other students followed their lead, approaching the windows slowly for fear of shattering glass. A hush fell over the room. The deadly light continued its dance across the sky.

"There are no clouds," a brunette girl said in awe. "Can you have lightning with no clouds?"

"Apparently, you can."

"Shut up, Jimmy!"

"Hey, look," Malcolm said. "In the parking lot."

He pointed toward a gray-haired woman moving between the cars. Every few feet, she looked into the sky and shook her head in dismay.

"Isn't that Miss Marcus?" Valentine said. "What's she doing out there?"

"Probably hoping the mother ship came back," Malcolm said.

"If it has, it's about the tenth one this month," Coach Boomer said. "This is crazy."

"You don't normally get these?" Valentine asked.

"Try never. Not until this past spring, anyway. They started slow, then just kept on coming."

A memory slipped across Malcolm's mind. Leaning forward, he exhaled and fog bloomed across the smooth glass.

"It's getting colder, Val," he whispered. "Just like that other storm. It's barely even fall, and that night there was frost on my window."

"Storms can affect temperatures."

"Enough to do that?"

Valentine shrugged. "Last year, I read about a place that has to burn down every year before new seeds can germinate."

"Uh, okay," he returned. "And that means . . ."

"It *means* some things are strange just because they *are*."

Malcolm grasped for a clever response but came up short. He wondered why he rarely won arguments with his sister. Did she know him too well? Did girls just play dirty? That was probably it. The one time he'd seen his parents argue, it had ended with his father dazed while his mother stormed away in a cloud of indignation.

Ice stabbed into Malcolm's chest, and the breath caught in his throat. He shoved the memory away in a flash of panic.

"You know what I mean?"

He gave his sister a blank look before realizing she'd been talking this whole time.

"Uhhh." He cleared his throat and swallowed, trying to catch his breath. Outside, the lightning dispersed, leaving behind a golden fall afternoon. He touched the window.

Warm.

"Hey." She brushed his arm. "You okay?"

Malcolm forced a smile. "Yeah. I'm just, you know, dazzled by your argument."

"Uh-huh," Valentine turned back to the window. "So, did you see any?"

"Any what?"

"Any strange faces. You know, in the lightning."

Malcolm glanced sidelong at his sister. She choked back laughter and turned to hide a devious grin. He knew then that he'd been right. Girls did play dirty.

VALENTINE pressed one hand against her stomach to quiet the butterflies. With the other, she picked up a brush. *It's just another night.*

Flame-red hair shimmered in the mirror, reflecting the amber glow of an antique lamp. She focused on the brush strokes. *One. Two. Three.* Just a few people hanging out. *Four. Five.* Nothing to be nervous about. *Six.* Except . . . the brush slowed. Except that tonight could make all the difference. What good was starting a new life if you did it with no friends? Valentine stared into the mirror, willing strength into her jade green eyes. *That's not going to happen. Seven. Eight.* The brush began again. Tonight would be perfect. She would talk and laugh. *Nine. Ten.* She would let people know her. Her butterflies danced, this time with excitement. *Eleven. Twelve. Thirteen. Fourteen* . . . and in no time, she would belong here.

Valentine tossed down the brush. Slipping on her favorite black jacket, she stepped into the hallway and glanced into Malcolm's room. Sprawled on his bed with a book under his nose, like usual these days. He hadn't moved since they'd gotten home, except now he was staring out the front window.

"Sure you won't come? They might have books, too."

"Ever wonder why no one talks about it?" Malcolm mused, sounding far away.

"Talks about what?"

"The house. Most towns have something weird, and there's

always legends or scary stories about it. But here, there's nothing. Like no one even notices."

Valentine bit her lip before a smart remark could slip out. "Mal, just come. You don't have to talk. Just be there."

He mumbled something like a refusal and put his nose back in the book. She studied him, hoping for some sign that he really saw her. That he understood.

He turned a page.

She sighed. "Good night, Mal."

Valentine backed into the hall and closed his door. She turned for the stairs and stopped short with a gasp. Oma Grace stood there in the hallway, a finger on her lips.

"How is he?" she whispered.

"Same." Valentine shook her head. "I thought he was getting better."

Oma Grace laid a hand on her arm. "Give him time. You've both been through big changes."

She clutched the hand, comforted by its warmth. "I just want the old Mal back. He never used to hide from anything."

Oma Grace led her toward the stairs. "And how are *you* feeling?"

She managed a wry smile. "I want the old me back, too."

Oma Grace chuckled. "You'll get there. It's only been a year, and what you're facing, well, it's one of the hardest things for a woman."

"What do you mean?"

They stopped at the top of the stairs and faced each other. "I mean letting go, dear."

Oma looked at Valentine's neck. She was clutching the silver pendant again. With effort, she uncurled her fingers and dropped the hand to her side, flushing hot with embarrassment.

"Oh, it's okay." Oma grasped Valentine's shoulders. "There's no forcing time in this house, my girl. Just keep trying and you'll get there. I promise."

Valentine nodded, unable to meet her gaze.

"Let me see that famous Gilbert smile," Oma Grace's knuckles brushed her downturned chin. "Come now, humor an old bat."

Valentine felt a bright spot of laughter grow inside her. She met Oma's twinkling eyes.

"There it is." Oma Grace turned Valentine toward the stairs and whispered in her ear. "Go show them how beautiful you are."

Valentine's smile blossomed—her real smile—and she bounded down the stairs.

VALENTINE called a goodbye to Oma Grace as she piled out of the car, wrestling with bulky bags of snacks. She stumbled onto the front porch with the awkward load, eager to get inside before the black storm clouds overhead burst open.

The doorbell hovered just out of reach of her elbow. She leaned over and barely rang it, when the bag of sodas slipped from her grasp and plummeted toward the ground. She lurched forward and managed to snag the plastic handle. Lightning flashed, disorienting her for a split second.

With horror, Valentine staggered and then flailed face-first toward the front door. The white wood loomed in her vision, and time seemed to slow. *So this is how I'll spend my first night here—bruised and mortified.*

The door swung open. Her face missed it by an inch as she careened across the threshold into a surprised pair of arms.

"Whoa!"

Arms wrapped around her shoulders, halting her momentum. She rested there for an instant to catch her breath.

"You know how to make an entrance."

Recognition hit hard as Valentine looked up at the face of her savior. She pulled away.

"Hi, John," she said, straightening her hair.

The slender, dark-eyed boy grinned at her. "Hello, Valentine. I see the rumors are true."

"Rumors?"

"About how the new girl flew halfway across the gym and danced her way to victory."

"Oh." She gave a nervous laugh. "You heard about that?"

"It's a very small town."

Valentine nodded. She glanced at everything around her, anywhere except John's eyes. Awkward fear gripped her insides, and the silence stretched on. *What are you doing? Say something!* She looked down at her feet. *Stop it! Look up!*

"You've come for the study session?" John asked.

She forced herself to look up. "Yeah. You?"

"I was just leaving. Bill and Nancy want a family evening, so I came to offer Winter my regrets."

"Oh. Okay." Through the fear, Valentine realized she was disappointed.

Moving through the doorway, John turned and held her eyes with his. "Will I see you here again?"

She nodded more enthusiastically than she'd planned. He gave her a little smile, then turned and stepped down the porch. "Perhaps we can talk more next time, then."

"Yeah. Hey!"

John turned back to her, more lightning arcing across the sky behind him.

"Um, thanks. You know, for catching me."

His eyes twinkled with amusement or irony or something like them. "It was my pleasure. Good night, Valentine."

Valentine stood in the open doorway and watched John cross the street. Chiding herself, she closed the door and followed voices toward what seemed to be the kitchen.

"Oh, thank you for catching me!" she mocked herself. *"I don't have anything smart to say, so I'll just giggle and stuff."*

She stopped as the voices poured through the kitchen door.

"I keep telling you, don't drink out of the carton," Winter's voice boomed. "If you keep doing it, I'm going to buy soy milk again!"

"NOOO!" a tiny voice wailed.

"That's right, just like when Daddy was a vegan. And we don't want that, do we? Do we?"

"YOU SUCK!"

Valentine dodged to the side as a tiny, black-haired girl barreled through the door. Winter stuck her head through the doorway.

"And you better not touch anything in my room, Summer! I mean it! Oh, hey Val. Come on in. Where's Malcolm?"

"Oh, he uh," she stammered. *Should've thought of an excuse on the way over.*

"Don't sweat it." Winter rolled over her in that brisk, nonchalant manner she pulled off so easily. "Grab a drink. Say hi, Brynne."

Brynne squeezed Valentine in a warm hug. "Hi, sweetie! Your hair is so cute! How do you get those curls?"

"Well, I brush it." Remembering why she was there, Valentine tried to return the hug.

"It's so pretty," Brynne exclaimed. She unwrapped herself

from Valentine and pulled her toward the table. "Here, set that stuff down. Are we ready, Winter?"

"Almost. John and Fred have stuff happening, so it's a girls' night, I guess. Just waiting on Carly."

Brynne's face fell. "Your brother's not coming, Valentine? He's cute."

"Brynne!" Winter reprimanded. "Inappropriate. That's the girl's brother."

"No, it's okay." Valentine smiled and unpacked the snacks. "He's busy, but maybe I'll tease him with a secret admirer."

"That's cold," Winter said. "Gotta say, though, Brynne's not the only one eying the new boy. I've heard a few . . ."

Valentine's attention wandered to the window facing the street. She could see John sitting on his front porch, conversing with a mustached man and a graying, willowy woman. Each held a steaming mug in their hand.

"He's single, you know," a perky voice said in her ear.

Valentine realized she was staring out the window. Both Brynne and Winter watched her in amusement. *How long was I staring?*

"Sorry, what?"

"John. He homeschools, but everyone knows him and he's never dated anyone." She pointed through the window. "That's Bill, his foster dad."

"*Adoptive* dad," Winter corrected.

"Oh, he's adopted." Valentine nodded. "Where'd he come from?"

"Who knows?" Brynne shrugged.

"He hasn't told you?"

"What? No. Remember, he—" Brynne's eyes widened. "Oh, you don't know! I forgot you're new. Winter, she doesn't know!"

Valentine glanced between them, puzzled. Winter shifted uncomfortably. Brynne shook with the excitement of sharing gossip.

"See," Brynne began. "John's got this thing where he doesn't know or—well, I mean, I'm sure he knew at some point, but now he just—well, he can't—"

"John doesn't know who he is," Winter cut in.

The power cut out.

"Seriously?" Winter said, staring up at the ceiling. "This happens, like, every week now."

Just enough light remained for them to find flashlights and set them in a circle on the table. They also added their cell phones, each turning on the camera flash. With the bright beams pointed at the ceiling, they fashioned a crude sort of lamp that cast the room in an eerie glow. Just enough light to see their snacks—though their study notes would have to wait.

"So, where were we?" Winter asked.

"John, sweetie," Brynne said.

"Oh, right."

Valentine shook her head. She'd spent the past few minutes unsure how to respond to Winter's revelation. "So, he has some sort of amnesia or something?"

Winter sank into a chair. "About a year ago, they found him wandering the streets downtown. Broken bones, clothes were all shredded. They figure he took some knocks on the head, too." She grabbed a brownie and munched on it. "When he woke up in the hospital, he couldn't remember anything but his name."

Brynne sat at the table across from Winter, in rapt attention. Valentine pulled out a chair and followed suit.

"Didn't anyone come looking for him?"

Winter shook her head. "They looked everywhere, but no

one ever came forward. So they figured he didn't have any family and asked for someone to take him in. That's how the Irwins got him."

"Wow," Valentine said. "Has he ever searched for a family?"

"Where would he start?" Winter said. "Carter isn't exactly rare. And what would he find that no one else could? He only knows the last year."

Valentine pondered this. "I can't imagine what that would be like."

"Questions," Winter replied. The tone made Valentine think the words weren't hers. "You'd have questions, and you'd be afraid of the answers."

"What sort of questions?"

"Did you ever have family? What were they like? Did something happen to them? Have they forgotten you, too? Are they dead?" She looked up at Valentine. "Or did they just abandon you?"

MALCOLM sat at the kitchen counter with his book while Oma Grace chopped potatoes for dinner. An old-style lantern sat between them, its warm glow just bright enough to let him read. The rest of the house sat in darkness—except for the continuous flashes of lightning.

The rhythmic sound of Oma Grace chopping might have lulled him to sleep, if not for the bacon and onions crackling in the pot behind her. The stove's blue flame kept dinner preparations on track despite the power hiccup. He breathed deeply, inhaling the smoky scent.

"Hey, Oma, what's with that house across the street?"

The sound of chopping slowed.

"Which house, dear?"

"The old one with no doors." He gestured through the window. "I thought you might know why it's there."

"Oh, so Granny must know about something old."

"No, I didn't mean it like—"

Oma Grace waved away his objections. "I'm teasing you, dear."

Malcolm smiled. "No one talks about it. Something that weird, shouldn't there at least be creepy rumors?"

"Who says there aren't?"

"I guess—wait, are there?"

"Oh yes." Oma Grace tossed the cubed potatoes into the pot. "The worst kind of rumors."

"Like what?"

"Well." She lowered her voice and glanced behind her. "They say that on a full moon . . ."

"Yeah?"

". . . The house comes alive and . . . *eats nosy teenagers!*" She stared at Malcolm, her face full of mock terror.

Malcolm rolled his eyes. "Okay, you got me."

Oma Grace chuckled. "Believe me, boy, the less you think about that place, the better."

"Is something wrong with it?"

"Any old place is dangerous," she said. "You start poking around, things are waiting to break, and before you know it the roof has come down to say hello. Then it's goodbye nosy teenagers."

Malcolm eyed the fading monolith through the window. "You don't think it's strange?"

Oma Grace paused and set her knife down. "Which do you think is stranger—a silly old house, or a healthy boy who won't make friends?"

Malcolm examined his hands, embarrassed. "I just—" he began, then cut off. He cast around inside, struggling to find the right words. "I . . ."

"Malcolm." Oma Grace rested her hands on his. He kept his face down. "Malcolm, look at me."

With effort, he raised his eyes to meet hers. It felt like lifting a boulder.

"I know you've been through so much, and everyone deals with things at their own pace." She leaned closer. "But you cannot get over the past by ignoring the future. You have to keep living. Don't you think that's what Emily would want?"

Malcolm broke his gaze and stared at the wall, fighting the heat building behind his eyes. He took a deep breath and blinked hard. "She danced today."

"Who?"

"Valentine. During gym—" His voice broke. Tears tore free and streamed down his face. "It came out of nowhere, and I wasn't ready for it."

"She danced?"

He looked back at Oma Grace. She was smiling, her own tears welling up.

"How was she?"

"Amazing, like always. Just like—she's better at all this, Oma, and I can't even . . ." He gave a frustrated huff.

"Valentine has her own struggles," Oma Grace said. "Same as you. She's just better at pretending things are okay."

Malcolm breathed deeply and pushed away the ache. It wouldn't budge. "I feel like glass inside."

She leaned down to catch his eye. "You will find your courage again, I promise. Both of you. You just need time, and each other, and friends. With those by your side, anything is possible. Okay?"

He nodded weakly. "Okay."

"That's better. Now, say it like a Gilbert."

Malcolm felt a smile tug at his lips. He raised his eyes and wiped his cheeks on a sleeve. "*Okay.*"

The power turned on.

Overhead lights flickered to life, and a familiar background hum filled the house as appliances and electronics woke up again. Oma Grace glanced at the ceiling, then winked and squeezed his hands before letting go.

"Now," she said, returning to the cutting board. "I know a few other things a growing boy needs. Is there one around who can help me with dinner?"

Malcolm smiled for real and stood to join her.

CHAPTER 7

Halfway through the school day, the twins made their routine locker visit to change out books and supplies. Valentine finished loading up and zipped her bag. As usual, Malcolm moved more slowly, so she took a moment to glance in the mirror and pluck at a tangle in her hair.

"That a new book?" she said.

"How do you do that? You're not even looking at me."

"I told you already, Mal. Girls have special powers."

"It's on the Renaissance. Never read much about it, which I've decided makes me a bad history geek."

"That's an excellent book," a new voice added.

Valentine froze at the mirror, and her insides twirled. Turning, she searched for something to say, but all her words disappeared.

"Oh, hi," Malcolm said. "It's John, right?"

"And you're Malcolm." John held out his hand.

Malcolm accepted it and hefted the history tome. "You know this book?"

"Yes, I enjoyed the chapters on . . ."

With John distracted, Valentine rummaged frantically through a small leather pouch in her locker. *Where is it?*

Her fingers closed around a plastic cylinder. A quick glance to see if they were still occupied, and . . . *GO!* She ripped off the cap and twisted the bottom. The color of her favorite lipstick slid into view. She leaned close to the mirror.

What are you doing? Why do you care?

I don't know, okay?

Color applied, she tossed the stick back into the bag and smacked her lips together. *You know he'll never get close. You won't let him.* She swiped hands through her fiery locks. *Just shut up!*

She closed the locker. "Hi, John."

John broke off mid-sentence and turned to her. "Hello, Valentine. Are you well?"

She nodded and his smile spread, touching his eyes. He had nice eyes. *Stop it.*

"Well," Malcolm interposed. "I suppose I'll be onto the next class. Val, see you there?"

Valentine met her brother's gaze. He was trying not to smile.

"Uh, yeah sure," she replied.

Malcolm nodded. "See you around, John." He gave the long-haired boy a last appraising look and melted into the crowd.

"Until next time, Malcolm," John said.

She struggled for something—*anything*—to say. "Um, I thought Brynne said you homeschool."

"I do. However, Winter forgot some notes for her newspaper. She's doing another story on Patrick Morgan's disappearance." He hefted a folder.

"Oh," Valentine said.

The fear clenched inside her as they stared at each other in silence. She shoved it away.

Then everything came pouring out. "Look, about when we

met—you talked about not knowing where you're from, and I remember that I laughed at it but I didn't know anything about you until Winter told me last week and I'm just . . . I'm sorry."

John's head tilted to the side as he watched her, looking amused. Her cheeks heated. She knew they must be red, and that made her flush more.

"Have you been concerned about that all this time?"

She nodded.

He chuckled. "Apology not necessary, but accepted anyway. How could you know? I didn't tell you. Most times it's just easier to make a joke."

"Yeah. Mal and I seem to do that a lot."

John nodded his understanding. "Anyway, I did come to find you for a purpose. After class, I'll be hiking to Misty Point with Winter and Fred, and we would love for you and Malcolm to come."

Valentine's interest piqued. "I've never heard of that."

"The sunset should be beautiful tonight, and it's the best view. We'll take blankets and spend the evening there." He grinned. "You know, basic small-town fun."

She laughed. "I could use some of that, I think. We need to check with our dad, but it should be fine. Meet you after last period?"

"I look forward to it."

THE stream of French words flowed past Valentine. Her mind wandered through the conversation with John. *What did I say again? How did I sound?* She remembered speaking, but not the words. Mostly, she remembered his deep brown eyes.

Madame LaChance's lecture picked up speed, interrupting her thoughts. Valentine had only learned enough basic French to catch pieces of it, though, and the teacher didn't allow English to be spoken in her classroom. At the moment, she was reading passages from an old history book—the woman loved reading to them about the French Revolution, so much that Valentine wondered why she wasn't teaching history.

Today's lesson centered around Charlotte Corday, also known as the Assassin of Marat. Apparently she'd murdered a radical political figure in his bathtub, claiming that her purpose had been to prevent all-out civil war and save her country from more violence. Though young, she'd gone to the guillotine for her crime.

Pausing between paragraphs, Madame LaChance copied key phrases onto the board that she wanted them to learn. As she wrote, her hips swayed in a skin-tight pencil skirt, and long chestnut hair brushed against the middle of her back. Valentine noted most of the male students were giving rapt attention. She tried not to roll her eyes.

Beside her, Malcolm tapped away at his phone. Her lap buzzed.

> **Mal:** *john seems nice*
> **Val:** *Course you'd say that. He liked your giant book.*
> **Mal:** *I doubt that's why he stopped, lol*
> **Val:** *What do you mean?*
> **Mal:** *why you pretending not to notice?*
> **Val:** *He invited us BOTH out. We're going on a hike with John :) Winter :) Fred >:(*

Valentine waited for a snarky reply, but her brother was focused forward. Following his eyes, she saw where he and every other boy was looking.

Madame LaChance faced the class, swaying side to side in her black stiletto heels. Her tight pink top showed a tease of smooth, tanned cleavage, and locks of silky hair fell across her eyes as she leaned over to read.

Val: *How are you enjoying the "lesson"?*

Malcolm jumped at the buzzing and looked down. A goofy smile played across his face. He glanced toward Valentine and gave a half-shrug, not quite managing to look embarrassed.

He bent over his phone to tap out a reply. Valentine focused on her own screen, waiting for whatever silly excuse he was planning to offer. If he even bothered to offer one.

She caught a flicker of movement in the corner of her eye, then jumped at a loud *crack*.

Madame LaChance had suddenly appeared next to Malcolm. The sound had come from a ruler, which she'd used to slap the surface of his desk. He gazed up at her, half in alarm and half in love, it seemed.

"*Vilain garçon. Tu connais les règles, mon cher. Donne-moi ça,*" she said, expectantly holding out an open palm. Malcolm handed over his cell phone.

She held his gaze. "*Tu peux l'avoir après la classe.*"

Cheeks reddening, he barely managed to nod.

This time, Valentine did roll her eyes. *Boys.*

VALENTINE pulled her jacket tighter. Following dinner they'd climbed into Fred's limo, and his driver—he actually had his own driver and butler—had taken them to Misty Point Park.

Emmett's Bluff was built on a plain, with flat grasslands stretching in three directions. The northern edge, however, sat at the base of tall and rocky, tree-lined foothills. For decades they'd been popular with hikers, artists, and gear-headed thrill-seekers alike. Trails crisscrossed their way into the hills, snaking through peaks and valleys as the terrain grew wilder.

Valentine slung her backpack over her shoulder, noting with disappointment that the path upward was paved and wide enough for cars. They followed along the chest-high stone wall that lined the right side, passing under tall street lamps. In the distance, the path swerved sharply west and ended at a lookout far below the more impressive peaks.

"Gotta admit, I pictured this differently," Malcolm commented from behind her. "I thought it'd be—"

"Woodsier?" Valentine offered.

"Yes! But it's so civilized."

"Aww," Fred said with mock sympathy. "Winter, they thought we were takin' 'em into the back country."

"Oh, they're not ready for that," Winter said. "We didn't even bring our guns."

They burst into laughter.

The lights flickered overhead. Their basketball-sized bulbs sputtered with an electrical hiss, leaping between dark and uncomfortably bright.

"See, now we're roughing it," Winter said. "Unreliable lighting? This is hard!"

"Alright, alright, we give," Valentine said. "But still."

"I said the same when they first brought me here," John said. He walked a few feet to her left, hefting his guitar case. Their eyes met and her stomach fluttered. *"Why put all this here? I thought. But then I saw."*

"True that," Fred said. "The road's just to sucker all the tourists."

"Real view's, locals-only," Winter said.

"Our spot's good for chillin', maybe takin' a date," Fred said too casually. He glanced back to catch Valentine's eye.

She fought to keep her expression neutral. *They're trying to be nice, and the night would probably end if I puked on him.*

The street lights sputtered again, pulsed bright, then all of them died at once. Evening darkness pooled around them.

"Hmm," Winter said. "That actually *is* kinda weird."

"There's still enough light," John said.

The electrical hum rose to a high-pitched whine. The lights surged to life, shining painfully bright and growing brighter and brighter. In an instant they were blinding, and Valentine heard a cracking noise.

The lights shattered, hurling shards of glass and metal through the air. Valentine dropped to her knees, covering her head with her arms. Someone screamed as fragments crashed down around them—it might have been her. The lights hissed and popped with arcing electricity.

The last pieces clinked to the ground, and all was silent.

Valentine took a deep breath, willing her body to stop trembling. She peered ahead to see Winter and Fred help each other up, carefully brushing fragments from their clothes and hair.

Thunder boomed overhead.

She slid fingers through her hair. Nothing. Puzzled, she clutched at the folds of her clothes. Nothing. Had she escaped completely glass-free? Then she looked up.

John crouched over her, holding the guitar case above them. His eyes were still closed and his arms were shaking. Valentine realized then why no glass had hit her. A warm glow touched her inside.

A bolt of lightning lanced between the clouds.

Tentatively, she reached out and touched his shoulder. "I think it's over now."

John's eyes popped open. "Oh. Okay."

Reddening, he stood straight. A layer of the crystalline shards slid from his back and clattered to the pavement. Valentine stood and plucked her bag from the ground.

"Mal, you okay?" she said.

"The glass ripped my shirt!"

"Fred," Winter said, "your hand."

"Aw man," Fred said as he wiped a small stream of blood from the back of his right hand. "That's the second time this week. Stupid glass, always cuttin' me!"

A web of light arced across the sky.

John fidgeted, his eyes darting everywhere but Valentine. His face was beet-red, flushed with . . . was it embarrassment? And something else was different. Searching the pavement, she found his dark-rimmed glasses among the debris.

"Here." She held them out.

"Oh. Th-thanks," John stammered, barely meeting her gaze.

"And, um, thank you. For what you did."

He nodded, but still wouldn't look at her.

Don't do what you're about to—

Valentine placed her hand on his arm and a thrill shot through her. Finally he made eye contact, managing a bashful smile. This was the first time she'd seen him less than confident, and the warmth inside her grew.

"Well," John said, clearing his throat. "Now that we're all sufficiently terrified, are we ready to continue?"

No one responded.

"Guys?" Valentine looked at her brother. He was staring at the sky.

Torrents of lightning raced from cloud to cloud. Valentine felt the urge to step back as thunder rumbled and cracked and built to a deafening crescendo. The ground trembled under its fury, and the oppressive air pressed down on them.

Then the lightning disappeared.

The thunder stopped.

They stood in stunned silence.

"Okay, *what* is going on these days?!" Fred demanded. "I mean, just what the—"

A pillar of lightning descended into the trees fifty yards ahead. Deafening cracks echoed through the forest as plumes of smoke and flame jetted into the sky. Valentine froze, wide-eyed, her bag falling from her grip. Malcolm cried out in shock.

Another bolt fell closer, and a tall pine exploded into a million pieces. Valentine flinched as the roar of destruction reverberated around her.

"HOLY—" Malcolm shouted.

A colossal bolt descended twenty yards from them, pulverizing a birch tree and hurling fiery fragments in every direction. Gusts of hot wind enveloped the group. Valentine felt hands grab her and pull. Shaking from her stupor, she spun as the group fled the way they had come.

"Run!" John shouted. "GO—"

A blinding flash burst in front of her and a boom shook the air. Ringing filled her ears. Terror gripped her heart, squeezing like a vise. Somewhere inside, Valentine realized her feet no longer touched the ground. The world tumbled silently around her.

CHAPTER 8

Valentine floated in a white void, wondering where her body had gone.

Whoa.

THUNK. Someone was knocking. She tried to call out that she was awake. Nothing happened.

Right. I don't have a body.

THUNK.

I'll be late for school.

THUNK. THUNK. THUNK.

Ow!

A sharp pain jabbed at her side.

The soft, floaty feelings retreated, chased away by a wave of agony. Valentine gasped as it slipped away, leaving the dull gray of dusk. She realized she was lying on her side, gritty pavement scraping against her right cheek. Her ears rang and her vision swam.

THUNK. THUNK.

Someone grabbed her shoulders and rolled her onto her back. She could barely make out the chunks of wooden debris falling from the sky. Nausea swept through her and she fought the urge to retch. She swallowed, closed her eyes, took a deep breath. When she opened them, Malcolm was staring at her and frantically mouthing something.

She concentrated, straining to hear him. *Am I deaf?* She shook her head to clear the fog. The ringing began to fade, and she immediately wished it hadn't. The first thing she heard was Malcolm pleading to know she was okay.

The second thing she heard was screaming.

Valentine forced herself up. Pushing away the ache that permeated her body, she nodded to Malcolm that she was okay. *At least, I think so.*

To the right, what had been a towering oak was now a flaming stump. The stone wall separating them from the tree had buckled, and chunks of wood littered the ground.

Her brother bled from dozens of cuts, his clothes practically ribbons, but he seemed alert. John was pulling himself to his feet, left arm held stiffly at his side. His face was a mask barely hiding the anguish. Fred sprawled on his back, trembling and white-faced as he cradled bloody forearms to his chest.

Winter sat hunched over on her knees, screaming and clutching her left ear. Her wide, frenzied eyes stared into space, and blood trickled between her fingers.

Malcolm moved to check Fred's injuries. John went to Winter and gently pried her hand from her ear. Wanting to help, Valentine set her hands on the ground and pushed up.

White-hot pain tore through her right shoulder. She dropped back to the ground, gasping and choking back tears. For the first time, she looked down at herself to see torn, dirty clothes and shallow cuts crisscrossing her body.

A jagged shard of wood protruded from her right shoulder.

Valentine trembled as she stared at the blood trickling from the wound. Panic seized her. *I've got to . . . I've got to . . .* She gripped the shard with both hands and heaved, rending it from her shoulder.

Three inches of bloody spike came loose from inside her. She collapsed onto her back as nausea and burning agony washed over her. John was suddenly there, ripping his button-up shirt into shreds. He lifted her shoulder off the ground and wrapped it in the soft green flannel.

Malcolm knelt on her other side, handing his phone to John. "Paramedics need to know where we are."

John put the phone to his ear. "Misty Point Park, at the eastern lookout."

VALENTINE squinted against the whirling lights of the ambulance. The EMTs had tended to her and Malcolm's wounds, and John's dislocated shoulder had been reset. She'd expected to be whisked to the hospital along with Winter and Fred but was patched up on the spot. Apparently these lightning storms had happened all over Emmett's Bluff, and their small hospital only had enough room for the serious cases.

John spoke parting words to Winter and Fred as the paramedics closed the back doors. They drove away with sirens blaring, and John rejoined the twins.

"Winter has a perforated eardrum. She's expected to be half deaf for months until it heals. And Fred." He shook his head. "Fred won't be competing in basketball this year. Both of his forearms are fractured."

Valentine's heart reached out to them. Even Fred.

"Since he has black eyes, they think he held both arms up to protect his face," John continued. "A piece of the tree hit them straight on."

Malcolm grimaced. "Ouch."

"How are you feeling?" Valentine asked John.

He studied her. "I was about to ask *you* that."

She shrugged, then winced. "I'll live. Half of me still doesn't believe this happened."

"And we were lucky. This could have been far worse." He locked eyes with her. "But I'm glad you were not badly hurt."

Despite her pain, she felt a smile bubble up. She wanted to respond but couldn't think of anything that didn't sound cheesy. Instead, she reached out and brushed his wounded shoulder.

He smiled back. "A few weeks' time and I'll be stronger than ever. In the meantime, Fred lent me his phone, so I will call his driver to return us home."

"Good." Malcolm hesitated, then held out his hand. "I saw the things you did back there. Thank you."

Valentine's face went hot. *What is he doing?* Suddenly, she wanted to crawl under the broken wall.

John reddened but took the offered hand. "Of course." He glanced away. "I should make the call now."

When he was out of earshot, Valentine whirled on her brother with an accusing glare. "What was that all about?"

"He did something nice, and I wanted to thank him," Malcolm said with a dismissive shrug. He moved to retrieve their bags.

For some reason, his calm infuriated her. "You made it awkward. Why did you have to say anything?"

Malcolm met her glare with hard eyes. "Let's be real for a minute. We should be dead. You, me, all of us—*dead*. That wall saved us from the worst of it. In all that chaos, I saw him leave his friends to check on *you*. Now, call me crazy, but you're my sister, so I guess I got a little sentimental. Okay?"

He stalked farther up the path, kneeling to gather items their friends had dropped. Staring after him, Valentine suddenly felt sick. And embarrassed. And ashamed. *Why did you have to snap at him?* She approached slowly.

"You're right," she said. "I'm sorry." He leaned forward, and she noticed that a few cuts were still seeping blood. It hit her then. *I never even asked if he was okay. I'm so selfish.* "How are *you?*"

He didn't respond, just knelt there clutching his backpack and staring at the trees. She put a hand on his shoulder. "Mal?"

"Val." He pointed at the trees farther up the path. "What do you see there?"

"What am I supposed to see?"

Malcolm stood. "I didn't notice until now. It looks like . . ."

Abruptly, he slung the bag over his shoulder and scrambled over the wall. He turned back to her. "Are you coming?"

Surprise had rooted her in place. "Coming where? What are you doing?"

"Testing a theory."

He headed northwest, where the hills rose higher. Valentine shook her head and scaled the wall, favoring her right shoulder. Malcolm waited at the base of a steep incline that rose nearly a hundred feet.

"I'll bet this is where we were heading tonight." He began to climb.

"Mal, what's gotten into you?"

"I have to see." He gazed back at her and his expression softened. "I know you're hurting. So am I." He held an arm out. "Here, I'll help you."

"What about John?"

"He has Fred's phone. I'll text him so he doesn't worry."

They scrambled up the side of the hill, grabbing onto rocks and roots for support. Every cut and bruise screamed at Valentine, and her lungs burned with exhaustion. Then they were there, standing on the peak and looking out over lower hills. They paused to catch their breath.

"Don't worry," Malcolm panted. "If I'm right, this'll be worth it."

"If you're not, I may push you over the side."

Chuckling, he shambled over to the outermost ledge. After sending a quick text, his gaze swept back and forth over the forest.

"There! Val, come look at this."

She sighed and joined him on the ledge. *If I pretend to see it, maybe we can leave.* Her eyes widened.

At least thirty trees had been blasted into charred stumps. The bolts had struck in concentric circles, traveling out from a central point. Smoldering husks now formed rings around a patch of open space in the forest. A spot where no trees grew.

"Whoa."

"Yeah. This just got a lot less random."

Valentine stared at the open center. "So, if that's where everything started . . ."

Malcolm nodded. "What exactly is in there?"

Their eyes met. Wordlessly, they spun and scrambled back down the hill as fast as their battered bodies would take them. They plunged into the forest, where fragments of shattered trees littered the ground in every direction. A smoky tang hung in the air and scratched at their throats.

They broke into the clearing—a circular patch thirty feet

across, carpeted with knee-high grass. Valentine moved to the center while Malcolm paced around the edge. Shuffling through the soft grass, she scanned the ground around her feet. Closer inspection revealed . . . grass.

Malcolm kicked a fallen branch. "I don't know what I expected, but it wasn't nothing."

Valentine ran her hands through the surrounding blades of grass. "Maybe we should go. It's getting dark for real now, and . . ." She trailed off.

Her palm was streaked with ash. Two minutes before, it had been clean.

Retracing her steps, Valentine knelt and studied the ground. In the waning light, she could just make out a blackened patch of grass, and beneath the blades was a scorched hole about six inches across—perfectly round.

"Mal, over here."

Approaching, Malcolm knelt by her side. She traced her fingers around the hole's edges.

"Still warm," she said.

"Hmm. Storms have been hitting all over town for months," Malcolm said. "And people say they're getting worse. So if this happened *here*, did it happen anywhere else?"

Valentine shrugged, then winced and rubbed her shoulder, the pain reminding her how exhausted she was. Her head felt twice as heavy. "Maybe, but right now this is just another weird mystery. I'm tired, I'm cut up, and I was just attacked by lightning. I'm going home."

Malcolm stared down at the hole, chewing his lip.

"All right," he said. "Nothing we can do tonight. The car's probably here anyway."

THE front door clicked shut. Valentine slipped off her shoes and padded over to the den with Malcolm trailing behind. As expected, Neil sat in a recliner, absorbed in a book while Oma Grace lounged on the couch with a crossword puzzle.

"Hey, kids," Neil mumbled, his nose practically between the pages. "Thought you'd be out longer. How was it?"

Valentine shuffled her feet, unsure where to begin. *How do we explain that lightning tried to kill us?*

"Well," Malcolm said. "It could've been better."

I guess that's a start.

"New friendships can be fragile," Oma Grace said. "Give it time and . . ."

She glanced up and her words trailed away. The puzzle dropped to the floor. With a gasp, she exploded from the couch.

"Oh, dear lord, what happened to you?"

She circled the twins, pointing at every cut and peppering them with questions. What did this? Was everyone all right? Why were there wood chips in Valentine's hair?

Neil pulled away from his book and went behind Oma Grace, re-examining each wound. Whenever he found a bad one, he made a concerned noise and brushed it with his fingers. Under all this examination, Valentine felt like a science project.

The twins did their best to answer everything, though Valentine noted that Malcolm left out their discovery. She decided to follow suit until they could talk more about it.

"We'll go visit your friends in the hospital tomorrow. Right now, you need to have those cuts cleaned again and re-bandaged," Oma Grace commanded. "Valentine, go upstairs with your father. And you come with me, young man."

Valentine trudged upstairs and changed into denim shorts

and a black tank top. Most of her cuts would be easily reachable now.

She gathered her fiery locks into a ponytail and stepped into the bathroom. Her father had flicked on the antique lamp, bathing the room in a soft amber glow. He dug through the cupboard for the first aid kit as she settled on the cool counter.

Neil found the kit and went to work. The room filled up with silence, broken only by his mumbled musings over her wounds.

It was almost too awkward to stand. *Will we ever talk like we used to?* Valentine tried to look him in the eye, but he avoided her gaze. *I guess one of us should give it a shot.* She took a breath.

"How were things before this happened?" Neil said. "Were you having a nice time?"

She stared at him. *Is he actually trying?* He looked up at her, and Valentine realized she hadn't responded yet.

"Um, yeah, it was good. We're kind of an odd group, but it works so far." Images of Fred's bloody arms and Winter's screaming flashed through her mind. Her stomach ached. "I hope they're okay."

"Me too. They're nice kids." He fell quiet again and bandaged another cut.

That's it? Valentine wanted more. She searched for something to keep the conversation going. "So, um, where'd you learn to do this?"

"Remember *Night Shift,* the thriller I wrote about a paramedic?"

"I'm not sure."

"Well, you were a toddler. I spent a month riding in an ambulance for research. They taught me a few tricks." He chuckled.

"One night, they got a call about a guy having seizures. I go in with Randy, one of the EMTs, and this guy on the couch starts shaking when he sees us. I'm feeling bad for the guy, but Randy starts laughing." He finished bandaging a deep scrape on her shin and started on a cut to her forearm. "Randy's coworker comes in and asks, 'What do we have here?' The guy on the couch stops and says, 'Hey man, can't you see I'm having a seizure?' and then starts shaking again."

Valentine burst into laughter. "He didn't!"

Neil nodded, laughing with her. "He did, and Randy knew right away the guy was faking."

He's actually talking! It felt almost like before.

"I swear, I'll never forget that." His fingers brushed over her bandaged right shoulder.

Valentine gasped, her laughter cutting off. White-hot pain lanced through her.

"I'm sorry! I didn't know it was that bad. Are you all right?"

Valentine shut her eyes and breathed slowly. Gradually, the pain ebbed and her muscles relaxed. "Yeah, it just hurt for a second."

Neil tilted his head to examine a cut near her neck. "This one goes pretty deep. EMTs must've been in a hurry—you need a couple more stitches." He retrieved a needle and thread from the kit and looked at her apologetically. "This'll hurt."

Valentine gripped her pendant. "Okay."

Her dad set to work while she turned away, trying to focus on anything else. The cool metal in her hand. That felt better.

"How does it feel?"

"Not too bad." Her voice came out strained.

A smile touched the corners of Neil's mouth. "You're a tough girl, Valentine. Always were." He finished the last stitch and reached for the shears. "Remember when you sprained your ankle at that dance recital? You were only eight, but you barely even cried."

"Yeah, I remember."

"You could hardly stand, but you still wanted to do your routine. That Russian teacher of yours said, 'Flower cannot stand on broken stem. Do not be fool.' And I had to make you sit down."

She grinned at the memory. "'We're fools whether we dance or not, so we might as well dance.'"

Neil stiffened. His face became a mask, still as stone.

Valentine's heart sank. *No no no!* "Well, I mean, uh . . ."

She grasped for anything, but felt frozen inside. Her father looked down again, avoiding her eyes. *Please, no.*

He set peroxide and a clean cloth on the counter. "Twice a day, for a week," he muttered, barely audible, and turned to leave.

He was slipping away from her, disappearing inside himself again. Her chest tightened. *Please, not again!*

"Dad." She grabbed his forearm. "Why can't you talk to me anymore? What did I do?"

Neil's face recoiled as if he'd been slapped. "Valentine, no. That's not—you didn't—"

She waited for more.

He just looked down, his face a mask of sorrow.

"Then what? What is it?"

He shook his head. "I can't. I just—I can't . . ." He seemed to grope for more, but nothing came.

She stared at him. The knot in her chest began to harden, turning darker. "So, that's all, huh?"

He finally looked up at her with reddening eyes. His silence stretched on, and her resentment solidified.

Fine. Setting her jaw, she nodded and walked to the door. "Forget it."

"I—" he called feebly. "I didn't . . ."

She fled to her bedroom and shut the door. As soon as it clicked shut, she leaned against the painted wood and sagged to the floor, face in her hands. The knot in her chest turned to tears. *Why?*

MALCOLM flipped through TV channels. Worry for his friends kept pushing into his mind, and he searched for anything that might distract him. He could still hear Winter screaming.

Soft steps made their way down the stairs, and Neil retrieved his book from the chair. "Feeling better?"

Malcolm stretched out both arms, displaying a dozen bandages. "Oma turned me into a mummy."

Neil nodded. "Hey, would you look in on your sister later? Just make sure she's okay."

"Happened again, huh?"

Neil looked away.

"You know, one of these days you're going to have to face this."

Neil's eyes flashed. "Oh? When did you become the parent?"

"Dad," Malcolm gave him a level look. "She doesn't even know what's wrong."

"And you do?"

"Yeah. But you won't admit it, and she's too hurt to figure it out. I mean, someone has to be the adult. Right?"

Neil stared him down. "Be careful."

Malcolm felt a pang of regret and glanced at the carpet.

"I may be down, but I'm still your father."

"Yeah, and things are fine between us, but Val barely feels like she has a father anymore." He stood and rested a hand on his father's shoulder. "You know I'm right, Dad. She needs you. Try harder for her."

Malcolm patted Neil's shoulder and headed for the kitchen in search of something sugary. A moment later the den lights switched off and Neil's footsteps hit the stairs. Malcolm waited in anticipation until his father's door closed with a click.

Go. Switching off the kitchen light, Malcolm slipped through the front door. The porch light was off, and moonlight snuck through breaks in the cloud cover, bathing the street in an ethereal glow. A chilly wind rushed through the trees. He pulled on the jacket he'd left by the door and darted across the street.

The old house towered over him, its front window glaring into the night like a skull's eye socket. Was that face behind the glass right now, staring at him?

Malcolm returned the house's glare with one of his own. "I know it was you today." He clutched the gate handle. "I know you did something." Its only answer was that same sense of wrongness.

He itched to walk through the gate, to examine the house up close. Was there a way inside? Heavy dread clamped around his heart, leeching away his determination. Even if there was, this wasn't like his books, and he wasn't that guy anymore—the guy who took chances and did things and lived.

"Who are you, huh?" he whispered to himself. Drawing up, he stared a challenge at the house. His hand flexed on the handle. "Come on, do it."

The handle began to turn. The fear drove deeper into him, wrapping itself around his heart. Malcolm pushed and beat against it, but it refused to move. His hand wavered.

His shoulders slumped. Sighing, he let go of the handle and looked down in shame. Turning his back to the house, he trudged home.

Back inside, Malcolm aimed for the darkened stairs at the rear of the house. Halfway there, he stopped dead in his tracks. The back door was swinging open.

A shadow slipped silently inside. Had someone followed him back? He snatched the nearest solid object, raised it like a club and flipped on the overhead light.

Oma Grace stood in the doorway, wearing a black track suit and a startled expression. Seeing Malcolm, her alarm turned to a smile.

"If you're going to swing that, young man, be sure you miss. It's my favorite."

Malcolm glanced at his hand. He held a tall porcelain figurine of some Victorian lady. Grinning sheepishly, he set it back down.

"Sorry, Oma. I thought you were ... uh ... something scary."

"Mm-hm." She swept past him and picked up the figurine. "What were you doing outside? It's after midnight."

"Oooh, I might ask you the same thing." She set the object on a higher shelf. "If you must know, I was visiting Mr. Crane next door. The man needs conversation, and I'm one of the few friends he has. But it's bedtime for both of us now. Go on, shoo!"

She pushed him playfully toward the stairs. Laughing, he started the climb. "G'night, Oma."

"Sleep well, my boy."

In his room, Malcolm tossed his shoes and jacket to the floor and grabbed a book, ready to read about the Middle Ages until he drifted to sleep. He glanced at Valentine's door, where light still glowed at the crack above the carpet, and mentally kicked himself. Dad had asked him to check on her, and she probably would need to talk.

"Val?"

Out of habit, he turned the knob and pushed inside.

She was sitting up in bed, half-buried under a fluffy comforter while a small lamp glowed on her bedside table. Her head snapped up in alarm, and she slid something under the covers.

"Knock much?"

"Sorry. I know something happened with Dad. You okay . . . ?" He trailed off, realizing what he'd seen, and examined her face. She was tense about something, and her hands were buried under the covers. "Is that what I think it is?"

She shifted. "Is what?"

His eyes narrowed. "You know what."

Sighing, Valentine pulled out a small book covered in worn brown leather.

"I thought you were going to pack that away."

"I am," she said. "Just not yet."

"Val, that isn't helping anything. Didn't you want to start moving on?"

Her eyes caught fire, and she clutched at her pendant. "I'm perfectly capable of reading a book and moving on with my life, unlike *some* people," she snapped. "When was the last time you did anything besides read a book? Because that's all you do now. You don't want to make friends or live a real life. All you want to do is hide. Or is that what you call moving on?"

The words scorched him. He paused to find a calm voice. "I'm not going to respond to that, because I know you'll regret it tomorrow." He closed her door, wishing he'd just gone to bed.

Back in his own room, he flopped onto the bed and grabbed the nearest book. Valentine's words echoed in his head, burning deeper. Through his front window, the house with no doors continued to mock him.

A surge of pressure built up inside as months of memories played through his head. A lightning storm matched perfectly by flashes from the house. A window frosted as sheets of energy fell from a clear sky. White-hot bolts raced after him, shattering trees and hurling his friends through the air. He flinched, once again seeing Valentine's limp body tumble to the ground.

The pressure grew to a burning. "So, all I want to do is hide, huh?" He stared hard at the house, then at his reflection in the glass. "Who are you?"

Malcolm snapped the book shut and dropped it onto the bed. Leaping to his feet, he donned shoes and jacket, then pocketed his phone and flashlight. His eyes fell on the Damascus steel daggers hanging on the wall. He crossed the room and plucked them from their mounts.

Gazing at them, he tested their weight in his hands. The banding on each blade glinted like flowing water. *This is crazy. Do you even know how to use them?*

He forced away the fear. *Sure I do. Don't grab the sharp end.* Malcolm slid the blades into their sheaths and clipped them to his belt—one on each hip, hidden beneath his jacket.

With the lamp switched off and the door closed behind him, he stalked toward the stairs.

CHAPTER 9

Malcolm clutched the iron handle and stared up at the dark window again. Thick clouds hurtled across the sky, casting inky shadows. He tried not to shiver in the gusting wind.

Do it. NOW.

He turned the handle and pushed, stepping inside the fence before he could change his mind. Thunder cracked overhead. He took a second step, and the swaying grass brushed near his waist. A third step, and the house loomed closer. Its faded white wood almost glowed in the moonlight.

Malcolm turned right and paced along the fence, searching for . . . well, he had no clue what. Something was very wrong here, so something had to be out of place.

The house looked tall enough for three stories, and each side seemed about fifty feet wide. A circular window sat at the top of each side, easily big enough for a person to fit through. Malcolm noted that each was one solid sheet of glass, and they didn't look the slightest bit warped or cracked.

After walking a full circle, he moved away from the fence and angled closer to the house. The wind howled and whipped at his clothes, and a heavy chill touched the air. It leeched into him, and each step forward grew more difficult, as if the presence of the house made the air thicker and heavier.

It's just a house. Only a house. Malcolm latched onto the thought that Valentine had been drilling at him for weeks. *But if it's only a house, why do I feel this way?* He forced himself forward until he stood inches from the west wall.

Pulse pounding, he swiped his fingers along one of the white planks. It was oddly warm.

A stiff gust hammered into his back. Malcolm reached out to steady himself against the house—and there it was. Under the pressure of his hands, he could feel it now.

"What in the . . . ?"

The house was vibrating. Subtle and easily missed by a casual touch, it seemed to pulse, rising and falling in a steady rhythm. He started walking again, tracing his hand along the house, and every inch vibrated with the exact same rhythm. *No way. Just . . . no*, he thought. But here it was.

Malcolm leaned in and placed his ear against the wall when a bolt of lightning stabbed across the sky. He jumped back from the wall and stared up at the window, waiting for a pulse of light. Nothing happened.

Somewhere along these panels, there had to be a hidden door. To have a chance at finding disguised cracks or hinges, he'd need to see every detail. He pulled out a Fenix LED flashlight, flicked it on, and leaned within a breath of the wall.

When he saw the truth, it was like a kick to the gut. Malcolm suddenly felt the full weight of what he was doing and what was happening around him. The night air seemed colder, the blustering wind more menacing, and he couldn't shake the feeling of being watched. He had expected a door, but this?

"It can't be," he whispered.

The entire wall was covered with impossibly small glass lenses and layers on layers of microcircuitry. They nestled into every inch of the wood, overlapping in intricate patterns.

It's like the circuit board of a computer.

He stepped back, shaking his head, and saw the pattern seemingly melt away. No wonder it looked normal from the street. *Who could've done something like this?*

This was more than a weird house—much more than he'd imagined. If he wanted, he could still walk away. *Should* walk away.

A tense moment passed as he stared at the house. The wind and the cold pushed him, urging him to go home. He steeled himself.

"Yeah, right."

Malcolm dug out his phone and held the camera up to the wall. He thumbed the shutter button, and after a discreet click he had a crystal-clear image. Satisfied for the moment, he flicked off the flashlight and pocketed it.

A deeper hum began to emanate from the house. Malcolm tilted his head and leaned his ear closer to the wall. The vibrations increased, pulses cycling faster and more intensely. The hum grew to a high-pitched whine, and he could almost feel the air vibrating around him. Lightning flashed overhead.

A bright circle of light burst from the wall. Malcolm cried out, shielding his eyes, and a wave of force crashed into his body. He flew back and hit the ground with a thud. Shaking his head to stop the world from spinning, he sat up with a groan and patted the soft grass in appreciation.

He looked up at the wall and froze. A spinning orb of

blue-white energy passed through the wood like it was air, leaving no mark. Taller than Malcolm, it rippled and crackled and flashed like lightning trapped inside flowing water.

The surrounding darkness warped and stretched toward the sphere. Shadows spun around it, wrapping it like a blanket of living darkness. Underneath, the brilliant orb shrank, twisted and winked out of existence. Only the shadow remained.

Wide-eyed and trembling, Malcolm gaped at the roiling pillar of shadow. It turned, and he knew it was looking at him. A deafening roar shattered the quiet night, tearing at his mind like a thousand voices shouting in fury.

The shadow raced toward him. Malcolm scrambled to his feet and backpedaled as fast as he could. The shadow closed the gap in seconds and lashed out, knocking him backward. He clanged against the iron fence and sharp pain blossomed in his back.

"YYYOOOUUU WWWIIILLLLLL NNNOOOTTT IIINNNTTTEEERRRFFFEEERRREEE!" The voices screamed into his head.

Malcolm tensed and mentally shoved back against the assault. The advancing shadow stopped in its tracks, as if surprised. Seizing the moment, Malcolm yanked out his cell phone and triggered the camera.

The shadow swiped at his hand, and the phone flew away in pieces. Darkness wrapped around his outstretched arm, and then he was airborne. His body cut through the air and flopped to the grass halfway back toward the house. Forcing himself to his knees, Malcolm pushed past the pain and drew the knife from his left hip.

With blinding speed, the shadow charged forward and

smashed into him. Malcolm tumbled backward and smacked full force against the wall of the house.

The air crushed from his lungs and the knife flew from his hand. Knees turning to jello, he fell back against the wall and sank to the ground. He gasped, desperate to find his breath.

Three copies of the shadow swam in his vision. Malcolm kicked out as it approached and connected with something hard. Wisps of shadow yanked him off the ground and pinned him against the wall. He shook his head and the three shadows coalesced back into one.

"YYYOOOUUU WWWIIILLLLLL NNNOOOTTT IIINNNTTTEEERRRFFFEEERRREEE WWWIIITTTHHH UUUSSS."

The onslaught tore at his thoughts. He stubbornly opposed it, clinging to his own mind and struggling to stay calm enough to think. Was there anything he could use? Ideas sprang into his frenzied mind and managed to click together. It didn't matter if they were true. He had to try *something*.

"Another kid goes missing, and you might get more than you bargained for!" he blurted.

He could feel the shadow examining him now. Had he actually been right?

"You know who I am, where I live. I disappear, where do you think they're gonna start looking? People know I've been watching this house!"

The shadow's hold tightened.

"There's a way out of this for both of us. Just show me what you're doing in there and the mystery's over. No more questions, no more snooping."

As Malcolm spoke those insane words, his right hand crept

slowly underneath his jacket. With his eyes adjusting to the dark again, he could see the attacker's silhouette against the moonlight. Its shape was familiar—almost human. The bands of shadow clinging to him could almost be arms.

The grip on his shoulders loosened. Malcolm dropped to his feet and leaned against the wall for support. He could barely stand, and every breath lanced pain into his side.

"*NNNOOONNNEEE OOOFFF YYYOOOUUU MMMAAATTTTTTEEERRR,*" it said. "*III HHHAAAVVVEEE SSSEEEEEENNN HHHOOOWWW TTTHHHIIISSS TTTOOOWWWNNN EEENNNDDDSSS. IIITTT WWWIIILLLLLL HHHAAAPPPPPPEEENNN SSSOOOOOONNNEEERRR TTTHHHAAANNN YYYOOOUUU TTTHHHIIINNNKKK.*"

It stretched toward him again. He could barely make out something metallic in its grip. A pinprick of light flashed within the shadow, pointing in his direction.

"*YYYOOOUUU WWWIIILLLLLL NNNOOOTTT BBBEEE—*"

Malcolm ripped the second knife from its sheath and slashed at the shadow. The blade dug into something solid and came back red. Screams of agony rewarded him.

He slashed again, driving the shadow back a step. With his free hand, he drew the flashlight and flicked it on. The beam blazed into the shadow, and the shadow backed away with a thousand shocked cries. The pinprick of light pointed at him again.

Setting his jaw, Malcolm dashed forward and slashed. The blade bit into something again, and the light disappeared. He drew back and struck at the shadow's center with all his might.

A jolt traveled through the knife and up his arm. With a

loud pop, sparks showered from where he stabbed. A voice shouted—one voice. The mass of shadows shrank and coalesced into the shape of a cloaked man. He struck out and Malcolm bashed against the wall again.

All strength gone, Malcolm oozed to the ground. He tried to lash out with the knife and realized his hands were empty. The dark man approached, Malcolm's dagger blade glinting in his hand. They stared at each other, both breathing hard.

Cloak and night hid his attacker's face. Malcolm glared where the eyes should be and summoned his last bit of courage. He beckoned the man closer.

"Come on, then. Let's get this over with."

He tensed, praying he could still defend himself. The dark man stepped closer.

KA-CHIK!

Malcolm turned and found himself staring at the barrel of a pump-action shotgun.

"Drop it and back away," Mr. Crane commanded.

The dark man moved an inch toward him. Mr. Crane hefted the gun and advanced, pointing it at his head.

"You get one warning," he barked. "*One.*" Steel eyes bore into his target. "Leave. Right now."

The cloaked man hesitated, then dropped the knife and slowly backed away. Mr. Crane came forward, placing himself between Malcolm and his assailant. When he reached the fence, the dark man vaulted it and sprinted into the fields beyond. His cloaked form seemed to melt into the night, and he was gone.

Malcolm released the breath he'd been holding. Mr. Crane grunted and lowered the shotgun, then marched back home without a word.

"Wait! Mr. Crane!" Malcolm pawed at the ground, not

leaving any items behind, then stumbled after his savior. "That guy was gonna kill me! How did you know?"

"Just saw the lights, so I came to check it out," Mr. Crane growled. "Didn't expect to find you getting robbed. Maybe next time you'll think twice about trespassing."

"He wasn't—well, if you hadn't come, I think I'd be dead."

He was in the street now. Malcolm jogged to catch up with him. "Did you see what he was doing with those shadows?"

Mr. Crane spun around. "What did you say?"

"The shadows. Almost like he was . . . *wearing* the darkness?" Malcolm felt foolish, but pressed on. "I've never seen anything like it."

Mr. Crane moved closer and stooped to stare him in the eyes. Malcolm shifted and tried not to look away. He felt like his insides were being sorted and catalogued.

Mr. Crane chuckled. "If you weren't Grace's boy, I'd think you were on the funny stuff."

Malcolm bristled. "I know what I saw."

Mr. Crane looked back at the towering house. "Well, fear can do funny things to your head. I remember once, back in . . ." he trailed off, catching himself. The scowl returned, and he fixed Malcolm with a hard stare. "Look, just go inside and stay out of trouble. Even small towns have bad people, and next time it might be worse than a mugger."

He swung around and stalked back to his front door.

"Thanks!" Malcolm called after him. "I'll—"

Mr. Crane's door slammed shut.

Malcolm closed and locked his bedroom door with shaking hands, leaving the lights off. Enough moonlight streamed in for him to see.

With the adrenaline fading, he gasped at the stabbing sensation in his side. If his ribs weren't cracked, they were at least bruised. His right shoulder and hip felt knocked out of place—he would be limping for days.

He had gotten off extremely lucky.

I could have died. Shivering, he collapsed onto the bed. His belongings tumbled to the floor, and he clutched the edge of the mattress for support.

That house, with its secrets; that man, with his control of things that couldn't be controlled; the voices digging in his head. What had he expected to accomplish?

As if in answer, another voice called out, calm and confident. *Who are you?*

No! Malcolm shoved it away. He was not a guy who wanted to end up dead. Pushing up from the mattress, he limped over to the front window.

"Okay, you win." Hands pressed against the glass, he stared directly into that round window. "It's over. I'm done."

Still shivering, Malcolm turned and sank to his knees, gathering the dropped items mechanically. The knives went back in their sheaths—one of them still red. Malcolm knew he should clean it, but he didn't want to think about having cut another person.

His fingers brushed something round and cool, metallic and partially smooth. He held it up to the moonlight.

An antique silver pocket watch gleamed in his hand—the kind with a fancy silver chain, designed to nestle in some old gentleman's pocket. The back side was shiny and smooth, with a delicate ring of scrollwork cut out of the metal. The front cover had a matching ring, with one difference—in its center sat a round, translucent jewel the size of a nickel, cut beautifully and glittering like a diamond.

He examined the jewel and his eyebrows climbed—in its center, microcircuitry swirled in a circular pattern, reminding Malcolm of a spinning vortex. He remembered the point of light in the shadowed man's hand and his pulse quickened. He eyed the release button warily. What could be gained from this except more danger?

"It's just a watch," he said aloud and thumbed the button.

The cover sprang open to reveal a black face with silver hands and roman numerals. Malcolm studied it, but compared to the casing it seemed unremarkable. *Another mystery bigger than me.* He sighed and reached for the cover. His thumb brushed across the glass face.

The watch sprang to life.

A soft blue glow emanated from the hands and the numbers. The hands shifted to six o'clock and began to spin, pointing in opposite directions. The spinning grew faster and the light grew brighter until the watch hands were a blur and he was bathed in blue.

Particles of light lifted from the glass and swirled in the air above the watch face. Malcolm almost laughed, scarcely believing what he was seeing. The watch was creating a hologram.

The light resolved into a pair of moving three-dimensional images. Malcolm easily identified the image floating to the left—the spinning Earth. The image on the right was less obvious, but it resembled a flowing river. Curious, he brushed the right image with his finger. More particles of light lifted from the face and resolved into words.

OPTIONS
COMMANDS

EXECUTE

Malcolm held his breath and touched COMMANDS. The words broke into tiny glowing fireflies and recombined, forming into different words. The submenu showed him what the watch could do.

He nearly dropped it.

"Oh my God."

CHAPTER 10

The next morning was gray and overcast. Feeling bleary and wretched, Valentine shuffled into the kitchen to find breakfast. Sleep had not come easily after her fight with Malcolm.

"Good morning, dear," Oma Grace said from two steps behind, following her into the kitchen.

Valentine jumped, then caught herself. "Hi," she mumbled. "You move like a ninja."

Oma Grace chuckled.

Somehow, cereal and milk found their way into a bowl. Valentine sagged at the table and ate mechanically. It didn't taste that good. *Junk food won't fix what you said.*

"Is Mal up yet?"

"Seems he's not feeling well. Left a note here, must've been earlier." Oma Grace slid a scrap of paper toward her.

> People of Earth,
> I have the plague.
> Signed,
> Malcolm Gilbert

"At least, I think that means he's sick. Your brother has an odd way with words."

Valentine nodded, certain that this was her fault. "Can we go see Winter and Fred after school?"

"Of course."

"Thanks." She bent over her bowl again, staring down into it. Though she was more awake and alert now, the feeling of ickiness wouldn't leave her. Like it was a coating of thick, smelly grime that refused to wash away. Grimacing, she pushed the bowl away and just sat there wallowing in how awful life could be.

"My dear," Oma Grace said, leaning down to catch her eye. "Are you all right?"

Valentine just shrugged. What was the point of doing anything else? Today was destined to be totally *not* awesome.

Oma Grace tapped her chin in thought. "You know, it occurs to me," she began, a twinkle in her eye, "if your brother can have a sick day, why can't you? How about we go see your friends this morning?"

Valentine dared to look up, this time with the barest of smiles. Maybe there was hope for today after all.

Malcolm stumbled out of bed at noon. Everything hurt. He wouldn't allow himself to take pain pills, though. He deserved the pain. It taught him humility.

At least his head was clear, even if his body was black and blue. He had a vague memory of Valentine knocking earlier and asking about visiting the hospital, but he'd been dead to the world at that point. It might even have been a dream. He wasn't sure.

After a long shower he almost felt like himself again, and his nerves weren't quite as raw. Plopping down in his desk chair, he spun in a circle while rubbing a towel on his wet hair. From the corner of his eye, he caught a glint where the pocket watch sat next to his laptop. Its jewel sparkled in the midday light, calling to him. What other secrets did it hold?

Once again, curiosity defeated his better judgment. Reaching out, Malcolm snatched the watch up and clicked it open. The hands spun after the same delicate touch, and in seconds he was examining the holographic root menu again. Last night he'd chosen the image of a flowing river. This time he brushed the option that looked like Earth.

The holographic image enlarged, taking the center spot. A submenu appeared, but he had no idea what it meant.

SKIP HISTORY

NEW DESTINATION

Let's see what exactly you can do. Malcolm's heart raced as he moved to choose SKIP HISTORY. He stopped short when a metallic *thunk* sounded from outside. He spun in his chair to see Mr. Crane in his driveway, half-disappeared under the hood of his vintage red pickup truck.

Good. Now he could accomplish today's real purpose. Closing the watch, he set it back on the desk and rummaged through the bottom drawer. The object he wanted sat under a pile of old papers. Standing, he slipped it into the pocket of his jeans. Malcolm owed a debt and he wanted to pay it immediately.

The October days were cooling off, so he pulled on a long-sleeved gray shirt. After leaving a note in the kitchen explaining where he'd gone, he slipped outside.

Funny—he'd faced death last night, but this still made him nervous. Pushing his jitters aside, he approached the neighbor's driveway just as the truck's hood slammed shut. Mr. Crane stood there with his usual scowl.

"Looking for another house to vandalize?"

Is that a joke? Malcolm tried to force a laugh but ended up clearing his throat. "Actually I came to thank you."

The old man's eyes narrowed. "You thanked me last night. Didn't ask for it then, don't need it now." He moved toward the truck's door.

"Wait!"

Mr. Crane stopped with his hand on the door handle.

"I thanked you, yeah. But not enough."

Malcolm produced a leather square the size of a wallet. Set into the leather was a bronze coin two inches across, embossed with the head of Abraham Lincoln. Above it, *1809–1909* shone in gold letters. He held it out.

Mr. Crane's eyebrows raised. He hesitated, then accepted it. "The Lincoln Centennial Coin," he whispered.

Malcolm nodded. "Never been out of the case, as far as I know. It's not as old as your Little Mack, but it's intact."

Mr. Crane turned it over, examining every corner. "These are rare. Where did you find it?"

"Buried in an antique shop back in Chicago." Malcolm smiled. "They didn't know what they had."

Mr. Crane stood dumbfounded. "I-I've never . . ." He wrapped both hands around the leather with reverence. "Thank you."

"You saved my life, Mr. Crane," Malcolm replied. "Thank you."

He turned to head back home, feeling uplifted. Hours of working up the courage for this moment—it had been more than worth it.

"Hold on a minute."

Malcolm turned back, puzzled. Mr. Crane was still standing there, looking as if he wanted to say something but hadn't figured out what.

"I . . . well, how's that project going? The one you inter-viewed me for."

Malcolm worked to hide his shock. "A little slow. We've been busy with, uh, other things, and there aren't many people to interview."

Mr. Crane stared at him, then nodded as if he'd decided something. Fishing keys from his pocket, he opened the truck door. "Heading into town if you want to come along."

Malcolm nearly fell over.

"You want some history? I'll show you the oldest man in town. Lunch first, though." He climbed into the truck. "You coming or not?"

Malcolm shook to his senses and jogged to the passenger side.

Nothing would be completely better until Valentine could talk to Malcolm. *I just want to apologize.* They fought so rarely, and nothing felt right when it happened. This would help, though—seeing her friends, making sure they were okay.

"Bye, Oma," Valentine called into the car.

"Call me when you're ready for pickup, dear," Oma Grace replied.

Grocery bag in hand, Valentine turned up the ramp to the hospital's main entrance. The doors whooshed open, sending out a rush of sterilized air. On reaching the fourth floor, she stopped at a door halfway down the east wing of the hospital. With a knock on room forty-two, she went inside.

"Whoa!"

She ducked as the remains of a dinner roll sailed past her head and smacked into the wall behind her.

"Sorry!" Winter called. "Thought you were John."

Smiling, Valentine went to hug Winter and sit on her bed.

"Good shot, though. S'up, Red," Fred said. Perched on the adjacent bed, he waved one of his thick casts.

Valentine pulled a plastic container from the bag and set it on the table between the beds. "Hey, Fred. Feeling better?"

He brightened at her attention. "Couple broken arms ain't keepin' me down. You can't stop the dawg that easy."

Winter tossed a ketchup packet at him. "Don't let him fool you. He's been crashing in my room all day, moaning about missing basketball this year."

Fred's brow furrowed. "Don't play, don't get a scholarship. You know that, girl."

"Whatever. What's in the box?"

"Oma Grace sent fresh cookies." Valentine popped the lid.

"Oooh, grandma cookies? Gimme." Winter plunged into the box and drew out a handful. "Uh, I mean thanks."

Valentine regarded Fred then, puzzled. "You're going for a scholarship?"

Fred nodded. "Yep. I gotta—"

"Hold on, quiet," Winter cut in.

She stared at the door and grabbed a fistful of ketchup packets. The knob turned. She waited an instant, then let them fly. The door opened and the condiment missiles slapped against John's chest. One fell into the sling cradling his arm.

He glanced down at them without breaking stride. "Hello, Winter."

Winter put on an innocent face. "Why'd you think it was me?"

"It's always you."

Her innocence melted into an evil grin. "That's right!"

"I showed your parents to the cafeteria. They will come back with dinner," John said. "Is your father flying home, Fred?"

"Naw, I told him I'm fine. Why should he come all the way back from London for a couple broken arms? I got it covered."

John nodded, then turned to Valentine and smiled. "Hello, Valentine."

She smiled back, praying that her cheeks weren't red. "Hi, John."

As he spoke, his gaze remained on her. "So, the doctor indicated that you're both staying one additional night. You'll check out tomorrow morning."

"Oh, come on," Winter protested. "I'm going crazy in here!"

"Why they keepin' us? We're good." Fred glanced down at his casts. "Sort of."

"Venturing a guess," John replied, "the cause of your injuries is unusual. They may want to ensure there are no surprises."

A heavy quiet fell over the room, and Valentine's mind went back to the events that led them there. The light. The explosions. The screaming. She could smell the burning wood, taste the bile rising in her throat as her friends fell. *Then you yelled at Mal, and then you were rude again before bed.* Another hot spike of guilt stabbed into her. *He was just trying to help. I'm the worst sister ever.*

"So," Fred broke the silence. "We gonna talk about what happened? Cause it sure wasn't natural, and we all know it."

Valentine sat forward. "Well . . ." she began, then hesitated, thinking of what she and Malcolm had found in the forest clearing afterward. If she told them everything now, would it help them or just put them in more danger? "I guess we'll never know for sure. At least we're alive."

Winter groaned and pressed a hand to her bandaged ear.

"Are you all right?" John asked.

"Meds are wearing off." Winter gasped. "God, this hurts." She clutched the ear tighter and squeezed her left eye shut, as if she were trying to block out the pain. "How am I supposed to work like this? I've got to keep digging if I'm going to find Patrick."

"Have they found any clues yet?" Valentine asked.

Winter shook her head, disheartened.

"I'll find a nurse for you." Valentine slid from her bed.

"I'll show you where they are." John joined her at the door and they left together.

Valentine walked next to John as he led the way to the nurses' station. She stole glances at him and her stomach fluttered. Why was it doing that?

Come on, you know why.

"I hate that Winter's in pain," she said.

"It's difficult for her to feel weak," John replied. "I believe that's more painful to her than the injury."

Valentine nodded. "I can understand that."

Okay, I admit it. He's cute.

"How is your shoulder?"

It's more than that, though.

She shifted, feeling the bandages flex. "It stings, and I have to be careful how I move. But everyone needs one cool scar, right? Aren't scars supposed to be sexy?"

She mentally kicked herself. *Why did you just say that?!*

John chuckled. "I believe I've heard that."

"Um, so, how's yours?"

He looked down at the sling. "Dislocations are painful, but

I'll be well soon if I leave it be." He gave an apologetic shrug. "Sorry, no sexy scars."

Valentine shook her head in mock sympathy. "Oh, that's too bad."

"I know," he played along, looking defeated. "How else could I attract a pretty girl's attention?"

She bumped against him and grinned. "I guess you'll just have to try harder."

What are you doing?

John held her eyes with his gaze. "I guess I will."

Blushing heat raced down Valentine's cheeks. She stared back into his eyes—into that intense stare he fixed her with sometimes—and the heat spread down her neck, across her chest. Would it reach all the way to her toes?

What are you DOING?

I like him, okay? I. LIKE. HIM. There, I said it.

On the outside, she playfully feigned indifference. "Oh, okay. I was just making conversation."

He laughed. "Well, I'm pleased we sorted that out."

THE road hummed, pulling Malcolm's battered body toward sleep. His mind played back the afternoon, which he still had trouble believing. True to his word, Mr. Crane had driven to a diner on the town square, where they'd talked over burgers and fries.

Their mutual love for history carried most of the conversation, but the older man had actually revealed a few things about himself. Born and raised in Emmett's Bluff, he'd rarely traveled for more than a few days. In fact, only three times had Walter Crane been away for long.

The longest had been during the Vietnam War, after which

he'd spent a year traveling abroad. The other two he hadn't seemed eager to discuss. The only real detail Malcolm had gleaned was how much Mr. Crane loved traveling. When he spoke about Rome, he actually smiled.

All the while, thoughts of the pocket watch swam through Malcolm's head. He'd seen a glimpse of what it could do, and his mind still reeled from it. And from what he'd observed today, the watch held even *more* secrets. Who could've built it, and what else might they be hiding inside that house? He kept shaking that question away. The house was off limits now; he'd sworn it. But what if the shadowed man came looking for his watch?

Malcolm shook from his reverie as they pulled into the parking lot of a wide one-story building. The red brick occupied a whole corner of an intersection on the northeast side of town. Its twelve bay doors of gray steel were all closed tight. On the far right, antique gas pumps decorated the outside of the front office. Through the office windows, Malcolm made out vintage road signs and license plates along the walls.

"Still the best mechanic shop in town," Mr. Crane explained as they exited the truck. "He's owned it for a long time now."

"Is it open?"

Mr. Crane nodded. "Doors are always closed, though. He'd never tolerate dust in his shop."

Malcolm followed him into the office, where they opened another thick steel door. Echoing clangs of machinery greeted him as they entered the shop floor.

He stopped short, taken aback by the sight. Gleaming slabs of steel and painted concrete, expensive-looking computer equipment, mechanics in sleek Formula One style jumpsuits—it looked like the shop floor of NASA. Every rack boasted expensive foreign cars.

The only exception was the bay closest to the office. Its equipment looked decades behind the rest, and the car was an old classic in mid-restoration.

Mr. Crane led them to the classic and stood next to a pair of legs that poked out from underneath. A young shop assistant saw Mr. Crane coming and stepped back, his face going pale. It seemed *everyone* was afraid of him.

"Hey, Kevin?" a muffled voice called from under the car.

"Yes, s-sir?" the assistant answered, voice cracking under Mr. Crane's scowl.

"You still got that socket wrench?" The voice called in a slow, smooth drawl. "I could use a hand down here."

"I thought Clive Jessop didn't need help," Mr. Crane said.

The clinking under the car stopped. "Hey, Kevin? You put up that *No Skinny Punks* sign like I asked?"

Mr. Crane chuckled. "Get up here, old man."

A tall black man with salt-and-pepper hair slid from underneath the car. "You givin' orders in my shop, old man?" He flashed an easy smile and raised his hand.

Mr. Crane pulled him to his feet. "Got someone for you to meet." He nodded to Malcolm. "Malcolm Gilbert, meet Clive Jessop."

Clive turned his smile toward Malcolm and they shook hands. "Gilbert. You must be Grace's kin," he said, winking at Mr. Crane.

Malcolm nodded. "Yes. Nice to meet you, sir."

"Pleasure, son. Any kin o' Grace can come here anytime." He noticed Malcolm eyeing the shop. "Not what you expected, right?"

"My sister would love this place. She'd want to know what everything does."

Clive nodded proudly. "Ain't a car we can't fix." His hand rested affectionately on the classic. "Still got a soft spot for the oldies, though."

"People come from all over the country to get work done," Mr. Crane explained.

Malcolm's eyes widened. "Just to have a car fixed?"

"Well, it's sure not for his charm."

Clive leaned toward Malcolm. "Sounds like *someone* doesn't want free work anymore, huh?"

Malcolm laughed.

"Speaking of that," Mr. Crane jerked his thumb behind him. "Your handiwork needs more work. Want to take a look?"

"You gonna be nice?"

"No."

Clive stroked his chin, pretending to weigh his options.

"Don't you want to show off for the kid?" Mr. Crane asked.

Clive's face brightened. "Don't mind if I do! Let's have ourselves a look."

Malcolm followed them out to the red truck, his aching body complaining with every step. He stopped next to Clive while Mr. Crane climbed inside to start the engine.

"How'd you do it?" Clive said quietly.

Malcolm looked up at him. "Do what?"

"Get him to like you enough to bring you here. Walter Crane's like a brother, but the man ain't exactly social."

Malcolm thought on Clive's query. "Well, I guess I just thanked him. He found me behind that weird house across the street. I was, um, really in trouble. He helped me out when I needed it." He chuckled. "Felt kind of like the lion and the mouse, except in reverse."

Clive's face grew thoughtful. He examined Mr. Crane

first, then turned an appraising eye on Malcolm. It was a look with weight behind it, and Malcolm began to feel uneasy at the scrutiny.

"What is it?" he asked.

Clive inspected him a moment longer. A slight nod, as if he'd figured something out, then his smile returned.

"Oh, nothing," he said lightly. "Old friend o' mine used to say something similar, that's all."

The truck rumbled to life. Mr. Crane climbed out of the cab and raised the hood to reveal a new-looking engine, every part gleaming. Clive approached, swiped a finger across the head and held it up.

"See, now, this is why you can't have nice things."

Mr. Crane rolled his eyes. "It's just a little dust. We can't all spend every minute under a hood."

"Yeah, I forgot—that busy retirement schedule o' yours."

"You going to take a look or not, old man?"

Clive flashed an impish grin. "Well, you know I can't see a thing without my glasses."

He drew a set of round, silver spectacles from his coveralls. Unfolding them, he slid the wire frames into place and peered at the engine. He placed a hand on it, staring as if he could see through it.

"Valves're knockin'. Timing's a little off. And you stopped usin' the oil I told you to."

Malcolm gaped. The diagnosis had taken less than a minute, and Clive hadn't used one tool.

"How'd you do that?"

"Oh, machines say what they need. Just gotta know how to listen." He closed and latched the hood. "Bring it in on Wednesday, Walt. I'll fix you up."

"Thanks."

Clive returned the silver spectacles to his pocket and fixed Malcolm with a stare. "Now that's all finished, you look like someone who came here for a different reason. 'M I right?"

Malcolm's eyebrows raised. "Yeah, actually. I'm doing a project on the town's history. I was hoping to interview you."

"Oh, really." Clive shot an amused look at Mr. Crane. "And why'd you think t'see me? You already came with the oldest man in town."

"Well, uh, it was . . ." he glanced at Mr. Crane, who offered no help. "I'd heard that—"

Clive gestured to Mr. Crane. "He tell you *I'm* the oldest? *He's* older by three months! Ain't that right, Walt?"

Mr. Crane shook his head. "Still sticking with that story, eh?"

Malcolm grinned, both at their banter and at the idea of them being the oldest men in town. Neither could be older than late sixties. It was just the way old friends teased each other, he supposed.

"Story, my eye." Clive turned toward the shop. "Come on, son. Bring Grandpa with you and we'll talk."

VALENTINE preferred this strip mall to the newer one across the street. It was quiet. The other place swarmed with shoppers, practically vibrating with the excitement of something new. That was rare for a small town, she supposed. *After this week, I'm starting to think excitement is overrated.*

Oma Grace had suggested this stop after leaving the hospital, though, and it wasn't often that she let herself shop just for fun. Maybe a little retail therapy wouldn't hurt. It would help keep her mind off yesterday, anyway.

Strolling along the deserted walkway, Valentine smiled.

She'd spent a leisurely afternoon buying a few trinkets and junk food in peace, and now she wandered past the last row of stores.

Oooooh.

She stopped at a window display. A mannequin stood behind the 50% *Off!* signs, wrapped in the perfect little blue V-neck top. She leaned against the glass to steal a better look. *So pretty.*

Yeah, and SO girly. Keep walking.

She turned from the window, reminding herself that she didn't care how pretty it was. She wore what was comfortable. Two steps away, thoughts of John flashed in her mind. She turned to glance at the V-neck again. Cut like it was, the top would hug her curves and maybe show a hint of cleavage. What would John think of her in that?

Her thoughts flashed unbidden to French class. Recently, Madame LaChance had worn a black cashmere sweater that clung to every curve, the top buttons undone to give a tease of cleavage. Her dark blue jeans could have been painted on, tucked into black leather boots with stiletto heels. A beret nestled in her silky chestnut hair. *How very French of her.* Of course, every boy had paid rapt attention, hanging on every word as if getting an A might make her fall in love with them.

Valentine peered down at her own body. At fifteen, she had some curves that she enjoyed, but nothing approaching the French bombshell. The boys' eyes practically popped out whenever the teacher walked nearby. Valentine saw them looking in her direction sometimes, but . . .

Have they ever looked at me like that? Valentine told herself she didn't really care what they thought of her. She knew it was a lie.

Forget it. Just go home.

Shut up.

Valentine threw her shoulders back and strode into the store. She emerged twenty minutes later with the V-neck and a little dress she hadn't been able to resist.

You're hopeless.

She grinned to herself. Yes, it seemed like she was. Somehow, if John liked it, she was perfectly fine with that.

Oma Grace sat waiting in the car, trunk open. Valentine piled the bags inside, careful to arrange the clothes to avoid any wrinkling.

There, perfect.

"Hello, Miss Gilbert."

Valentine shrieked, smacking the back of her head on the trunk lid.

"Apologies, I didn't mean to frighten you," Mr. Carmichael said. "Are you hurt?"

She sighed in relief at the tiny man. "Geez, you scared me. I didn't hear you walk up."

"It appears I owe you extra credit on your next lab assignment." He grinned. "Not that you need it."

She laughed weakly. "Are you shopping here?"

"Even world-class teachers need to eat. But I saw you here and, well, I just couldn't wait until Monday."

"To do what?"

"To extend an offer. You see, the Science Department will choose one exceptional student to be my teaching assistant next year. Traditionally, I would wait until next semester to make the choice. Really, though, who could even hope to challenge you?"

Valentine's heart leapt. "Are you saying . . . ?"

"You have a brilliant future, Miss Gilbert, and I am proud to offer this to you."

"I'll get to work with you next year? Help you teach?"

He smiled warmly. "You'll even receive extra class credits."

Valentine put a hand to her mouth. She wanted to laugh, or cry, or maybe both. *It's finally happening!* All the work, all the passion and study, and someone had finally noticed.

"So." Mr. Carmichael clasped his hands together and assumed a formal air. "Do you accept my offer?"

"Yes!" she said as a giant bolt of lightning flashed in the distance. They both flinched at its intensity, and at the crack of thunder that followed. It had even lit up the daytime sky.

Mr. Carmichael stared up at the sky, his eyes narrowed. "How strange. What could possibly . . ." He shook his head. "Lightning always gave me chills. In any case, I must be going. I'll see you in class."

Valentine waved goodbye and walked to the passenger door on cloud nine.

CLIVE led Malcolm and Mr. Crane through the office and out a back door, which opened onto a sprawling fenced-in property. The rectangular plot of land covered at least an acre, half of it packed with orderly rows of classic vehicles. Each sat in a different state of repair, from rusted shells to gleaming masterpieces. Malcolm saw everything from motorcycles to dragsters to pickup trucks, and even military vehicles.

Clive led them across the yard toward a smaller building in the back. Along the way, he pointed out favorite models.

"Here's a 1939 Kuro Hagane motorcycle from Japan, real rare. '51 Studebaker Champion convertible. '67 Ferrari Dino 206 GT, original red. Amazing how rich folk give up cars they're tired of or don't wanna fix."

"Show him your new project." Mr. Crane stopped at the first vehicle in a middle row.

"Wow," Malcolm said.

Most of the other cars could fit inside this one with room to spare. Tall and boxy, it looked like a huge old pickup truck, except it was fully enclosed where the bed should be. Thick tires stood nearly to his waist. Malcolm noted the paint was half green and half primer white.

"Ah, the 1950 Dodge Power Wagon," Clive beamed. "Model got used for all sorts o' things, but this one was a soldier transport. Served plenty long 'fore they threw it in some junkyard." He caressed the blocky grille. "Tough as nails, these things. A lot o' love, some parts and fresh paint, it'll run like new."

Malcolm nodded in appreciation. "Looks like fun."

"Oh, you bet." Clive gestured toward the back building. "Come on, let's have a sit."

A smaller copy of the main shop, this building had only one bay door next to the regular one. Clive slapped a button on the wall and the door rose smoothly into the ceiling.

The inside consisted of an open space the size of two of Malcolm's classrooms. A large round poker table dominated the center. The bay door took up one corner, and the other corners boasted a pool table, a flat-screen TV with couches, and a small kitchen.

"Welcome to my li'l getaway."

Clive sauntered to the kitchen area and pulled open the fridge. Malcolm followed Mr. Crane to the table and settled into one of the cushioned leather seats.

"Who wants a beer?" Clive's voice echoed from inside the fridge.

"Right here," Mr. Crane said.

"I'm fifteen," Malcolm said.

"Good t'know. So, you want one?"

Mr. Crane chuckled quietly to himself.

"Well, uh . . ."

Clive sat down and set a beer in front of each of them. "Take that as a yes." He took a long gulp from his. "Ah, that's good." His eyebrows raised at Malcolm's untouched bottle. "Last I heard, they don' bite, son."

Malcolm looked quizzically at the older man. He seemed genuinely puzzled why Malcolm's age would make a difference. The product of an older era and a small town, he supposed. Still, he left the bottle alone. One of the men would probably drink it.

Clive settled back just as a giant bolt of lightning flashed in the distance, followed by a crack of thunder. "Huh," he said, exchanging a glance with Mr. Crane, who was setting up the old record player. "Now, what can this old man tell you 'bout our town, young man?"

Oh, right. In all the fun, Malcolm had almost forgotten why he was there. He drew his iPhone from a pocket along with the sheet of questions.

"So, can we start with what the town was like when you got here?"

"I was born here, actually," Clive said as an old Miles Davis tune began playing in the background. He took another swig of beer and began his story. "But that's not even the best part."

As evening darkness fell, Valentine entered her brother's room with a plate full of hot food. Dinner—the ultimate peace offering for a teenage boy. In minutes, the plate would be empty and hopefully she would be forgiven.

But all the lights were out and Malcolm was gone. Only the lightning from the storm brewing outside lit up the room. She switched on his desk lamp.

"He's out with my friend Mr. Crane, dear," Oma Grace called up the stairs. "I just found the note."

"Oh. Okay."

Valentine's forehead scrunched. *Mr. Crane? Really?* She'd have to get that story when he got home. Maybe he'd manage to find out more for their history project. She clicked on his desk lamp, thinking to leave the food on his desk, but then thought better of it. There was no telling how long he might be.

A reflection caught her eye, the lamp light glinting off something she'd never seen before. Curious, she set down the plate and picked up the object, examining it from all sides.

When did Mal buy a pocket watch?

Normally he would show off any antique he'd found, but not this one. The jewel and scrollwork in the silver elevated it from an average antique to a work of art. It sparkled with a fine polish, every facet and curve catching the light.

Valentine thumbed the release button and the cover clicked open with a fluid motion. On its black face, the silver hands and letters sparkled—almost shimmered—in the faint light. *What are those made of?* With her thumb, she brushed specks of dust from the face.

The hands spun, blue light sprang from the watch, and Valentine's eyes nearly bulged from her head. Light particles floated above the face and resolved into two images. To the left floated a spinning model of Earth.

The right image resembled a river, except the current looked more like energy instead of water. Bright pinpoints of light floated in the current, and a menu floated beside it.

OPTIONS
COMMANDS
EXECUTE

Valentine shivered. *Mal, what did you find? Do we even* have *real hologram tech yet?* She licked her lips, wanting to explore it but afraid to touch the wrong thing. *But if it were dangerous, he wouldn't have kept it.*

She swept her finger through COMMANDS. The menu scattered into dancing light particles and resolved into a new submenu.

HOP
SKIP
JUMP

She touched JUMP. The model Earth shrank, the river grew bigger, and the menu scattered and reformed as another submenu.

JUMP HISTORY
NEW DESTINATION

Some sort of travel guide? She touched JUMP HISTORY. *Let's see where you've already been.* The pinpoints of light inside the current pulsed brighter. She touched the nearest one, bringing up a date, location, and a window of full-motion video.

January 1945: Führerbunker

Valentine watched, mesmerized, as the video played out. Judging by the stacked crates, the footage had been shot from some old storage area looking out on a heavily-trafficked hallway. She could see armed soldiers and men in military uniforms hurrying to and fro.

It's a holographic history book! Punch in a date and time, you get information and video. Why program this into a watch?

Another menu appeared under the date and location.

EXECUTE

CANCEL

Valentine wiped her hands on her jeans. They'd been sweating as her heart pumped double-time. *Calm down, calm down. Let's just see what it does.* She touched EXECUTE.

The blue light disappeared and the watch hands stopped spinning. As the watch cover snapped closed, a whirring sound emanated from deep inside. The watch vibrated, then grew cold. In her shock, Valentine nearly dropped it.

Blue-white energy bubbled out from the watch and formed a shimmering sphere around her hand. To Valentine, it appeared as if she were seeing the hand through a rippling mirage. Goosebumps rose on her skin as the room's temperature dropped.

The energy sphere expanded, circling her entire body. She gasped, wanting to run, but was fearful of the consequences. The sphere spun around her, arcing with electricity, swirling faster and faster until she could see nothing but the glowing ripples. Dazzling beams of blue light flashed from the watch and filled the inner sphere. Valentine swayed as a wave of disorientation washed over her.

Then the watch darkened and the sphere disappeared.

Valentine gaped at her surroundings. The light show had taken maybe five seconds, yet Malcolm's room was gone. She found herself standing in a storage area—the same place she had just witness in the video.

WHERE AM I?!

"*Hast du das Licht?*" a voice said from the hallway.

German? She thought she had recognized one word—*Licht,* or *light.* Scrambling to the back of the room, she crouched behind a wall of crates.

Too late.

"Ich sehe jemanden! Jemand hier!"

Booted footsteps stomped into the room. *Oh, God!* She clicked the watch open and swiped her thumb over the dial. The hands spun and the menu hovered in front of her face again. She worked back through the options as quickly as possible, pulse pounding in her ears.

"Suche das Zimmer!"

Footsteps drew closer to her hiding place, and Valentine risked glancing past her cover. Six armed soldiers entered the room, machine guns ready. *Wait a minute. Isn't that . . . ?*

She squinted at their uniforms and her insides melted. The patch on their arms was a swastika. The destination she had chosen exploded in her mind. Führerbunker, January 1945—the last command center for Hitler during World War II. The soldiers hunting her were Nazis.

Did I just travel to 1945?!

She stifled a gasp and opened the JUMP menu. *Got to get out of here!* No time to learn how to choose her own destination. JUMP HISTORY would have to do. She touched the menu option and the flowing timeline—it must be a timeline—moved into view. She stabbed another point of light, accessing a new time and place.

"Ist etwas glühende da drüben?"

She waited the eternal seconds while the watch processed her commands. A mechanical clatter sounded above her head, and Valentine found herself staring down the barrel of a Nazi machine gun.

"Wir fanden den Spion!" the soldier shouted at her. *"Kommen von dort! Lassen Sie die Waffe und Hingabe!"*

EXECUTE pulsed at the edge of her vision.

Five soldiers and an officer converged on her, shoving their weapons in her direction. They cocked their guns and shouted commands at her.

Dear God, please work!

Valentine thumbed the command and cried out in relief as the sphere enveloped her. She could hear shouting and gunfire coming from outside. It seemed the bullets couldn't reach her here. The lights and a wave of disorientation hit her again.

The sphere disappeared and the watch deactivated, depositing her in a green field surrounded by massive trees. Lush vegetation stretched in every direction and the quiet air smelled fresh, reminding Valentine of pictures she'd seen of Costa Rica or Hawaii. She bent over, resting her hands on her knees.

"Holy crap!" she gasped.

Who on earth would travel to Hitler's stronghold? When she got home, Malcolm was going to get the verbal beating of his life. After she caught her breath and calmed her nerves.

GRUNT.

SNORT.

Valentine stiffened at the noise behind her.

THUMP. THUMP.

A tremor passed through the ground. She forced herself to turn around. One hundred yards away, an animal carcass as big as a car lay on the ground, twisted and half-eaten. Above it, a monster crouched with flesh hanging from its teeth. As tall as her house and nearly as long, it stood on muscled, scaly hind legs and sniffed the air.

It stared right at her.

Oookay, yeah, that's a T-Rex.

She backed away slowly. Flipping the watch cover open, she accessed the main menu while keeping an eye on the beast.

Come on, just a few more seconds.

The dinosaur reared to its full height, maw open wide. A roar shattered the air and vibrated through Valentine's body. She gripped the watch hard, struggling to quell her panic, and continued to back away. *Don't provoke it; just get out of here. It's a football field away—*

With one spring, the *T-Rex* leapt over its prey and charged. Powerful legs drove into the ground, chewing up yards and shaking the earth with every step. Valentine screamed and ran.

No, finish the jump!

She skidded to a halt, knowing she could never tap the right commands at a flat-out run. Instead she let her fingers work while every instinct screamed at her to flee.

The *T-Rex* closed half the distance in seconds. Valentine touched JUMP HISTORY and pinpoints in the timeline glowed brighter. *Which one do I choose?!* So far, both choices had been death traps. Where might the next one take her? *Just pick one!*

Her vision shook as the predator pounded closer, roaring again, hunger in its eyes. Forty yards away. She couldn't escape death three times in a row—this choice had to be right. Her insides twisted.

The first choice showed up as 539 BCE: Babylon. *The year Persia invaded Babylon? No thanks!* She canceled the jump, silently thanking Malcolm for drilling her with useless history.

Thirty yards away.

Wait, what's this? Below the image of the timeline, a third option floated in smaller, darker letters.

JUMP KEY

She stabbed the option and the pinpoints faded, new ones taking their place. Date and time descriptions floated above each, with what appeared to be priority numbers. Hope blossomed in Valentine. *They're bookmarks.* Carefully chosen and ranked destinations in history, waiting to be activated.

Twenty yards away.

She could smell its hide and see the jagged points of its razor-sharp teeth. Her heart pounded close to bursting. A destination drew her eye—the number-one priority.

Present: Home

Please don't be a death trap! Please don't be a death trap! Valentine held her breath and chose the destination.

Ten yards away.

She touched EXECUTE before the letters even finished appearing. The prehistoric monster loomed above her with massive jaws open wide. Steaming hot breath jetted down at her. She could see half-eaten bones protruding from its teeth.

An energy sphere formed around her hand—only this one was red. Massive jaws descended, opening wider to pluck Valentine from the ground. A shriek erupted from her and she dove to the grass.

The rippling red light enveloped her. The *T-Rex*'s jaw clamped around the sphere, roaring as it tried to swallow her. Red light burst from the watch, Valentine's head swam, and the beast was gone.

She found herself lying on a rough wooden floor, a persistent electrical hum filling the air. She hugged herself, shivering with terror. *Oh God oh God oh God I almost died.* Lying still, she forced herself to breathe evenly.

After an eternity, her pulse slowed. She opened her eyes and sat up to examine her surroundings. Wherever she was, it wasn't Malcolm's room, which meant she could still be in danger. She clutched the watch tightly—her one lifeline.

Valentine sat near the center of a square room fifty feet across. *At least I made it out of Jurassic World,* she thought. But why had the time bubble changed color? Maybe because she'd traveled forward this time, instead of back?

The wall in front of her held a window looking out into a dark night. *Is that a bullet hole?* She shook her head and refocused on the important details. In each corner flanking the window were two ten-foot-tall black cylinders, blinking with indicator lights. Industrial power cables sprouted from their casings and snaked along the walls and floor toward the center of the room. To her right, a set of stairs led to a lower level.

The watch called this place home. Maybe this is where it came from.

A *clink* echoed from behind her. Alarmed, she came up to a crouch and turned toward the noise. *What in the . . . ?*

In the center of the room, four curved metallic panels stretched from floor ceiling. They faced each other like the points of a compass, or the corners of a hollow sphere. Their shiny inner surfaces were speckled with circuitry and multicolored lenses, and many of the cables snaking along the floor attached to their backs.

In their center, the floor was replaced by a ten-foot circular hole. Wire bundles ringed the opening, along with hexagonal plates made of an unusual-looking red metal. Their surface almost seemed prismatic, reflecting the dim light at unexpected angles, like pictures Valentine had seen of satellite panels.

Valentine peered to the other end of the room, and her heart leapt into her throat. Stifling a yelp, she flattened against the nearest panel and peeked around the edge. On the far side, a mass of cobbled-together computer equipment covered the wall from floor to ceiling. Dozens of screens displayed technical schematics and scrolling data feeds. Two laboratory tables, covered with unfamiliar and exotic devices, filled the space between the panels and the computers.

A tall, dark-eyed man sat at the table to the right, scowling down at a tablet computer. Its casing had been cracked open and wires connected it to a flat, shiny surface in the middle of the table. He tapped on the screen.

"Prepare test protocol twelve, live specimen," he said with a husky, rough-accented voice.

Light particles lifted from the shiny surface and spun, resolving into a scale model of the panels she hid behind. Valentine glanced down at the watch. *Looks like you did come back home.*

The man grabbed a box by his feet and turned a hawklike stare on the panels. Valentine ducked behind her cover again.

"Engage test."

The electrical hum leaped to a high-pitched whine. Lights on the giant cylinders flared to life, and the panel she hid behind began to vibrate. She took a step back, careful to keep it between herself and the man.

Beams of red energy shot from the top of each panel and converged on the hole in the floor, combining into a glowing orb. The prismatic plates tilted to face left, and the orb began to spin.

The four panels came to life—gadgets clicked and whirred, and lenses turned toward the orb. The energy spun and warped, flattening into a disk that filled the opening in the floor, like a glowing whirlpool.

Valentine's hand went to her mouth. *Who can do something like this?*

The man reached inside the box and drew out a squirming white rabbit. Casually, he drew back and tossed it into the machine. Valentine's hand clamped tighter to muffle a scream.

The rabbit tumbled around the vortex as its energy grew brighter, and the high-pitched whine reached a crescendo.

"Execute."

In the blink of an eye, the disk collapsed on itself and shot through the open floor, disappearing. White light burst out from the hole like a blazing sunbeam, and Valentine shielded her face until the room darkened again. When it returned to normal, she glanced around the panel's edge. No vortex, no rabbit.

Outside, lightning crackled and thunder shook the sky. Valentine stopped short. *Wait a minute.* A storm had been building when she'd found the watch in Malcolm's room.

She whipped around and stared at the nearest wall again. In its center, between the black cylinders—were they generators? Batteries?—was a window. A large, round window.

It can't be.

Staying in shadows, Valentine crept toward it. Outside, rain poured and treetops swayed in the distance. Sweat dotted her forehead, and she tried to quell her fear as she inched closer.

Outside the window, across the quiet street, sat Oma Grace's house. *Her* house.

Valentine felt lightheaded, suddenly unable to stand being within these walls anymore. She returned to her hiding spot and clicked open the watch cover. With a swipe across its face, the menu rose to greet her.

At the computer banks, a klaxon rang out. She heard the dark-eyed man move, and she rushed through the watch's root menu. She knew where and when she was now, and couldn't bear to travel through time again. Home was right across the street!

Come on, you must be able to do more!

The COMMANDS submenu appeared.

HOP

SKIP

JUMP

"Source of breach?" the man said.

He knows I'm here. She guessed the watch's activation had set off the alarm, and he was probably reading about it on his screens. *Stupid stupid STUPID!*

She stared at the three options and did her best to reason through them. *JUMP took me to a new place and time. I just want a new place. Okay, HOP!*

"Temporal anomaly? Display location." A pause, then she heard a clatter and running.

Oh, no!

She pressed HOP and waited for a destination menu to appear. Instead, the watch closed and the energy bubble sprang up around her. It spun more slowly, in a different direction, and the glow seemed dimmer. *What does this—?*

She fell through the floor.

Valentine's insides whirled as she dropped to the floor below. She smacked onto a mattress, crashing through the thin wooden bed frame. A groan seeped from her lips, and she rolled onto hands and knees to catch her breath. Footsteps stomped overhead.

She forced herself to her feet. *Okay, so HOP seems to phase through things.* She dove through the menus and landed on SKIP. *Please be the right one!* She tapped the command and the spinning holographic Earth enlarged, taking the center spot. A submenu appeared.

SKIP HISTORY

NEW DESTINATION

Okay, SKIP HISTORY! A finger tap sent the watch zooming into the United States, then deeper into the Midwest, then into their state, and finally it became a three-dimensional map of Emmett's Bluff.

"Locate intruder!" her hunter shouted.

Valentine heard a beep, and tracer lights lit up in the walls and floor. Every light coursed in her direction and drew a luminescent circle around her feet. She dashed away and the lights followed her. *Great.* Dragging the watch's holo-map to the far east side of town, she pinched and zoomed the image, and *there* they were—her street, and the pinpoint of light inside the image of her house.

Footfalls hit the stairs and swiftly descended toward her. She tapped the hologram of her house. *Hurry up!*

"Countermeasures!"

The walls came alive, sprouting angry-looking machinery from hidden panels. They trained on her, powering up. Valentine trembled with panic. *I'm so close!*

EXECUTE pulsed bright, and she stabbed it with a pleading cry. The sphere wrapped around her and spun. Valentine looked up and shrieked as the tall man barreled angrily toward her. She raised her arms and backed away screaming. He snarled and lunged for her, hands stretched toward her throat.

The man faded away, light and dizziness swept over her, and Valentine kept backing away until she collapsed onto Malcolm's chair. She yelped and sprang away from it. In the center of her brother's room, she turned in frantic circles, certain that her attacker would leap from the shadows.

Her head swam and her mind raced. Three brushes with death in . . . how long had she been gone? Twenty minutes? *Feels like twenty years.* Every second crashed into her at once. She tried to stand still, but the room kept spinning around her. The walls blurred and her thoughts grew muddled.

The floor is wobbly . . .

Valentine collapsed to the carpet. Darkness enveloped her.

CHAPTER 11

The night of listening to stories and old records with Walter and Clive had gone much later than Malcolm had expected. The red truck eased into Mr. Crane's driveway after dark. He set the gear and switched off the throaty engine.

"Hope you weren't bored sitting with a couple old men."

"No way," Malcolm assured him. "Clive had some great stories."

"He's got plenty more. I've kept you out long enough, though. Better get home."

"Sure. Thanks for bringing me along and everything. Really."

Mr. Crane nodded. He kept his eyes on the steering wheel. "Don't mention it, kid."

Gratitude made him uncomfortable, it seemed. Malcolm made a mental note of that and opened his door. Halfway out, he stopped and turned back. "Hey, Mr. Crane?"

"Walter, kid. Call me Walter; it's okay."

Malcolm tried and failed to mask his surprise. "Okay. Um, Walter?"

"Yeah?"

"I'm just curious. When we talked, it seemed like you love traveling, so, well, why come back here? Why stay all this time?"

Walter kept examining the wheel. "I had things to do here. Never did get to see the Parthenon."

"Why didn't you go after you were finished?"

A wistful smile crossed Walter's face. "When I'm finished, maybe I will."

ON tiptoes, Malcolm stole down the hallway toward his bedroom. In a family of insomniacs, any creak would surely wake someone. The afternoon had turned out far better than he'd hoped, but his tired body ached like it had been beaten.

Actually, it was *beaten.*

He noted that Valentine had forgotten to shut her door for the night. Odd—she treasured her privacy as much as he did. A light was on in his room, though. That was doubly odd. His door was half-closed, and he pushed it open.

Valentine lay face down on the floor. Malcolm jumped back in shock and then rushed to her side.

"Val!" He shook her. *"Val, wake up!"*

He relaxed as her glazed eyes opened.

"Mal. Where?" she said thickly. "Am I . . . floor?"

"Did you hit your head or something?" He sat back on his heels.

"No, I—" With a gasp, she sat bolt upright. "It's real. I didn't believe you, but I know now—it's all real!"

Relief flooded him. "You finally saw what the lightning was doing? I knew eventually you'd—" Malcolm trailed off as his eyes locked onto the watch in her hand. "How did you find that?"

Valentine shoved it in front of his face. "How did *you* find it? Do you have any idea what this thing does?"

"I know exactly what it does, which is why I didn't show anyone. Why did you snoop in my room?"

"I wasn't snooping; I was bringing you dinner!" she snapped, then stopped and stared at the wall, clutching the pendant at her neck. After a moment, her words came out more calmly. "You left it on your desk. I was just curious about it."

Malcolm began to respond, then stopped short. "Wait, you asked if I knew what it does. You didn't use it, did you?"

Valentine grasped for words, but he saw the truth on her face.

"Oh, no. Did you touch anything? Talk to anyone?"

"No!" She examined the watch, avoiding his eyes. "I mean, not really."

He slapped a palm to his forehead. "Geez, Val!"

"Well, I didn't know what it did! I just looked at the dates. How was I supposed to know it would actually take me there?"

Malcolm's mind reeled with the implications of what his twin might have done—might have changed—if things had gone worse. They were playing with forces that couldn't be fathomed.

"I saw inside the house, too."

"What house?"

She nodded toward the window. "The house. I didn't know what *Home* meant, and I was kind of panicking after running from Nazis and that *T-Rex*."

Malcolm gaped. "T-Rex? Why would he jump back so far?" He wondered aloud. "Testing the watch's limits, maybe."

"I don't know. It just kind of happened." She slid closer. "Mal, I saw him. The man you must've seen in the window. He's doing something big, and he's got this machine—I've never seen anything like it before. It made this big energy *thing* and a rabbit disappeared, and . . ." Her voice dropped, filling with desperation. "I don't know what it all means, but I was so scared. He would've killed me, I know it."

Malcolm crossed to the window and stared out at the darkened house with a furrowed brow. It mocked them, daring them to challenge it.

"Did he see your face?"

"Not sure. He nearly got me, but it was pretty dark." She hesitated. "I think he's from somewhere else. And I don't mean Chicago."

Malcolm nodded. "Figured that when I realized what the watch does. He's got to be from somewhere else. Or, I guess I should say some*time* else."

"So, what's he doing here?"

Malcolm grimaced. Of course she'd want to find out everything now. Hadn't *he*, before his close encounter? Still, this had to stop.

"It doesn't matter." He turned from the window. "If he's not from here, then maybe he's just passing through. So, let's leave him alone."

Her eyes narrowed at him. "What are you saying? That we should just ignore this?" She shook her head. "You didn't see what I did, Mal. This is about way more than lightning storms."

Malcolm sighed. Knowing Valentine, she would never stop without a good reason. So, she would have to see. He lifted his shirt over his head.

"Uh, what are you doing?"

Next he peeled away the tape covering his ribs. Tossing it aside, he raised his arms and turned in a slow circle, allowing Valentine to see the bruises covering his torso.

"What happened to you?"

"After we argued, I decided to do some investigating.

Whoever's inside didn't appreciate that. But I did find something." Stepping over to the desk, he rummaged in the bottom drawer and withdrew a sketch of circles and jagged, overlapping lines. "The house is covered with these, every inch of it. Tiny circuitry and some kind of lenses."

"I saw something like these lenses on the machine, only a lot bigger."

"I took pictures, and this shadow monster *thing* came through the wall and attacked me. I managed to cut up the guy inside it, but he kept coming until he had me. Might've killed me, I think, except Walter chased him off."

"Did Walter see what happened?"

"I don't think so. But after that, I made a promise—to leave this whole thing alone before someone got killed. That's why I didn't show you the watch. Every time I see it, I want to do something stupid."

"But if we don't figure this out, who will?"

Malcolm gently pried the watch from her fingers and slid it into his pocket. "There's curiosity, and then there's just asking for it. If someone wants to hide in a weird house and do crazy experiments, does it really matter?"

He took Valentine's arm and moved toward the door.

"And what if it's more than just experiments? Don't you care that he might hurt people?"

"You know I care, but we've got no clue what his intentions are. It's better to mind our own business." He guided her through his door. "Night, Val."

She rested her hand on the door, stopping him from closing it. "Mal, I . . . I really wasn't snooping. I only came in here to—"

"Yeah, I know." He gave a tired smile. "It's okay."

Relief warmed Valentine's face, and she threw her arms around him. He returned the hug.

"I'm sorry for what I said."

He chuckled. "I said it was okay."

"I know." She pulled away and wiped her eyes. "But I still needed to say it."

After saying good night again, Malcolm shut the door and rested his back against it. The wood felt cool against his sore body. Sighing, he pulled the watch out and ran his thumb over the sparkling jewel. What purpose did that serve?

That was a dangerous question. He squashed the thought and closed his fist around the device. Though now that it was in his possession, he wasn't sure what to do with it. He and Valentine would need to figure something out. For now, though, his dominant feeling was exhaustion. He glanced down at the watch.

"I've got to hide you better this time."

CHAPTER 12

Saturday morning found Malcolm at his desk, typing out more notes for their history project. He'd have to ignore the most interesting thing in town from now on—the old house looming across the street—but they still had to finish the assignment. Halfway through, he heard a knock.

"Yeah?"

Valentine opened his door and leaned against the doorjamb. She yawned. "It's nine in the morning. You're productive way too early for a Saturday."

He grinned. "Guess I felt ambitious."

His phone buzzed on the desk. He reached for it while Valentine dug in her pocket for hers. They each read the same text message.

Winter: *Movies tonight? Your turn to host*

"Wow. She hits the ground running, doesn't she?" Malcolm said. "She was in the hospital a few days ago."

"And she's probably hoping to forget about that. You do want to do it, right?"

Malcolm stared down at the desk. Despite his fears, it

seemed Winter and the rest were becoming real friends now. Still, he felt like running away.

"Mal," Valentine began in her lecturing voice.

"Yeah, I know. I know." He let out a sigh. "Okay. Just tell her yes before I change my mind."

His sister tapped a reply and planted a quick kiss on his forehead. "You won't regret it."

"Yeah, right," he said, but couldn't hide a smile.

"You're on the project, so I'll ask Oma if she can drive me to the store for snacks and stuff." Valentine crossed to her room.

"I like Swiss Cake Rolls," he called.

"When have I ever forgotten that?"

The fear clenched inside Malcolm's chest again. He closed his eyes and tried to will it away. Just a quiet night with friends, that's all. *Friends.*

"How's it looking?" Valentine called from the living room.

Malcolm stood back and surveyed his work. Snacks and drinks covered the wide kitchen counter. "We've got enough carbs to last a year, so I'd say we're ready."

"Perfect." Valentine entered the kitchen with her bag slung over her shoulder. She picked at a few locks of wavy red hair, teasing them into place. "Got the first movie loaded."

Malcolm did a double take as she set her bag on the counter. Something was different.

"Forgot I had a couple things in here, too," she said.

A bottle of iced tea and a package of M&Ms joined the rest of the spread. She slid the bag over to the counter's far corner, out of the way.

He squinted, examining her. She was wearing lipstick and

eyeliner! That blue shirt—had he seen it before? It clung to her far too tightly.

Valentine noticed his attention. "What?"

Malcolm's face split into a grin. "Well well, Val. I do believe that's what they call a man-gettin' outfit!"

A fierce blush colored her cheeks. She looked down at herself. "I'm not sure what you—"

"Val," he interrupted. "You can stop pretending. We all know. Actually, I think we knew before you did." His grin widened. "Good for you."

Her face relaxed and she giggled nervously. "I can't believe I'm doing this. It's so not like me."

"Well, it's not like he's the usual jock type, right?" Malcolm said. "Not many like him."

Valentine gazed into the distance, her eyes sparkling. "I've never met anyone like him."

The doorbell rang and Valentine practically sprinted for the door. Malcolm made a mental note to watch closely and remember all the new things to tease her about.

A moment later, they filed in—Winter with her half-purple hair pulled down to cover the bandaged ear, Fred with a basketball jersey that seemed ironic now with his double casts. John and Valentine entered last, already deep in conversation. John's temporary sling was gone, and he wore a black trilby hat pulled low, with thick-framed, horn-rimmed glasses.

They busied themselves piling snacks onto plates and pouring drinks for the first movie. Winter and Fred spent half the time stealing food from each other, while Valentine and John seemed content in their own conversation.

Eventually the group drifted into the living room. Valentine led the way to get the movie started, and Malcolm brought up the rear. He was surprised to see John linger until he got close.

"Thank you for hosting, Malcolm," he said. His eyes shifted around the room. Was he nervous?

"No problem."

John hesitated. "Will we be meeting your family?"

Realization dawned on Malcolm. What guy wouldn't be nervous meeting a girl's father? He smiled. "Not tonight. Dad's on a research trip for his book, and Oma's visiting friends. We've got the house to ourselves."

Tension left John's face. "We could use some relaxation."

THE pizza smelled like cheesy heaven. Malcolm pulled the pies from the oven and set them on the stove to cool. After the first movie, the others followed him to the kitchen to refill drinks and await the main course.

"Bein' lazy makes me thirsty," Fred said.

He reached across the counter to grab an unopened bottle of soda. His bandaged fingers only half-gripped the neck, and the bottle slipped from his grasp and plopped sideways onto the counter. It rolled away and knocked into Valentine's bag, tipping it onto the floor upside down.

"My bad. I'll get it." He rounded the counter to the other side.

"Fred, don't worry about that," Valentine called from the doorway.

"No sweat, girl, I got this."

He bent to rescue the bag while Valentine hurried into the kitchen, her face tightening.

"Fred, really, I—"

As Fred lifted the bag, its contents spilled out and scattered onto the floor.

"Figures," he muttered, and scooped the smaller items back in. "Hey, what's this?"

Malcolm stiffened. Fred held up a small leather book, open to the first page.

"It's nothing," Valentine insisted. "I'll take it."

Fred's eyes lit with mischief. "Is this a diary?" He flipped to the next page. "All your childhood secrets in here?"

Malcolm knew he was trying to make a joke, but Valentine's expression darkened.

"Give it back." She reached for the book, but Fred slipped away.

"Here's a good one! *We sat together today. I'm going to marry him, I know it.* Aw, now that's romantic."

"Fred!" she cried.

"Fred, give it back to her," Malcolm said.

He turned the page, oblivious to the mood in the room. "Ooh, now this one's called *First Kiss.*"

"Boy, don't be an idiot," Winter said. "Give it back."

"*I feel so safe when he holds me,*" Fred read.

John stepped forward. "Fred, perhaps it's time to—"

Red-faced, Valentine stalked toward Fred with furious tears in her eyes. He stopped reading and backed away in alarm. She drove forward, backing him into a corner until he bumped against the wall.

"Hey, I was just—"

Valentine yanked the book from Fred's grasp and smacked him hard across the face. She whirled and fled the kitchen. Malcolm heard footsteps as she disappeared up the stairs.

Fred massaged his red cheek. "I was just playin'. Thought it was old. How am I s'posed to know she still writes in it?"

Malcolm rubbed his eyes and sighed. He suddenly felt exhausted. "She doesn't write in it. It's not hers."

"Then why she so upset?"

"Shut up, Fred, or I'll hit you with my stun gun," Winter snapped. She turned to Malcolm. "Whose is it?"

"It's our mother's journal, from when she was young."

"Oh," Fred said. Then his eyes widened as he realized he'd never seen or heard a word about their mother. "*Oh!* Man, I'm so sorry. I'm such an idiot! Was she, like . . . I mean, did she walk out on you guys or something?"

Malcolm felt crushed by a wave of anguish. He forced himself to look at Fred and say the words.

"She died last year."

Stunned silence fell over the room. John turned and left the kitchen, and a moment later Malcolm heard his footsteps on the stairs.

VALENTINE sat cross-legged on her bed, facing the window with watery eyes. Hugging the book to her chest, she struggled to push away the bitter grief twisting her insides.

High up in the clouds, lightning flashed.

A faint knock sounded on the open door. She didn't answer. Soft footsteps came close and John settled next to her. The hat and dark glasses were gone, and his eyes radiated concern.

"My mother . . ." Valentine began.

He nodded, as if he already knew. She opened her mouth and words came tumbling out. "I feel like I'm starting to forget her. Sometimes when I think about her now, I can't remember her face." She looked at him in desperation. "What does that mean?"

John thought for a moment. "Perhaps it means you're beginning to heal." His deep voice caressed her. "Which would please her, I'm certain. A mother would want you to have a life beyond the memories."

Valentine choked back tears. "I've tried so hard to move on. But every step I take away from her, it feels like she's dying again." She stared at the book. "I can't talk to my dad. The truth—we moved here because he couldn't handle it. After she died, he just shut down. Like he's not even there anymore."

She covered her eyes. "The worst part is . . . I'm scared that I'm like him. That I might just keep hurting and keep closing up, and I won't know how to stop. Sometimes I feel like it's already happening."

Tears broke free and streamed down her cheeks. She struggled to breathe through the sobbing. John leaned close and wrapped a warm, comforting arm around her shoulders. She pressed into him, burying her face in his shoulder.

"I feel so broken. It's like . . . I don't know, like . . ."

"Like, how are you supposed to heal when your heart is in two places?" John whispered. "In two times?"

She nodded into his shoulder.

"Like you were meant to have this whole other life," he continued. "You had a future. Then something took that future away, and a part of you is suddenly gone. But inside, it still feels real. Like in some other world, that life still exists." She felt him take a deep breath. "So you find yourself living in two worlds—the one that's real, and the one that *feels* real. You can't bear to let one go, so you drift between them, never really living one whole life. And before you know it, both lives have passed you by. You wake up one day and realize you're living in a world you don't recognize, in a body that doesn't feel like yours."

John fell silent and Valentine peered up at him. He stared out the window with heavy, sad eyes. Then she realized he hadn't only been speaking about her—he had confessed something about himself, too. He knew her pain deep inside. Even drowning in sorrow, her heart reached out to him.

John brushed a thumb across her cheek, wiping away the tears. "I'm sorry for your pain."

Valentine intertwined her fingers with his. She nestled against him, savoring the comfort of his warmth.

"I miss her so much. I'd give anything to talk to her one more time."

John leaned his head against hers. "Tell me about her."

She fought to ignore the anguish. Right now, in John's arms, she wanted to remember.

"She was so beautiful. A dancer, an artist, so earthy and bright to be around, it was like she glowed. Everywhere she went, her spirit lit up the room. Everyone wanted to be near her." She wiped away more tears. "Even when she got sick, it was *her* comforting *us*. To the last day, right when the cancer took her, she was making sure *we* were okay. She . . ."

Valentine tried to say more, but the words choked in her throat. She clung to John, exhausted.

"She sounds like a special person," he said.

"She is."

Any chance of salvaging the evening was gone. Fred—the big dumb oaf—had been apologetic and eager to leave, and Winter had thought it best to go with him. Only John remained.

Back in his room, Malcolm glanced out the window. The

night was growing angry. Wind whipped at the house and howled through the trees as lightning pierced the clouds. The first rumbles of thunder rolled.

The watch seemed to call to him, but he stifled the urge to retrieve it from deep inside his desk. It needed to stay out of sight until he could figure out what to do with it.

Sneaking into the hallway, he stopped to check on Valentine. She and John sat at the window, wrapped around each other, conversing softly. Malcolm smiled and made his way down the stairs and out the front door.

Gusting winds tore at his clothes. Booming thunder shook the ground, and crackling lightning strafed across the sky. He fought the urge to run for cover, pushing aside the memories of his last encounter with the lightning.

Now outside, his attention crept across the street. Tall and foreboding, the house glared down at him with cold menace. Bright beams of light pulsed from the windows, matching rhythm with the storm. He stood mesmerized by the beautiful, dangerous light.

The storm's intensity surged, multiplying in the blink of an eye. Bolts of energy seared the air. Thunder threatened to shatter the sky and rain it down in pieces. Malcolm covered his ears and ducked away from it all. His instincts screamed to hide until—

The light in the windows sputtered and quit.

The storm dispersed.

Just like before, when they nearly died. Panicking, he sprinted to the closest cover—Mr. Crane's porch—and crouched against the door. Silence stretched on while he waited for the inevitable onslaught. None came.

Malcolm stared into the sky, brow furrowed. *What happened?* The storm had been growing and then suddenly stopped, like someone had pulled a plug. He reminded himself that he was done with it. Anything else would get him nowhere but dead.

Then why haven't you thrown the watch back at that house? To his chagrin, he had no answer for that. *Still sure that you're done with all this?* He mentally shoved the questions away. Of course he was done—he had to be. Anything else was asking for trouble.

As he leaned back against Walter's door, it clicked and swung open to reveal a dark interior. Alarms rang in Malcolm's head. Walter would never leave his door unlocked and half-latched. He peered inside, his senses on high alert.

No movement, no sound, no lights. He pushed the door open and slipped inside, his foot bumping a half-broken bottle on the floor.

Could the shadowed man have returned to seek revenge? Heart pounding, Malcolm crept down the medal-adorned hallway to the back of the house. At the end, he turned into the study. Sounds of breathing echoed in the dark.

"Walter?"

He grasped for the nearby lamp and twisted the switch. Dim yellow light bathed the room and his friend, slumped in one of his leather chairs. The small table next to him held a tall glass and a half-empty bottle of bourbon. His right hand clutched something small.

Walter's eyes traveled sluggishly up to Malcolm's face. "I let you in?" His words ran together.

"Your door was open." Malcolm sat across from him. "Walter, what's going on?"

"Anniversary."

"Oh. I never knew you were married."

"No." Walter shook his head. "Different anniversary."

"What do you mean?"

Walter swallowed hard. His words came sluggishly. "We caught 'em by surprise. Key position, had to be taken. We're good at that. Surrounded the camp, caught 'em in their beds."

He grew restless and reached for the bottle. "Thought one tent was empty. I'm running by it, and . . . soldier comes out. Something in his hand. I know it's a grenade. His last resort. I shoot him square in the chest."

Walter took a long swig and leaned back in the chair. "Went close to make sure . . . make sure he's dead. No grenade. Just . . ." He opened his hand. "Just a picture of his family. I really look, and he's just a kid. No more 'n sixteen."

In Walter's hand rested an old, faded family photo. On top of it sat a Silver Star, the medal he wouldn't talk about. "I looked in his face as he died. Broke my heart. I just sat down right there and cried, hoping to God someone would come . . . finish me off, too."

Malcolm covered his mouth. To carry this horror inside for all these years—he couldn't imagine what that would be like. Sadness filled him. Sadness for his friend.

Walter grimaced. "They think if they give you a medal, somehow you'll believe it had honor. They gave me a medal for killing kids." He dropped the picture and the medal on the table. "Happened today . . . forever ago."

"God, Walter," Malcolm gasped. "I . . ."

Walter waved his words away. "No one's burden but mine, kid." He pushed against the chair and stumbled to his feet. "Old man needs his rest now."

He took a step forward and nearly toppled. Malcolm rushed to his side and slid a shoulder under his arm.

"Come on, I'll help you."

"Don't need to be tucked in, boy," Walter grumbled.

"Yeah, but I need my 'Help a Drunk Old Man' merit badge."

Walter chuckled and his lined, worn face lifted just a little. They stumbled through the doorway to the bedroom. Malcolm held the tall man up just long enough for him to topple into bed, eyes closed.

Malcolm grinned down at him. "Do you want some juice and a story before you go to sleep?"

Walter opened one eye. "Come closer and I'll put *you* to sleep."

Malcolm reached for the light switch. "No, thanks."

"Malcolm."

He turned back toward the bed. Walter's other eye opened.

"No one knows that story. Please."

Malcolm got the message. "I wouldn't dream of it. Good night, Walter."

He switched the light off and let himself out.

THIRTY miles north of town, Rayner Nuclear Power Plant sat next to a winding river, its twin stacks ascending from a deep basin between rocky foothills. Barry Oliver, senior reactor operator for the skeleton night crew, strolled alongside the massive steam turbines.

"I got nothin' here, Sal," he said into his radio. "Sure you're readin' the right numbers?"

"We been watchin' these dials for ten years, Barry," a gravelly voice replied. "I'm tellin' you we're losin' juice. Past couple months, we've been puttin' out a little less power each week, and tonight the losses spiked."

"And you're sure the problem's here?"

"I ain't sure o' *nothin'*. Yer the senior on this crew, remember? Figure it out."

He rolled his eyes. Everything looked as it had for a decade—nothing out of place, everything humming along like clockwork.

"All checks out on this side. S'pose it could be the generators."

"Yeah, maybe so."

"You wanna come help me look?"

"Now, why would I do that?"

Barry meandered toward the electrical generators linked to the turbines. "You don't get off that fat butt, I'll stop bringin' in my wife's cherry pie."

"She'll give me some anyway," Sal retorted. "Annie loves me."

"Annie hates you, and she thinks you smell."

"That ain't what she said last night."

Barry snorted. "Fine, sit there and get fatter. I'll check it out."

He clipped the radio to his belt and ducked under a cluster of pipes, hunting for anything out of place. The sounds of his footsteps were drowned under the whirring of the massive machines.

He rounded a corner and stopped in his tracks. The first generator stood ten yards away, and the cover to its primary access panel lay on the ground. A dark-haired man knelt in front of the open panel, his back to Barry. A large duffel bag sat beside him, unfamiliar tools and varieties of wire protruding from the unzipped top.

A surprise inspection? Couldn't be—he wasn't wearing the green uniform of a Rayner tech, or the business suit of a shareholder. Just a long black coat with a hood, and sleeves rolled up so he could reach inside the panel.

The man pulled an exotic-looking silver tool from the bag, along with a short length of copper wire. He held them in the air and examined them. Barry winced at the man's left forearm, crisscrossed by two deep, angry red cuts.

Pulses of energy arced from the tool and bore into the panel, burning a focused hole in the delicate instrumentation. Barry shook himself from stunned silence and broke into a sprint.

"Hey stop, you can't do that!"

The dark man whirled. His scarred arm smacked against something metallic on his chest, and shadows twisted and stretched toward him. In an instant, a mass of darkness enveloped him.

A cloak made of shadow.

Barry's eyes bulged and his feet ground to a halt. A thousand angry roars exploded into his mind. Crying out, he clutched his ears and dropped to his knees.

The shadow charged. In a blink, Barry flew from the ground and clanged against a metal support beam. He struggled to keep his composure, but panic clouded his thoughts.

"Wha—wha—" He stared into the shadow, laboring to catch his breath. "What do you want?"

The shadow roared and flung him into the air. He skipped like a stone across the concrete and skidded to a stop against the open access panel. The shadow stalked toward him.

"MMMOOORRRREEE *PPPOOOWWWEEERRR!!!*"

Barry pulled up to his knees and clasped his hands together. "I can get you more power! I will!"

Steps away, the shadow stretched toward him. The tapered end of that exotic-looking tool protruded from the black and pointed straight at him.

"No, please!" He tried to scramble away, but smacked into the generator. "Please, I can help you. *I said I can help you!*"

The tool crackled and glowed, ionized air shimmering around it. Barry yanked the radio from his belt and put it to his lips.

"SAL!"

A blazing beam pierced the air. The radio clattered to the ground.

CHAPTER 13

Early Sunday morning, Valentine bounded into the kitchen. She finished pulling her wavy hair into a ponytail, then sat at the table to tie her shoes.

"Morning."

Oma Grace stared at her over a crossword puzzle. "Good morning, dear. You do know it's Sunday? I thought you kids turned to dust if the sun hit you before ten."

Valentine grinned. "I'd like to go into town, if you have time."

"What for, may I ask?"

"Oh, just, uh, some stuff for this history project. I'd like to see some old places in town and try to interview people. Plus, it'd be good driving practice for my permit. Is that okay?"

"Next time, more notice would be appreciated, but yes."

"Thanks! I'm going for a run first."

Valentine hopped toward the front door in short bursts to warm up her legs. Exiting the house, she paused on the front steps to check her resting pulse. The crisp morning air smelled like autumn.

A black limousine sat in the driveway. Fred had just climbed out from the backseat and closed his door, and he blinked at her in surprise.

"Hey, Val."

Valentine stiffened and approached warily, glancing at what he held in his arms. "Hey. What's up?"

"Oh, um." Fred shifted the massive bouquet of roses clutched awkwardly between his casts. "These are for you." They faced each other uneasily, then he rushed forward and pushed them into her arms.

"I know you're into silver." He glanced at her pendant. "So, sterling roses. They're rare—I ordered them from the city."

She accepted them numbly. The roses were unlike anything she'd ever seen—instead of red or pink or white, these were a soft, silvery gray with thornless stems.

"You brought these in all the way from Chicago?"

Fred dipped his head low. "Thought if I brought you something pretty, you might forget what a jerk I was." He shuffled his feet. "I got a mouth, we all know that. I say dumb stuff. But I never woulda read from that book if I knew." He glanced up at her. "I'm sorry I hurt you."

Valentine's heart melted into a puddle. Fred Marshall, the loud-mouthed buffoon, was actually being sincere with her. He seemed subdued and embarrassed and genuinely worried about her feelings. *Maybe there's a real person in there, after all.* She smiled at him. Her real smile.

"True friends are hard to come by. I'd hate to lose one over this." She sniffed the roses. "They're beautiful."

His expression brightened. "You and Mal are awesome, and you're part of us now. Group wouldn't feel the same without you." He paused to gather himself. For some reason, he still seemed nervous. "I know the timing's horrible, but maybe you'll let me do more to make it up to you. Dinner tomorrow night?

There's a café on the north side. You can see the hills, and it's the best at sunset."

"Oh." Valentine's brow furrowed. *Why would he—OOOOH! I'm such an idiot.*

She grasped for her pendant. Fred had proven to be better than she'd thought, but nothing inside her felt romantic toward him. How could she explain her feelings without hurting him? Her thoughts flashed to John—his deep, quiet voice and those eyes that reached out to consume her. She tried to speak.

"Look," Fred interrupted. "I know what people think of me. Yeah, I throw parties and I'm popular, whatever that means. But to most people I'm just this rich wannabe player. A clown. Sometimes they're right I guess." He gazed earnestly into her eyes. "I wish you could see past all that. Because when I'm around you, Val, I don't want to be that guy anymore. I want to be better."

The words tugged on Valentine's heart again. "Fred, I—thank you so much. You have no idea how that makes me feel."

Fred raised his eyebrows. "But?"

I don't want to hurt him. "I already—"

He nodded, as if he'd expected it. "John."

Heat spread across her cheeks. She nodded.

Fred gave a wistful smile. "Thought that was coming. It's okay. He's the better man—I've always known that. Deserves you more'n I ever will." He sighed. "I promise I won't get in the way. It's just, I needed you to know how I feel. Once."

Valentine gave him an appraising look. *He really is more than I thought.*

Fred stepped away from her. "I'll see you guys 'round soon, right?"

Valentine nodded. An impulse came over her, and she rushed forward to hug the lanky boy. He gasped, then wrapped his arms around her.

"What's this for?"

She smiled and stepped back with a shrug. "Because you're a good guy, Fred. Really."

"Well, that's something. I'll take it." He walked back to the limo, his usual swagger returning. "Oh, one thing." He put on ridiculously blinged-out sunglasses. "I know you'll tell Mal, but please don't tell anyone else I came spillin' my guts like some drama major. I got a reputation. 'Kay?"

She chuckled. "You're safe with me."

"Cool, see ya."

Fred hopped into the black monstrosity and disappeared down the street. She stood in the driveway, dumbfounded.

The sound of Fred's car faded, and Valentine's real purpose for the morning sprang back into her head. Her face grew serious again as she refocused on the task. It would take some maneuvering to keep Oma Grace in the dark, but it had to be done. If her theory was right, what she might find would change everything.

MALCOLM shivered and pulled on his jacket. His phone bleeped on the desk.

> **Winter:** *Guess the hostilities are over. Movie night, take 2?*

He stared at the message with furrowed brow. Did something happen that no one told him about?

> **Malcolm:** *Sounds fine, but what do u mean?*
> **Winter:** *You haven't heard? Fred came to your house, talked to Val. Said they made out and everything's fine now.*

A shock jolted through Malcolm. He gaped at the phone.

> **Malcolm:** *He said they WHAT?????????*
> **Winter:** *?*
> **Winter:** *Oh sorry, they MADE UP and everything's fine.*
> *Stupid autocorrect.*
> **Malcolm:** *going to kill your phone*
> **Winter:** *LOL. So you in for tonight?*

Just then, he heard Valentine's feather-light footsteps padding down the hall. She moved with a dancer's grace, but he could feel her presence with his mystical twin powers.

Malcolm jammed a hand in his front pocket, then leapt onto the bed and pulled a thick book about the French Revolution under his nose. He'd bought it after learning it was Madame LaChance's favorite, which Valentine had teased him for mercilessly. Denying the reason had only made her laugh harder.

Valentine rushed into his room and set a map on his desk. "You've got to see this."

"Hey, can you give me a few minutes? I was, uh, just about to change."

She unfolded the map. "Can you wait? This is important."

"Actually—"

The phone beeped.

> **Winter:** *How about Fred's house?*
> **Malcolm:** *Yeah, no prob*

"I haven't changed since I got up. Winter invited us to Fred's just now, and I don't want to go in pajama pants. Just give me five minutes?"

"Wow, you keep it cold in here." Valentine fixed him with a curious look. "Aren't you wondering where I was? I've been gone with Oma for hours."

Malcolm faltered. "Well, yeah, of course. But—"

She grabbed his arm and pulled him to the desk. "Just look!"

They stood over a map of Emmett's Bluff. His sister had drawn lightning bolts in a dozen spots and scribbled notes next to each.

"After the lightning up in the hills, we found that round hole without a bottom. Right?"

"Yeah."

"Remember how it was scorched?"

"Yeah." He raised his eyebrows, impatient.

"I searched local news online and found something, then went into town and saw for myself." She pointed to the lightning bolts. "There are eleven more places where the identical thing happened. Four would've been way out in the woods, so I'm only guessing about their location, but eight were right in town. I saw a burned-up hardware store, a broken front porch, a melted truck that they tossed in the junkyard." Valentine locked onto him with a significant look. "The guy who owns the hardware store said his dogs burned up inside, and someone was *in* that truck when it melted."

Malcolm felt a heavy weight press on him. Now he realized the point she'd been building to.

"This guy may not be looking to hurt people, but he sure doesn't care if it happens. I mean, look at—"

"You're right," he broke in, his insides twisting. She had to go now! "Can you please just go get ready or something?"

"What's the big deal? We can be five minutes late." She went to sit in his desk chair and then glanced around the room, puzzled. "Hey, where's your chair?"

A timed alarm rang out from Malcolm's phone. "Move!" He grabbed Valentine and dashed toward the window.

A glowing red sphere flashed in front of the desk, right

where they'd been standing. The sphere spun for a half-second, collapsed into a point of light and winked out of existence. A cold wind rushed over them. Malcolm's chair now sat in front of the desk, spinning gently.

Valentine yanked from his grasp. "What did you do?"

He looked away embarrassed and pulled the watch from his pocket.

"I, uh, may have sent my chair ten minutes into the future." He put up his hands in defense. "I tried to leave it alone, but after what happened to you, I couldn't resist. I was just going to use it once and hide it again, but, well, that's when you came home."

She half-grinned. "You little sneak. I went through all this to get you back in the game, and you were already there?"

"No!" Pushing away the chair, Malcolm stared down at the map. He sighed. "I was going to hide it and never look at it again. Part of me thinks I still should."

"Before you decide, look at this." Valentine grabbed a pencil and a ruler. "See how the marks are arranged?"

Malcolm nodded. "A perfect circle, like a twelve-pointed star." He rethought that. "Or a clock."

"Exactly. Now watch this." Valentine drew a line between the northern- and southern-most marks, then drew another from east to west. "Right there, where the lines cross. Look familiar?"

Malcolm's jaw dropped. "That's our street!"

She pointed out the window. "That house is dead center in the middle of everything. If he can do this, what else can he do? Something bad is coming, Mal. I can feel it."

Malcolm knew exactly what she meant. He suddenly felt as if their whole future boiled down to this one choice. Was he ready for that? Was this what the point of no return felt like?

Staring down at that map, he knew he couldn't turn away.

Someone had to do something, and there was only them. The choice had already been made. They had to see it through, to whatever end.

He gave a resigned shrug. "I guess we should figure out what to do next."

With a relieved sigh, Valentine embraced him. "I don't think I could do this alone. I have the next step figured out, but first we have to convince the others we're not crazy."

Malcolm stepped back. "Whoa. Others?"

She looked at him as if it were obvious. "Yeah. John, Winter, and Fred need to know, and we need help."

"Val, this isn't some piece of gossip we can spread around. It may get dangerous."

"Have you forgotten what they've gone through? The lightning hit them worse than it did us. They deserve to know and to have the chance to help."

She had a point.

"You know they're going to freak out," he said.

"They'll come around. Both of us did, right?"

He nodded grudgingly. "I guess it would help if we could show them one of the holes."

"Got that covered. This spot?" She pointed to one of the northern markers. "Guess whose giant property it's on."

"You've got to be kidding me."

Valentine grinned. "You remember how big his estate was, right? I don't know why I was surprised."

"Unbelievable." Malcolm shrugged like a man going to the gallows. "Okay, now can I change so we can go to Fred's?"

CHAPTER 14

The black limousine turned onto Fred's driveway. Lounging in the backseat, the twins spoke softly in the presence of Fred's driver. Malcolm folded the map, refolded it with trembling hands, and slid it into his backpack.

"Nervous?" Valentine said.

"Well, we're kind of in uncharted friend territory. *Hey guys, I know we just met, but can you help us defeat a time-traveling super villain?*"

The driveway felt twice as long this time. There were still hundreds more trees and some low foothills to wend through before the house would rise into view.

Valentine nodded agreement. "So, how did you do that with your chair? When I jumped through all those times, the watch stayed in the middle of that bubble. As long as I was near it, I jumped with it. But you didn't jump with the chair, and neither did the watch."

Malcolm pulled out the device and showed her the jewel mounted in the cover. "I poked around in the Options menu and realized I could channel the energy through the jewel instead. Like a remote emitter, sort of. It shot out a beam that touched the chair, then there was a bubble, then the chair was gone."

"Why would he build it to do that?"

Malcolm's mind flashed back to his encounter with the shadow. "I can guess one reason." He shivered. "He could use it on a person. I think he tried to with me."

Valentine pursed her lips. "Why would he do that?"

"Maybe it's part of his experiments. Or just a convenient way to get rid of someone without killing them."

They fell silent as the implications sank in. If they kept on this course, a confrontation seemed inevitable. Were they ready for that?

The limo rolled to a stop. Calling a *thank you* to the driver, the twins climbed out of the car and shuffled slowly to the giant front door. Given what they were about to do, Malcolm didn't mind taking their time.

"I found something else, too," he said. "No clue what it means, though. When I jumped my chair, I could've sent it thousands of years into the past, but ten minutes was the farthest it could go into the future."

"That can't be. I traveled a lot farther into the future than that. I do think the red color is based on forward travel, though."

Malcolm held up a finger. "That's what I thought at first. I mean, you're probably right about the color. You said it was blue when you traveled backward, right?"

"Yeah. I mean, it makes a weird kind of sense, if you look at the whole cosmic redshift and blueshift thing."

He shrugged. "I'll take your word for it. But you also said the menu read 'Present: Home,' which means you traveled to the watch's present. Since you came back to this time, that must mean the watch's present is also *our* present." He held up a second finger. "So technically, you just traveled from the past back to the present, not really the future." A third finger raised.

"I'm guessing it's because the watch was built sometime in our *past*, not our future."

"Hmm," Valentine said. "So if the watch was built in our past, then this may be the farthest forward in time it's ever been. This would be its present, just like it's *our* present."

They stopped at the door and faced each other. Valentine bit her lip, pondering the theory. "If it was built in our past, would that mean he's done this at other points in history?"

"Maybe. Who knows? And why is it so much harder to move forward in time?" He touched a hand to his temple. "This is so far beyond my level."

"Mine too." Valentine rested a hand on his shoulder. "Let's just concentrate on getting through tonight. We can worry about that stuff later."

As usual, she was correct. They had to take this one problem at a time or it would overwhelm them. He turned to the door and reached for the bell. His hand stopped inches away, trembling again.

"Remember why we're doing this," Valentine said. "They deserve to know, and we need their help."

Malcolm nodded. Counting down from three, he jabbed the button. When Fred came to the door, he was still holding his breath.

"S'up, y'all!" Fred pulled them into a vigorous hug. "Just in time for the movie."

Malcolm offered a stunned half-hug in return. When Valentine had told of Fred's confession, she'd made him sound so normal. Modest, even. Now it seemed the loud-but-friendly oaf that they knew had returned, decades-old slang and all.

"Thanks for having us again, Fred."

"Um, yeah thanks," Valentine said.

Fred grinned. "For friends, it ain't nothin'. Come on, everyone's already here."

They followed Fred down to the gym-sized expanse that had served as a dance floor during his party. Now dotted with furniture, expensive art, and the biggest TV Malcolm had ever seen, it felt more like a regular living room. A giant, opulent, museum living room.

Winter and John lounged on a plush white sectional. *Monty Python and the Holy Grail* played on the TV, and the two were practically in tears from laughter. They called greetings to the twins, John's eyes lingering affectionately on Valentine.

"Don't know how you can watch that mess," Fred complained. He plopped onto the couch next to Winter. "Ain't even funny." That only made them laugh harder. "Can we pick a *real* movie now?"

Malcolm didn't sit. If he relaxed, he'd never have the guts to do this. Apparently Valentine felt the same, so they stood on the opposite side of the coffee table, facing their friends.

"Would you like a seat, Valentine?" John indicated a space next to him.

"Yeah, take a load off," Winter said. "We're supposed to chill out tonight."

Malcolm exchanged an uneasy glance with his sister. Her eyes shared the same conviction, and the same fear. It had to happen now. He picked up the remote and paused the movie on Brave Sir Robin.

"Aw, that's my favorite scene!" Winter cried.

She quieted as John placed a hand on her knee. He leaned forward and examined the twins.

"Are you two all right?"

Malcolm moved to speak, and hesitated. Winter and Fred sat forward now, too. Valentine's presence was tense at his side.

"What's wrong?" John prodded.

Swinging the bag from his shoulder, Malcolm set it on the floor and pulled out the folded map. With a deep breath, he met their eyes.

"We need to talk."

"No way," Winter said. "It's not possible."

Malcolm gestured to the map. "Valentine saw several with her own eyes. Trust us, they're real."

"This is so awesome." Fred pointed to a southeastern lightning bolt on the map. "I think this one is—"

"No!" Winter snapped. "Everyone knows this stuff doesn't happen in real life. Why are you doing this?"

Malcolm paused to gather his thoughts and shake off Winter's attack. As he and Valentine had explained their discoveries, each of their friends had reacted in drastically different ways. Fred had seemed excited by it all, like he was watching it happen in a movie.

John had fallen silent from the first moment and hadn't uttered a word since. He just listened with his brow furrowed. As cerebral as John seemed to be, that wasn't a surprise. Malcolm had expected him to take in everything before reacting.

Winter had shocked him. She was their resident conspiracy theorist. Yet, after listening to Valentine recount their discoveries, she'd repeatedly implied either a naïve misunderstanding or outright deceit on the twins' part. Now her eyes took on an almost frenzied anger.

"Well?" Winter demanded. "What's this really about?"

Valentine held up her hands in a placating gesture. "I know this is crazy. But why would we lie?"

Winter leaped to her feet. "That's what *I'd* like to know!"

"Hey." Fred touched her arm. "Chill out, girl. What 'bout the lightning we saw? Few months ago, that woulda seemed impossible, too."

"Totally not the same thing!" She shook his hand away and narrowed her eyes at the twins. "We were all there for that, so we know it's true."

"Here, look at this." Valentine pointed at another symbol. Malcolm could hear her struggling to stay soft and reasonable. "Someone *died* here. We couldn't make that up."

"I don't care—" Grimacing, Winter looked away and put a hand to her bandaged ear. Her eyes welled up. "I don't want to hear this right now. I can't! I jump at every sound. My ear won't stop hurting, and every day I'm terrified it'll never work again." Angry tears spilled down her face. "How are we supposed to move on when you bring up stupid stuff like this? I thought you were our friends!"

Malcolm cast a pleading look at John. Why wasn't he saying anything? Usually he could even Winter out, but now he just stared at the map.

"They must be tellin' us for a reason," Fred offered. "Just hear 'em out."

"No! They're lying, and I want to know why!"

Sighing, Malcolm stood and reached into his pocket. "Set a timer for thirty seconds."

Valentine nodded and pulled out her phone. They had known it would come to this eventually, but Winter was forcing them to show everything at once. When everyone saw, there would truly be no going back.

Across the room, an eight-foot-tall metal sculpture dominated one corner. Malcolm fixed his eye on it as he drew out
the pocket watch. Opening the lid, he swiped across the glass
face and brought the device to life. From the corner of his eye,
he caught Winter's mouth working silently as the holograms
spun in the air.

"Wha—what?" she managed to say.

"Dude, what *is* that thing?" Fred finished for her.

"Just keep watching."

Having practiced, Malcolm navigated swiftly through the
menu system now. In a handful of seconds the watch was ready.
He pointed it at the sculpture.

John finally unfroze his stare from the map. His eyes settled
on the watch and sprang open like saucers. He half-stood from
the couch. "Malcolm, where did—?"

Red energy burst from the watch and struck the sculpture.
The familiar sphere sprang up and enveloped the tall hunk of
metal, spun on its axis, and disappeared. The sculpture was gone
with it. Goose bumps rose on Malcolm's arms as the air chilled.

"Whoa!" Fred yelped.

He leaped over the couch, away from the watch and the
missing sculpture. Winter collapsed stunned onto the cushions,
staring agape at the empty corner. John came the rest of the way
to his feet, eyeing the watch as if it were a snake.

"Where did you get that?" he demanded.

The lid snapped shut in Malcolm's hand. "Counting down?"

Valentine nodded. "Twenty seconds."

Malcolm faced his friends. "The man who attacked me
was carrying this. With it, you can jump through time, teleport
through space, or phase through solid barriers. We know because we've done it. That's the truth."

"Ten seconds."

Focusing on Winter, he let his stare bore into her. "We didn't do this to upset you. You deserve to know because he's hurt you, too. Because whatever he's doing in there, it can't go on. And because we need your help."

"Three. Two. One. Ze—"

A rushing cold breeze washed over them as the sphere's glow filled the corner again. It spun and disappeared, depositing the sculpture exactly where it had been before.

Fred stood from his hiding place. "That. Was. *Awesome!*" Cackling, he vaulted the couch and grabbed Malcolm's watch hand.

"And scary," Valentine said.

"For sure, but still awesome!"

Winter shook from her stupor. Malcolm watched tensely as she rose from the couch and edged toward them. In her emotional state, would she accept what she'd seen?

Fresh tears spilled from her eyes. Reaching out, she pulled the twins into an embrace. Her face buried in Valentine's shoulder and sobs came softly.

"I'm sorry. I'm sorry."

Malcolm held on while Valentine whispered comforting words and stroked her back. His heart went out to her. Winter always worked hard to appear bulletproof. Her shield was convincing enough that most would believe it. Yet here she was, allowing them to see her so vulnerable. Despite her earlier words, it was obvious how she really felt about them.

Winter pulled away and wiped her eyes. "I said such awful things."

Valentine shrugged. "Who hasn't? We're friends. Don't worry about it."

She smiled gratefully. "It actually kinda makes sense. This town hasn't felt right all year." Her eyes widened. "Patrick! The boy just vanished. Do you think, maybe . . .?"

"I think anything's possible," Valentine said. "Who knows what else this man has done, or who he's done it to?"

Winter's face went grim. "When we track this loser down, I'm going to have some serious questions for him."

"Malcolm." John approached with an outstretched hand. "May I see it?"

Malcolm set the device in John's open palm. His hand quivered, as if he were afraid it might explode. He turned it over and over, examining every corner.

"This can't be happening."

"I know," Malcolm said. "I about fell over when I realized what it does."

"I passed out," Valentine added.

John pushed the watch into Malcolm's hands and backed away from them. "I need some air," he muttered, and retreated toward the stairs.

They heard his footsteps ascend the spiral staircase and disappear through the front door. Valentine's face was a mask of worry.

"He just needs time," Winter said. "You know he's been through some crazy stuff." She rubbed her arms. "Did it get colder?"

Malcolm shared a glance with Valentine.

"Actually, we think that's from the watch, too," she said. "I haven't seen any battery indicators, and this thing is doing powerful stuff." She shrugged. "Maybe it pulls heat from the air and runs on the thermal energy."

"I noticed the same thing outside the house when I snooped," Malcolm added.

"Wow," Winter said. "That actually makes sense."

Malcolm smiled. "Who knows if it's actually true. This is all like a weird movie anyway."

Fred rubbed his hands together, a glint in his eye. "So, what now? We gonna pound this guy into next century?"

"One of the northern tunnels is on your property," Valentine said. "First thing, you guys should see it."

"Food first, though," Winter said. "I need pizza therapy."

The twins agreed, and they moved to the kitchen. Fred poured them all drinks while they talked about anything except what was really happening. After ten minutes, Valentine leaned close to Malcolm's ear.

"Be back in a few."

He nodded with a knowing smile, and a bashful grin reddened her face. She slid from the stool and left the kitchen, no doubt headed for the stairs.

THE front door clicked shut. Valentine found John's silhouette leaning against one of Fred's cars, peering up at the sparkling night sky. She wandered toward the boy, gravel crunching underfoot. John's head tilted toward the sound, and he slid over to make room.

Did he know it was me?

"The sky here is so pretty." She stopped next to him and leaned back, mirroring his posture. "Never saw this many stars in the city." John nodded, but said nothing. She slid closer, his scent filling her nostrils—earthy and clean, like the forest after a rain. "You okay?"

He stared at the stars for a long moment. "I didn't anticipate that. I don't know how to process it at the moment."

"If it makes you feel better, I don't either. Even Mal doesn't, and he saw it first." She brushed her arm against his and a thrill swept through her. "You were there for me when I needed it, John. What can I do for you?"

He smiled faintly. "I'll be fine. This isn't an everyday occurrence, that's all. Makes you question things." John turned, leaning his side against the car, and gazed down at her. "But I'm calmer with you near me. Right now, I feel as if I could hear the most insane thing and it would be okay."

Valentine flushed, heat spreading across her face and chest. He was so close, she could feel his warmth on her skin. Deep inside, she longed for more of him. "When I'm with you, I feel quiet inside. Like everything bad hears your voice and just goes away." She smiled. "It's so peaceful."

Does he feel this as much as I do? John's eyes caressed her with tenderness and warmth and desire, and Valentine knew in her heart that he did. He glanced down at her neck, and his face lit up with recognition.

"I realized what you're wearing."

She touched the silver pendant, wrought in the shape of two interlocked hearts topped with a crown. "You did?"

"It's a Luckenbooth pendant." Shy embarrassment crossed his face. "I may have searched for it on Google. It said this was from old Scotland, often given as a betrothal gift. Yes?"

He cared enough to search about my pendant. Valentine swallowed a lump and nodded. "My dad couldn't afford a ring when he proposed. So he gave my mom this. She left it to me, after . . ."

"You treat it with so much love." John's eyes pierced her. "That's wonderful."

Valentine's gaze slid to the ground. She wanted to drink him in until there was nothing left. The feeling filled every corner inside her, terrifying and beautiful and exhilarating. A few stray hairs fell across her eyes.

"What is it?" he asked.

She kept her eyes down. "It's just that, when you look at me like that . . . you make me feel beautiful." She drew in a deep breath. "I'm not used to that."

Gently, John slipped his fingers under her chin. He tilted her face up and searched deep into her eyes. Into her soul. "You are beautiful."

He brushed the stray hairs aside and his touch lingered on her skin. Her heart leapt and her stomach fluttered like a thousand butterflies.

"No matter where we are, you are the first thing I see," he continued. "And when I go to sleep, you are the last thought in my head. You make me—"

Valentine fell against John and locked her lips with his. His words cut off and they melted together like one being. With her eyes closed tight, his touch sent electricity through her. The earthy scent of him filled her senses, and his soft lips chased away every thought.

John leaned into the kiss and wrapped his arms around her waist. Valentine grasped his neck with her fingers and they pulled tighter against each other. She never wanted to let go, and in her mind the moment stretched into eternity.

Finally they parted. Valentine's legs wobbled and her vision swam. She rested against John's chest, not trusting herself to stand. He held her tight and stroked her hair, his soft breath caressing the back of her neck.

A giggle bubbled up from inside her. "Maybe we should go inside. They're probably wondering about us."

He chuckled. "I doubt it. They probably knew this was happening before we did."

Valentine giggled again and hugged him tighter. She could feel his steady heartbeat, his presence wrapped around her like a warm blanket.

"Still, I suppose we shouldn't miss all the excitement." John leaned down to look her in the eye. "Shall we?"

Valentine nodded dreamily. After one more kiss—okay, maybe two—they released each other and wandered slowly toward the front porch. Mid-stride, John reached out and their fingers interlaced.

They stepped through the door together.

CHAPTER 15

Flashlight beams stabbed through the darkness. Malcolm swept his Fenix across trees and hills, searching for a swathe of scorched earth.

"Hey, see that?" Winter's flashlight pointed up an incline, at a stand of young trees. "Those look different than the rest."

"Let's check it." Fred leapt up the hill with the rest of them in tow.

Malcolm glanced at Valentine and smiled to himself. She hadn't released John's hand since they'd left the house, and she practically glowed when he looked at her. It warmed Malcolm's heart to see her happy. If there was any order to the universe, she would stay that way.

Breaking into a jog, Malcolm caught up with Winter and Fred as they neared the top of the incline. Something had been nagging at the back of his mind.

"Fred, I'm curious."

"Yeah, man?"

"Val told me you're playing for a scholarship."

"That's the plan, dawg."

"I'm just wondering why. Don't take this the wrong way, but aren't you . . . ?"

"Rich?"

"Uh, well, yeah."

Fred snorted. "Same thing my dad says. 'You don't gotta do this, son. Where you wanna go? I'll write a check.'" He tossed his hands in front of him, as if pushing the idea away. "Please. A man's gotta do *somethin'* for himself. He buys what I want, lets me have parties and stuff." He looked pointedly at Malcolm. "But gettin' into college—I'm gonna do that on my own. Ain't gonna run to daddy for everything."

Malcolm nodded. "Wow. Good for you."

Fred shrugged it off. "Way I roll."

They reached the top of the incline, and Malcolm saw that Winter had been right. "It *is* different here, but I think we're too late to see anything."

"What do you mean?" Winter said.

"He's right," Valentine observed. "All the trees around here are big and old, except for this patch. And see the rectangles in the grass? It's new sod."

"Aw, man!" Fred said. "Stupid landscapers musta fixed it already."

"Which means the tunnel is probably under a bunch of dirt and grass," Winter lamented.

Malcolm nodded. "Yeah. I wonder if—"

A low, rolling rumble rose from beneath them. The ground shuddered, leaves whispering as they danced on shaking branches, and birds took to flight with alarmed caws. The friends stared wide-eyed at each other.

The earth bucked under their feet and Malcolm danced quickly to the side, struggling to keep his balance. His shoes caught on each other, and he fell to his hands and knees.

The tremors stopped.

"Whoa," Winter said. "We never get earthquakes here. Never."

"Then perhaps this is for the best," John said as everyone regained footing, except Valentine, whose dancer's balance must have kept her upright. He held up a defensive hand when they all stared at him. "As a warning, I mean. You all seem eager for the adventure, and I understand that. But do we have the slightest clue what forces we are toying with?"

"This isn't about adventure, John," Malcolm returned. "It's about defending the town."

"I appreciate your intentions, Malcolm. However, you have only fragments of knowledge. Have you considered that interference may turn things worse?"

Malcolm knew John was right. The twins had managed to uncover a few details, but the big picture still eluded them. Without real facts, none of his arguments would seem logical. So for now, he'd just have to go with illogical.

"I know you're trying to protect us, but you haven't seen what we've seen. It doesn't matter how big this is—I have to try."

Valentine squeezed John's hand. "So do I. This is our home now, and something's very wrong here."

John studied the ground with a sigh. He stroked his chin, deep in thought.

"Don't punk out on us, dude," Fred said. "We need *one* sane person in this group."

John chuckled before looking at Valentine and squeezing her hand back. "I'll remain with you, but I *will* speak up if this goes too far."

Valentine smiled and nestled closer to him.

"So, what's next?" Winter asked.

"I guess we could find another tunnel," Malcolm said.

"Do we really need to?" Winter shrugged. "I believe you saw something real. That's good enough for me."

Fred and John nodded their agreement. Malcolm cast a questioning look at his sister. Of anyone, she'd witnessed by far the most.

Her brow furrowed in thought. "Some of them may be different, which could tell us something. I'd hate to miss any clues. There should be one in the northern hills, by an old warehouse. "

Malcolm agreed. "I want to know everything we can, so let's start with that. Can your driver keep quiet, Fred?"

"Uh, thing is," Fred began. "See, I thought y'all were stayin' overnight, so I sorta sent him home."

The group stared at Fred in stunned silence. Winter punched him in the shoulder.

"Moron."

"So we're stuck here." Malcolm's shoulders fell. "Things are getting worse. I don't think we'll have many chances to do this."

Fred's eyebrows raised. "Well, I could—"

"No!" Winter stopped him. "I know that look, Fred. No way."

He flashed an innocent face. "What, girl? I'm just sayin'. You got a better idea?"

Valentine looked from one to the other. "A better idea than what?"

THE north end of town gave way to tall, rocky hills. Fred charged a huge black SUV—one of his dad's many vehicles—up a steep, winding road toward their destination. Malcolm squeezed the armrest in a death grip as they tore around another sharp curve.

The road cut into the hill and snaked between large, flat plateaus that dotted the hillside. Climbing higher, the group passed everything from radio towers to high-rent vacation con-dominiums built to take advantage of the view. Tonight, they aimed for a spot near the top.

"Found it!" Fred veered off the main road and jammed on the brakes. The wheels kicked up a shower of gravel and dust, skidding to a stop inches from a tall chain-link fence. "Slammin' directions, Val."

"Fred, you moron!" Winter snapped. "You're not a secret agent. Quit driving like one."

"You'll live." Fred threw his door open. "Come on, I wanna see this thing."

The rest of them climbed gingerly from the vehicle. Malcolm wondered if they were shaking as much as he was. "First time I've ever wanted to hug the ground. I can't believe we're doing this."

Valentine stopped beside him, hand-in-hand with John. "This seemed less stupid back at his house."

They gathered at the fence's wide gate and peered onto the property. The flat, two-acre expanse was ringed on three sides by the gray metal chain links. The fourth side was a sheer rock face that rose into the sky.

Behind the fence sat a one-story building with corrugated steel walls, discolored and sagging with neglect. The faded *Veidt Industrial Storage* sign hung askew near the door. A wa-ter tower perched to the right of the warehouse. It might have been impressive if not for its obvious lean, or the faded and pit-marked exterior.

"So, this is why we risked fiery death at Fred's hands," Winter said. "Not so impressive."

"I'm pretty sure it's the place, though," Valentine said. "See the black streaks everywhere? They could've come from lightning. And the way the building sags there at the corner—maybe that was the center."

Winter glanced at her. "Maybe?"

Valentine shrugged. "It's not an exact science, and the place is locked down." She gestured to the gate's chain and thick padlock.

John examined the top of the ten-foot-tall fence. "Could we climb it?"

"Wait, I got some'n better." Fred strolled to the back of his SUV and popped open the hatch. Malcolm heard clinking metal, and Fred re-emerged with a set of shiny red bolt cutters.

Winter rolled her eyes. "You *would* be carrying those around."

Fred offered the handles to Malcolm. "Here, I can't cut nothin' with these casts."

Malcolm accepted it out of reflex, then stood staring at it. His insides recoiled. "Um, breaking and entering seems like a big step."

Fred inclined his head toward the warehouse. "This place look like anyone cares?"

He did have a point, Malcolm admitted. They'd probably be the first people to enter the building in a decade. So having a look around shouldn't be a big deal. Right? Still, he stood there.

"Oh, just do it," Winter said. "We can all find out what juvie's like."

Fred shook his head. "Always so dramatic." He reached out for the cutters. "Here, I can try if you ain't into it."

"No." Malcolm clutched the handles tighter. "No, we're mostly here because of me. It's my responsibility." He faced the padlock and steeled himself.

The cutters were new and sharp, the lock old and brittle—one swift clamp and it crumbled away. A wave of anxious excitement overcame Malcolm. In the past year, his idea of danger had been finding rare books about the Franco-Prussian War. Now here he was, in uncharted waters. He grinned.

The warehouse sat fifty feet back from the fence. In that open space, the grounds were littered with busted crates and containers, discarded scrap metal, even a few rusted shells of construction machinery. The group picked their way through the debris.

"So, how do we find what we're looking for?" Malcolm asked Valentine. "Should we walk around the building first?"

"The water tower sits high," John offered. "Perhaps we could climb it and search from above."

"Or," Winter pointed to the bolt cutters. "We could add to our heinous crimes and just bash in the door with—"

The sky exploded with a barrage of lightning.

Halfway to the building they stopped in their tracks. Silvery lances raced from cloud to cloud and thunder shook the air. Malcolm froze in place and someone beside him yelped.

A bolt struck the roof of the warehouse, blasting chunks of debris into the air. The bolt cutters dropped unnoticed from Malcolm's hands.

"Holy crap!" Winter yelled.

Another strike pounded the roof, turning metal to slag and flinging more jagged projectiles. They stumbled back again, too shocked to flee as the night sky glowed like daylight, sizzling with a web of electricity. A third bolt hammered the roof, then a fourth. The structure began to sag under the assault.

"We should never have come here," John said. He grabbed Valentine and whirled back toward the fence. "We've got to go *now.* Come on, before this gets worse!"

Malcolm shook to his senses and yanked Winter and Fred's shoulders, turning them to follow John's retreat. The group broke into a run and aimed for the gate.

"Look at that!" Fred pointed ahead of them.

Malcolm's heart froze in his chest. Lightning formed a perfect ring in the valley beneath them, cutting right through the center of Emmett's Bluff. The storm stretched for miles, bombarding town and country with its fury.

The fence stood just a few yards away. Malcolm aimed for the gate, planning to open it for his friends and follow them through.

A rumble rose from beneath their feet, violently rattling the chain links. The ground bucked and shuddered, and Malcolm lost his footing. He tumbled to the ground and rolled to a stop near the fence. With a groan, he clutched the ribs that hadn't fully healed while the others sprawled on the grass around him.

"Feels like the whole mountain's coming down!" Winter yelled.

John grabbed Fred's shoulder. "Can you drive us out of here?"

"Are you nuts? You want to drive during an earthquake?"

"We can't just wait here!" Valentine shouted.

"We've got to go!" Malcolm agreed. "Give me your keys and—"

A screech split the air like ripping metal and crushing stone, as if Earth itself cried out in agony. The warehouse windows exploded out, hurling hot darts of glass. A beam of blue-white energy as wide as a car shot from the ground, lanced through the half-collapsed roof, and stabbed into the sky like a blade of light.

Malcolm stared at the unnatural sight, trying and failing to make sense of it. Winter and Fred hugged each other in terror. Valentine and John did the same, with John covering his ears and yelling something that was lost in the wind.

Malcolm lurched to his feet and snatched the keys from Fred. Someone had to protect them, and no one else was moving. It was up to him now. He charged toward the gate, intent on ramming the SUV through it and picking them up.

The tremors worsened. Malcolm stumbled over the undulating ground and fell to his knees against the chain links. The lightning intensified, searing the air with crackling static electricity.

Behind him, the giant beam began to pulsate, and waves of pressure jumped through the air like a rising tide. His hairs stood on end, and every inch of skin puckered into goose bumps. Malcolm couldn't resist it—he had to see. Bracing against the fence, he turned to look back.

The beam was spinning, and it was expanding. Like a giant drill bit, it twisted and writhed and tore at earth and sky. Wider and wider it expanded, vaporizing anything in its path until it had grown to a twenty-foot wide firestorm.

Malcolm felt an invisible force pulling him toward the beam. The others must have felt it, too—in a panic, they scrambled to the fence and latched on. He stared in horror as hulking chunks of the building tore loose and spun in the air, orbiting the beam like a tornado, then plunged into its glowing heart and vaporized. The loose debris and machinery in the yard went airborne next and joined the swirling maelstrom.

The pull grew stronger, like a predator tearing at him. Malcolm clutched the fence tighter and metal links dug into his hands, drawing lines of blood.

"Don't. Let. Go!" he yelled, praying they could hear him.

They couldn't make it to the car now, and they couldn't run. Only one way out remained. Releasing the fence with one hand, he reached into his pocket and withdrew the watch. He would transport them somewhere safe.

The ground bucked underneath them. Malcolm stumbled dizzily, his grip slackening for an instant, and the beam's pull ripped the watch from his hand. It shot into the air like a bullet and plunged into the angry light.

Malcolm's heart broke to pieces and dropped into his stomach. He wanted to scream. He wanted to cry and curl into a ball and wish this all away. Their one advantage was gone, and now they were trapped!

A sound of groaning metal reached his ears. Their stretch of chain-link fence bent and twisted, then ripped from its anchor poles with a jolt. It hurtled through the air toward the giant beam with Malcolm and his screaming friends attached.

Halfway across the yard, Fred's bandaged hands slipped from the chain links and he spun apart from the fence. Winter reached for her friend and lost her grip as well. They skidded along the grass and smacked into the warehouse wall with a metallic clang. Malcolm hoped that what was left of the wall would shield them from the beam.

The fence caught on a corner of twisted steel protruding from the warehouse, and with the sudden stop they flopped down onto the battered roof. Rattling, the fence strained against its bonds as if eager to plunge into the burning light.

Panic forbade Malcolm from letting go. He swallowed hard and mustered his courage, knowing this might be his last chance. One by one, the tangled chain links were breaking under the strain.

Valentine clung to the fence, and to John, with equal

ferocity. He wrapped a protective arm around her shoulders. His glasses had long since fallen into the beam. He stared up at Malcolm with determined eyes and pointed, once at Valentine and once over the edge.

It seemed they had the same thought. With a nod, Malcolm silently agreed—family came first. He inched closer to Valentine, reached out and wrapped his arms around her waist. She looked up at him with questioning eyes.

John let go and Malcolm rolled away with his sister clutched tightly to his body. She screamed and stretched a hand back toward John. Ignoring her cries, Malcolm rolled along the rippling fence to the precipice of the roof, swung Valentine over the edge and released his grip. He clung to the fence again before the beam could suck him away.

Red hair flailed as Valentine dropped twelve feet to the ground and smacked into the grass. Malcolm winced as she curled into a ball and cried out. Her ribs may have bruised, or even broken, but hopefully the warehouse wall would shield her.

Malcolm slid back toward John. A precious few chain links still clung to the roof, stretched nearly to breaking. John waved him away.

"Go back!"

Malcolm ignored him and offered a hand. John shook his head and pointed downward. Malcolm shook his head back and offered the hand again.

John pointed more forcefully. This time Malcolm looked, and his face fell. A section of fence had tangled around John's leg and dug into his flesh.

John saw the recognition in Malcolm's eyes. He nodded, shook his leg to show it was truly stuck, and pointed back to the ledge. The message was clear. *I'm lost. Get out while you can.*

That wouldn't do. No way. Shouting in wordless fury, Malcolm tore at the bonds trapping John's leg. The strong metal links resisted, yet he kept attacking them.

John helped pry at the fence, then yelled into his ear, "She can't lose us both!"

"She's not losing anyone!" Malcolm snarled. "Now, pull!"

Overhead, metal screeched and ripped again. Malcolm gasped as the water tower broke from its base and spun around the beam. Its shattered legs swept through the air, bursting through other floating debris.

The tower's bulbous top swung low and bashed into the warehouse roof. Still it kept spinning around the fiery lance, tossing up chunks of brick and steel as it smashed through what little of the building remained.

It swung right toward them.

Malcolm's teeth chattered with the force of every impact. Struggling to quell his panic, he pried harder at the links holding John.

"Pull the whole fence over the edge!" John shouted.

"I tried before. It's too heavy!"

"Then go! Help your sister."

"I'm not leaving you! Just keep trying!"

The water tower's leg swept underneath them and smashed through the last supports anchoring the roof to the ground. The fence shook free of its bonds and surged upward, spinning around the giant beam, carrying Malcolm and John with it.

A dreamlike feeling overcame Malcolm. While his insides panicked and struggled to survive, his outer self felt almost calm, lulled by the wind in his hair and the sensation of flight. They swirled closer to the deadly beam, like the last orbit of a doomed planet.

On their last spin, Malcolm gazed out across the valley to drink it in one last time. His stomach soured at the sight. Across Emmett's Bluff, eleven more identical beams pierced the sky. He could see their fire from miles away, forming a perfect circle—like the points of a clock. Valentine had been right.

In the center of the storm, on a patch of land that should be dark, one tiny spot lit up like the sun. Four blazing beams emitted from it, pointing in opposite directions. In his broken heart, Malcolm knew they came from a house with no doors. Right then, the truth was clear. Whatever the scientist had been planning, he had just won.

They spun back inward, turning away from the view of Emmett's Bluff's demise. The pull on them tightened, and they plunged toward the relentless beam's white-hot center. Light filled Malcolm's vision, and he closed his eyes.

His clothes began to sizzle.

CHAPTER 16

The light and terrible noise disappeared. The dark of night flooded back in. Trembling, Valentine forced herself to her feet and clutched her aching side.

"Oh my God, did you see what happened?" Winter called. She and Fred limped toward Valentine, leaning on each other.

Valentine shook her head. "Almost blacked out when I hit the ground. My head's still spinning."

"That *thing* picked them up," Fred said. "John and Mal—it took 'em into the air."

Sinking dread slammed into Valentine. *No.* "Mal! John!" She shouted over the half-collapsed wall.

Nothing.

"Maaaal!"

She tugged on the door handle. Locked. She searched for an opening in the sagging steel wall, her insides quaking. What if they needed help? Marching to the door again, she kicked with all the strength she could muster. The rusted frame tore loose, and the door buckled inward with a metallic screech.

"Come on," she commanded.

The warehouse roof was completely gone, and except for a few support columns, the inner structure had disappeared, too.

Even the concrete floors had been ripped away, leaving the soil underneath churned up like a giant child's sandbox.

Valentine scrambled over hills of dirt. "Mal! John!"

A faint scraping sound reached her ears. Then, just barely, a strained voice. "*Here. Over here!*"

Valentine's heart leapt. Climbing over the last hill, she found the heart of the carnage. A round crater had been blasted into the scorched earth, big enough to swallow a bus. The chain link fence lay at the crater's edge, one end tangled around a twisted support beam, the other end wrapped around John's leg. He sprawled out toward the crater, gritting his teeth.

Malcolm hung over the crater's edge, dangling above the black pit. He clung to John's arms, straining to lift himself out. With every motion, more dirt broke away from the edge and he sank deeper into the crater.

Valentine broke into a sprint. Skidding to her knees next to them, she reached over the side and gripped Malcolm's belt. Winter and Fred arrived to help, and inch by inch they lifted him onto solid ground. He flopped onto his stomach and hugged the dirt.

Exhausted, Valentine slumped onto her back and allowed relief to flood her body. They had survived. Barely.

"We thought you were dead," Winter gasped.

"Me, too. Beam stopped right before we hit it." Malcolm gripped Valentine's hand. "Thank you."

She squeezed his fingers. "Don't you two ever do that again."

"No promises." He squeezed back. "Family protects each other."

Rolling onto her hands and knees, Valentine crawled to John and examined his leg. "Are you okay?"

He nodded, but stayed silent. The others joined her in prying at the links digging into his leg. He winced and groaned as the last of the metal pulled from his flesh. Valentine tore a strip from her ripped shirt and pressed it around the puncture wounds.

"These need to be cleaned and wrapped. Have you had a tetanus shot?" she asked. He shrugged mechanically and looked away. "How's everyone else?"

"Bruises and cuts." Winter hugged herself. "And my ear's killing me."

"Cracked one of my casts." Fred held up one arm and a chunk of fiberglass flopped loose.

"Dirt gave us a soft landing, fortunately," Malcolm said. "How are *you?*"

"My ribs are pretty bruised," Valentine replied, her eyes fixed on John. She stepped closer to her . . . boyfriend? She supposed he was now. "John?"

He stared at the ground. Valentine knew they were all shaken, but John had always been so steady. Now he seemed switched off.

Malcolm pulled out his phone. "Dad's calling. Probably wants to make sure we're not dead." He considered, then put it away. "I'm not ready to talk to anyone yet."

The rest of them got their own phone calls, none of which they answered. What could they say? John made no move for his pocket, and Valentine remembered his aversion to technology.

Malcolm took her gently by the arm. "Come on. We should get out—" He cut off, his head whipping skyward.

Just then, a whistling sound reached Valentine's ears. She stared up at the night sky, but nothing appeared against the blackness. The whistling grew louder, drawing closer each second, and instinctively she backed away to search for cover.

Winter grabbed her ear and grimaced. "Don't tell me another one's coming."

A glint of metal flashed and something struck the ground ten yards ahead, casting up a plume of dirt. They jumped back in alarm, Valentine holding her breath in expectation of an explosion or something equally terrible. After a tense moment, Malcolm moved toward the hole that the—whatever it was—had created in the ground.

"Hey, man," Fred shifted uneasily. "Why don't we just leave it?"

Malcolm shook his head and kept moving. *Alone,* and after he'd just stared death in the face. Gathering what remained of her courage, Valentine moved to catch up.

They came to a stop together over the tiny crater. Valentine peered inside and her mouth fell open.

"No. *Way.*"

Malcolm reached down and the brown earth crumbled away to reveal a dusty silver watch. Lifting it by its chain, he wiped off the grime and held it in the air for all to see.

"I *saw* this hit the beam. How could it survive that?"

Valentine examined it in awe. "Maybe because it came from the same place?"

Her brother nodded. "Everyone else was vaporized. So maybe it was designed to survive something like this."

"Just more questions." Winter shuffled toward the door. "Come on. I can't take this right now."

PLUMES of fire and smoke rose in a ring around Emmett's Bluff.

The faint wail of sirens floated up to them. Malcolm gasped at the sight and rushed toward the edge of the plateau.

Valentine hurried after him with the others in tow. "What is it?"

He sank to his knees at the edge, tears in his eyes. "I thought that was it. I thought we were all dead."

"So did I." Kneeling, she placed an arm around his shoulders. "But it's over now. We're okay. Sort of."

"No. I mean, I thought we were *all* dead." Malcolm wiped a forearm across his eyes. "When we were flying into that thing, I knew he'd won." He smiled. "But everything's still here!"

Examining her brother, Valentine realized his tears weren't from grief or fear. They were from relief. He was actually *happy.* "What do you mean?"

"The town is still standing. Whatever he's planning, I don't think he's finished." He came to his feet. "This was just the beginning."

"Mal, look what he did. What else could he possibly be planning?"

"The *what,* I have no idea. But the *why* . . ." He faced their friends. "Why do I think there's more coming? Because what did this gain him?"

"Destruction," Winter stated.

Malcolm shook his head. "No. Val saw him running tests, not just destroying things. If he's some kind of scientist, then he's looking for a result. Twelve craters are not a result."

Valentine thought on this. "He's right. A scientist would have a reason. But, what is it?"

"That's what I'd like to know." Malcolm's gestures grew animated and his voice took on a new life. "He wouldn't do this without being close to his goal. That means time is running out, and we can't just poke around anymore." He pointed southeast. "We have to take this to *him*—find out what he's doing, and stop him before he does something worse. Look, I know we're tired and we're hurting." He stepped closer to their friends, meeting each of their eyes. "But we're not finished. This has to stop *now*, and I can't do it alone."

Silence greeted him.

They shuffled their feet, looking anywhere but at him. Even Valentine felt herself warring inside. Exhausted, aching, and terrified, she just wanted to find a dark corner and hide. Yet, what would happen if they did nothing? That terrified her, too. It didn't help that John seemed broken.

Malcolm's shoulders slumped. "No one?"

Finally, Fred cleared his throat. "I hate dyin', and it's almost happened twice when I stuck my nose in this." He shook his head. "I just don't know, man."

Winter leaned against Fred and closed her eyes. "I can't even think with this headache. My brain feels like oatmeal."

Malcolm looked to John, his face pleading for support. John just stared into the distance, his face an unreadable mask. Valentine knew he could hear them, but it felt like he was seeing something they couldn't.

"John, please." She brushed his hand. His whole body trembled like a leaf in the wind. Standing close, she searched his face. "Look at me."

With effort, he met her eyes. Valentine gripped his hands and searched for the right words. What could she say to bring him back? So much of him was still an enigma. Her lips parted, but nothing found its way out.

His fingers slid from her grasp. Valentine tried to hold tighter, but John backed away.

"I can't," he whispered, dripping with desperation. "I can't. I'm . . ." He turned away and retreated to Fred's SUV. Climbing inside, he shut the door behind him.

Valentine stared after him, feeling as helpless as she'd ever known. She realized one hand had stretched out toward him, so she put it back at her side. Winter appeared next to her and slid an arm around her shoulders.

Valentine leaned gratefully into her friend's embrace. "Did I do this to him, dragging him out here when he didn't want to come?"

Winter snorted. "John Carter does what John Carter wants. He'll say it was worth it to protect you. He's old-fashioned that way."

Over the past year, Malcolm had shown similar reactions to stress and fear. Sometimes you just had to let a boy be for a while, she supposed. Still, every fiber in her wanted to run to John and make it okay.

Malcolm offered a sympathetic smile. Then he eyed everyone in turn and his expression hardened. Valentine knew he wanted to shake them to their senses.

"Okay, here's what's happening." He palmed the pocket watch and clicked it open. "It's eleven o'clock now. I'm taking a shower and a nap, then at four a.m. I'm going inside that house. Val used this to do it before, and I'm betting I can do it again."

Dread settled in the pit of Valentine's stomach. Memories of tracer lights and "countermeasures" flashed through her memory.

"I don't want your answer now," he continued. "Anyone who wants to help, text me and I'll use the watch to come get you." He took a deep breath and his tone softened. "If this is too much, I'll understand. We're friends no matter what."

Winter and Fred nodded but seemed at a loss for words. Valentine knew how they felt. What could be said that would make all this seem okay?

"Fred, can you get Winter and John home?" Malcolm asked.

Fred test-flexed his arms. "Yeah, I can drive."

Winter rolled her eyes and dug the keys from Fred's pocket. "*I'm* driving, we'll be fine. What about you?"

"We've got planning to do." His thumb brushed the watch, and its blue glow lit his face.

The thought of using that *thing* again sent a tremor through Valentine. She cast a longing glance toward John, then reluctantly stood beside her brother. "This is all insane," she whispered.

Malcolm didn't answer.

The glowing blue sphere spun around them, and a wave of disorientation washed over her. Seconds later, the spots faded from her eyes and she stood in her own backyard. No lights were on inside.

Except for the fires, the city had gone dark.

CHAPTER 17

Any other time, Malcolm would've made a joke to lighten the mood. Tonight, he didn't. With his serious face on, he stared around the back corner of their house, eyeing their target across the street.

"I know what I said, Val, but I really don't want to go in there." His voice fell to a whisper. "Why couldn't I just stay buried in my books?"

She put a hand on his arm. "Maybe you're remembering who you are. The last thing I want is to go in there again, but you're right—who else is there? The government'll be busy with the craters, and it takes adults forever to do anything important." She shrugged. "We're all this town's got."

"Yeah. Who'd listen to a bunch of teenagers, anyway?" He moved toward their back door. "We should get some rest. Four a.m.'s going to come fast."

Valentine pulled him into a hug. Their arms wrapped tightly around each other, and his presence soothed her frayed nerves. She let their shared warmth comfort her in the chilly night air.

"Okay," she said. "First, let's go tell Dad we weren't vaporized."

NEIL sprang from the couch as the back door swung open. Before the twins were fully inside, he gathered them in a crushing embrace.

"Oh, thank God!" He released them and leaned back, concern creasing his face. "Were you caught in it? How'd you get back?"

For the first time, Valentine realized how terrible they must have looked—bruised, clothes torn and dirty. "Uh, yeah a little. Fred's driver brought us back."

"Got too close to one of those . . . whatever it was," Malcolm said. "Where's Oma?"

"She went to check on Walter." Neil examined them closely. "Are you hurt? What about your friends?"

"Just sore," Valentine said.

"So, are they saying what happened?" Malcolm deflected.

Neil led them to the kitchen table, where a battery-powered portable TV cast the only light. "Power's out for most of town, but national news is blowing up with the story. Cell phone videos are already on YouTube. They say the National Guard and the FBI are coming to investigate." He scrubbed a hand through his hair. "This is unbelievable. Downtown is like a war zone."

They fell silent and watched a montage of footage. The twins saw repeats of what they had witnessed on the hill, only these had been far worse. The beams sucked up cars, houses, a shopping center, even pedestrians helpless against the titanic pull of that deadly energy.

Malcolm's voice was subdued. "How many were hurt?"

"Hundreds, probably more." Neil shook his head. "Some are dead."

Valentine clutched her stomach. Her heart reached out to

those people, and her insides roiled at the power that had ripped through their town. Power they would soon face.

Malcolm tugged at her sleeve. "We should get some rest. G'night, Dad."

"Glad you two are safe," Neil said. "Schools are closed, but I'm sure everyone'll be helping out tomorrow."

Staring at her father, Valentine hesitated. Words bubbled to her lips—words that had to be said—but his eyes stayed locked on the screen, and finally she followed Malcolm upstairs.

THE shower did little to calm her, and there was no point in trying to rest. She knew sleep would never come. Her body shook with nervous anticipation. By the end of this night, would things be better? Or would she regret her choices?

Valentine stood in front of her father's closed door. Despite it being two in the morning, a light still glowed at the edges of the doorframe. Steeling herself, she knocked lightly.

"Come in," came the muffled reply.

Go. Not letting herself think twice, she turned the handle and stepped inside.

Neil sat with his back to the door and the TV on his desk. "Thought you'd be sleeping by now."

Valentine cleared her throat. Neil whipped around in surprise, and his expression grew uncertain. "Hey there. Everything okay?"

Obviously, he'd thought she was Malcolm or Oma Grace. She tried to ignore his disappointment. *After all, how often do I come in here voluntarily?* Hefting a bag of Sun Chips, she forced a smile.

"Thought you'd like a snack."

"Oh. Well, uh, thanks. I do like those." He just sat there, staring at the bag but not reaching for it. After a moment, she gave up and set it on the end table next to his lamp.

Studying the floor, she took a moment to summon her courage. "Um, I was sort of hoping to talk a little. Some things have been happening lately with . . . well, a boy. A few other things are happening, too, and they're kind of big, so . . ."

Her dad looked stunned. "Oh, I didn't know. A boy, wow . . ." He trailed off, avoiding her gaze. "Uh, don't you think Oma Grace might be better at this? I mean, she's got advice for everything."

She had seen it coming, but it still cut like a hot blade. *Why is he doing this?* Her thoughts flashed back to the night of the lightning storm, when she had tried to talk to him then. *Why do I keep trying?* Her pain turned sour, and she fixed him with a bitter glare.

He fidgeted. "What's wrong?"

She felt acid drip onto her heart. "What's wrong is huge things are happening, and I can't talk to my own father about them. I mean, do you notice me anymore? Do you even—" She cut off, knowing he didn't really hear her. *So, that's how we're going to leave it. Fine.*

She whirled toward the door, swiping at the Sun Chips and adopting a new plan to eat every chip in the bag. An edge caught on the lampshade and ripped down the side, spilling chips across the carpet. She wanted to keep running but sighed and knelt to scoop them up.

Behind her, Neil stood. She felt his eyes on her and regretted stopping for anything. All she wanted was to get out and never think of this again. Just a few more chips and—

"You look so much like your mother."

Her hands slowed. She kept her back to him.

"I forget she's gone sometimes. I catch myself wondering what she'll want for dinner. I still hear her voice." He sounded so weary. "Then I see you, and I remember all the things I loved about her. Every little detail that made her . . . *her*. I keep feeling myself push you away and haven't known how to stop."

Valentine found herself turning to look on her father. He stared at the ground, ashamed, his face soured with grief.

"You have her eyes. Her laugh." Neil stared silently into space for a long moment. Wearily, he rubbed his face. "I look at you, Valentine, and it's impossible not to miss her."

His words stung her heart. Yet, she understood them. She had felt those things, too. She straightened and he took a step toward her.

"I have been so selfish. Drowning in my own grief, ignoring what I still have. All this time we could've helped each other, but I shut you out because I was afraid to remember. But look at what's happening out there. Look how easily I could've lost—" He cut off, his voice breaking.

Tears welled up in his eyes. Valentine felt her own eyes brimming. Still, pride and anger coursed through her, and she shoved the tears back inside. *You will NOT make me cry!*

"I . . . I want things to be like they were before," he sniffed, and tears streamed down his face. "I want to see you smile like *she* used to. I want to be there when you need me." He implored with desperate eyes. "I know you're angry, Valentine, and I can't be perfect, but I just want to be your dad again."

Valentine's heart broke open and tears burst from her eyes. Rushing forward, she plunged into his arms. They clung tightly and cried into each other. The anguish of the past year rushed through her, like so many times before. Only this time it felt a little less tragic.

"I missed you, Dad."

Neil hugged her tighter. "You're all the best parts of her, Valentine. And she'd be so proud of the woman you're becoming. Just like I am."

They held each other and soothed away the pain just for a moment. Valentine basked in warm comfort, knowing that no matter what happened today, she had her father back.

CHAPTER 18

Malcolm pulled on a black jacket and covered the daggers strapped to his belt. Valentine waited with him, rubbing her hands against the cold and her nerves. He checked his phone for the fiftieth time.

"They'll do it," she said.

"Wish I had your faith."

Valentine smiled, a full-faced expression that burst from deep inside. She was happier than he'd seen in many months. He took comfort in knowing that, whatever else happened, his family was healing. Malcolm grabbed hold of that feeling of solidity. If they were going to succeed tonight, he would need to be stronger than ever.

The clocked ticked by. He fidgeted, got up to pace the room, sat down again and drummed his fingers on the desk. His cell phone chimed 4:00. Then it was 4:01. Then 4:02.

Nothing happened.

Valentine's shoulders slumped. "I guess I don't blame them. This *is* kind of crazy."

"Kind of?" Malcolm stood and opened the pocket watch.

Valentine joined him in the center of the room. "It's all right. We can do this."

She rested a hand on his forearm to offer support. He paused to quell his anxiety, then swiped across the watch face. "Ready?"

Valentine nodded. He noted she was holding her breath. "Okay. Time to—"

His phone chirped.

Fred: *ready now. come to my billiard room*

THE blue glow winked out, and a chill wind rippled their clothes. Disorientation faded, and the twins stood in a dark wood room between four pool tables.

"S'up, dudes?" Fred and Winter sported dark clothes and ski masks. Fred tossed ski masks to the twins as well.

Malcolm approached and offered his hand. "You came through."

Fred accepted it. "Apparently."

Valentine and Winter hugged in greeting.

"Don't let him fool you," Winter said. "He can't wait to see what's in there, and he's *so* excited to wear his mask."

Fred shook his head. "Always callin' me out. If we're gonna spy, we gotta do it up legit, like ninjas. That's just common sense."

Chuckling, Malcolm turned to Winter. "Did you bring what I asked you to?"

She nodded and patted her jacket.

Valentine surveyed the room and her face fell. "John?"

Winter shook her head and sighed. "Reminds me of when they first found him. He just kept saying, 'I can't.'"

Malcolm couldn't let his sister dwell on John. Moving quickly, he set a wide sheet of paper and his flashlight on one of the pool tables. The others gathered around and examined the markings.

"This is what Val saw. We're guessing it's the third level." He pointed to each area as he described it. "She jumped in next to these panels. Those are computers and work tables on the other end. To the side is a staircase, and these are possibly batteries or generators. Remember, this is not an invasion. We observe, that's all. We've done our job if no one realizes we were there."

"And how are we supposed to do that?" Winter challenged.

Malcolm looked to Valentine, and she stepped up to the paper. "Okay, here's the plan."

BE *strong,* Malcolm told himself. *Be strong for them.* They faced each other in a tight circle, waiting as he worked through the watch menu. Their destination came into focus, and his finger hovered above EXECUTE.

Malcolm took a long, slow breath and examined each of them. He wanted to really see them, and for them to believe he meant this.

"Thank you," he said. "Thanks for doing this."

He cast around inside for something eloquent and meaningful to say, but found nothing. Plain gratitude would have to do, then.

"Okay." Standing straighter, he held the watch in the center of their circle. "Here we go."

He touched EXECUTE.

THE bubble deposited them on the exact spot Valentine had appeared before. They sprang into action, splitting into pairs and slipping to their cover behind the panels.

Malcolm unlocked his phone and tapped out a group text. They had agreed to run silently for the entire mission, not knowing if even a whisper might give them away.

Malcolm: *hold for distraction.*

Reaching into his jacket, he withdrew a tiny RC truck and handheld remote—a childhood remnant that he'd rediscovered during the move. He set the toy on the floor and flicked at the controls. Its rubber wheels pointed left, then right, then crept forward with a mechanical whir. Malcolm nodded, satisfied. If all went to plan, he'd be able to grab the good scientist's attention and lead him downstairs.

Now to gauge where he needed to drive this thing. Heart hammering in his ears, Malcolm peeked around the panel's edge. Computers were *there*, lab tables were *there*, and the scientist was—

Wait a minute.

Malcolm spun back around and tapped out another message.

Malcolm: *no one there. only computers.*

The group glanced at each other, at a loss for what to do. No one had expected this. In fact, they'd assumed one of them would be spotted eventually and planned for it.

Even a mad scientist had to sleep sometime, Malcolm supposed. So, do they wait for their enemy to move? Do they check the lower level to see if they're truly alone? Valentine noticed his hesitation.

Valentine: *already here. keep going. one guards, others search.*

Winter: *that works*
Malcolm: *ok. 5 minute intervals. Fred first watch?*

They tiptoed from their hiding places and approached the far side, where enough equipment was active to bathe the area in soft light. Fred crept to a place halfway between the tables and the staircase. The spot left him in shadows but able to see or hear anyone coming up the stairs and give a warning.

The multitude of cobbled-together equipment reminded Malcolm of Frankenstein's laboratory. He recognized most of the gadgets, but they'd been reworked into technology with uses he could only imagine. Whoever this man was, his knowledge had to be immense.

Valentine moved to the wall and tapped a keyboard attached to a rack of computer servers. A giant screen came to life, and she typed more commands. Winter floated around snapping pictures with her phone.

Malcolm chose a lab table to begin his own search. One side was littered with handheld tools and gadgets—cell phones, tablets, radios—all gutted, rewired, and conjoined with other devices; a silver tube with buttons, dials, and what looked like some kind of emitter on the end; even a few everyday tools like pliers and a soldering gun. Next to the table sat a glass-topped laser cutter on a wheeled stand.

In the center of the table, one small object drew Malcolm's eye—a pair of round, black-framed spectacles. Why would something so ordinary be here?

Pushing aside questions, he snatched up the frames, slid them on and held his breath. Nothing happened. The lenses didn't even change his vision. It was just like looking through a window.

Winter appeared by his side and snapped a photo of the

table. Malcolm flinched at the bright flash, blinking twice in quick succession.

The glasses sprang to life and glowing outlines formed around every object on the table. Malcolm stared in amazement as data scrolled through the air next to each gadget, telling basic descriptions of their uses. He thought about the watch, how it had been activated by a simple touch. Had his blinking activated these?

He focused on the silver tube and blinked twice. The glasses overlaid the device with a grid, which broke into pieces to reveal every component inside. Next to each piece appeared detailed data about origin, core technology and application, and new uses it could be adapted to.

Must be some kind of active database, Malcolm figured, *built to scan and break down technology.* The perfect tool for someone wanting to build things that shouldn't exist yet.

A muffled gasp broke his concentration.

Valentine: *Found it!*

Malcolm reluctantly left the glasses on the table and moved to her side. Winter joined them as Valentine gestured wildly at what she'd uncovered. He leaned closer to read the screen.

His heart skipped a beat. She had been right!

Every scientist keeps a record of their work, Valentine had stated during their planning. *If that's what he is, then we've* got to find it.

A detailed timeline scrolled across the screen with dates, locations, experiments and results, and what could only be described as egomaniacal ravings about his genius and the things he would prove to them. Malcolm gripped his sister's shoulder, mirroring her excitement. This could be the key to everything.

Fred: *5 min done. Next?*

Malcolm indicated for her to keep working and went to take Fred's place. The tall athlete moved to the opposite side of the lab table he had occupied, where an iPad rested with its casing cracked open. Wires sprouted from it to connect with a flat, shiny surface in the middle of the table. Fred picked up the tablet and tapped the screen.

Malcolm leaned against the wall, letting the darkness absorb him. His eyes shifted constantly between his friends and the staircase, and he strained his ears toward the slightest sound. If anyone ambushed them, it would not be on *his* guard.

His stomach flipped at what they were doing. Yet, watching his friends as they worked, he couldn't help but feel proud. The situation had escalated from weird to insane, yet here they were, putting themselves on the line. How many others would do the same?

Fred: *Guys*

Fred looked up from the iPad with a bleak expression.

Fred: *Watch this*

With a tap on his screen, the shiny flat surface on the table lit up. Like a large-scale version of the pocket watch, it emitted particles of light that danced and spun into a moving image.

Eighteen inches above the surface, the lights resolved into words: *Simulation 8, Vent Creation.* Below them appeared a model of Emmett's Bluff and the surrounding landscape. They hovered motionless, like a three-dimensional photograph made of light.

Twelve miniature columns of light burst from the simulated ground. Buildings crumbled, streets imploded, and fires broke out across the city. Smaller particles spun around the columns and were slowly sucked in, just like they had witnessed at the warehouse. In the center of it all, a tiny house lit like a flare.

The beams disappeared, leaving simulated carnage behind. New words floated above the town. *Projected Destruction—19%.* Smaller text scrolled beneath the percentage, detailing elements of damage to buildings, water mains, gas lines, and power.

Winter: *That's exactly what happened*

Malcolm silently agreed. The simulation had guessed perfectly, down to the percentage, what would happen when those beams hit the town. It had called the craters "vents." What was being vented, and why?

Fred: *Wait. More.*

Fred tapped again and the image subtly changed. The town remained damaged, but fire and smoke faded away. The overhead caption broke into glowing particles and resolved into *Simulation 9, Final Jump.*

The house glowed again, growing brighter until it became difficult to look at. Malcolm held up a hand to partially shield his face. Columns of light rushed through the twelve craters, lancing higher into the sky. Again, particles spun around them as more of the town vaporized.

This time, the beams didn't stop. They grew taller and brighter, taking on a life of their own and rushing from the craters in a torrent. They widened more and more, devouring streets and buildings, then entire neighborhoods. In the center of it all, the house with no doors shone like the sun. The simulated ground around it buckled.

A massive wave of light exploded from the house. The wave swept through the town and surrounding country, annihilating everything in its path. When it dispersed, left in its wake was . . . *nothing*. Emmett's Bluff had been razed to the ground. New words appeared.

*Projected Destruction—*100%

Malcolm felt his knees turn to jelly. He pressed a hand against the wall for support. They had finally found the truth, and it was far worse than he'd imagined.

If they failed, Emmett's Bluff and everyone in it would disappear.

CHAPTER 19

Winter: *oh god*
Valentine: *he's going to kill EVERYONE??*

Fred tapped the tablet. The image broke into spinning particles and faded, leaving only dim light. Malcolm silently thanked him for turning it off.

Fred: *that's messed up*

The magnitude overwhelmed Malcolm. They knew the stakes now, and he wished they didn't. Could four high schoolers really handle this? Shouldn't they just—*no*. He squashed on the thought—the stakes didn't matter now, and neither did the odds. There was no going back.

Wind gusted outside and the old house groaned. The sound yanked Malcolm from his thoughts, and he turned back toward the darkened staircase. His guard duty wasn't over, and the longer they stayed, the bigger the risk of—

A tall, dark-eyed man stood two feet from him, yawning and rubbing sleep from one eye. He stopped short and his other eye widened in shock. For an instant, they stared at each other.

The man leaped forward and swung his fist.

"Here!" Malcolm yelled.

He backpedaled as the blow caught him in the shoulder, spinning him into the lab table with shocking force. The table tilted sideways and dumped its contents onto the floor.

The tall man loomed overhead, fist raised. Malcolm lifted his foot to kick out. An iPad soared from the darkness to smack his attacker in the face, and he stumbled back clutching his nose.

Malcolm scrambled away and put the table between them. His friends were at his back now, and he heard them rushing to put their emergency plan into action.

"Hey!" Winter called.

Malcolm heard an electrical sizzling. *Right on cue.* Last minute, he'd asked Winter to bring the stun gun her mother made her carry. Now it hovered precariously close to the large rack of computers.

Valentine grabbed cables that snaked from the rack, wire cutters in hand, and Fred stuffed a length of power conduit into the laser cutter. The man took in the scene and stood his ground, glaring at them.

"You want to keep all this safe." Malcolm held up his hands and backed away. "We just want to leave. So let's trade."

The dark-eyed scientist gave Malcolm a reappraising look. Was that a hint of admiration? It lasted an instant, then split into a malicious smile. A booming laugh exploded from him, and his hands came together.

Malcolm noticed metallic bracers peeking from underneath his long sleeves. Black and bronze with intricate scrollwork, they covered half of each forearm. The man twisted his left bracer and something beeped.

"Spotlights!" he yelled.

Ceiling compartments opened and high-powered LED lamps lowered into the room. A lamp oriented on each of their faces and blazed to life. Malcolm cried out and covered his eyes.

He felt himself shoved to the floor, pain blossoming in his side, and opened one watery eye in time to see their enemy move like the wind. In a blur of motion he kicked Fred square in the chest, smacked Valentine away from the computers, and knocked the stun gun from Winter's hand.

Valentine and Fred hit the floor. The scientist gripped Winter by the throat and shoved her against the computer rack, his face twisted into a snarl.

Their clever plan had been busted in seconds! Malcolm tore the watch from his pocket and opened the cover. This might be their only chance now, but for it to work he had to keep his distance.

Winter kicked and scratched at her assailant's iron grip, to no avail. Panic and tears filled her eyes. Malcolm willed her to hang on—just a few seconds, that's all he needed!

Valentine grabbed a length of thick pipe, charged forward and swung with all her might. The pipe bounced off their foe's back with a clang. The scientist spared her a brief glance and casually smacked her to the floor again.

Malcolm's fear spiked and he forced himself to refocus on the watch. One more adjustment and . . . there! He closed the lid.

BLAM!

Fred regained his feet, pointing a 9mm pistol at the ceiling. What was he doing with a gun?!

"Drop her, fool!"

The man huffed and turned back to Winter. Fred's eyes caught fire. Rushing forward, he poked the gun into his target's back.

"I'll do it! Drop her!"

Malcolm leapt to his feet. "No, don't!"

In a blur, the scientist dropped Winter and spun. One hand grabbed the gun, while the other tossed Fred with bone-shaking force. Flipping the weapon, he pointed it back at Fred and pulled the trigger.

Malcolm's insides and everything around him slowed to a crawl. Holding the jewel outward, he lifted the watch and aimed toward the gun. A cloud of gunpowder slowly billowed from the barrel. Deep inside, Malcolm felt a *shift* as power surged through the watch and a blue-beam sliced through the air. He stared in amazement as it crossed directly in front of the outstretched gun.

The boom of the shot rippled through the room and Fred's expression began to morph into the terror of realization. The bullet exploded from the barrel, collided with the crackling beam, and disappeared in a bubble of warped time and space.

The flow of time returned to normal.

Fred crashed into the laser cutter and fell in a tangle. Valentine scrambled over to help Winter, who had crumpled gasping to the floor.

The scientist ignored them. He turned an accusing glare on Malcolm, and at the device in his hand. Now they had his attention.

"Yeah, you know what this is." He pushed aside his own shock and pointed the jewel at their enemy. "Drop the gun or you'll end up back in the Middle Ages."

He gestured to a stool. Grudgingly, the scientist let the gun clatter to the floor and sat. In the light, Malcolm saw him clearly now—lean and wiry, with tanned skin and close-cropped black hair, he could have come from anywhere.

Malcolm beckoned the group over, wanting them close

to the watch, their one remaining lifeline. Valentine helped a teary-eyed Winter to his side, followed by Fred after he retrieved the gun.

"Middle Ages," their enemy said in a guttural accent. Was it German? "Been zere before. Perhaps ve vill show to you one day, yes?" A malevolent smile crept over his face.

Malcolm's thoughts screeched to a halt. Did he say—

"*We?*" Valentine asked.

The man spat at her. "You vere here before! Still, you learn nothing."

Malcolm barely heard, his mind caught in a whirlwind of hazy memories. The sphere of light. A man cloaked in shadows, with inhuman strength and speed. Clearest of all, he heard the scream of a thousand voices in his head.

YYYOOOUUU WWWIIILLLLLL NNNOOOTTT IIINNNTTTEEERRRFFFEEERRREEE WWWIIITTTHHH UUUSSS.

"Lift your left sleeve and take off the bracer," Malcolm said. The man's eyes narrowed at him. "Do it!"

Slowly, the man complied. Malcolm stared at the exposed forearm, and his heart dropped into his stomach. All this time, he thought he'd been figuring things out. He thought they'd been facing *one* enemy. He couldn't have been more wrong.

"We have to go." Valentine's voice quivered, understanding. "*Now.*"

"What's goin' on?" Fred asked.

"I cut the one I fought, but *he's* not wounded." He shot Fred a significant look. "There's two of them!"

Fred's face whitened. Winter groaned in despair.

"Come on, Mal." Valentine eyed the watch. "We—"

Shadows wrapped around her from behind and flung her through the air. Tumbling head over heels, she smashed into the wall and flopped to the floor.

Malcolm sprinted toward her. Billowing blackness yanked back on his shoulders and kicked his feet out from under him. The room spun as he crashed onto his back.

Shots rang out. Fred shielded Winter with his body and emptied his clip at the swirling blackness, hitting nothing but air. The shadow zigzagged toward him with impossible speed. In one fluid motion, it knocked the gun away and tossed Fred skyward. His body bounced off the ceiling and plummeted to the floor with a sickening thud.

Winter charged forward with the stun gun hissing in her hand. *"Where is Patrick Morgan?"* She swung and the shadow dodged. *"What did you do to him?"* She swung again and it danced to the side. Twisting, she plunged the weapon into the cloud of darkness.

Her arm stopped short, and rage turned to fear. The shadow gripped her arm, bent it back toward her body, and jammed the sparking weapon against her chest.

An inhuman scream exploded from Winter. Her body seized and convulsed, and her teeth clacked together. The shadow let go, and she crumpled like a rag doll to moan on the floor.

As Malcolm tried to rise, the dark-eyed man appeared and punched him in the temple with an iron fist. Stars exploded behind his eyes and he lurched onto his side. The scowling face of his attacker circled above. Light footsteps came close, and the shadowed man appeared.

"*Y Y O O O U U U H H A A A V V V E E
S S S O O O M M M E E E T T H H H I I I N N N G G*

TTTHHHAAATTT BBBEEELLLOOONNNGGGSSS TTTOOO MMMEEE."

Setting his jaw, Malcolm held the watch to his chest and squeezed tighter.

The dark-eyed man laughed. "Zis one shows spirit. And potential."

Potential for what?

The shadow regarded Malcolm. *"NNNOOOTTT EEENNNOOOUUUGGGHHH."*

Bending, it reached out to him. He recoiled from its grasp.

An earsplitting boom shook the house. A rippling wave of force slammed into their captors, hurling them to the floor.

What was that?! Malcolm sat up and searched the darkness. Behind him, the scientist and the shadowed man regained their feet.

"Get back down!" a voice yelled.

He flattened onto his back, and a sound like thunder split the air. Another wave of distortion passed above him and blasted their enemies onto their backs.

Four figures emerged from the darkness, hooded and dressed in black. Three of them carried a bulky heap slung over one shoulder. Malcolm realized with alarm that the heaps were his companions.

The fourth figure plucked him from the floor as if he weighed nothing. Battered and dazed, he found himself slung over a stranger's shoulder and as they rushed toward the center of the room. But were these hooded phantoms friends, or just different enemies?

A commotion sounded behind them and Malcolm lifted his head to see his adversaries rise in a fury. The figure next to him spun, and light flashed between its gloves. Another deafening crack sent a shockwave at the shadowed man and the scientist, and again they staggered.

Malcolm caught sight of the four metallic panels looming closer. Between them was a black abyss—the circular hole that opened down through all three levels of the house. They would need to swing past that to reach the stairs. Only, they weren't swinging past it. They were running toward it!

"No!" he blurted.

The floor fell away and Malcolm's stomach leapt into his throat. Blackness opened up and swallowed them.

STARS twinkled overhead.

After the dizzying plummet into darkness, they had spent what seemed like hours traveling through an earthen tunnel. At an abrupt dead end, they had ascended a long rope ladder and come out of the round crater in a wide clearing surrounded by thick trees.

His sister and friends had shaken awake during the journey. They sprawled next to him now.

"Mal." Valentine clutched at his sleeve.

"You okay?" he whispered.

"I'm alive. You?"

"Same, I guess. They took our masks"

"So much for anonymity."

The hooded figures loomed overhead, staring down at them like silent judges. Backlit by the starry night, their hoods appeared as faceless pits.

"*OONN YYOOUURR FFEEEETT,*" one of them commanded.

The sound vibrated around them like a room full of voices, threatening to dig into Malcolm's mind. Winter and Fred leapt up, their faces contorting with the agony of sudden movement. Malcolm shared an uneasy look with his sister. What power did this voice have over their friends?

The speaker approached the twins. *"OONN. YYOOUURR. FFEEEETT!"*

As beaten and helpless as they were, Malcolm decided defiance was a foolish choice. Valentine seemed to agree, and they helped each other stand. He brushed a hand on his jeans, and relief flooded him as the round shape of the watch pressed through his pocket. Impossibly, he'd managed to keep it.

"HHAANNDDSS IINN TTHHEE AAIIRR. AANNDD TTAAKKEE TTHHOOSSEE SSTTUUPPIIDD MMAASSKKSS OOFFFF."

Winter and Fred complied swiftly, as if eager to please. The twins followed more slowly.

"LLEEFFTT FFOOOOTT IINN TTHHEE AAIIRR."

Winter and Fred's left feet sprang from the ground. Malcolm saw that Valentine's expression was as dubious as his own, but they complied. What was going on here?

"NNOOWW DDAANNCCEE."

Winter and Fred twisted and shook to a rhythm only they could hear. An otherworldly laugh drifted from under the hood.

Malcolm had had enough. Planting his feet, he forced himself to stand taller. Valentine put her hands on her hips and glared at the speaker.

"That's enough horseplay," another dark figure said. Stepping forward, it slid back its hood. "Turn them loose."

Malcolm blinked. "Walter?"

His friend nodded at him. "Kid."

"Well well, *someone* still wants to be the boss," the

interrogator said, only the voice sounded normal now. Miss Marcus pushed back her hood. "Don't you, Buster?"

Valentine gasped and reached for her pendant.

"You gotta be kiddin'!" Fred exclaimed.

A third stepped forward. "They look foolish enough without your help, Blue." Clive pushed back his hood. "Save your tricks for later."

Malcolm gaped. *"What in the—"*

"No bad language, young man. Show some respect." The fourth figure threw back its hood, revealing Oma Grace. "Lord knows you've caused enough trouble already."

Malcolm felt something explode in his mind. All his words fled, and he stood there like stone. At his side, Valentine fainted.

CHAPTER 20

"What did you think you were doing?" Oma Grace glared back at them from the front passenger seat.

"What were *we* doing?" Malcolm retorted. "What were *you* doing?"

Valentine rubbed at her eyes, wishing away the pain. She ached for the comfort of John's presence.

After a brief rest, they'd marched back to Clive's restored military Jeeps at the edge of the forest. She and Malcolm had been shoved into one with Walter and Oma Grace, while Winter and Fred had taken the other with Clive and Miss Marcus.

"In case you missed it, young man, we were saving your lives," Oma Grace snapped back.

"You kids have a real problem with gratitude," Walter said.

Valentine's eyes popped open. "You know what he meant. You came prepared, which means you've known about that place."

"And we weren't alone, obviously. Except *you* ran into danger without the slightest clue what you were doing!" Oma Grace shook her head. "Now look at you."

Valentine glanced at Malcolm. Head bleeding, clothes dirty and torn, and every move came stiff and labored. She knew she must look just as terrible. Her ribs caught fire with every breath, and every thought felt sluggish.

"We thought we were the only ones who knew," Malcolm said. "But you *did* know I was watching that house. If you'd told me the truth, maybe this wouldn't have happened."

"I didn't tell you because you're children."

"Grace," Walter said quietly. "That might not be the best way to reason with them, considering."

"Considering what?" Valentine asked.

Oma Grace ignored her. "I don't care what happened before, Walt. They shouldn't be involved."

"We both know it's too late for that."

They locked eyes, and her glare seemed to soften a little. The corners of her mouth turned down. Was that a hint of guilt?

"Have to admire their guts," Walter continued.

Oma Grace gazed at them, uncertain now. "Close your eyes and rest until we get there."

"Where are we going?" Valentine asked.

"Somewhere safe."

THE Jeep pulled to a stop. Malcolm jolted awake and memories flooded in. What had possessed Fred to bring a gun? What happened after the scientist pulled that trigger? Did time *really* slow down, or did it just feel that way? What about that weird *shift* sensation?

"We're here," Walter said.

Malcolm woke Valentine and followed Walter into the chilled early morning. Next to them, the other four climbed out of their own Jeep. Winter needed Clive's help, and Malcolm felt a rush of sympathy for what she'd endured. He wondered if he'd ever forget that scream.

"Hey." Fred came up beside him. "They tell you what's goin' on?"

"Not yet, but I know this place." He nodded at the wide brick structure. "It's Clive's shop."

Clive led them across the rear grounds to his makeshift clubhouse. Opening the door, he ushered them inside, where a single light burned over the table.

Fixing the four of them with a hard *just-see-if-I'm-kidding* expression, Walter stabbed a finger at the table. "Sit and wait."

Malcolm lacked the strength to argue. Or think, or move. He shuffled over and eased gingerly into a chair. Valentine and their friends followed suit, groaning like old men as they sat. The four adults gathered in a corner and whispered.

"So, what do we do now?" Clive said.

"Perhaps their memories—" Miss Marcus began.

"No," Oma Grace interrupted. "Don't you use that thing on them again."

"You know it'll work."

"We said you could only use it *one* way, Blue," Walter said. "Don't push it."

Clive nodded. "Then they need to know everything."

"They're children. Just order them to go home." Miss Marcus said, and the other three eyed her flatly. She shrugged. "I don't care if it's hypocritical. They're a complication."

"They managed to get inside without help. We underestimated them." Clive grinned. "Ironic, don't you think?"

Winter smacked a hand on the table. "We're right here, you know!"

"What can they do?" Miss Marcus continued. "After tonight, they're in no condition to finish it with us."

Though he'd never say it, Malcolm agreed. They couldn't survive another night like this.

Oma Grace held out her left hand. "So we'll help them."

Another significant look passed among them. Miss Marcus nodded agreement, and each of them held out their left hand. Malcolm watched with intense curiosity. What were they all talking about? Then he saw it.

Each wore an identical ring on their left middle finger.

"Just for tonight," Walter said.

He gripped his ring and twisted, the others following suit. A faint whir-click sounded and the rings expanded, somehow doubling in circumference. They fell loosely into the palms of their owners.

Moving to the table, they took the remaining seats and slid their rings to the center. Malcolm noted that they moved more slowly, sitting heavier in their chairs. For the first time tonight, they looked tired.

Closer examination revealed the rings to be anything but ordinary. To Malcolm's eye, they resembled tech or machinery. Tiny segments of black metal arrayed in a seemingly random pattern, yet they managed to cling together.

"Put these on, please," Oma Grace said. The four of them hesitated. "That means *now*."

Malcolm reached for Walter's ring and the others took one for themselves. The moment it slid onto his finger, the metal segments rearranged and snapped into place in an overlapping pattern, constricting against his finger.

He gasped as a comforting warmth spread from his hand and traveled across his body. The pain numbed, exhaustion faded, and he felt stronger than ever. By his friends' expressions, they were feeling it, too. He sighed and settled back in his chair, relishing the relief.

"Keep them on until tomorrow," Oma Grace instructed. "They will help you heal and make you stronger."

"So that's how you carried us and jumped off a three-story building." Malcolm stared down at the ring. "Where did you—?"

"We know you have questions," Clive said. "We'll get to them soon."

"No," Valentine protested. "I want to know what's going on *now*."

"You need rest first. Afterward—"

"Hey!" Winter snapped. "You have any idea how many times we've almost died?"

Fred crossed his arms in defiance. "I ain't goin' nowhere, I ain't doin' nothin', until I finally know what's happenin' here. Get me?"

Malcolm's head wound stopped bleeding and his thoughts came clearer now. He leaned staunchly forward, showing his agreement. "We're not going anywhere."

The adults drove hard stares back at them, but they held their ground. The time for mysteries was over.

A tense moment passed, and then Walter nodded to Oma Grace. She rested both palms on the table.

"Everything that's happening now—it happened before. The storms, the beams of light." She looked pointedly at Malcolm. "Strange things in the window . . ."

". . . of a house with no doors," he finished in a whisper.

She nodded. "We were about your age. We saw things, but no one would listen to a group of silly kids, so it was up to us. We learned all we could and did our best to fight back."

"Fight back against what?" Malcolm said. "Who are they?"

"And what do they want?" Fred added.

"They're scientists. That tall one with the cruel eyes is Ulrich, and he is merely an underling. The shadowed man—he's the real mind behind everything."

"The shadowed man," Valentine said. "You don't know who he is?"

The adults shook their heads.

Malcolm sighed. "That was going to be my next question."

"His method was more primitive in our time," Walter said. "It only made him blurry, but that was enough to disguise him. That's why we used fake names. Figured if he could hide himself, we should try to do the same."

"As for what they want," Miss Marcus said. "They simply want to get home. Back to their own time, centuries in the future."

Despite their situation, Malcolm felt a swell of satisfaction. "So, we were right. They *did* travel from the future."

"They didn't travel," Clive corrected. "They were banished." Pushing back from the table, he walked toward the back wall. "We only know pieces, but in their time the shadowed man was first to pioneer somethin' he called temporal dynamics." He pressed on an empty spot on the wall and a disguised compartment popped open. "In ordinary man's terms, they studied the flow of time, what made it work and why. Started a whole new branch o' science and then, well, things turned ugly."

"Ugly how?" Winter asked.

Miss Marcus took over. "Seems they got big in the head and decided to try more extreme experiments. We have no clue what they were, but they broke every ethic there is. When they were discovered, they insisted that it was all for good. That they were creating a better world, and moral dilemmas were inevitable. The shadowed man saw himself as heroic."

"Ulrich, however, had no such illusions," Oma Grace continued. "He wiped out an entire police force before they took him down." She stared into the distance, as if remembering something. "He *likes* to hurt."

Clive rejoined them with a worn leather-bound book. "They were captured, but as much as they knew about technology, no prison coulda held 'em. Death penalty'd been abolished by then, so what to do? Then someone got the bright idea—use their own inventions to send 'em back in time. Put 'em so far away that the closest they'd come to technology was the wheel." He slid the book to the center of the table. "That's when he started writing this."

"A journal?" Lunging forward, Valentine snatched the book and flipped through the pages. "I recognize this part from his computer! They were sent back to the Middle Ages first, right?"

Clive nodded. "That's only the beginning."

"No one knew the full extent of their work," Oma Grace said. "Over the years, they implanted themselves with cybernetic devices. Details in the book are vague, but after their banishment, they dug these devices from their flesh and somehow used them to access the time stream and take a small jump forward."

"Since then, they've repeated the process dozens of times," Walter explained. "Jump forward, find better technology, build better machines, and jump farther the next time."

"With a few detours," Clive said. "He's gone anywhere that might have tech he could use. Everything from ancient Egypt to Nazi strongholds in World War II."

Walter nodded. "Using today's machines, though, he's within

range of his own era. One more jump is all he needs to get home. And if he does that, it's all over."

Fred frowned. "But why not just let the fool go?"

"Remember that simulation," Malcolm reminded him. "If he jumps, everything's gone."

"That's what's messed up here." Fred leaned forward. "It don't look like he destroyed the town last time. Why's it happening now?"

"There's some kind of shield around their original time," Walter said. "We don't know how, but it's there."

"Best guess is folks in that time aren't takin' chances," Clive said. "They really don't want these two back."

"But they found a way back anyway," Walter said. "And it takes a city's worth of power to do it. That's why they're stealing energy from the nuclear plant and storing it in batteries. They're going to jump to that shield and punch a hole right through it."

"*That* is why Emmett's Bluff is in danger," Miss Marcus said. "Imagine what it would take to build a shield within time itself. Imagine the destruction if all that energy were released. Where do you think it will go?" She pointed to the floor. "Back through his open portal to *our* time. The shadowed man is convinced it will happen, and therefore so are we."

"They're really willing to do that?" Valentine asked. "Wipe out thirty thousand people just to go home?"

"That's why they're more dangerous than ever," Miss Marcus replied. "They're so close now, it no longer matters who gets hurt."

"Read that book and you'll see," Clive said. "He's convinced himself that the future won't survive without him."

"Vents," Malcolm blurted. Everyone stared at him. "The

simulation called the tunnels *vents*. All that energy that blows back—he's going to channel it away, isn't he?"

Oma Grace nodded. "Just long enough for him to get through the shield. He started with a test, making very small holes. But tonight was about blasting the real vent tunnels in preparation for his jump. Eventually, though, even they won't be enough to contain all that power. Then we'll all be gone."

Silence fell and again Malcolm felt the weight of responsibility. They were responsible for an entire town now? He pressed down on his mounting fear. *No fear,* he repeated. *Fear is a killer.*

"No way," Winter broke the silence. "Sorry to be the skeptic again, but I write for the newspaper. I know town history, and I've never heard of this. Why wouldn't there be records? Why doesn't anyone talk about it?"

The adults bristled.

"Perhaps, young lady, you are not as clever as you think," Miss Marcus lashed out. "For your information, there *was* no newspaper here when it happened."

Winter snorted. "The paper goes back to the thirties. You want us to believe they forgot to mention it?"

"That's enough disrespect, girl." Walter's voice cracked like a whip.

Walter's words washed over Malcolm unheard. A dozen memories clicked together in his head as if they'd been waiting for one unifying question. He fell back in his chair, feeling struck to the core as the question streaked through his mind like a meteor.

"Oma," he said. "How old are you?"

Oma Grace stared at the table, uneasy. Could he have been right?

"Oma," he repeated.

Taking a deep breath, she forced herself to sit up straight and meet his eyes. "I was born July 28, in the year 1905."

CHAPTER 21

Winter fell back in her chair, wide-eyed.

Fred pointed at her and grinned. "You got *told.*"

Despite the heavy mood, everyone chuckled and some of the tension broke. Clive looked at Malcolm and jabbed his thumb toward Walter.

"Told you he's the oldest man in town."

"You're going senile," Walter retorted.

"Dear," Oma Grace caught Winter's eye. "It happened October 7, 1918. No one talks about it because everyone who saw it is long dead. Everyone but us. Okay?"

Winter glanced down at the table, seeming embarrassed, and gave a nod.

"How?" Valentine cut in. "What happened to you?"

Walter cleared his throat. "We had a plan. Well, Albert had a plan and we followed. He always was the smartest."

"Albert?" Fred asked.

Walter studied his hands. "We all grew up together, went to school together. We were the same age. But it wasn't always just four of us. Once, there was another, and he figured out how we might beat them."

"That's why we went in the house that first time," Clive said. "Al figured there'd be plenty o' things we could use against 'em, and he was right. We got away with this book and any li'l gadgets we could grab. Then we used what we stole, plus one we built, and attacked before they could make the jump."

Valentine sat forward. "Wait, you built something? How?"

He hesitated. Walter gave a nod, and Clive reached into his coat. From the inner pocket he withdrew silver spectacles and set them on the table.

Malcolm sat bolt upright. "There's another pair like those in the house, except black!"

"Didn't think I was born a master mechanic, did you?" Clive flashed a mischievous grin.

"The lenses show you holograms," Malcolm explained to his friends. "Put them on and look at tech or machinery, they break it down into components and show you how to use it."

Clive nodded. "They got a massive database. Most of it we ain't even invented parts for. But with some, you can use a little trickery and build something that works."

"So, you could build your own time machine?" Winter asked.

"I said master mechanic, not genius. Or miracle worker." Clive scoffed. "Even with these, I could only make simpler stuff." His expression grew dark. "But that *house*—I looked at it through these once, looked *real* close. There's tiny lenses over the whole thing, and with these I figured out why."

"I've been dying to figure that out," Malcolm said.

"Half of 'em pull in energy—heat, magnetic energy, that kind o' stuff. The other half." He shook his head. "Now, here's where it gets crazy. The other half project a field that plays with your head, makes you wanna stay away and ignore the house." He waved his hands in a circle. "Plays with air an' light somehow so people wanna forget about it."

Malcolm thought back to the beginning, when they only noticed the house after weeks of living across from it. That whole time, they were being manipulated. Anger sparked inside him. He didn't like being controlled.

Valentine fidgeted, then snatched up the glasses and put them on.

"Blink twice," Malcolm told her.

Looking down at her ring, she blinked twice and her eyes went wide. With a gasp she held out her hand, no doubt reading every detail the glasses showed her about the ring. A smile crept onto her face, and she leaned toward Clive with a hungry expression.

"What else do you have?"

Malcolm smiled inwardly. Even in the face of destruction, his sister was a scientist at heart.

"Managed to steal one o' those," Clive said, pointing at her finger. "Built the others after studying it. We call 'em accelerator rings. Kicks up your strength and healing tenfold, but there's a price. You can't wear one for too long or it'll drain you, and you're exhausted after using it a lot."

"That's why you all look so old and tired now," Winter quipped. The adults shot her icy stares. "What? You know it's true."

Oma Grace shuffled in her chair. "I suppose it's my turn now."

She pulled up her right ankle and slid a linked silver anklet into view. Unsnapping it, she set it on the table and gave it a push toward the middle. Malcolm noticed a honeycomb pattern etched into the shiny material.

"Watch and listen."

She snapped once, twice, three times, each time moving her hand closer to the bracelet. Four snaps, then five, then—nothing. She was still snapping, but as her fingers approached the metal, Malcolm heard only silence.

Valentine shook her head and smiled. "We always said you move like a ninja. The glasses say it's some kind of silencing field?"

Oma Grace grinned. "You'd be surprised how it comes in handy."

"You did somethin' to us in the woods." Fred poked an accusing finger at Miss Marcus. "So I know you got one, too."

"Do I, now?" she returned. "Are you certain, boy?"

"Come on, Blue," Clive chided. "They've earned it."

Miss Marcus gave an exaggerated shrug and slid her hand next to Oma Grace's anklet on the table. She rested the hand there for a moment, then drew it away with a satisfied smirk. In its place was a small silver pin.

"The caduceus," Malcolm said. "Thought so."

"Oh, wow," Valentine muttered and touched her temple. "The glasses are going crazy."

"Yes, Old Ironsides, the symbol of Hermes," Miss Marcus announced with dramatic flair. "You've heard how the shadowed man speaks? Voices yelling into your mind, and for some reason you just *have* to obey? This is the same, except less potent."

"And you made us dance with it," Winter said, an edge to her voice.

"After tonight, you deserved to be humbled."

"The glasses call it a time prism," Valentine said. "Whatever that is."

"When you hold the pin, it channels your voice through that prism," Clive explained. "Somehow it slices up your words and broadcasts them through multiple points in time. Somethin' 'bout that breaks through the mind's defenses, makes anyone more likely to obey." He looked pointedly at the twins. "Well, except for you two, which sure is a puzzle."

Malcolm exchanged a glance with his sister. It was true that he'd felt the pin—and the shadowed man—trying to break into his mind. Yet, he'd been able to resist, and apparently so had she. What could that possibly mean?

"Anyway, never built one o' those myself. Too complex."

"So, what did you build?" Malcolm asked. "You said it was part of your plan before."

Walter reached for the book and flipped to the back cover. Resting between the last pages was a folded slip of paper, yellowed with age. Unfolding it, he revealed a hand-drawn schematic resembling an oval blob of metal segments—similar to what comprised the black accelerator rings.

"Albert used the glasses to build this. No idea how he figured it out, but we called it the Spike." Walter stared at the paper as if remembering, then lifted his head. "We couldn't beat them, but we couldn't let them destroy the town. And if we broke their time machine, they'd just rebuild it. So, Albert thought, why not trick them? Make them *think* we're trying to stop them, when really we're forcing them to jump away. So we attacked to force them into action and to distract them so Albert could attach this to their machine."

"Wait, how'd he know where to attach it?" Valentine asked.

Walter flipped pages to another set of diagrams—four curved

panels arrayed around a circular opening. Malcolm's jaw dropped. That *thing* they'd seen was the time machine!

"He studied these," Walter said. "They gather energy and channel it into this opening until it forms a vortex. When there's enough power, it pierces through time and space. Ends up looking like a funnel cloud, or water spinning down a drain. Albert figured out how to intercept that power."

"Smarter than all of us combined," Miss Marcus muttered.

"Why would you want them to jump?" Winter challenged. "I thought that would destroy everything."

"The Spike forced the machine to draw more and more power," Clive explained. "So they had to jump or the machine would overload and vaporize itself. We knew that's where we'd get 'em, because the Spike had a second stage. When the machine created a portal, the Spike was built to release most of that energy. Vent it away."

"By that point, they'd already be in mid-jump," Walter said. "Nothing they'd be able to do about it. Losing power meant they'd fall short of the shield. We thought, let them jump ten or twenty years ahead, and we'll use that time to figure out how to stop them for real. But—"

His voice cracked and he cut off. He tried to speak again but no words came. Malcolm noticed Miss Marcus dabbing at the corners of her eyes.

Oma Grace patted Walter's hand and took over. "They had surprises we hadn't anticipated, and we were losing badly. But Albert . . ." She paused, pulling herself together. "He fought past them and increased the intensity of the Spike. It forced them to retreat and jump through the portal before their machine destroyed itself. He saved our lives. But then . . ."

"Drawing extra power had a price," Clive said slowly. "I

'member the ground shakin'. Size o' the vortex doubled in a blink. Spike got overwhelmed, vented too early, and all that raw power just exploded." He exhaled sharply. "One second, Al's standing next to that machine. The next, he's just . . . gone in a flash o' light. Never got to say goodbye. Never got to thank him."

A tear ran down his cheek. Miss Marcus cried in earnest, covering her face with her hands. Malcolm noticed Walter and Oma had joined hands, offering each other comfort.

All this time, the four of them had seemed like such an enigma, as if they each hid a shameful secret. Now Malcolm knew why—they still carried the guilt and the grief. They held it close, kept it fresh and raw as if it were a penance for their mistakes. His heart reached out to them for all they had sacrificed. If the time came, would he be strong enough to do the same?

Clive wiped the tears away. "It was over. Enemy was gettin' away and our friend was dead. So we ran. Went down through one o' the tunnels, hopin' it'd lead us out before they finished the jump. But then, this wave hit us."

"Because the Spike failed, we knew they jumped more than twenty years," Walter said. "We'd kept them from breaking the shield, but a time disturbance that big still caused an equal reaction *here.*"

Oma Grace spoke up. "Which, we think, is what has kept us young all these years. Instead of perishing from the shockwave of a broken shield, we bathed in the pure energy of Time itself. It touched us, left something behind, and has sustained us for all this time."

Malcolm's mind reeled. "Wow," he managed to say. "That's . . ."

"I know, my boy," Oma Grace said. "I know."

Clive squeezed Miss Marcus's shoulder. "Miranda, tell 'em the next part, will ya?"

She nodded and forced herself to sit up, attempting a regal, authoritative demeanor.

"The next day, children, we made a vow to each other never to abandon this town. To protect the people and deliver justice for Albert." Her eyes turned inward, her expression twisting. "If I couldn't be with him, I would live to avenge him."

"So, we've watched and prepared," Walter finished. "Waiting for the day when the lightning would come again."

With their story told, the adults sat back, faces drawn and shoulders slumped as if they'd run a marathon. It had obviously hurt a great deal to remember.

Winter was the first to break the silence. Her elbows clanged onto the table and she leaned forward. "So, how are we going to do this?"

Malcolm couldn't hide a grin.

Clive tapped on his watch and pursed his lips. "Six in the mornin' now. Feds and the National Guard'll descend on this town any minute. They'll study the tunnels, but they won't get far. Shadowed man's sealed the openings with force fields by now, and they won't think to look for the epicenter until too late."

"So they'll be around but won't be a factor," Walter added. "We'll find a place outside town, dig down and intersect with a tunnel farther underground. From there, we'll get inside and attack."

"With what?" Malcolm asked.

"We built a new Spike based on Albert's design and managed to figure out some improvements. It'll work exactly how we want."

Miss Marcus sighed. "Even with machines, digging will take time. This would be so much easier if we still had the watch."

A jolt raced through Malcolm. He locked eyes with Valentine, who looked as shocked as he felt. Fred and Winter gaped.

"What watch?" Malcolm demanded.

"Albert claimed the most powerful object we stole—an antique pocket watch with unimaginable powers." Miss Marcus shook her head. "During our battle, they took it back. If we still had it, getting into that house would be as easy as, well, you wouldn't believe what it could—"

Standing, Malcolm dug the watch from his pocket and placed it on the table. The adults stared at it in wide-eyed silence, as if looking at a ghost.

"Is that it?" he asked.

Still, they said nothing. Finally, Miss Marcus reached out and grasped the watch with trembling fingertips. The touch was soft, almost tender. Drawing it closer, she clutched it to her heart.

"Oh my god," she whispered. "Albert . . ."

CHAPTER 22

Emmett's Bluff was broken.

The morning sun exposed every detail of the carnage. Valentine stared through the car window and thought about John for the thousandth time, praying that he was okay.

Malcolm's revelation that he'd fought the shadowed man before, and that Walter had been involved, had sent shockwaves through the group. Oma Grace had taken it worse than anyone. A dark cloud hung over her in the front passenger seat, and she shot Walter a series of fiery glares.

Walter stole furtive glances at Oma Grace. "We've got the watch back," he finally said. "That's the important thing."

Oma Grace shifted to face away from him.

Walter's shoulders fell in defeat. "It wasn't my story to tell, Grace. I didn't think he'd understand what was happening anyway."

Valentine's gaze rested on Malcolm, who had fallen asleep with his temple pressed against the frosty window. How close had he come to dying? The thought of losing him pierced her through. What would she do without her other half?

"We'll have words later," Oma Grace said. "In the meantime, this does give us an advantage. A welcome one, since we used up the shockwaves rescuing the children."

That must be what they used in the house. Apparently, they were gloves that generated thunderclaps and force waves, but they only held limited charges before burning out.

Walter nodded. "With the watch, we can slip inside and plant the Spike before we attack. They'll never know until it's finished."

Valentine's face scrunched in confusion. The adults had explained broad strokes of their plan, but she still didn't grasp how *this* Spike was different. Apparently, it was designed to send the time travelers somewhere specific, but no one had said where or when.

She rubbed her temples. Maybe it was just the fatigue, and a few hours' sleep would clear things up. The Jeep turned a corner and flashing lights filled the windshield.

"The Guard's here," Walter said. "They move faster these days."

Soldiers waved flares and directed them through a series of blockades and detours. They must have expected heavier traffic, but hardly a soul stirred. Valentine felt like she was seeing a live news feed from a war-torn country, only this time it was her home. Even knowing they had a plan, it was difficult not to feel bleak.

Malcolm startled awake. "What's going on?"

"National Guard."

Malcolm grunted, then caught sight of something out his window. "Val, look," he said, pointing. "The library was right there. Remember?"

Valentine followed his line of sight a hundred yards to their left. A raised circle of earth—the ring around a crater—sat where the town square had once been.

"Yeah, and the cafe next to it. They made those nice little

sandwiches. Fresh-baked cookies." She swallowed, awash in a sense of loss.

"I'd been planning to go back sometime and never got around to it." Malcolm's head dropped. "Now no one will."

The ground shook beneath them. In the crater's direction, a blue flash arced fifty feet into the air, flinging a military vehicle in its wake.

Valentine recoiled. "What was *that?*"

"Force fields." Oma Grace shook her head. "They never did *that* before. It appears his methods have improved."

"Guard'll never break through that," Walter said. "But if it's something new, maybe we should take a closer look."

"Yes, to avoid any surprises," Oma Grace said, sounding every bit the soldier that Walter did. "You two come along. Knowledge may save your life."

Walter found a gap in the detour barricades and parked the Jeep behind a half-collapsed restaurant. They continued on foot to the raised earth surrounding the crater mouth. As they approached, bustling sounds of activity reached them.

"Stop right before the crest," Walter instructed. "Just high enough to see over it."

Halting at the designated spot, Valentine scanned over the edge. Her jaw dropped at the sea of uniforms around the crater mouth, assembling temporary structures and bank after bank of test instruments.

Where an empty hole once gaped, there was now a curved dome of pulsating energy. On the far side, a twisted heap of metal decorated the hill. She guessed it to be the vehicle they'd witnessed on its maiden flight.

"Two people did this by themselves," Malcolm whispered. "And we're about to challenge them to a duel."

"I'm trying to ignore how crazy it is," she whispered back. "But I wish we had the glasses. Can you imagine what's going on with that force field?"

Malcolm reached into his jacket and handed her the silver frames. "Clive had a feeling you'd want them."

Despite the danger, a thrill raced through her. She accepted the spectacles with reverent care and slid them on. Two blinks later, the lenses came alive, and multiple readouts cascaded across her field of vision. She wondered if some of the military tech was classified.

As the data scrolled, her face fell. "I can't read the force field. It's like the glasses don't even see it."

"The source is likely back at the house," Oma Grace explained. "You wouldn't pick up any details here."

"Oh." She shook her head in frustration. "I still feel like we're missing important details."

"That's war," Walter said. "You make do with what you have."

"Hey." Malcolm pointed toward a center of activity. "Is that who I think it is?"

A tall, gray-haired man in an FBI windbreaker skimmed the edge of the bubble, stopping to examine it every few feet. A line of younger agents and soldiers followed behind and peeled off to carry out his commands.

Mr. Carmichael marched next to him, gesturing vehemently. In his sport jacket, the tiny man looked out of place next to trained operatives. He appeared to be engaged in a passionate speech, and the FBI agent appeared uninterested.

The teacher swung around to face the agent, standing in his path. Valentine couldn't hear the words, but his voice grew more insistent. Mid-sentence, the agent cut him off with a shout and pushed past him. The entourage moved on, leaving him dejected and shaking his head.

"What on earth is he doing here?" Valentine said.

As if he'd heard, Mr. Carmichael's gaze came up in their direction. With renewed enthusiasm, he trotted toward them.

"You survived!" He gathered the twins in an affectionate hug. "I worry for my students, and now two favorites appear unharmed." He pulled back and nodded a greeting to Oma Grace and Walter. "However, I must know why you haven't abandoned this place. We can't know if the danger has passed."

Valentine cleared her throat. "Um, just trying to help out, I guess."

Mr. Carmichael gave a tired smile. "That is admirable. I've been attempting to convince the authorities to evacuate everyone. With an occurrence this strange, is it possible to be too cautious? Apparently, though, I am a teacher and not a 'real scientist' and can therefore be ignored." He cast a resentful glare back at them. "Small-minded fools."

This was the first time Valentine had seen her teacher so discouraged. Angry, even. "At least you're trying."

He nodded gratefully. "And I must continue trying. The dullard in charge here cannot be the final authority. You two I am able to help right now, but only if you promise to leave. Just get in your vehicle and drive and do not return until the danger is gone." He squeezed their shoulders. "Please. For me."

The twins exchanged a glance, and Valentine weighed the possible responses. Agreement may not be honest, but what else could they say?

"We'll try to leave as soon as possible. Promise."

He smiled. "You give me hope, and I will enjoy seeing you in better times." Stepping back, he gave a formal nod to each of them. "Farewell for now, friends."

The teacher turned and headed toward a group of half-standing buildings on the edge of the blast zone. In moments, he disappeared among the maze of alleyways.

"Odd man," Walter observed.

"Super smart, though," Malcolm said.

"Smartest man I know," Valentine agreed. "And he's trying to help, even though he's not from here." With those words, an idea struck her like a bolt. She grabbed Malcolm's arm with urgency and emphasized every word. "He's smart. He's determined. And he wants to help."

Malcolm's expression morphed to match hers. He clutched her arm in return. "He's obviously open-minded and not afraid to stand up to people."

"And we can show him proof about what's happening!"

"What are you two saying?" Oma Grace demanded.

"Oma," Valentine said. "Let's add another ally to our team."

"Absolutely not!" Walter snapped.

"Walter, he's smarter than all of us," Malcolm said. "And we trust him."

"The more people involved, the more chance of our plan going belly-up."

"You would've said that about *us* a week ago," Valentine countered. "And we proved you wrong."

Walter stared her down. "Careful, girl. You managed to stay alive once, but don't forget who's still in charge here."

She bristled. "Well, I don't recall asking you for permission."

He took an aggressive step toward her. "If you think for one second—"

"Walt." Oma Grace rested a hand on his arm. "Listen to them. I don't care for it either, but they've earned some trust. Allow them a decision and things may even work out for the better. Can you do that?"

Valentine hid a triumphant grin as Walter hesitated, then looked away and nodded. Few could stand against Oma Grace, with that earnest tone and pleading expression.

"You saw which way he went?" Malcolm asked.

"Yeah," Valentine pushed Clive's glasses farther up the bridge of her nose. "If I run, I can catch him."

THE connecting alleyways formed more of a maze than she remembered. Valentine slowed to catch her breath. Noise from activity around the crater echoed off the walls, and she strained her ears to catch any footsteps.

Rounding a corner, she stepped into a dead-end passage at the meeting of three buildings. A wooden utility shed sat in one corner of the dead end, while a large metal dumpster occupied the opposite corner. Her teacher stood next to the dumpster. *Found him!* Valentine began to approach, then stopped short.

Mr. Carmichael retrieved a small backpack from behind the dumpster and stripped off his jacket. It went inside the bag, leaving him in a short-sleeved button-up shirt, which he also began to unbutton.

Valentine's eyes fell on his exposed skin and her heart dropped into her stomach. Disbelief shattered her thoughts.

His left forearm was crisscrossed with two angry-looking red cuts—deep, painful, and *recent.* She watched him flex his left hand absently, as if working out the discomfort by habit. She held onto enough sense to duck back behind the corner and peek around at him.

Okay, wait. Coincidence. You didn't even see what Mal did to the shadowed man. He just described cutting something like an arm. You're getting paranoid.

She chided herself for overreacting. This was Mr. Carmichael, not a time-traveling super villain. Shaking her head at her own foolishness, Valentine rounded the corner again. At that moment, he finished unbuttoning his shirt and let it fall open.

Clive's glasses went crazy.

Readings cluttered her field of vision. Glowing grids appeared over a six-inch, rectangular metal plate strapped to Mr. Carmichael's chest. The image magnified and broke into pieces, revealing a myriad of buttons and the functions assigned to each. She recognized some of them.

Hop.

Skip.

Power.

Speed.

Lightning.

Silence.

Valentine's thoughts screeched to a halt at the last function. *Shadow.*

She leaned against the wall, praying for it to hold her up. *It can't be. This CAN'T be happening.* But in her aching heart, she knew.

Mr. Carmichael was the shadowed man.

CHAPTER 23

How could I have been so wrong? Valentine shuffled, swimming in a haze of confusion.

Loose gravel crunched under her feet and Mr. Carmichael whipped around. In her shaken state, Valentine had stopped in full view of the teacher. She snapped to attention and their eyes locked. For a tense moment they stared in silence, each seeing that the other knew the truth.

"You . . ." she began. Fiery anger and hurt and betrayal distilled into one echoing thought.

STOP HIM.

Then she was sprinting, not *away* like her instincts screamed, but *toward* him. With the accelerator ring on, her muscles pumped harder and she ran faster than should have been possible. Valentine plowed into the small man and drove him back against the dumpster with a clang. She clutched his collar in her fists.

"Why?" she shouted, slamming him against the dumpster again. "WHY?"

Scorching emotion pushed her forward. The metal at his back bowed from the force. *Don't,* a voice inside whispered. *Don't kill him.*

He wants to destroy us all!

Don't do it.

Desperation gripped Valentine like a vise. Here was the man trying to destroy her home, her family and friends. She had a chance to finish this. *It's up to me.*

She gripped his throat and began to squeeze. "Not going to let you . . . not going to . . ." She whispered in a frenzy, her thoughts a whirlwind, not sure if she spoke to him or herself. "Can't let you. Can't—"

She was falling apart inside, and she knew it. Everything felt jumbled and broken. She tried to make herself squeeze harder, struggled to *want* to kill him. Tears flooded her eyes and she choked them back with fury, willing herself to harden, to do what was necessary.

I can't do it.

She couldn't save them this way. She wasn't like him. Her determination ebbed and she searched his eyes for something to bolster her resolve. To push her to the edge.

Mr. Carmichael's eyes drooped with grief, the corners of his mouth turned down. Gently, he grasped both of her wrists and pulled them away. Somewhere in her mind, Valentine realized the device on his chest made him *much* stronger than her ring. He didn't attack—only held her at bay.

"I'm so sorry, Valentine. I don't want to hurt you, or anyone." He shook his head. "I just want to go home."

His words quenched her rage, leaving confusion in its wake. She had expected venom and violence, anything but this. Was it real?

"My people, my time—they need me," he said. "They're naked without me, without my guidance. Please try to understand, I only want to save them!"

She hesitated. *What would Malcolm do now?* From behind, she heard an outcry and a loud whooshing sound, like a fire flaring up from too much gasoline. The ground trembled.

"They'll never get through my shield." The teacher leaned closer. "Run, Valentine. Leave this place and *live.* I cannot bear to think of this world losing you."

"Then call this off!" she pleaded. "Find another way. Or stay. Stay here and make a life. Help us!"

"I wish it were that simple." Mr. Carmichael stared at the ground and sighed. "But . . . *shadow.*"

Valentine blinked. A razor-sharp edge replaced the sadness in his eyes, the chest plate beeped, and her glasses confirmed that a function had been activated. Then she understood.

"The fact is," his voice altered as blackness slid from dark corners and flowed around his body, "this town died long ago. *TTTHHHEEEYYY JJJUUUSSSTTT DDDOOONNN'TTT KKKNNNOOOWWW IIITTT YYYEEETTT.*"

The storm of shadow enveloped him. He moved away from the dumpster, pushing against her with ease. Valentine's heels dug into the pavement as she struggled to hold him back.

Her arms disappeared into the darkness. She tried not to be unnerved by the ice cold shadows touching her skin. *He's just a man. Just a man with fancy toys—flesh and blood.* She focused on his treachery, gritted her teeth, and shoved harder.

Staring into the shadows with defiance, she looked where his face should be. "We are going to stop you."

"*TTTHHHEEERRREEE IIISSS BBBRRRIIILLLLLLIIIAAANNNCCCEEE IIINNN YYYOOOUUU, VVVAAALLLEEENNNTTTIIINNNEEE,*" the voices shouted. "*BBBUUUTTT TTTHHHAAATTT'SSS*

NNNOOOTTT GGGOOOIIINNNGGG TTTOOO SSSAAAVVVEEE YYYOOOUUU."

Valentine felt herself lifted off the ground by her arms. Then she was flying. Head over heels, she tumbled across the alley and crashed through the utility shed. The front wall splintered, and she rolled to the floor in a heap.

Grateful for the ring's power, she ignored the pain and sprang to her feet. Dizziness lingered and lights flashed behind her eyes. Still, she kept her fists up and stumbled out of the hole.

Lucius Carmichael was gone.

Her brow knit. He'd had her beaten but chose to leave. How much of what he said was true? How much had been meant to manipulate her? *So many questions.* Through the jumble, however, two thoughts rang out like a bell.

First, we can't go home. His identity is compromised. Who knows what he might do to protect it? Everyone in the group, all our families—we have to get somewhere safe where we can plan.

She knew the perfect spot. Gathering herself, Valentine charged out of the alley and aimed toward her family.

Second, the plan has to happen TODAY. We've run out of time.

CHAPTER 24

"Dad's okay. He's helping around town." Valentine flipped her phone closed. "He thought we were still home in bed. I wish I could've told him to leave town." She frowned and flipped the phone open again.

"He'd never go without us." Oma Grace turned to Malcolm. "Right, young man?"

Malcolm snapped to attention. Planted on Fred's enormous couch, he'd been trying to absorb the news that his chemistry teacher was actually a time-traveling super villain. Of all the high school problems they warn you about, this was *not* on the list.

"Uh, yeah. If we stay, he'll stay."

Oma Grace turned to Winter and Fred. "And what of your families?"

"Out of town seeing a cousin," Winter replied.

"Dad's gone on business a lot." Fred sank onto the couch next to Malcolm.

Until now, Winter and Fred had busied themselves with closing the blinds on every window and door. They had hours to hide and wait since the attack wouldn't happen until the cover of night.

Malcolm knew in his gut that it wasn't enough time. "What's next?"

"We finish the plan and get ourselves ready." Clive descended the curved staircase, clutching long rolls of paper.

Walter followed behind him with a military duffle bag. "And we've got to move fast."

Lucius. Malcolm refused to think of him as *Mr. Carmichael* anymore. He wasn't their teacher—he was a murderer, and he'd attacked Valentine. Well, technically she'd attacked him, but that was beside the point. He was the enemy now.

"Where's the best place to lay all this out?" Clive asked.

"Billiard room, that way." Fred pointed to one of the long hallways.

Malcolm recognized it as the hall that led to the kitchen, sitting rooms, and game rooms. Strange, Fred's party seemed like so long ago. Had it really only been a few months? He peered at his sister, but her back was turned as she murmured into her phone.

"Your family's back home?" Oma Grace called after Clive.

"Safe and sound two counties over."

Walter paused at the hallway and shot her a questioning look. "Miranda?"

"I called her an hour ago." She frowned. "Can't imagine what's keeping her."

Walter shrugged and followed Clive down the hallway.

"What about *his* family?" Winter asked. "Are they safe?"

Oma Grace gave her a soft smile. "That remains to be seen, dear. We *are* his family. Or, as near to family as he's got."

Valentine turned back to them with a frustrated huff. She stuffed the phone into her front pocket and pulled Clive's spectacles from her jacket. The frames had bent from her impact with the shed. She pried gently at the bridge, seeming desperate to do something with her hands.

"Still no answer?" Malcolm asked.

She shook her head. "I feel like I've left twenty messages. Where could he be?"

They'd driven by John's house, but found it locked and dark. Since then, Valentine had been edgier than ever. Malcolm had no answers, so he searched for something to change the subject.

"So, why Fred's house? Not that I mind," he added quickly with a glance at Fred. "But you said it was the perfect spot."

"Yeah. Well . . ." Valentine shifted, eyeing Fred with embarrassment.

Fred grinned. "Bet I know why. Wanna hear?"

She relaxed and smiled with gratitude.

"Carmichael don't think a lot of me. Val's the favorite, but he thinks I'm grade-A useless. So, no way could I bring anything to the group, right? It's the last place he'd look." He raised eyebrows at Valentine. "That about right?"

"Yeah. Sorry, Fred, I'm just trying to think like him."

He waved away her apology. "Don't sweat it, girl. It's a good idea."

Malcolm's eyes drifted between his companions. On the surface, everyone had dealt stoically with Lucius's true identity. They had a job to do, and they would put their lives on the line without hesitation.

However, as quiet fell and they settled into their own thoughts, subtle emotions played across their faces. The shock of betrayal. The weight of knowing that time had run out. The possibility that this night would be their last.

He couldn't help feeling responsible. Logically, any pain or loss was worth saving thirty thousand people. Still, when it came down to it, they were all here because he'd been unable to ignore an abandoned house across the street.

Whatever happened tonight would be unpleasant. In the years to come, would they be able to leave all this behind? Could they have normal lives?

Walter rounded into view and caught his eye. "We could use you now."

Malcolm nodded and stood. Valentine startled to attention and moved to join him. "No, it's okay." He gave her a gentle downward push. "Rest. You can check it out later."

With a weary and grateful smile, she snuggled back against the cushions.

"I'll give them a little more time," Oma Grace said. "Then we'll fix breakfast."

Oh, that's right. Food. Malcolm couldn't remember the last time he'd eaten. Ignoring the hollow sensation in his stomach, he slipped the spectacles from Valentine's grasp and followed Walter.

In the billiard room, two of the four pool tables hid under a sea of diagrams and scribbled notes. Malcolm noticed hand-drawn renderings of Lucius's house and various gadgets, and page after page of battle plans. Curtains were drawn across the French doors leading out to a side patio, and only a small overhead lamp illuminated the tables. It reminded Malcolm of a darkened war room in some movie.

At the far table, Clive pored over Lucius's journal and jotted notes on a drawing of the house. "How are they?"

"Shell shocked," Walter replied. He moved to stand over Clive.

"Figured as much. Go on, Mal, have a look around. Just finishin' some thoughts, then we can talk."

Malcolm wandered to the nearer table. The Spike sat on one corner, a shapeless jumble of metal. When placed in Lucius's machine, though, it would rearrange itself into the proper form. The faded paper bearing Albert's original design rested nearby, next to renderings of this new device.

"Walter, I've been thinking." Malcolm bent to examine the drawings. "The war you fought in, all those medals. It wasn't Vietnam, was it?"

From the corner of his eye, both men stiffened.

"No," Walter said. "I fought in World War II."

"And if people knew, they might wonder why you look so young. Might start asking questions. Right?"

"Something like that."

Even to his untrained eye, the two Spikes looked different. Yet, he was still unsure what exactly *made* them different. *Can't afford to have questions at this stage. I need to understand.*

With a flick of his wrist, he opened the spectacles and pushed them on as best he could. After two blinks, a three-dimensional outline of the Spike split into pieces and lines of technical data scrolled across his vision.

"Look, Malcolm," Walter said. "I'm sorry for lying to you."

He waved it away. "You didn't really know me. I'd do the same in your—" A piece of data caught his eye, and he leaned closer. "Wait a minute. What is *this?*"

He met guarded expressions from the two older men.

"You said this Spike would send them somewhere specific, not just cut their jump short." His eyes narrowed at them. "I kept asking, but you never said *where* or *when*."

"Maybe you should stop pokin' at that, son," Clive said. The lines around his eyes tightened.

"No." Malcolm's body tensed. "I know what I just saw, and

I want to hear it from your own mouths. *Where are you sending Lucius and Ulrich?*"

The men exchanged a long, hard look. It seemed like an entire conversation happened in those few seconds. Then Clive shook his head and stared down at his notes with resignation. Walter turned that steel-gray stare on Malcolm.

"We're sending them straight to the gates of Hell."

Malcolm felt as if he'd been punched. The original Spike had been designed to vent the time machine's energy and interrupt Lucius's jump. This new Spike *appeared* to have the same purpose. Except instead of venting the energy, it would force the machine to keep drawing more and more power until it exploded. When that happened, nothing near the house would survive.

This Spike would turn the time machine into a time *bomb*. The adults weren't just planning to defeat Lucius and Ulrich.

They were planning to kill them.

"OKAY, everyone." Oma Grace stood. "The others are hard at work, and now it's our turn."

Valentine forced her leaden eyelids open. With a yawn and a stretch, she dragged herself from the sofa.

"Come on, sleepyheads! We're on breakfast detail." Oma Grace grabbed Winter's arm and pulled her up with twinkling eyes.

Valentine marveled at her grandmother. *How is she doing this while we're dragging?* Her smile seemed brighter and more eager. She moved with purpose and strength, as if she were waking up from a long sleep. Like all this time she'd been waiting for the chance to set things right. *She almost looks young again.*

Winter rubbed her eyes. "What're we making?"

"We took what we could from Clive's kitchen." Oma Grace led them toward the staircase. "The bags are in the car."

Fred stumbled to the steps behind them. "You know I got a huge kitchen, right?"

"Yes, my boy. We'll combine our supplies and make a meal to remember. One should never battle evil on an empty stomach."

Valentine's stomach rumbled. *When's the last time I ate?* She hadn't the faintest idea, and her mouth watered at the prospect of a hot meal.

"What on earth are you *thinking?*"

Walter's eyes narrowed. "Careful, Mal."

"Careful about what? Making you angry? This is our fight, too, and you're keeping this a secret!"

"Ain't like we can wait around for 'nother try, son," Clive defended. "We can't risk that they'll get by us again."

"Well, if you're so eager to kill," Malcolm asked Walter, "why not just shoot him when you found us behind the house?"

"I wasn't about to blow a man's head off in front of a teenage boy," Walter snapped. "And there would have been a body. People would have asked questions. Then we'd still have Ulrich to worry about. So I waited. I stuck to the plan so we could accomplish everything in one move. No witnesses, no questions, no enemies."

"And you decided to just keep lying to us. Why?"

"'Cause o' this," Clive indicated Malcolm's whole body. "'Cause we knew how you'd feel. And 'cause it ain't your burden. We gotta finish what we started."

"Yeah," Malcolm said bitterly. "And you had no problem letting us help you do it." His accusing glare switched to Walter. "I trusted you!"

"You're too young to understand."

"To understand what?"

"To understand that war is a terrible choice, but sometimes it's the *only* one. After all these years, everything I've seen, I'm ready to accept the burden if it saves lives." Walter's fists clenched. "And I refuse to let the past repeat itself."

Malcolm crossed his arms. "And what would Albert say about this? Do you think he would approve?"

Walter's eyes burned like hot coals. In a blink he crossed the room and stood inches from Malcolm's face. His arms flexed as if he struggled to keep them at his sides.

Malcolm's blood raced, pulse pounding in his ears. He stood his ground, barely resisting the urge to jump back. *He could probably kill me with a finger.*

Stifling tension hung thick in the space between them. The silence stretched on as Malcolm struggled to keep his fear controlled, his breathing slow and even. *Be strong. Don't show him you're afraid.*

Then Walter's face fell. He stared at the floor, anger crumbling away like a shell he could no longer hold together. His shoulders slumped and his mouth turned down in a grimace.

"Albert was the best man I ever knew. Better than I'll ever be. We all lost something when we lost him." His voice came out thick as he battled to hold back tears. "But I couldn't save him. He was my best friend, and I miss him . . . *every day.*" He regarded Malcolm with eyes full of sorrow. "And you remind me of him."

Peering up at Walter, Malcolm realized he was seeing a side that few people ever witnessed. The vulnerable, human side that he kept hidden away. It turned out that underneath all the grit and steel, Walter Crane was just a man who missed his friend.

Turning his back to Malcolm, Walter slumped against the table and stared down at the Spike. "If he were here, he'd have found another way. When we were planning, he'd always remind us, 'We are constant as the northern star.' That no matter what happened, we should never lose who we are." He scraped a forearm across his eyes. "But I can't find another way."

Malcolm's heart battled with itself. There should be a better way. But was there, or had they run out of options? He rubbed his eyes, feeling more lost than ever.

"I . . . I've got to think this over." He moved toward the open doorway.

"Perhaps I can help you decide," a new voice said.

Malcolm's head whipped toward the far side of the room, where a dark blur detached from the shadows and charged toward him. Eyes wide, he raised his arms to defend himself. Then he was hurtling backward.

They found—!

Wood paneling splintered as he crunched against the wall. Air crushed from his lungs and light exploded behind his eyes. He dropped hard to the floor.

Footsteps approached him.

CHAPTER 25

"Ain't cooked a day in my life," Fred protested.

"Well, young man, this is the perfect day to start." Oma Grace gave him a lighthearted shove. "Scoot."

Valentine stood next to her grandmother as Fred approached the front door with his key. As always, Winter stayed by his side.

"Oh yeah, *perfect* day," Winter said. "Right when we're about to—"

The front door caved in, exploding into wooden shards. Valentine screeched and shielded her face from flying debris.

"What in the—?" Fred cut short with a choking sound.

Valentine brought her arms down and fear knifed into her chest. Ulrich stood in the doorway, clutching her friends by their throats, his bracers gleaming in the morning light. Dripping with disdain, he regarded them as if they were fleas.

"Idiots," he spat. "Not vorth my time."

With a casual flick, he flung them through the doorway. They skipped across the gravel driveway and spun out of sight.

"You, though," he said to Valentine and Oma Grace. "I *am* here for."

How did he find us?! Valentine ran a thumb across her

accelerator ring as Ulrich drew closer, praying that it would help her survive the next few moments. Gathering her courage, she rushed forward.

Oma Grace jumped in front of her.

"Oma, no!"

Ulrich pointed at her. "Zat vas you, years ago. Yes?" He flashed a predatory grin. "I remember."

"Run, girl. Warn your brother," Oma Grace said over her shoulder. Her eyes lit with anticipation. "I've been waiting for this."

Pushing Valentine toward the stairs, she stalked forward and brought up her fists. Ulrich moved to meet her, while Valentine stood rooted to the floor. *Should I help? Should I go?* Everything was happening too fast! *What do I do?* Then another thought flooded her with horror. *She doesn't have her ring!*

Oma Grace and Ulrich collided, raining blows on each other. Valentine cringed at the hollow thump of fists on flesh and bone. She reached out instinctively, desperate to do *something*.

Oma Grace bloodied Ulrich's nose and knocked the wind from him with a rabbit punch to the solar plexus. She withstood two blows to the jaw and swung forward with abandon, driven by decades of grief and anger. Ulrich countered with a haymaker, knocking her to the side. By the time she recovered, he was on her. One blow to the eye, one to the stomach, a vicious overhead chop to the collarbone, and Oma Grace crumpled to the tiles in a heap.

Valentine cried out and lurched toward her. Ulrich blocked her path, clutching his nose and drilling a murderous glare at her. Crashes echoed from the direction of the billiard room, and she remembered Malcolm and the others with alarm.

"Oh, yes. *He* is here, too. None of you vill last ze day."

"So, you'll just kill us now? Why didn't your boss start with me in that alley?"

"You vere all crucial to his plan. Now you are together and ve can move forward." He grinned again. "And he orders me, no kill. Only *cripple*."

We're crucial to his plan? What does that mean? Valentine pushed the questions away and steeled herself. "So I'm next, right?"

She brought her fists up, heart threatening to pound through her ribs. *Okay. This had to happen sooner or later. Make it count, Val.*

He advanced on her, then a blur of motion exploded from behind him.

Ulrich's feet flew out from under him, and his shoulders yanked backward. He smacked onto the tile with a sickening plop. Wrapping her legs around Ulrich's knees, Winter yanked his foot until the ankle twisted at an unnatural angle. He gasped and cringed.

From behind Ulrich's back, Fred put a scissor hold around his arms, pinning them helplessly to his sides. His feet crossed over Ulrich's chest and dug into his rib cage. Fred swung wildly with both fists, bringing them down on Ulrich's face and punctuating each strike with a shout.

"Don't—you—touch—my—FRIENDS!" Chunks of his casts broke away under the assault. He didn't notice. Breathing hard, he looked up at Valentine with frenzied eyes.

She stepped back involuntarily, stunned by their ferocity. Her mind could barely process the sight of Winter and Fred intertwined with their enemy like a pretzel.

"Focus, Val," Winter commanded. "We heard what he said. Go help Mal."

Valentine hesitated.

"Go, girl!" Fred insisted. "We got this."

With effort, she seized control of herself again. The terror began to fade, and she felt purpose replace her confusion. *They're right. I'm the only one who's fought Lucius. They'll need me.*

Nodding gratitude to her friends, she charged down the stairs.

MALCOLM came to his knees, rattling his head as a mass of darkness approached. Steps away, the darkness receded and Lucius stared down at him with an eager glow.

"Hello, Malcolm."

The light switched off, plunging the room into darkness, and something whistled through the air above Malcolm's head. Wood splintered and Lucius grunted in surprise.

"*Now* it's even," Walter declared.

By the faint light spilling in from the hallway, Malcolm barely made out three figures locked in battle. A storm of fists and feet struck out with fury.

"Enough!" Lucius shouted. His dim outline exploded into motion.

Something cracked and Clive cried out, followed by a crash. Walter's body jerked and spasmed under a flurry of blows, then lifted high into the air. He came down with an ear-splitting boom.

The fight had lasted a matter of seconds.

Light flooded the room. Clive sprawled on the carpet,

clutching his left arm. The nearest pool table had buckled in the middle and folded in on itself. Walter lay dazed at the center of the crack, as if he'd been used as a battering ram.

Lucius stood by the wall switch, his lip split and bloody. He glared venom at Walter.

"See, now, that's one thing you never understood, *Buster,*" he spat. "We'll *never* be even." He held up a hand, and Malcolm realized with a start that he clutched the Spike. "Still trying the same old tricks?"

Shaking his head in mock dismay, Lucius crunched the Spike in his iron fist, reducing it to a tangled mass of useless metal. Malcolm's heart sank—it was an evil thing, but it had been their only chance. *It's over. We just lost.*

Lucius flung the broken device toward Walter's prone form. Flaring with anger, Malcolm leaped to his feet and smacked it away, placing himself between Lucius and Walter.

"No!" he said, pointing at Lucius. "You don't get to—"

Lucius closed the distance. A fist connected with Malcolm's jaw, snapping his head to the side, and another blow sank into his stomach. Disoriented, Malcolm stared at his enemy in shock as a wave of nausea assaulted him. Lucius kicked his feet to the side and he tumbled limply to the floor.

"H-how did you . . . ?"

"You're in a dark room with a door to the outside, hiding from a master of shadow and silence? Perhaps you truly *are* a simpleton. As for how I found you, that will be clear soon enough. In the meantime," he knelt beside Malcolm. "You have something that belongs to me."

With a flick of his wrist, Lucius ripped open Malcolm's front pocket to reveal the pocket watch. Malcolm snatched at in desperation. *No no no no!* Lucius smacked his face, sending stars across his vision, and stood with the prize in his hand.

Malcolm lurched to his knees and reached out for the watch as Lucius backed away, examining it with affection.

"Thank you for guarding this for me," he said with a hint of irony. "However, the time has come—"

A pair of hands latched onto Lucius's shoulders from behind, and then he was flying. Like a rag doll, he tumbled across the hall and through a doorway, skidding into the sitting room until he crashed into a coffee table. He came to rest in a heap.

Valentine stood in his place, red hair flying. "You okay?"

Malcolm nodded, unsure what to say.

"He's mine!" she growled, and sprinted toward their adversary.

Malcolm could only stare after her.

HE'S stronger. He's faster. He's smarter. Attack and don't stop, keep him on the defensive!

Already he'd untangled from the table and risen. Valentine charged forward and leaped into a front handspring. Her pointed toes drilled Lucius in the chest, and he stumbled back a step.

She leaped again and swung fast, smashing his eye, then crunching against his nose. Drawing back again, she struck toward his throat.

He smacked her fist to the side and lashed out with an uppercut to the stomach. Thunder exploded through her body as she lifted off the floor.

Vengeance fueling her, Valentine cracked her fist against Lucius's temple, feigned a left hook and brought a knee into his gut. As he bent forward with a gasp, she drove her forehead into his nose.

Lucius fell backward and snapped a spin kick against her neck. Rolling with the strike, she tumbled to the floor and cartwheeled to her feet again. The entire side of her head throbbed, and she forced air into her tired lungs. *Keep going keep going!*

Snatching up a marble figurine, she flung it toward Lucius and dashed in behind the makeshift projectile. While he dodged to the side, her fist came around and bashed into his ribcage. Her wrist and knuckles went numb like she'd punched a brick wall.

He struck like a cobra, catching her twice between the eyes. Valentine's head snapped back, and her vision quaked. She stumbled back and threw a desperate kick. Smacking it to the side, Lucius pressed forward and boxed her ears. Flashes of light and pain burst in her head.

Planting her feet, she swung hard through the disorientation, fists hitting nothing but air. Lucius twitched and the force of a mountain crushed against her chest. A kick caught the side of her leg, and she fell hard to one knee. Another shot blasted her temple, and she crumpled to her hands and knees.

Dark edges crept into her vision. *Don't stop! Don't go down!* Valentine lurched to her feet and lashed out wildly. *Please, let me just . . .*

Impossibly strong hands wrapped around her from behind. Her arms were pinned to their sides, and she felt Lucius's breath on her neck.

"It doesn't have to happen like this," he said through heavy breaths.

Her vision cleared, and she realized with despair that the pocket watch was in his hand. The air chilled, and a blue energy bubble enveloped them. She struggled against his iron grip.

"There's another way!" he insisted, holding her fast. "Just for you."

"What are you talking about?"

"My admiration for you was never false. You are so rare a talent, Valentine, that I have altered my plan to include you. Simply help me succeed here, and I will bring you to my time as my student."

Valentine snorted and kicked his shin.

Lucius gripped her tighter. "There are wonders there, such that you could never imagine them. However, if that is not to your liking, I have another bargain."

Outside the bubble, Fred's living room disappeared and scene after scene went flashing by. She wasn't sure how she knew, but the sensation of a *shift* told her somehow—they were moving backward in time.

"Here we are," Lucius whispered.

They stopped in a small room with two cribs, golden light and gentle breezes pouring in from an open window. A pale woman danced and laughed along with the babies she clutched to each hip. Her yellow sundress twirled out from her lithe form as she spun on pointed toes. Long red hair floated around her bright, sparkling eyes.

Valentine's heart seized. "Mom?"

CHAPTER 26

Fred gritted his teeth and squeezed harder while Winter wrenched Ulrich's ankle. He twisted and bucked, his superior strength battling against their leverage.

"Tell me where Patrick Morgan is!" Winter snapped. "Tell me or I'll break your foot off!"

"You are *nothing!*"

"Look who's talkin', dude." Fred punched his head. "You're a *sidekick.*"

"Dark-age scum!"

Ulrich threw his head back, cracking Fred in the nose. A wave of disorientation washed over him. His injured forearms screamed and his limbs went slack. Reaching over his shoulders, Ulrich grabbed Fred and flung him upward with titanic force.

The floor sank away and he collided with the wall—no, he realized, with the *ceiling.* Fred crashed through layers of wood and plaster and broke into the level above the foyer. Cartwheeling, he smacked down next to the new hole in the floor.

He threw me into Dad's gym!

Fred's father had built this floor as a gymnasium that stretched the length and breadth of the house. Shuttered floor-to-ceiling windows looked out on the backyard, while the other walls were covered in mirrors.

Shaking the static from his brain, Fred rose wearily to his feet. *She's gonna need me down there.*

"Oh, *wrong* move, future-boy!" Winter shouted.

An instant later, Ulrich blasted through the floor and cart-wheeled to a stop in the middle of the gym, face-down.

"Whoa!" Fred peered through the floor as Winter brushed the dust from her shirt. Her left eye swelled and a trickle of blood spilled from her ear. A groan and a shuffle sounded from the middle of the room, and Fred saw that Ulrich was recovering.

"Ain't got much time," he said to Winter.

She nodded grimly, and he knew she'd caught his meaning. *No time to run to the stairs.* Centering herself beneath the hole, she crouched and raised her arms.

"You better catch me."

Fred sprawled onto his stomach and stretched out his arms. "Go!"

With a shout, Winter leaped and accelerator ring–fueled legs propelled her high. Her hands latched onto his, sending hot pain through his arms. Cringing, Fred pulled her up and they stood panting beside the hole.

Ulrich rose to his hands and knees and spat drywall from his mouth. Winter eyed him, and Fred knew they shared the same desperate thought. *How do we survive this?*

"We can do this," he whispered. "We just gotta—"

"Cheat?"

Fred raised an eyebrow. With a glint in her eye, Winter nodded toward a rack of disc-shaped iron weights—at least thirty of them, in multiple sizes and weights. Fred's face split into a wicked grin. *That's why you're my oldest friend, girl.*

They dashed to the rack and Fred snatched up a forty-five pound disc. With the ring on, it felt like lifting a coffee mug.

Winter grabbed its companion and flashed her own grin. "You like frisbee, right?"

Ulrich regained his feet and stalked toward them as if unencumbered by pain or exhaustion.

They let loose simultaneously. The weights sliced through the air like ninja stars and clanged against their enemy. Winter's swiped his thigh and Fred's caught him full-force in the chest. Ulrich stumbled back, clutching his ribs.

"Again!" Winter shouted.

They loosed another volley of forty-fives and Ulrich dove to the side, barely dodging the iron missiles. Twisting, Fred picked up another weight with the opposite hand and loosed it.

Winter mirrored his movement, and they forced Ulrich to retreat from the constant hail of iron. Fred's next shot thwacked against his shoulder, Winter's clipped his knee, and he stumbled to the floor again.

Fred hurled a twenty-pounder that sailed past Ulrich and crunched against a set of shutters. Wooden slats broke away and a wide crack spread across the thick glass. Winter's ten-pounder connected with Ulrich's forehead. He clutched at the wound with a frustrated growl.

"Keep goin', we got him!" Fred reached back, but grabbed nothing but air. The rack was empty! He felt a sinking dread. *We tossed 'em all and just barely put this dude down. What now?*

A whirring sound interrupted his thoughts. Rising again, Ulrich tore his sleeves away to reveal the bracers that lent him his power. The rear half of each bracer began to spin around his arms.

Winter gasped as the room grew colder. Fred eyed the

bracers, remembering something similar with Malcolm's watch. Dark laughter erupted from Ulrich as the front half of each bracer split and rearranged to form hollow tubes.

What in the . . . ?

Planting his feet wide, Ulrich pointed at them and the bracers stopped spinning. A glow emanated from the "tubes" and suddenly Fred understood. *Not tubes—barrels!*

He shoved Winter. "Move!"

Thunder reverberated through the room. Beams exploded from Ulrich's barrels and sliced toward them, carving deep furrows in the walls and flinging equipment like toys.

Blinding light enveloped Fred, and a force hammered against his body. He sailed through the air to slam against the front wall. Mirrors and drywall shattered, slicing into his skin and rocketing in every direction as he dropped to the floor. A heartbeat later, Winter crashed against the wall and collapsed next to him.

Fred clung to consciousness with the fingernails of his mind. "Stay with me, girl."

Winter lifted up on her elbows, pale-faced as she eyed Ulrich. "He's recharging."

Fred spotted him at the opposite end of the room. The bracers were spinning again and a thick layer of frost coated his surroundings. He fixed them with a predatory stare.

"He ain't slowin' down."

Winter shook her head. "Least we made him think twice."

White-hot grief stabbed at Fred's heart. His best friend lay thinking she was about to die. He set his jaw. *No way is that gonna happen.* He searched around them for any weapon, any advantage. Nothing.

Fred studied Ulrich again, grasping for ideas. Then his eyes slipped past the tall man, to the wall behind. One set of shutters hung askew from the impact of Fred's disk, the glass behind it cracked like a spiderweb.

The glass behind it . . .

An idea blazed in his head. But how to do it? They couldn't take another blast, and they had nothing left to throw. Was there any way to get close to him?

Winter braced her hands on the floor and pushed up, trying to rise. Fred watched with sympathy, wishing he could lend her strength. He eyed the black accelerator ring on her finger. *Wish we had more of those things.*

His thoughts screeched to a halt as he stared at the ring. It was a crazy idea, but could it work? Reaching out, he grasped her hand.

"Fred, what—?"

"Squeeze hard. Just trust me."

Interlocking their fingers, he squeezed as tightly as he could. Winter followed suit and her eyes popped open. Her ring was now wrapped within Fred's hand and touching his skin, while *his* ring also touched *her* skin. Warm relief cascaded through his body and the pain in his side lessened. Winter's face brightened as if she'd discovered an untapped well of strength.

Fred grinned. As he'd hoped, he and Winter now shared their rings' power with each other.

"Can't take this fool in a fair fight," Fred gestured toward the cracked glass. "Feel like takin' him for a ride?"

Winter eyed the glass with grim satisfaction. "Oh, you have *no* idea."

They helped each other to their feet and turned toward Ulrich.

"We don't stop, we don't fall, we don't quit," Winter said. "This is it. It ends here no matter what."

Fred nodded, eyes trained on their target. He tensed to run. "Call it when you're ready."

Ulrich regarded them with amusement. "Still trying to win?" He pointed his bracers. "Come, then."

"*Now!*"

Hand in hand, they charged. Fred ran harder than ever before, feet pounding against the floor as he threw himself forward. At his side, Winter kept pace with all the speed she could muster.

Ulrich unleashed his weapons. Fred cried out as a beam struck his chest with bone-shaking force. He willed his legs to keep pumping through the relentless assault. Step after step, he bolted forward while the energy exploded against his body. His foot caught on a crack in the floor and Winter pulled him along until he regained his balance.

Winter caught a beam in the stomach. Retching, she fought back a wave of nausea and poured the pain into her resolve. She would not quit! She battled the urge to double over and vomit, and Fred pulled her forward until the sensation faded.

They stampeded wildly toward their adversary. As they closed the last few yards, Fred saw the fear in Ulrich's eyes and allowed himself to smile.

Fred and Winter collided with Ulrich, lifting him off his feet with the force of their charge. They closed around him in a mighty bear-hug and kept running. His beams carved wild arcs in the air as he struggled desperately to blast them away. Then he saw where they were running.

"*NO!*"

They took a last leap forward and smashed through the window.

Fred's world slowed around him. Wind rippled his clothes

and flying fragments of glass glinted in the sunlight. From over thirty feet in the air, he observed the stone patio beneath them.

He watched as their momentum turned downward, and the ground rushed up to meet them.

"She's so young," Lucius whispered into Valentine's ear. "So healthy. And she was so easy to find."

From inside the time bubble, Val trembled like a leaf at the sight of her mother. Lucius must have done something with the bubble so that Emily couldn't see or hear it. Twirling with baby Valentine and Malcolm on each hip, she glowed as if the sun shone from inside her.

Valentine gazed at her with longing. Her knees weakened until the only thing holding her upright was her enemy's grip. "Please don't hurt her!" she begged. "Please—"

"I'm not threatening her, Valentine," Lucius insisted. "I'm offering to extend her life. I will give you the means to cure her illness, and you will have your mother back for decades to come. All you have to do is help me get home."

Valentine's resolve crumbled to pieces and a flood of tears streamed down her cheeks. She reached toward her mother, desperate to embrace her again. To talk to her one more time. *I'll do anything. Anything . . .*

A faint voice struggled through the torrent of emotions. *But what's the real price?*

Valentine stopped short, latching onto the thought like a life preserver. *Yes. What is he bargaining for?* Taking hold of herself, she labored to focus on what was real. *He wants my help.*

And what does that really mean?

She forced herself to think out the words. *I'd have to fight my brother. Oma Grace. My friends. Then help kill thirty thousand people. All for him to get home. All to save one person I love.*

Lucius cared nothing for her mother. For him, she was only a means to manipulate Valentine. The memory of Emily Gilbert was his final, desperate bargaining chip.

Valentine focused on that thought—it gave her clarity. And with that clarity came molten rage. Her outstretched hand closed into a fist and she sucked in a deep, shuddering breath.

"No," she said. "You will *not* use her against me!"

Valentine's fingers clamped over Lucius's open hand and squeezed. The watch pressed against her palm and the image of her mother wavered.

"I only want to—" he began.

Throwing her head back, she cracked against his nose and stomped his right instep. He gasped, his grip on her slackening. Keeping her grip firmly on the watch, Valentine whipped around and planted an open palm against Lucius's chest. Her eyes bore into his, and she saw him through a veil of red.

"*Don't ever go near her again!*" she roared. Her anger swelled until it became a living beast. The watch vibrated in her grip, and power burst through her body like a living fire.

She shoved hard against Lucius, shouting in fury. His jaw dropped as she propelled him away from her mother. She pressed harder and he fell back again. With another *shift* sensation, the bubble turned red and the scene outside changed.

Snarling, he pushed back against her. His face recoiled as he failed. Her expression twisted into a bitter, humorless smile at the look in his eyes. *Fear.*

Valentine's will took on a life of its own. The watch glowed in her thoughts and she seized it with her mind like a burning star. Again she advanced and Lucius retreated, and again the scene outside changed. They *shifted,* flying forward in time. Deep inside, she knew it was somehow because of her.

Step after step she battled Lucius, pushing him farther from her mother, flashing them through scene after scene as time ticked by. The changing scenes stopped at Fred's battle-scarred living room.

The energy bubble burst, depositing them in the present. Valentine's shout rose to a primal shriek, and she shoved with everything she had. Lucius burst through the living room wall like a bullet, toppling hard to the kitchen floor.

Seething, she followed him through as he stumbled to his feet. Before he could recover, she dealt a wicked snap-kick to his chest.

Lucius crashed through the glass doors facing the backyard. Tumbling to the patio, he spun across the stone and slid to a stop. The pocket watch left his grasp and skittered in another direction.

With the watch out of her hand, she felt the hot surge of power slowly diminishing. But she had enough left.

He'll never stop. Valentine paused at the doorframe, which had splintered from the impact of Lucius's body. Grabbing a thick length of wood, she wrenched it free and stomped toward her foe. *Unless I stop him.*

She stomped down on his shoulder with a booted heel. Clenching his jaw, Lucius snaked a hand inside his jacket.

"*DDDOOONNN'TTT DDDOOO TTTHHHIIISSS, VVVAAALLLEEENNNTTTIIINNNEEE,*" he commanded. "*III'VVVEEE AAALLLWWWAAAYYYSSS BBBEEEEEENNN YYYOOOUUURRR*

*FFFRRRIIIEEENNNDDD. YYYOOOUUU
MMMUUUSSSTTT—"*

Lifting her foot, Valentine reached down and grabbed him by the jacket. With a yank, she brought him closer and swung. His head rocked to the side as the makeshift club splintered against his temple. He stared at her bewildered.

"HHHOOOWWW DDDIIIDDD YYYOOOUUU—?"

She brought the club down again, silencing him with a crack to the ear. "Stop it!"

More chunks of her weapon broke away until all that remained was a sharp wooden stake, the narrow end pointed straight at his heart. Lucius held up his hands in surrender, then reached inside his jacket again.

"It appears you have hidden talents, Valentine. Just like your brother."

She had no clue what that meant, and in this moment she didn't care. *I can finish this right here.* The stake felt *right* in her hand, with the tip pressed against his chest. Her muscles tensed and she willed herself to push harder. But she couldn't move.

Just do it! End it! She tried and failed again. Her hand shook, the stake's tip wavering. A desperate sob escaped her lips. *I can't . . . I can't . . .*

"You see?" Lucius said. "At this moment, thousands of lives depend on you. Think of all the people you could save by killing me right now. But you won't do it." He shook his head. "Even you don't think they're worth it."

Valentine pulled Lucius closer, glaring. He tensed, keeping an eye on the point of the spike. It seemed his self-assuredness had been more smoke screen than truth. *He's not sure what I'll do.* Trembling, she battled within herself. *But neither am I.* Her thoughts a whirlwind, she drew the weapon back and willed herself to strike.

Glass shattered somewhere overhead. Valentine flinched as glistening shards rained down around them. She and Lucius regarded the sky in puzzlement.

Three figures crashed to the ground at their left. Valentine heard a sickening crack and nearly forgot her own battle. Ulrich had fallen flat on his back against the stones, with Winter and Fred bracing themselves on top of his body.

Winter's elbows buckled and she rolled to the side, unconscious. Valentine saw that Fred's forearm casts had broken completely away. Then she looked closer and her heart jumped into her throat.

"Fred!" she called.

Sunlight glimmered along the edge of a long, thick shard of glass. It protruded from Ulrich's chest, then lanced upward to pierce through Fred's right shoulder. The two of them lay connected by the deadly sliver.

Fred's chest heaved as he gasped for air. He pushed up, attempting to lift himself off the bloody shard. Ulrich's hand shot up and gripped the back of his neck.

"You are . . . *nothing!*" Ulrich spluttered, blood painting his teeth. Tightening his grip, he pulled down on Fred's neck and forced the glass back through his shoulder.

Fred cried out and pushed harder against the stones. Valentine yearned to run and help her friend. *But if I let go of Lucius, this is all for nothing!*

"Come *on,* man," Fred gasped. "It's over!"

"Y-you might as vell . . . die here," Ulrich spat, his chest heaving. "I have seen future—seen history books. Your—" He hacked and retched. "Your names are not in them. Nothing you do vill . . . e-ever be remembered."

Fred collected himself and gave a defiant grin. "Guess that means we can do whatever we want."

Tensing, he struck his fist against the shard. The glass smashed into a thousand pieces, showering Ulrich's face and chest.

Fred drew up to his knees and glared grim victory at his enemy. Ulrich coughed and shuddered and struck at Fred with his last bit of strength, his breaths growing shorter and shorter. Then they stopped, and Ulrich was silent.

Fred exhaled and his eyes rolled back. He crumpled to the stones next to Winter.

Valentine could scarcely process what she had witnessed. *Oh . . . my . . . God. They beat him.* She blinked. *Winter and Fred beat Ulrich!*

Her attention returned to Lucius. He stared at Ulrich's body, mouth agape, his lower lip trembling and tears welling in his eyes.

"Ulrich," he muttered softly. "I . . ."

He seemed confused, as if he couldn't remember what to do. Valentine fought down a pang of sympathy, reminding herself what these men really were. *They're evil. Can't let myself—*

Lucius's eyes snapped back to her, brimming with unbridled hatred. He shifted under her grip, and Valentine spotted what she'd been too distracted to notice. Somehow his hand had crept back inside his jacket.

Thunder cracked and the sky arced with lightning. Cruel satisfaction darkened Lucius's visage, and suddenly she knew what his counterattack would be.

In a panic, she released her captive and fled toward the kitchen doors. Three strides later, the ground shook and her teeth rattled. The air flashed and sizzled as a bolt struck the stones between her and Lucius.

A shockwave slammed into Valentine and she collapsed in a daze, the world around her muffled and blurred. Over the ringing in her ears, she barely caught the sound of footsteps on broken stones.

Valentine rolled onto her back. Lucius loomed overhead, regarding her with cold eyes and a bitter twist to his lips.

"All right," he said to her. "New plan."

His foot connected with her chin.

CHAPTER 27

Thunder boomed and the house rumbled around Malcolm. *Got to get moving! Val's going to need my help with Lucius.* As he came to his hands and knees, a foot connected with his flank, flipping him onto his back. He clutched at his side, laboring to breathe.

Lucius towered overhead with a frenzied look in his eye, his face bearing the marks of a fight. *She made him angry.* Then he saw Valentine slung over Lucius's shoulder. Desperately he lunged for his sister, but a heavy foot pinned him to the floor.

"You got what you wanted! Let her go!"

"Oh, I think not," Lucius spat. "Your plan is lost, your friends are broken, and still my purpose moves forward. Oppose me and the consequences will be on your head." His voice grew to a shout. "Believe me when I say that you *cannot imagine* the horrors I will visit upon this girl if I see your face again!"

With that, he disappeared inside a sphere of energy, leaving Malcolm to wallow in defeat. *No.* He pushed up from the floor. *We're not done yet!*

Fred eased stiffly onto a lounge chair by the pool and released the breath he'd been holding. Oma Grace rechecked the bandage on his shoulder, making sure it wouldn't rip against the glass.

"Gotta tell you," Fred said, "I ain't a real big fan o' glass lately."

"How do you feel?" Malcolm asked.

Fred managed a weak grin. "Shoulda seen the other guy."

Any other day, Malcolm would've laughed. Instead, he stared down at the object in his hand with growing fear. *Valentine's accelerator ring.* He'd discovered it on the patio, in a circle of broken stones. *She has no protection.*

"You sure he was dead?" Clive asked.

"Wasn't breathing when I woke up." Winter hugged herself. "Lucius took him away, I guess. I don't know why he left us."

"Because he thinks we're finished," Oma Grace said.

Malcolm understood why. Fred was stabbed. Winter sustained two sprained wrists and a concussion. Oma Grace also suffered a concussion and a broken collarbone. Lucius had fractured Clive's left arm and his left foot.

By some miracle, Malcolm and Walter escaped major injury. As a group, though, they couldn't have presented a sadder picture. Malcolm wracked his brain for a new strategy, anything to give them a fighting chance. There had to be a way!

"Miranda never made it," Oma Grace continued. "We never found John either. I fear *they* may have found them first." She shook her head in despair. "What are we supposed to do now?"

Heavy silence pressed down on Malcolm's companions. As they took stock of their condition, the glimmers of hope began to die.

Oblivious, Malcolm's mind worked overtime. *I'm missing something key. Something that doesn't add up. What did he really come here for? Wait a minute—he told me!* He stared down at the ring. *That's it!* In his arrogance, Lucius had revealed more than he'd intended.

"Guys," he began.

"I wanna pound that dude into dust," Fred said. "But look at us."

Winter nodded agreement.

Malcolm held up the ring. "Why did he leave this—?"

"Even with the rings, Grace an' I wouldn't last two minutes now," Clive interrupted. "Can't fix broken bones in a day."

"I will get to Valentine, no matter what," Oma Grace insisted. "I won't let her face the end alone."

Walter regarded her with uncharacteristic softness. "I'll look after the rest of them, Grace," he assured her. She thanked him with a fond smile.

Malcolm stared at her. "Hold on. What are you saying?"

She regarded him with teary eyes. "We gave it everything, my boy, and we lost." She gave a desperate huff. "We have nothing left to challenge him with! The least I can do is be with my granddaughter in the final hour. He may allow me that."

Clive studied the ground. "Grace said he thinks we're finished. Maybe he's right. Maybe we oughta think about gettin' the rest o' you outta town."

Malcolm blinked in disbelief. "So, that's it? He won? We're just going to run while he kills thirty thousand people, including my sister?"

His insides cracked, and he felt steam rising up. Fear of losing Valentine collided with bitter fury, and his blood began to boil. "Walter, you're just going to let this happen?"

"Malcolm," Walter said wearily. "He's got us from every angle. It's checkmate."

"It's checkmate because YOU'VE GIVEN UP!"

They recoiled from his verbal assault. He didn't care. A part of his heart burst open—the part that had lain buried since last autumn. It suddenly dawned on him how he'd spent the previous year—wallowing in loss, letting others control the course of his life. He'd let them because it had been easier than feeling something.

Those days were over.

Malcolm shoved Valentine's ring under Walter's nose. "Look at this! He took the watch from me, but left this behind." He pointed at Oma Grace. "And Ulrich told you we were all part of Lucius's plan. Don't you see?"

He met a sea of blank faces.

"He's had us figured out from the start! But attacking before now would've just given us time to plan a counterstrike. So instead, he distracted us. He let us use some old gadgets. He let me have the watch, knowing I'd stay occupied but never fully master it. All the while, time ticked by and our window to prepare got smaller. And then the day came—*this* day, when he's planning to jump. Attacking us now means we have no time to recover." He held up a finger. "But he gave us one fatal clue."

Again, Malcolm faced slack-jawed expressions.

"Why would he leave the rings behind? Why take the watch and nothing else? Because it's the only one that matters! He must *need* the watch for his final jump."

"What are you saying, Mal?" Oma Grace prodded.

"Knowing what he needs tells us where he's weak. If we get inside and find how he's using the watch, we may have a chance to disrupt it."

He peered into a void of bleakness. It seemed Lucius had also achieved something unintended. He'd broken their spirits.

It didn't matter—Malcolm was in charge now, and he would get their lives back.

"We still can't fight," Winter moaned.

"You and Fred are going to a hospital." Malcolm turned to Clive and Oma Grace. "You take them. They need a driver, and you both need a doctor anyway. Don't go to our hospital."

"Why not?" Clive asked.

"Because if we fail, I want you out of the blast radius. Take them to another town, maybe Winnick or Abilene. Tell the hospital you got hurt during the blasts and were afraid to stay in town. They'll buy it."

Oma Grace and Clive exchanged glances with Fred and Winter. Slowly they nodded to each other, coming to silent agreement.

"Okay." Clive gave Malcolm a reappraising look. "You be careful, son."

Malcolm nodded, then turned to Walter. By the look in the old soldier's eye, he knew what came next. "Just you and me against the future, huh?"

Malcolm nodded grimly. "I'll need your help for what I have planned."

Walter looked amused. "So, you actually have a plan?"

"For the first part, at least. We're getting my sister out. Then, well, we'll see if I'm right about all this."

"Can't just walk inside, now that the watch is gone," Clive pointed out. "Craters are under guard. How you gonna get in there?"

"Got that figured out, but I'll need a key to your shop."

Clive dug in his pocket and handed over a jangling key ring. "You've more'n earned my trust."

Choking back sobs, Oma Grace slid past Clive and wrapped Malcolm in a tight embrace. He returned the hug just as hard. *Is this the last time I'll get to do this?* He pulled her in tighter.

"You come back to me, boy," she breathed. "Hear me? And bring that foolish sister of yours. I want to see you both smiling again."

He nearly broke right then. Tears burned at the back of his eyes, and he felt his chest heave with thick emotion. He stomped on it. *Not now. I need to be strong for them.*

He grasped her good shoulder and held her at arm's length. "I'll get her out. I promise."

Her hand clutched his, and he looked down to see that she'd given him her anklet. Her one advantage, and she was giving it to him. After touching his cheek one last time, she wiped away tears and moved to help Winter. Clive supported Fred, and the two pairs hobbled toward the stairs.

"Wait!" Fred beckoned stiffly to Malcolm and wiggled his fingers. "Here, take it."

Malcolm shook his head. "Fred, no. You need the ring more."

"Psh. Thing's probably just keepin' me awake, an' I'd rather be out cold. You'll need any advantage you can get." He wiggled his fingers again. "Come on, man."

Malcolm reluctantly grasped the ring. With a twist, the black metal segments snapped open and slid from Fred's finger. He readied himself to catch Fred, but he showed no signs of passing out.

Maybe these things leave a residual effect. It fades away slowly.

Fred grasped Malcolm behind the neck and pulled him closer. "You make him feel it!" he hissed. "When he knows he's gonna lose, make it *hurt*. Understand?"

Malcolm met Fred's hard stare with one of his own. He set his jaw and held up Fred's ring. "I'll tell him the first punch is from you."

Satisfied, Fred nodded and turned back toward the doors.

"Hey," Winter said, and held out her hand.

"You sure?"

Winter's exhausted expression morphed into her trademark *you're a moron* stare. "Take this thing so I can go get some painkillers."

Malcolm stepped up and her accelerator ring fell into his palm, clinking against the others. Winter's hand lingered near his, and he noticed she was studying him.

"You look different."

He paused. "I feel different."

Winter smacked his arm. "Good. Tell that loser it's from me when you kick him in the—"

"All right, my dear, it's time we were off." Oma Grace rolled her eyes and half-dragged Winter toward the staircase.

Moments later they were alone, and the quiet almost echoed in Fred's mansion. Malcolm still pictured it packed with his partying classmates. Now it looked more like a war zone.

"The man worked us over good, didn't he?" Walter said.

Malcolm gave a dark chuckle. "That's for sure."

"So, how are we going to finish it?"

"By outsmarting him."

Walter cocked an eyebrow. "We're going to outthink the time-traveling genius?" He grimaced. "I'd rather just punch him."

Malcolm slid Valentine's ring on, relishing the warm relief. The aches faded and his muscles pulled taut and ready. Even the sunlight shone brighter.

"We'll outsmart him because he thinks we're stupid. Since we're only stupid compared to *him*, that works in our favor. As for punching . . ."

He flicked his wrist and the two remaining rings sailed toward Walter. The soldier snatched them from the air.

Malcolm grinned. "I'm planning on that, too."

Walter put them on, and his eyes lit up with the rush of power.

Malcolm hefted Clive's keys. "Let's get to the shop. I don't think we have much time."

"What does Clive have that we need?"

"The key to Lucius's house."

THE chain dug into Valentine's wrists, tethering her to a thick metal ring bolted to the floor. She leaned against the west wall of Lucius's house, hands behind her back. If she sat up, she could just manage to peek out the window.

Why did he bother to tie me up? This place had an acute lack of doors, and the only real exit was occupied by a red energy vortex. It spun like a tornado, stretching from the top level all the way to the tunnels below the house.

Lucius stood at the center of his vast computer array, typing furiously, fingers flying as he jumped from one computer to the next. At random times one hand would reach out to flip a switch or throw a lever while the other kept typing as fast as ever. Despite her hatred for this man, Valentine couldn't help but be impressed at his ability to divide his attention so skillfully.

The silver panels whirred, tilting half an inch to the right. Lucius paused for a brief moment to gaze at his creation. "Beautiful, isn't it?"

She shrugged. "I've seen better."

He snickered, then resumed his furious pace. "Upon reaching our destination, you certainly will."

He almost reminded Valentine of the old Mr. Carmichael—the enthusiastic scientist, the man she'd come to admire. An air of giddy anticipation vibrated around him. *He's excited to go home.*

She shuddered at the implications. "Why are you taking me? You know I won't help you."

"Every master needs a student," Lucius said. "It grounds them. And since your friends killed my last one, you will take his place." He flipped more switches and the tall batteries across the room began to hum. "I forgive you for opposing me. Soon you will see I've been truthful, and in time you will be ready to learn from me again."

The mouth of the vortex expanded to fill the opening in the floor. Outside, thunder cracked and flickers of lightning danced between black clouds. Valentine examined the room again, determined to find something to use against Lucius. She pulled at the chain and winced as it chafed against raw flesh.

"Please let me help my family. They'll stay until they find me, and if the blast wave catches them—"

Lucius kept working, his fingers a blur. "Do you realize how many calculations are necessary to achieve my goal? I have little time left, and my machine *must* be ready."

Her lips curled in contempt. "I spared your life!"

"And for that I am grateful. If it gives you solace, they will not feel pain. They will simply cease to exist."

Lucius slid over to a computer he hadn't touched before and typed in a series of commands. Between the lab tables, a disguised panel on the floor slid open. A metal cylinder ascended from the aperture, standing four feet tall and a foot wide. At its top, facing the massive time machine, was a small round depression.

Dread filled Valentine as Lucius pulled the pocket watch from his jacket. *Malcolm had that!* She longed to know if her brother was okay. What about Oma and her friends? What about John?

Stop it. She shoved away the rising anxiety and focused on the here and now. *Can't help them until you help yourself.*

Lucius pressed the watch against the round depression. It clicked into place and spun twice, nestling into the cylinder as if they'd been made for each other. Valentine shook her head. *He needed it the whole time, and we let him waltz in and take it.*

"You look surprised," he said. Brimming with self-satisfaction, he resumed typing. "You didn't think I'd let you discover *all* my tricks, now did you?"

She feigned nonchalance. "So you like toys. So what?"

"Toys?" He jabbed his finger toward the watch. "This toy is the master control unit for my entire machine, Miss Gilbert. It's been under your nose all along, and no one recognized it—not even you. Which, I have to say, disappoints me slightly."

He wants to gloat. A classic flaw of every egomaniac. They all want an audience to acknowledge their brilliance. *Okay. So I'll let him, and he'll tell me everything.*

"I don't know what that means," she lied. "Why would you need a remote control?"

Lucius tapped out more commands, then hit the last key with a pronounced jab. A bright red beam shot from the watch's jewel and lanced into the center of his machine. The swirling energy *shifted.* Valentine couldn't grasp exactly how, but she felt it deep in her bones. The rhythm of the red vortex changed, and the storm outside worsened.

"Have you ever heard of resonant frequencies?" Lucius asked. "This is a similar principle. The technology of your barbaric era prevented me from building a machine with the necessary power *and* a sophisticated guidance system. In your terms, it is a shotgun when I need a sniper rifle." He gestured at the watch. "That's where the master control unit comes in. A smaller device with much finer tuning, it is able to pinpoint the exact moment and location I desire."

How do I use it against you? "So why not just use *that* to go home? Why go to all this trouble and murder so many people?"

Lucius shook his head. "I need the power to catapult us that far and break their shield." His tone dripped with venom. "The watch will tell the machine exactly where to drill through time and space. It may take time, but eventually the shield *will* break."

She let the lightbulb turn on in her eyes, as if just beginning to understand. "So, whichever time and place you choose with the watch . . ."

"The machine will change its orientation to match," he finished. "As long as the energy of the watch intersects with the energy of the machine, you can direct its path."

"And why are you telling *me* all this?"

Lucius studied her for a long moment, then bent over his computers again. The keys clicked at what seemed like a thousand words per minute.

"As long as you're my student, Valentine, I will never hold back knowledge from you. I respect you. Please do not forget that." An alert sounded and his face brightened. "And here we go. We begin our assault on the shield . . . *NOW!*"

He tapped a key and another beam lanced from the watch. The vortex spun faster and the house shuddered as Lucius pumped every ounce of power into his machine. Outside, the sky erupted. Valentine gasped, her insides twisting as if she could feel his assault through the timeline.

"We are home, Valentine!" Lucius cried. "We've done it!"

He continued entering more commands and throwing more levers, fine-tuning his assault. Valentine marveled at him. *In his mind, he's already home and I'm his loyal servant. He can't imagine that I'll use any of this to destroy him.* She examined her surroundings again and wondered if she was the one fooling herself. *No one's come yet. Are things worse than I've been willing to imagine?*

Am I going to die alone, in some other time?

Outside the window, a mechanical rumble carried above the sounds of the angry storm, drawing closer until it became a roar. She rose to her knees and peered down at the street.

A gigantic old truck charged into view, half faded green and half primer white. Tall and boxy with thick tires as tall as her waist, it barreled down the street in their direction. DODGE was emblazoned across the grille in thick red letters—a warning or a challenge. Memories awoke of Malcolm describing Clive's automotive projects.

Valentine smiled. *You're not home yet!*

CHAPTER 28

Sheets of rain pelted the Dodge Power Wagon as Walter veered onto their street. Squinting through the torrent, Malcolm could see the windows of Lucius's house glowing red.

Walter stomped on the gas and the massive engine roared. They pressed back into their seats and Malcolm gripped his armrests, bracing himself. Swerving to the right, Walter hopped the curb and aimed the Power Wagon directly at the front corner of the house.

Malcolm eyed him. "Should we ring the bell?"

The wrought-iron fence crumpled under their wheels.

Walter grinned. "Nah, we'll just let ourselves in."

The armored transport plowed into the house with a thunderous boom. Wooden planks imploded and layers of microcircuitry sparked as they flew to pieces. The transport crunched to a stop, two-thirds of its long frame embedded in the house.

"Bet that got his attention." As Malcolm leapt to the ground, he marveled at the destruction. He kicked a side view mirror that had broken off the wagon. "And we finally gave this place a door."

Walter exited on his side and stood transfixed by the energy piercing the center of the room. "The last time I saw this, Albert died." Shaking himself back to the present, he joined Malcolm at the crumpled grille. "We get your sister first?"

Malcolm nodded. "Then I'll deal with Lucius while you both find my dad and get as far away as possible."

Walter frowned. "I never agreed to that."

"Which is why I didn't say it earlier. I know it's selfish, but my family comes before this town."

Walter's expression clouded with objection.

"I realize this sucks, but I'm asking for your help. Please."

Walter considered, then gave a grudging nod and gestured to the staircase. "We'd better move fast. You know he'll be waiting."

"Actually, the truck was just misdirection. I have something else in mind," Malcolm said with a grin. "How about we remodel this place a little more?"

GRINNING, Valentine shook off the dust falling from the ceiling. *There's still a chance.* The impact had cast Lucius to the floor, but he had quickly recovered and resumed his frantic work on controlling the great machine. Cracking his knuckles, he paused to adjust a knob on the plate underneath his jacket.

"Your former allies are becoming a true annoyance," he said. "But they will not prevent my return home. I have surprises in store for—"

Behind Valentine, the window shattered inward. A dark figure sailed through the opening, rolled across the floor, and came to his feet. Valentine's heart soared as Malcolm set himself between her and Lucius.

"I'm not interrupting, am I?"

Lucius glared at her brother. All the while, he kept typing. "Attack me at your own peril, Malcolm. I do *not* have time for your tantrum."

"Well, here it comes."

Malcolm leapt over the table separating them, swinging as his feet hit the floor. Lucius flipped another switch, typed another command, then danced back from Malcolm's attack at the last instant. Reversing direction then, he went on the offensive.

They collided in a mass of flying fists and boots. Seconds later, Malcolm slammed onto his back with a thud. Valentine lunged forward, desperate to join the fight, but the chain snapped her back into place.

Instead of pressing his advantage, Lucius slid away from Malcolm and typed on two separate keyboards at once. Valentine felt the vortex *shift* and adjust itself again, ever so slightly.

"This is delicate work, boy," Lucius chided, kicking Malcolm's side without even looking. "You're distracting me."

Seething, Malcolm leapt up and drove at Lucius again.

A shadow fell across the window. Valentine whipped around as Walter crept silently inside, a glint of silver showing at his ankle. *Oma's anklet!* Putting a finger to his lips, Walter knelt next to her and grasped the end of her chain. With a sharp tug, it snapped it free.

Her jaw dropped. Noting her expression, he showed both hands. *Two rings? What did I miss?* She realized then that no one else was coming through the window.

"Where is everyone?" she hissed.

"Come with me," Walter whispered.

"No, we've got to help!" Valentine sprang to her feet, then swayed as her vision spun.

"Your brother's in charge, and he says we get you out!" Walter clutched her by the waist and stepped to the window. "Just hold on tight."

Mal's in charge? What happened back there? She followed numbly, too weak to give real resistance. As much as it pained her, Walter was right—in her state she'd only be a liability.

"Okay, let's go," she said.

Mechanical whirring came from behind, and a wave of chilled air rolled over them. At the window, rain droplets crystallized and clinked frozen to the floor. Valentine looked back toward the fight.

Ulrich's bracers! Lucius had donned his old partner's weapons, adding their power to his chest plate's, and now they spun around his forearms with a high-pitched whine. Valentine realized then the pounding that Malcolm must be taking. Even with two rings, he'd feel every blow in his bones.

The spinning stopped as the bracers reconfigured into a tubelike shape. Lucius broke free from grappling with Malcolm and danced two steps backward, leveling his hands at Malcolm's chest.

"Mal!" Valentine shouted.

With a crackling boom, twin beams blasted him square in the chest. He flew back like a cannonball, heading straight for them. Walter whirled them toward the window and shielded Valentine with his body.

A colossal force struck them. The window filled her vision, and then they were falling. Wind and rain swirled around her like a billowing blanket, wrapping her in the sensation of floating. Walter spun them again, turning his own back toward the ground.

They impacted the rain-soaked earth, Valentine croaking

as air fled from her lungs. Released from the cocoon of Walter's embrace, she turned onto her hands and knees and forced herself to suck in a rush of air.

"Thank you," she wheezed.

"Help me with your brother."

On Walter's other side, Malcolm sprawled face down in the mud, unmoving. Valentine's chest seized and she scrambled to his side. Walter flipped him onto his back while Valentine felt for a pulse and placed her ear near his mouth.

She gasped in relief. "He's breathing!"

Walter lifted Malcolm onto his shoulders and they scurried through the gaping hole in the house. As they reached the truck's back door, Malcolm stirred with a violent coughing fit. Valentine rested a hand on his chest.

"Easy, Mal. Breathe slowly." Valentine opened the door and stepped aside as Walter laid Malcolm across the wide backseat.

"Need to move fast," Walter said. "He'll be down here any second."

Valentine shook her head. "He'll never leave that machine now. It takes all his attention, and he's too close to his goal. He must have something else to—" She cut off, Lucius's words echoing in her mind. "He said he had surprises waiting. What did that mean?"

"It doesn't matter now. You two get out of town. I'll hold him off as long as possible."

"No! We're in this together. No one's leaving you."

"Kid, we don't have time to argue."

Footsteps interrupted them, echoing from the stairwell. Valentine crouched and braced against the cracked floor, ready to attack. Walter raised his fists. The footsteps shuffled around the truck, then a familiar face came into view.

Valentine relaxed. "Miss Marcus! If you can help, I know something to use against Lucius."

The teacher stared at them in silence, her left hand balled into a fist.

"Miranda, we need you now," Walter said. "Are you ready?"

Tears welled up in Miss Marcus's eyes as she turned to Walter. *"KKIILLLL HHEERR."*

Valentine gaped. "What—?"

Walter's hands closed around Valentine's throat.

Valentine kicked out and tore at his grip with her fingernails. Looming overhead, Walter's face contorted and his body shook. He groaned with exertion.

Valentine knew he was fighting Miss Marcus's power. Her silver pin commanded the deepest parts of his mind, and with the rings he could have easily crushed her windpipe. Somehow, he was resisting just enough to keep her alive.

"Miranda, stop this!" Walter rattled his head from side to side. "What are you doing?!"

Miss Marcus sobbed. *"HHEE SSAAIIDD HHEE'DD FFIIXX IITT, WWAALLTTEERR! HHEE SSAAIIDD WWHHEENN TTHHIISS IISS OOVVEERR, WWEE CCAANN GGOO BBAACCKK AANNDD SSAAVVEE AALLBBEERRTT! HHEE CCAANN BBEE WWIITTHH UUSS AAGGAAIINN!"*

Through the haze falling over her mind, Valentine recognized that brand of bargaining. Lucius had offered her something similar. *He wants us all against each other.*

"He's . . . a liar and a devil, Miranda!" Walter forced out, his grip tightening. "Don't make me do this!"

"Please . . ." Valentine begged with the last of her air.

Walter's eyes bulged. *"You.* You told Lucius where we were, everything we've been doing. He knew because of you!"

"II'MM SSOORRRRYY! II HHAADD TTOO—"

"Stop!" a powerful voice commanded.

In unison they turned toward the hole in the wall. A figure stood in the rain, silhouetted by the constant flash of lightning. The figure stepped inside and the red light of the vortex illuminated him.

The tinted glasses were gone, the long hair had been cropped short, but Valentine would know that face anywhere. Hope swelled inside her. *JOHN!* He came closer, his attention on Miss Marcus.

"Constant as the morning star, Miranda," he said in a reprimanding tone.

Walter's face went white. Miss Marcus blinked and her knees quivered. She managed only one word.

"Albert!"

Valentine's mind burst like a storm cloud. *WHAT?*

"What happened to you?" John said. "Betraying everyone for the promise of a madman?" He raised his arms and turned from side to side, inviting her to examine him. "See for yourself—I am not dead. Lucius bought you with cheap lies." He shook his head with regret. "And I was coming to help you defeat him."

"B-but, you're supposed to—" Miss Marcus stammered. She swayed, looking as if she might topple over. "He said you were . . . he promised." She sagged to her knees. Dropping the pin to the floor, she covered her face and broke into bitter sobs.

Walter's grip disappeared. Valentine crumpled to the floor, coughing and massaging at her throat. The air never tasted so sweet.

He knelt over her. "I'm sorry."

She shook her head. "It wasn't you."

John appeared at her side, and his hand intertwined with hers. "Thank heaven I arrived in time. Are you injured, Valentine?"

She shook her head, eyeing him distantly.

Once again, he fell in sync with her thoughts. "I will explain everything when this is finished. I promise you, I am still the person you know."

"Al!" Walter reached out to clutch John's shoulders, tears in his eyes. He stared at the younger man, making sure he was real, and pulled him into a tight embrace. "Oh my God, Al. You're—"

"Yeah, Walt. It's me." John laughed with joy, shedding tears of his own. He returned the hug with vigor. "Sorry I didn't come to you sooner, my friend."

Valentine's head spun. *This is . . . I don't even know anymore.*

"It was all for you," a tiny voice whimpered.

The three of them turned toward Miss Marcus. She rose to her feet, the truck's broken mirror clutched in her hand. Valentine realized with alarm that her other hand held the silver pin again.

"For *you*, Albert!" She gazed at John with longing. "To save your life. To save our love!"

John reached out to her. "Come to me, Miranda. We'll work through this together."

"No!" She shook her head violently and backed away. Her eyes cast about in a wild, erratic pattern. "No no no it's too late it's too late!"

"Miranda, please," John beckoned softly. "We need you."

"Can't do it—can't let myself! Must save you—save you from *him*. Save you from *me*."

Trembling, Miss Marcus held up the mirror and stared into her own eyes. Her other hand closed tightly over the pin. *"FFOORRGGEETT,"* she commanded her reflection. *"FFOORRGGEETT WWHHOO YYOOUU AARREE. FFOORRGGEETT TTHHIISS PPLLAACCEE AANNDD TTHHEESSEE PPEEOOPPLLEE. FFOORRGGEETT EEVVEERRYYTTHHIINNGG. WWAALLKK AAWWAAYY AANNDD NNEEVVEERR LLOOKK BBAACCKK."*

She stiffened. The mirror dropped to the floor, followed by the pin. Blank-faced, the shell that was once Miranda Marcus marched mechanically toward the open wall.

"Miranda!" Walter called after her.

"She's . . ." John hung his head. "Miranda is gone, Walt."

The former Miranda Marcus left the house and disappeared into the pouring rain.

CHAPTER 29

Valentine stared after Miss Marcus in disbelief. *She was never evil—just desperate. Lucius twisted her into something ugly.* She eyed the silver pin glinting on the floor, and moved to retrieve it.

"Why couldn't we move to a normal town?" Malcolm mumbled. Sitting up with bleary eyes, he stared out at the storm. "She didn't even take an umbrella."

With a shaky laugh, Valentine rushed back to his side and double-checked him for injuries. "Are you okay? How long have you been awake?"

"Long enough to get the important stuff." Malcolm gently pushed her hands away. "I'm okay. He just caught me off guard. What'd he do to me?"

"Took you down in five seconds, then shot us all out the window," Walter said.

"So that explains all the mud," John said.

Malcolm gave him a respectful nod. "Nice to see you back, uh . . ."

He smiled. "You can still call me John."

"Lucius has Ulrich's bracers. That's what he hit you with,"

Valentine said. "And while I was up there, I learned something else."

Quickly as possible, she explained what Lucius had shown her about the watch and how it controlled the time machine. "If we get the watch and force him into the machine, we can use the jewel beam to send him anywhere we want," she concluded.

"Where can we send him that'll neutralize him?" Walter mused.

Malcolm stood. "How far back did the watch take you, Val?"

"Not sure, but there were dinosaurs. If we send him that far without any toys, there's no *way* he could threaten anyone again."

A muffled boom shook the house from above. They stared at the ceiling as a second boom followed close behind.

"That didn't happen last time." John moved protectively toward Valentine.

"We need to get moving." Malcolm looked at John. "Can you get everyone to safety?"

"Not everyone. I'm staying to finish this, too," Walter said. Clicking open one of his rings, he offered it to John along with the keys to the truck. "Get yourselves as far away as possible, and use the ring if you hit trouble."

John stared at Walter's outstretched hand. "No, Walt. I came to help end this, and I'm not leaving until it's done."

The house rattled with another boom.

"You are helping," Malcolm assured him. "You and Val need to find our dad. With my family safe, I don't have to worry. I can do whatever's necessary." He turned to Walter. "And you *know* one ring isn't enough to stand up to him. Go with them."

"Never," Walter said.

"Two rings aren't enough, either, Mal," Valentine reasoned. "You can't do this by yourself. Let me have the other two and we'll do this together."

John and Walter voiced protests at the same time, speaking over each other with objections until their words ran together. Valentine kept her attention on her twin and the dangerous look in his eye. The look of a boy planning something foolish.

Pleading with her eyes, she shook her head. *Don't do it, Mal. Listen to them!* He met her gaze with silent reassurance, looking eager yet almost sad. Reaching out, he pulled her into a tight embrace.

"Look after them, Val," he whispered into her ear.

"Whatever you're thinking, don't—"

"You've all done your part. Now it's my turn." He pulled back and kissed her on the cheek.

"Mal, I—"

The words died in her throat as she stared at him. Malcolm gave her one last grin, then sprang into action. Darting forward, he snatched the ring from Walter's outstretched hand and socked him hard in the stomach. The older man doubled over with an *oof.*

Malcolm leaped over the hood of the truck and bounded to the staircase. Climbing to the top step, he faced them all again. The third ring clicked onto his finger.

"Sorry, Walter," he said. "But you know you'd have done the same."

Walter cast an accusing glare at him. "You crazy son of a—"

Malcolm smiled. "Get yourselves away from here. The last round is mine."

With a leap, he disappeared into the upper level.

MALCOLM ascended to the third level, making no attempt at silence. The time for stealth was over. To his left, Lucius worked at a keyboard, no doubt making final preparations.

The vortex spun like an angry red tornado. From deep in its center, a bluish-white glow radiated upward. As Malcolm watched, a crescent-shaped sliver of light flew from the center and exploded against the ceiling like a cannon. Seconds later, another followed with a boom. Droplets of rain began to seep through the cracks overhead.

"Shards of the time shield," Lucius explained. "My device is shredding it faster than I'd hoped. It won't be long now." He glanced up at Malcolm. "Ready to challenge me again?"

Adopting a casual air, Malcolm paced nonchalantly around the giant machine. "No, I plan to win this time."

Lucius chuckled. "Do you honestly believe that is an option?"

Outside the far window, the Dodge Power Wagon made it to the street and sped away. Malcolm covertly watched its escape and breathed an internal sigh of relief. He focused back on Lucius.

"Well, after you ambushed my team, destroyed the Spike, and ruined our plans after learning them from my *other* double-crossing teacher, I'll admit to a moment of doubt. But then I realized something."

He wandered closer to the lab tables. Peering between them, he saw that the metallic cylinder Valentine had described was missing. *Must be back inside the floor. I'll have to break through it.*

"You see, I'm a straightforward guy," Malcolm continued. "I don't need elaborate plans. My goal is simple."

"Really."

Malcolm nodded. "I'm just going to kick the crap out of

you and break all your toys." He gestured to the time machine. "Including this one."

Lucius's smile twisted. "Or I could use one of my *toys* to vaporize you right now."

"You probably could." Malcolm shrugged. "But you won't."

"Oh? And why not?"

Malcolm circled around the second table, noting objects he could use as projectiles. "First, because despite everything, you don't consider yourself a killer. Second, because somewhere deep inside, you're curious if I'm good enough to beat you. And what scientist can resist a great experiment?"

Lucius drove a hard stare at Malcolm. *Looks like I've hit a chord.* He returned the stare, packing all the confidence he could muster.

"What now, then?" Lucius said.

Shield fragments poured from the vortex and a boom shook the house, then another, then another. The center of the roof shredded, spewing fragments into the sky as rain gushed in through the hole. Lucius's eyes flashed to his machine for an instant.

Malcolm plucked a random object from the table and snapped it in half. "There goes one." He grabbed another in each hand and crushed them. "And two more." *Have to make him think I have no plan.*

Lucius came within arm's reach and Malcolm drew back a fist. Forcing all his might into the blow, he slammed against Lucius's jaw like a sledgehammer.

Lucius barely moved.

A flash of distress hit Malcolm. He struck again as Lucius watched him stoically. He attacked again and again until his knuckles ached, and his enemy stood unaffected. Doubt crept in. Had he misjudged his chances so badly?

With a malevolent smile, Lucius crushed his palms against Malcolm's chest. He flew backward to crash through layers of wood and circuitry, head and shoulders protruding through the side of the house. In a daze, he stared at the sky while cold water droplets drenched him.

Hands gripped his jacket, and then he was yanked back inside and tossed to the floor. Malcolm slid to a stop next to the time machine. Groaning, he clutched his chest and willed himself to stay conscious. *There's still a chance. There's still . . .*

Lucius towered over him. Rain fell on them both, soaking through their clothes. As if he were relishing the moment, Lucius ripped his jacket to shreds and flung it away.

Steel-braided cables snaked out from the chest plate to wrap around his torso and arms, ending in new connections with Ulrich's bracers. *He found a way to combine them!* Malcolm knew then where Lucius's titanic strength came from.

Lucius pressed a boot against his chest. Strength flowed back into Malcolm, and he silently thanked the accelerator rings for keeping him in overdrive.

Catching the boot, he kicked up and caught Lucius hard in the groin. The scientist seized with a guttural groan, momentarily stunned. Malcolm leapt to his feet and aimed for the softest parts he could get at. A jab to the throat, an elbow to the eye, and Lucius fell back a step.

Malcolm paused for an instant to catch his breath. It was all Lucius needed. His fist hurtled upward and caught Malcolm under the chin, lifting his feet off the floor.

Stars exploded in Malcolm's eyes. Lucius swept his legs to

the side and brought a fist down on his chest like a wrecking ball. He crashed down and floor planks shattered under the impact.

Whole thoughts and complete sentences fell beyond Malcolm's grasp. Only instinct remained to guide him, and it shouted one thought over and over. *THE PLAN. FIND THE WATCH.*

Malcolm pulled himself from the hole in the floor and crawled between the lab tables. Hands trembling, he summoned his little remaining strength and pried open the floor panel. Waiting underneath was the shiny cylinder that Valentine had described. A thrill raced through him and he reached inside, grasping for his prize.

The watch was gone.

No no no no where is it? Where is it? I NEED IT!

A singular sound carried above the storm and his pounding heart: Lucius's laughter.

Resigned, Malcolm rose to meet his opponent eye-to-eye. One hand braced against a table to hold himself upright, the other closed into a fist. He prayed the rings would keep him alive long enough.

Lucius grinned with mock pity. "Were you looking for this?" The watch glimmered on his left palm. "Or perhaps this?" His right hand clutched a ten-inch spike of jagged glass, crusted over with dried blood. *The glass that killed Ulrich.*

"You said I wasn't a killer, Malcolm. You were right."

Lucius became a blur. Malcolm blinked and they were face-to-face. Something thumped against his ribs.

Suddenly he couldn't breathe. He clawed at the air with his lungs but drew nothing in, as if a boulder were pressing on his chest.

"Until today."

He blinked. *Something's wrong.* Lucius stepped back and Malcolm looked down to see the last inch of glass poking out from between his ribs.

Lucius had pierced him through.

Malcolm's strength melted and he collapsed to his knees. Lucius regarded him with cold satisfaction.

"You will not be remembered." He clutched Malcolm's throat and lifted him from the floor. Together they moved to the edge of the vortex. "So you might as well disappear."

With a flick of Lucius's wrist, Malcolm flew into the swirling maelstrom and tumbled around inside like a toy in a whirlpool. Weakly he grasped at the makeshift dagger, managing only to slice his fingers on the razor-sharp edges. His lungs refused to work and blackness crept into the edges of his vision. A last thought echoed in his fading consciousness.

I'm going to die . . .

CHAPTER 30

The time shield shimmered beneath him.

Malcolm tumbled around the edges of the vortex like forgotten laundry. Below him, it ripped through centuries' worth of time and space and ended at the borders of the shield. He saw the shield's radiance waver under the assault of Lucius's machine.

All strength spent, Malcolm stopped pulling on the glass and let his arms float free. Distantly, he knew that if the wounds didn't kill him soon, the next broken piece of the shield would. It would explode against him as the others had against the roof, and everything would be finished.

A sinking sadness filled his belly as he thought of Valentine, of Oma Grace and his father, of Fred and Winter, the unlikely friends who'd stuck by them when the world had gone crazy. *I'm sorry. I tried.*

The air vibrated as a sliver of the shield broke away. He watched it tumble end over end, flying toward him at breakneck speed. *Okay, then. This is it.* Malcolm willed his mind to relax and open himself to accept it with peace. The sliver collided with his torso.

Then he absorbed it.

The sliver sank deep into his flesh and dispersed, its energy infusing new life into every cell. Malcolm realized he could breathe again. Every inhale carried a stab of hot agony, but the air flowing into his lungs had never felt sweeter.

What . . . ?

Another shard broke away. Tentatively, Malcolm opened himself to accept its ethereal light. As it slipped into him, cuts and bruises healed and his skin rejuvenated. He accepted another and glimmers of new life swirled inside, healing muscle and mending bone. His mind accelerated past normal and his thoughts raced with elation and puzzlement.

What is happening to me?

The vortex shuddered as a massive section broke away from the shield. Malcolm saw it with his eyes, then felt it in his mind. The shard spun wide of him, threatening to veer away, and somehow he reached out in his mind to beckon it in his direction. As if hearing his call, the shard curved toward his body. They merged in a burst of dazzling light.

His strength soaring, Malcolm grasped the end of the glass dagger and withdrew it from his chest. Energy converged on the open wound, and in seconds the bleeding stopped and the gash healed over, leaving only a scar.

Malcolm's attention returned to the shield as several fragments broke off at once. As if it were practiced habit, he reached out and commanded them to converge on his body. They obeyed, and he overflowed with unbridled power.

A million questions repeated over and over again. He found he had no answers. Then he found he didn't care. All that mattered was this power, and what he could do with it.

Malcolm's thoughts turned to the past year, memories playing out in a blink. Rage ignited inside him. Rage at storms. Rage at lightning and earthquakes, at death beams and time travel and cancer and grief and futility.

This year had already taken his mother. It would *not* take anything else.

Malcolm threw himself out of the machine. Bursting through the wall of red energy, he landed squarely in front of the lab tables. Lucius sat enraptured by a screen high on the far wall, fingers blurring as he clicked out commands.

A robotic voice rang out. *"Fifteen minutes to shield failure. Sixteen minutes to final jump."*

With a flick of his wrist, Malcolm sent the spike hurtling into the center of the display. Lucius jerked away as the screen spewed a shower of sparks.

"Should've finished me yourself."

Lucius turned toward him slowly, as if beholding a ghost. Observing the scientist with new eyes, Malcolm realized he felt no fear. *He looks so small to me now.*

Lucius swallowed. *"No. No, it can't be,"* he said, half to himself. "You *can't* be one of the—"

Malcolm fumed at the man trying to destroy everything he loved. In that moment, he cared nothing for the plan or the answers Lucius may possess. He cared only for four words that Fred had spoken.

MAKE HIM FEEL IT.

I like the sound of that.

Malcolm moved forward.

Lucius rushed at him, wide-eyed and desperate to strike the first blow. Malcolm focused his will and, with a *shift*, Lucius slowed to a creep. His body pumped with everything he had, yet to Malcolm he appeared to move through thick syrup. Finally within arm's reach, Lucius launched a barrage.

Malcolm stepped between the jabs and kicks as if he were dodging falling leaves. Lucius redoubled his efforts, shouting in frustration.

Then it was Malcolm's turn.

His elbow connected under Lucius's chin with a boom and lifted him from the ground. With a swift kick, Lucius burst through the back wall.

Malcolm dashed to the hole and watched his enemy plow into the ground, carving a divot in the mud with his body and breaking through the wrought-iron fence. He stumbled to his feet, scraping the filth from his clothes.

Malcolm jumped the thirty feet to the ground, landing as if he'd stepped off a curb. Self-doubt had burned away, and he waited while Lucius regained his senses.

Now is when he pays.

Lucius caught sight of Malcolm and took a half-step back, his face a mask of uncertainty. They stared at each other for a long moment, like two figures of stone in the howling storm.

Stubborn determination clouded Lucius's face. Snarling, he sprinted to the broken fence and ripped the bars from their welds. Black metal filled the air as he hurled them like spears. They cut through the wind, driving straight at Malcolm.

He slipped between them without breaking his stride, and they sailed past to punch through the side of the house. Stalking close, Malcolm batted away the last spear and grabbed Lucius in a vise-like grip.

Lifting the scientist off his feet, Malcolm spun and flung him back toward the house. Lucius embedded into the wall with an earsplitting crash.

Closing the distance between them, Malcolm locked molten eyes on his prey. "This is for my sister!"

He shoved upward. Lucius flew up like a bullet, carving a furrow in the thick planks as wood and circuitry blasted away. His body broke through the roof overhang and soared high above the house.

Malcolm crouched low and then launched into the sky like a guided missile. Slicing through the rain and buffeting winds, he slammed an outstretched knee into Lucius's middle with a devastating boom. The scientist crumpled around his knee, moaning, the air crushed from his body.

"Would you have hurt her?" Malcolm smacked Lucius across the face.

Their ascent slowed, then turned back toward the ground. The house hurtled up at them with deadly speed.

"Would you have KILLED her?"

Locked together, they rocketed into a nosedive. Flipping them over until Lucius fell back-first, Malcolm drove his enemy down.

"WOULD YOOOUUU?!"

They smashed through the roof with impossible force, tore through the third level like paper, blew through the second, and blasted a crater into the bottom floor. The ground shook and the house shuddered under the assault.

Malcolm leapt up, towering over his enemy. "You'll never threaten *anyone* again. You understand? It's over, Lucius!"

Lying at the bottom of the crater, Lucius hacked and spluttered. The metal plate sparked against his chest, half of its knobs and buttons broken off.

"I'll give you this, Malcolm," Lucius rasped, chuckling. "You've got vengeance down cold."

Malcolm drew in a slow breath and forced his fists open. Though it still burned like acid, he pushed the anger aside. Deep down he knew he didn't want a man's life on his conscience—even a man like Lucius. *Back to the plan, then.*

Plucking Lucius from the crater, Malcolm leapt high and sailed up through the house. Landing on the third level, he tossed Lucius to the floor and regarded him without sympathy.

"You were so arrogant. Now look at you." He reached out a hand. "I'll take the watch now, if you don't mind."

With a wistful smile, Lucius drew the silver watch from his pocket and gazed at it with affection. "I first built this as a multitool. After every jump, I gave it new abilities. You would be surprised at everything it can do."

Malcolm shrugged. "Doesn't matter to me."

"It should." Lucius's expression sharpened. "Because this is *far* from over."

With a double-tap on the chest plate, thunder cracked overhead and lightning arced down in a blinding flash. The bolt struck against the plate. Its sizzling energy channeled down the steel cables, collected at the bracers, and fed straight into the watch. A massive beam exploded from the jewel and hurled Malcolm across the room.

He bashed against the north wall and stumbled to his knees, momentarily stunned. *Stupid stupid stupid! You did just what he did—assumed you'd already won.*

When the room stopped spinning, Lucius was back on his feet. He tapped the chest plate again, and a hail of lightning streamed from the sky to feed him its power. He fired again.

Malcolm moved to dodge, but the brilliant beam crushed him back against the wall. What remained of his jacket and shirt burned away. Skin and hair scorched under the assault, and he could feel the power he'd absorbed begin to leech away.

Doubt regrew in his mind. *Did I waste my one chance*

to—NO! Malcolm stomped on his fear. *He's not going to win. I won't let him!*

Summoning his remaining power, Malcolm leaned into the beam and took one step forward. The searing energy exploded harder against him. He willed himself to ignore the pain and take another step. Another step and his nemesis drew nearer. He drove forward with abandon, forgetting his body, forgetting the consequences, focusing on Lucius and the desperation on his battered face.

Ten steps away now. Malcolm felt muscles tear from the strain. Nine steps, then eight. A rib cracked, then another. Seven steps. Six. Hot agony filled his senses. Five. He forgot what the absence of pain felt like. Every moment except this one disappeared. There was only the next step. Four. He marched forward. *I am a weapon. I am unstoppable.* Lucius bellowed in rage. *I am your reckoning.* The beam split apart as he advanced through it. Three steps. Two. ONE.

Malcolm clamped his hands over the watch, trapping the stream of energy under his grip. Lucius yanked back but failed to break his hold. Malcolm squeezed tighter and dazzling light streamed from the cracks between his fingers. For an instant, it looked as if he'd trapped the sun in his fists.

Seeking an escape, the power backfired and surged through Lucius's devices. The bracers overloaded and shredded to pieces, the cables burst, and the chest piece vaporized in a flash.

The blast wave of raw energy blew a massive hole in the house, flinging the opponents in opposite directions. Malcolm tumbled head over heels and bounced to a stop under the north window. Sometime during their fight, it had shattered, too.

He lay among debris, the strange power completely spent.

Thick rain fell through the window, dropping onto him in slow motion. He turned onto his side, dazed and utterly drained, and a welcome glimmer caught his eye.

The pocket watch rested face-down in his hand. He breathed a sigh of relief. *We just might have a shot.*

Malcolm drew up to his knees and peered across the twenty-foot gash in the side of the house.

Limping and stumbling with every step, Lucius dragged himself to the computers and tapped out commands.

"Eight minutes to shield failure. Nine minutes to final jump."

Malcolm's attention returned to the watch. *Need to fix the settings now, so I'm ready.* Flipping it over, he froze in shock. *NO!*

The jewel had shattered.

All that remained was a small round hole where the gem had once rested. *Those blasts must've finally broken it.* He sagged, deflating as the implications sank in.

There was only one way to do this now. The watch would have to be carried *into* the machine and activated there. Then at the last second, it would have to be tossed away to ensure that no technology traveled back with Lucius.

A task like that would leave no time to get out of the machine. He would be banished along with Lucius. *So this is really it, then.*

Hanging his head, Malcolm allowed himself a moment of grief. Today was the last day he would see his family, his friends, and his home. Silently he said goodbye to them all, wishing them every happiness.

With that, Malcolm shook away his sorrow. *Time to go to work.* The accelerator rings slid from his fingers and clinked to the floor. *No tech at all—not even these.*

As he began to rise, a shadow fell across the floor next to him. He looked up in alarm. Walter Crane stood there with a faint smile, offering a hand.

Shaking his head, Malcolm accepted it. "You never left, did you?"

"You needed backup," Walter said.

He glanced down at the watch and frowned. His eyes locked with Malcolm's, and it felt like a whole conversation passed between them. He understood.

"How long?"

"Maybe six minutes." Malcolm hesitated, pushing down a swell of emotion. "And I do need something. Once it's done, promise to look after my family."

Walter's expression tightened, but finally he nodded. "Of course. But I can help you now, too." He beckoned for the watch. "I know a setting that may buy you time."

Malcolm held out the watch. As Walter grasped it with his left hand, his right balled into a fist and slammed into Malcolm's stomach. He teetered on shaky legs, gasping up at Walter in shock.

The old soldier socked him again, and he collapsed to the floor in a breathless heap. He clutched at his middle, assaulted by a wave of nausea. Fiery accusation shot from his eyes.

"Wha—?" He couldn't finish. *Please, not another double cross. Not Walter.*

Walter confirmed that the settings were in place, then clicked the lid shut. His attention returned to his Malcolm and he gave a wistful smile. "You were right, Mal. I would have done the same."

The horrible realization slammed into Malcolm. Walter intended to take his place in the machine.

"No!" he cried. "Walter, don't! I've got to do this!"

"You're going to be there for Valentine," Walter replied. "You're going to live a real life, free from all this."

"No!" Malcolm reached for the watch. "I can finish it!"

"You can barely move. You're spent." Crouching next to Malcolm, Walter regarded him with tender eyes. "And you make me proud to be your friend."

Malcolm stopped, taken aback by the honest moment. Walter's face was the softest he'd ever seen it. Sad, yet somehow satisfied.

"The way you watch over your friends, you remind me of everything I wanted to be." Walter stared into the distance. "I tried, all those years ago. Tried so hard to protect them. But I wasn't strong enough."

"Three minutes to shield failure. Four minutes to final jump."

Walter cocked his head toward the voice, then looked back at Malcolm. "I've spent my life trying to make up for that. Every day, I wonder if I could've done more." Rising, Walter twisted his fingers and the ring dropped to the floor. "Today, I'll find out."

Malcolm stared in stunned silence as Walter turned toward the center of the room. Steps away from the machine, he looked over his shoulder.

"Goodbye, Malcolm."

Marching with the strong gait of a soldier, Walter circled around the time machine and strode into Lucius's work area. The scientist faced a computer with rapt attention.

He turned at the sound of footsteps and recoiled. "What are *you*—?"

Walter smashed him in the face with a battle-hardened fist. Lucius rocked back against his table with a gasp. Leaping on him, Walter squeezed the smaller man in an iron bear hug and turned toward the machine.

"What are you doing?" Lucius demanded. "This jump must be carefully controlled! I need to make adjustments!"

"One minute to shield failure. Two minutes to final jump."

He struggled against Walter's grip. "Release me!"

Then Lucius saw the watch in Walter's hand, its lid open and displaying the new destination. He froze, then exploded in a frenzy of desperate rage, screaming and cursing their names and tearing futilely at his bonds. Walter pressed EXECUTE and a sphere of energy emitted from the watch.

"Thirty seconds to shield failure. One minute to final jump."

Walter broke into a sprint and hurled them both into the center of the machine. Malcolm's insides leaped with them as they disappeared into the red vortex. The shimmering light of the time shield faded away, and the vortex *shifted.* Its blood-red color changed into a crystal blue.

"Shield assault aborted. New destination locked."

Clambering to his feet, Malcolm peered into the machine. He could hear Lucius threatening and screaming and begging to go home. Walter cut him off with a sharp growl.

"You're *never* going home! We're going for a ride *together.*"

"NoooooOOOOOOO!"

A metallic glimmer flashed at the edge of the vortex, and the watch slid to a stop at Malcolm's feet.

"Jump initiated."

Everything went white and silence filled every corner of the house. The world hung in suspended animation. An instant later, a deep *THRUM* vibrated through Malcolm and he was blown off his feet by the backwashing shockwave.

Vibrations rattled the house and passed into the earth far

below. Malcolm's mind traveled with the wall of energy as it raced through the tunnels and burst from twelve crater mouths, lancing high into the sky once again.

The shockwave passed, leaving the tunnels silent and dark. Outside, thunder and lightning disappeared and the heavy rain slowed to a drizzle.

Alone in the quiet, Malcolm breathed a heavy sigh. Walter had changed the machine just in time. *We won.*

He lifted his head and studied the machine to confirm what he already felt. Walter and the vortex were gone. So was Lucius.

And the town was safe.

CHAPTER 31

The house twisted with an ear-splitting crack.

Malcolm roused himself from the floor. Something far beneath shuddered and the house lurched to the side. *It's going down!*

Scooping up the rings and the watch, he dashed to the front window and hurled himself through. In mid-flight, he clicked a ring onto his finger. A glimmer of strength supported him as he tumbled to the mud and rolled away. Flipping to his feet, Malcolm sprinted across the street and skidded to a halt in his own front yard.

As he turned back, the towering structure imploded and sank into the collapsing ground. Rending to pieces, it buckled and folded into the deepening crater. With a creaking death moan, the fragments of Lucius's lair disappeared under mounds of churning earth.

The last echoes of destruction faded, and silence settled over everything like a blanket.

Malcolm slipped the ring from his finger. For now, he'd had enough of being strong. Staring at the crater, he fell to his knees as burning tears streamed down his face.

I'll never see him again.

Silently, he cursed Walter for leaving and thanked him for saving their lives. Wherever—and whenever—his friend was, Malcolm hoped he knew what he'd done for them all.

A profound weariness sank into Malcolm's bones, as if he could sleep for a year. The surrounding quiet cradled and comforted him, promising peace. Allowing himself a moment to rest, he sprawled on the wet grass and closed his eyes.

"Mal!"

He startled awake, fists coming up as his eyes darted everywhere in search of Lucius. Overhead, the sky had cleared to a crystal blue. Valentine gazed down at him with relief.

"Oh, thank God!" She fell against him.

Malcolm wrapped his arms around her, tears flowing with gratitude that she was alive and safe. Somewhere, a bird chirped in the morning breeze.

"Walter's gone," he said through the tears.

"He made us go without him." Valentine examined him with a grimace, her fingers tracing the scar on his chest. "What happened, Mal?"

Malcolm sat up and noticed the Power Wagon idling on the curb. John waited inside, giving them a moment of privacy. He reached for Valentine's hands and she helped him stand.

"Let's find the others. I'll tell you everything on the way."

They would learn later that Lucius's machine had overloaded the nuclear power plant, causing an emergency shutdown. With public power and cell service down, the twins couldn't know which town to search. So they determined to try *every* hospital until they found their friends. During the drive, Malcolm and Valentine each laid out the events of the day from their point of view. They sat in the backseat while John drove the steel behemoth.

"I can't believe this." Valentine shook her head.

"I know. It just happened and already it doesn't feel real." Malcolm hung his head. "I miss Walter."

She took his hand and leaned against his shoulder. "I'm sorry, Mal. He was a good man."

"He was the *best*."

Peering to the front, Malcolm saw John glance at them through the rearview mirror. Tears brimmed in his eyes, too.

"Was it . . . did it end well for him?" he asked.

Malcolm flashed back to the look on Walter's face. "He went out protecting his friends. It's what he wanted."

John's shoulders relaxed. Though tears still fell, he looked comforted. Studying him, it occurred to Malcolm that he still didn't understand part of the story.

"You look pretty good for your age, John."

John's expression grew uncomfortable. "Technically, I'm still only fifteen. Lucius's machine pulled me in, and I just missed a blast that should have killed me. It threw me forward in time."

"But you've been here longer than Lucius."

"A little. I've been here just over a year."

"We think that since he jumped first, his path split from theirs," Valentine said to Malcolm.

"I'm sorry for concealing the truth," John said. "I thought people would lock me in an institution. So I pretended not to remember anything except the name I adopted."

"Why that name?"

A hint of a smile touched John's lips. "Before all this began, I read *A Princess of Mars,* where a normal man suddenly finds himself in a strange new world. His name was John Carter." He shrugged. "It felt right at the time."

Malcolm considered this. "I don't blame you for using a cover. But why not go to your old friends?"

"A century has passed. I couldn't know if they would believe me, or even remember me." His voice grew heavy. "The truth—I was afraid to try, and I needed to forget everything that happened to us. So I homeschooled to avoid Miranda, grew my hair out. Tried to hide from everything."

"That's why you were nervous at our house. I thought you were scared to meet Dad. But you weren't, were you?"

"No. I feared seeing Grace again."

Malcolm thought he understood now. "You just wanted a normal life, but it started happening all over again."

John winced. "I tried to help, but . . . it felt like going back to war. To my shame, I fell apart. Remember, for me, it happened only a year ago."

"It sounds like post-traumatic stress to me," Valentine said, affection and protectiveness pouring off her in waves. "And you've been dealing with it alone."

"There's nothing to be ashamed of, John," Malcolm assured him. "You came back right when we needed you."

John smiled in gratitude. "Thank you. This past year, I have felt like a real John Carter. I found a home, loyal friends." He reached back to grasp Valentine's hand. "And I met a princess."

The truck's cabin fell quiet again. Malcolm sank back, lulled by the hum of the road and the comfort of his sister's presence.

Outside the window, he watched a burned and broken part of their town slip by. In the golden light of the sun, it didn't look so bad.

"We'll get it back, Mal," Valentine said. "The town, I mean. We're going to bring it all back. Only it'll be better."

Malcolm knew she was right. With a contented sigh, he turned to look through the windshield. As Emmett's Bluff slipped into the distance, a wide, green country opened before them. Their friends were out there somewhere, healing from their own battles and waiting to be reunited.

They didn't have long to wait.

past year. "You were right before, you know. About me. I *did* stop living. If you never move, you never have to feel." He shook his head with regret. "Those days are over. I'm starting to feel like myself again."

"Good. I need my brother back." She grinned, then her brow furrowed. "Now we can figure out what's happening to us."

Malcolm raised his eyebrows.

She gave him a level look. "You know what I'm talking about. The weird sensations we felt, those . . . *shifts*. And the things we did back there—me with the watch, you with the time machine."

Malcolm flashed back to his battle with Lucius. "I think, somehow, we bent the energy of Time to our will. Ever since, I don't know how, but . . . I feel something I didn't before. I can't see or explain it, but I know it's out there. Sometimes, I can almost touch it." He locked eyes with his twin. "What is happening to us?"

"We'll have to figure it out together. Later, though. For tonight . . ." She gestured at the crater.

Malcolm nodded. "Later."

Footsteps crunched through the snow behind them. Shadows approached from the sidewalk, resolving into five people. John shook Malcolm's hand warmly, then gathered Valentine in a tight embrace. Grinning, she kissed him and caressed his cheek.

Malcolm greeted the others in turn—Oma Grace, Clive, Fred, and Winter. After all these months, their casts were gone and their wounds had healed. The deeper scars of battle would only fade with time and care. Still, they were smiling. Happy. And every step of the way, they would be there for each other. His heart warmed as he watched them.

"I think it's time," Clive said softly.

CHAPTER 32

Six Months Later

Snow was falling.

For the fourth night in a row, it danced down to blanket the countryside. The deeper cold had delayed for months, likely due to Lucius's tampering with the sky, and now winter frolicked in the air.

Malcolm switched off the porch light and shut the front door. A full moon illuminated his path across the street. Valentine waited for him at the edge of the crater, where a house with no doors had once stood.

"Did you bring it?" she asked.

"Yeah. I thought it'd be hard to choose, but . . . it's the right one."

"Good." Unzipping her coat, she tugged at the collar of her sweater. "This thing Dad bought me is itchy."

Malcolm glanced at her throat and smiled. Catching his look, she blushed. The silver pendant was gone from her neck.

"It was time," she said. "It's still in a box, but . . . I think she'd have wanted me to let it go."

"I'm happy for you, Val," Malcolm said with admiration. He stared down into the crater, considering the course of the

The companions stood shoulder to shoulder at the edge of the snow-dusted crater. Below them, jagged bones of the old house jutted through layers of earth. Clive glanced at Malcolm and nodded.

Drawing in a deep breath, Malcolm gathered himself. He paused, not knowing what to say. *Nothing flowery*, he reminded himself. *Just the truth.*

"How do I describe someone like Walter?" he began. "He was gruff. Reclusive. A lot of things annoyed him, especially teenagers. The second time we met, he pointed a gun at me."

The others chuckled.

"That sounds like Buster," Oma Grace said with a bittersweet smile.

Malcolm laughed too. For the first time he could think of Walter without feeling overwhelming sadness. *Tell them.*

"I've thought about him a lot these past months. About my last moments with him. They used to make me sad. They *still* make me sad, but they make me glad, too. Glad to have known him, to have learned who he really was. In that last moment, I wish I could've said what he meant to me. I wish he were here now, so I could see that look on his face again. The look that said he knew he'd saved us all.

"More than anything, though, I just miss my friend. I think I'll miss him for a very long time." He looked up at the sky, blinking back tears. "He wouldn't have changed it, though, so I won't wish for it either. To protect his friends was all he ever wanted."

Reaching into his pocket, Malcolm withdrew Walter's Silver Star and held it over the edge. "You had more honor than ten men, Walter. We'll miss you every day."

The others quietly said their own goodbyes. When they

finished, Malcolm let the medal fall into the crater. With a faint thump, it disappeared into the snow and buried itself among the remains of the house.

A moment later, Winter stepped forward and tossed in what looked like a small piece of computer circuitry. Malcolm shot her questioning glance.

"We lost other friends, too," she said, her eyes glistening. "I couldn't find Patrick. If he's still out there somewhere, I just hope—I have to believe he's okay."

John and Fred put their arms around her, offering comfort.

"Then we'll believe it, too," Fred said.

Together, all the companions gazed into the abyss. Long moments of silence passed in remembrance of what they'd all shared. What they'd all suffered. And what they'd all overcome.

"So," Fred said eventually. "Same time next year?"

They agreed without hesitation. Then, knowing that Walter would roll his eyes at them for standing in the cold to talk about him, Malcolm turned back toward the street. The others followed suit.

A *BOOM* shook the air behind them. The ground rumbled and a rushing wind gusted from inside the crater. Whipping around, Malcolm and the group faced forward again.

A second *BOOM* vibrated through their bones. In his mind Malcolm felt something intangible *shift* and then rip. Inside the crater, the air split open and bright light poured out of the tear. Something solid shot out and dropped to the ground, and the light disappeared in a blink.

Returning to the edge, Malcolm peered into the crater. He caught sight of a small mound that hadn't been there before. The mound shifted and groaned.

"Someone's in there!" Valentine exclaimed.

Malcolm, Valentine, and John slid down the embankment and scrambled across the dips and rises in the crater. Dodging past remnants of the house that jutted from the ground, they halted above the figure of a tall, armored man covered in thick frost. In a ten-foot circle around his body, the snow had frozen into a solid sheet of ice.

"What on earth . . . ?"

Hesitantly, Malcolm removed the man's helmet. Shoulder-length black hair spilled out to frame a young face, lean and olive-complexioned. His right temple was heavily bruised, and blood seeped from a jagged gash at the edge of his scalp.

"He's young," John observed. "Eighteen, maybe."

"Mal, look at this." Valentine touched the plates of ornate silver armor, etched with fine scrollwork in a flowing, wavy pattern. Underneath was a layer of chainmail—a mesh finer than any Malcolm had seen.

"Where's this guy from?" she said.

"Where?" John gave them a significant look. "Or *when?*"

"I've never seen armor like this before," Malcolm said. He leaned in to get a closer look. "Whoa, this guy's hurt!"

A wide gash split the armor's right flank. Valentine parted the layers, and they winced in sympathy. A deep slash had cleaved the man's side open, leaving a seared red wound. Oddly, while the rest of him was covered in frost, the wound radiated heat.

"Call an ambulance!" Malcolm shouted.

Fred pulled out his phone. "On it."

"Should we move him?" Valentine asked.

"It could hurt him," John said.

The armored man's chest heaved with guttural hacking and

his eyes fluttered open. Hollow and glazed over, they locked onto Malcolm with wild terror. He lunged forward and grabbed onto Malcolm's arms.

"He's coming! He's—" he cut off with a grimace and sucked in a breath. "The Black Tempest is coming! No stopping him! You've all got to run. *Run!*"

Spasming, he slumped to the ground and his eyes rolled back. His breathing grew more labored, and the small bit of color in his cheeks drained away.

"Does he mean Lucius?" Valentine's eyes darted around warily.

Malcolm shook his head vehemently. *"No way.* Lucius is out of the game. We made sure of it this time." He glanced up at the sky. "He's talking about someone else. Maybe someone wherever he's from."

Malcolm forced himself to relax and slide out of arm's reach. The instinct to defend himself with force had not yet faded, and he didn't want to hurt an already-injured man. Sitting in the snow, he tried to digest what he'd just heard. Valentine's brow was furrowed, and he knew she was pondering the same thing.

"A year ago, I'd have said he's delirious and doesn't know what he's saying," she said. "But now?"

"Yeah," Malcolm said. "And we've seen too much to think he's just crazy."

"So, if it's true, who's coming and why should we run?"

"I don't know. But if it *is* true," he looked pointedly at Valentine. "We'd better get ready."

ACKNOWLEDGEMENTS

Given my fear of the acknowledgements page—specifically, of forgetting to include someone important and spending the rest of my life in a shame spiral—I'd like to start by thanking every single person who has ever lived, or will ever live, on planet Earth. Seriously, I couldn't have done it without you.

Okay, now to get more specific . . .

No book comes to life because of one person, and I'm ridiculously grateful to those who were there along the way. To the beta-readers who showed me how to make this book even better, thank you for all that you taught me—Jolene Perry, Brenda Drake, Steph Funk, Darci Cole, Elena Jacob, Cortney Pearson, and any others whom I may have forgotten. Thanks to Laura Register for helping with Valentine's point of view, to Amy Shaw for schooling me in French grammar, and to Trent Stokes for guidance on military procedure and nuclear power plants. Huge thanks to Morgan Shamy, one of my oldest friends in the writer community. Your tireless support, advice, cheerleading, and determination have often been the fuel that kept me writing through trials and discouragement. This book belongs to you, too.

To the Parking Lot Confessional—Amy K. Nichols, Amy

McLane, and Stephen Green—thanks for always helping to replenish my creative energy, and for the ridiculously fun time podcasting and geeking out about books.

To everyone at SCBWI who made an unpublished but eager writer feel welcome and part of such a great group of creators, thank you Jodi Moore, Evelyn Ehrlich, Kim Sabatini, Jeff Cox, Christa Desir, Karen Akins, Allie Brennan, and Liz Briggs. Thanks to Austin Aslan, Tatum Flynn, Ryne Pearson, and Ellie Ann Soderstrom for cheering me on, and for welcoming me into the fold when this book was announced. And thank you, Jonathan Simon of Lightning Octopus, for spotlighting my work long before I was ever published.

Thank you so much to the musicians who helped me find the soul of this story. Murray Gold's score from *Doctor Who* helped me define the tone. James Newton Howard's *Unbreakable* soundtrack helped Winter and Fred defeat the villainous Ulrich. Jeremy Messersmith's earnest ballads set the mood for Valentine's first kiss. John Powell's triumphant *Hancock* score gave power to Malcolm's final fight and Walter's sacrifice. Finally, Ryan Bingham's theme to *Crazy Heart* gave depth and a breath of hope to Walter's funeral.

Thank you Magneto, Professor Moriarty, and the Operative, for teaching me how to write my favorite kind of villain; and Green Arrow, for constantly going toe-to-toe with villains who are stronger than you because it's the right thing to do. Thank you, Joss Whedon, for teaching me how to balance humor and tension. Thank you, *Batman* 1989, for creating the moment that told me I'd be a geek for life.

To my awesome superhero editor Zach T Power, to executive editor and amazing cover artist Christopher Loke, and to the whole team at Jolly Fish Press, thank you so much for believing in this book and giving it a home, for being such incredible partners and making this whole experience the dream that I'd hoped it would be.

To my parents and brother—even though most people only experience my weird humor and random ideas in little pieces— you've had a front row seat for my entire life. Thank you for not only tolerating them but allowing them to flourish, for believing eight-year-old Ryan when he declared that someday he would publish books, for letting me conjure up years' worth of crazy stories and silly jokes on the path from *dreamer* to *author,* and for just going with it when I pull the car over to jot down an idea before I lose it. I'm here in this moment because of all those times and a thousand more just like them. Thank you forever.

Finally, thanks to YOU, the person holding this book. You're a part of the dream now, and I hope you'll come with me all the way to the end.

This book will self-destruct in five seconds . . . but the gratitude will remain.

RYAN DALTON either wears a cape and fights crime abroad, or he writes about it from his red captain's chair at home. Perhaps he's a superhero that's trained with the world's finest heroes, or he's a lifelong geek who sings well and makes a decent dish of spaghetti. It's also plausible that he's been plotting to take over the world since he was ten, or that he's since been writing novels to stir the heart and spark the imagination. Either way, he lives in an invisible spaceship that's currently hovering above Phoenix, Arizona.